THE RAIDAN AWAKENING

The Death Hunting
Book Two

By Emma Steinbrecher

For anyone who has ever wanted to be the villain—if only for a moment.

Dear reader,

It is my desire to ensure that everyone who picks up this book feels comfortable in doing so. Because of this, I have provided a list of trigger warnings below.

Trauma
Explicit Sexual Scenes
Death
Graphic Violence
Torture
Alcoholism
Physical Abuse
SA
Negative self-thoughts
Betrayal

As you know, I try to provide a complete list of trigger warnings. If you feel that something is missing, feel free to reach out. It is also helpful if you add trigger warnings in any review you may write.

The Wasteland
Vulcan
Ohriid
Adhara
Ascella
Zora
Namid
Tiranna
The Court of Shadow
The Court of Light
Nashira
Debnar
Velas
N
The Fae Realm

Death

A palace made of skull and bone held nothing but sorrow and subdued shadows.

It also imprisoned Death.

Matthias sat chained to the floor. Iron shackles clung to his wrists, forged by the demon who had taken him here. The metal stole his power by suppressing the dark magic coasting through his veins, and it sucked away every ounce of comfort—leaving Death with no hope to hold on to.

Jagged bone embedded in clay stood to create the crude walls of the hellhole. The ceramic tiles were suspended from the ceiling, ancient runes carved and glowing blue. They were unfamiliar symbols—even to the god of death. The marks glowed with eerie magic, an immense power that unsettled him as he stared at the blue light for hours, trying to pass the time.

Footsteps tapped the gray stone floor beyond but quickly approached. Matthias sat with his back leaning against the dead remains of fae and human alike. Sweat beaded on his brow, dripping down his temple and chilling his blood. He looked at the polished black shoes, refusing to meet the gaze of the monster before him.

The demon crouched with elbows on his knees. The dim light highlighted his black suit and the fog rising from the floor by his feet. Cold hands gripped Matthias's chin, making him shudder as he looked into the glowing amber eyes. The creature was waiting for a reaction. Matthias clenched his teeth, barely holding back the snarl of feral rage intended for his kidnapper.

The monster inspected its prey, tilting Matthias's head to either side and analyzing Death. There was a hint of satisfaction in the upward tilt of his smug smile—as if capturing the god of death were a true accomplishment and tell of his power. The scrutinization had Matthias reaching for the shadows, but there was nothing to answer his call. He pulled against the confining metal, chains rattling as the cuffs bit into his skin—icy burns burrowing into his soul.

"Eat," the gravelly voice commanded, tossing Matthias's chin out of his grip before standing.

Matthias watched the polished shoes retreat into the darkness, only to return to toss a lump of charred bread onto the floor. The sound echoed across the chamber, traveling along the stone floors, up the walls, and across the tiled ceiling. Matthias swore the blue runes pulsed from the vibrations, fueled by whatever wickedness clung to the monster in the room.

"What are you offering Inara?" Matthias asked, his eyes blazing and glued to the monster. His tongue dragged slowly over the roof of his mouth, the dryness feeling like coarse sand. A bitterness simmered in his gut—calm and collected—waiting to release the wrath of a god.

The demon crouched again, a smirk pulling up at the corner of his thin mouth. His long gray hair fell below his shoulders in waves. The man's gray beard shifted as he spoke. "I offered her blood." The monster took a small knife from his pocket, pressing it to the skin of his palm before slicing a clean cut along his flesh. He didn't flinch. His finger dipped into the red liquid, and he drew another rune in blood on the stone floor in front of Matthias. "Blood. Perhaps, more powerful than my own," he added while pocketing the knife. A gleam entered those amber eyes. Matthias couldn't prevent the chill that ran down his spine. "And you're about to find out exactly how powerful I am."

Matthias's brow furrowed as he tried to place the symbol on the floor. He didn't recognize the painted rune, but it was glowing now. The crimson stain turned to blue light that emanated power. The man was a monster.

"And who the fuck are you?" Matthias called out. The sandy feeling coating his throat returned, the rasp evident in the way his voice traveled through the dungeon. Matthias let his eyes burn into the demon's back as he retreated. Breathing deeply, Death willed his gaze to keep the monster here—force him to answer his questions. He had nothing else.

The monster paused with stiff shoulders. "Death should dare to speak my name?" He turned his head and growled. "Death is meaningless to the gods of old."

"Who are you?" Matthias repeated.

"Raidan."

Raidan disappeared into the darkness beyond the rune, pulsing with power. Everything smelled of iron and mist—the same white fog that trailed behind Raidan as he departed.

When his image faded into the darkness, Matthias's skin began burning, his world alight with the ancient magic. Everything within him cried out in pain as he screamed in agony. The feeling of fire invaded his veins, his chest—his mind. The pain was unbearable and left him thrashing on the ground—chains rattling.

And how does one kill a god?

Her voice cut through his screams. It was echoing loudly in his mind, acting as a reminder of the woman that consumed his thoughts. Where was she? What was happening in his court? Had she gotten his message? Would she even come?

"Not like this," he rasped. The answer echoed through the dungeon and disappeared. It was a senseless nothing added to the stinging air and pulsing power.

Death felt his skin ripping and stitching back together. There was nothing left but the pain of torture.

He fought the scream threatening to rip from his already raw throat. Matthias could feel his muscles straining as fire licked up his flesh. His spine arched off the stone floors. Fear was foreign and unyielding. As he realized the immense power held by the monster that took him, Death allowed himself to break apart in the ancient temple.

Nothing but his echoing screams and the ghastly palace decorated in bone.

One

Despite the crimson stains of blood and wrath, her hands steadied at her sides. There was nothing left in her aside from exhaustion and the hollowed numbness of what she had just done—who she had just murdered.

Morana sat in the dimly lit tavern littered with quiet patrons tending to their breakfasts. In the realm of fae, they didn't notice the elaborate dress she still donned. And she was thankful her appearance didn't draw attention—especially since she hadn't had time to change.

Ronan had taken on the responsibility of cleaning up the throne room and sent her out. She knew he was buying her time, something she wasn't used to accepting.

Her hand, scrubbed pink after cleaning up in the tavern bathroom, wrapped around a large mug filled with steaming coffee. She watched the smoke rise from the liquid, twisting in a way that reminded her of the shadows. Her power rippled beneath her skin as if called by the thought, comforting her. The anger was gone, as well as the biting sting of betrayal that had marinated in her blood.

Every feeling that had swarmed in her the moment Axton shoved her face to the concrete had disappeared.

Soft murmurs quieted her thoughts. She tapped a nail on the oak table, slouching in her seat and sighing. Ronan had allowed her to come and escape her thoughts, but as she glanced at the delicate red dress with black overlay and felt the cloak draped over the high-backed chair behind her, she couldn't help but lose herself in her own memories.

When her mom had left and her father had fallen into his depressive state, there was no room to feel. She picked herself up—even at seven—put her head down, and moved forward. Her life was a never-ending list of tasks that didn't leave room for sorrow. Even now, there were things to do. The Wastelands still imprisoned Matthias in the north, leaving The Court of Shadows without a king. And despite his absence, Inara was still hunting her.

Morana ran a finger along the scar scored across her cheek. The skin was almost as numb as her tired soul. Her thumb ghosted over the snake tattoo, a permanent reminder of Axton's death. Closing her eyes, she breathed in deeply.

"The crown suited you." Morana jumped as Elivira wrapped slender fingers around the back of an empty wooden chair, sliding it across the hardwood floor and sitting with her elbows on the oak surface of the table.

A forced laugh left her lips when her startled heart steadied. She needed to be more aware—not so lost in her own thoughts, especially as her enemies held Death—

enemies she didn't fully understand. "It was all for show." Morana glanced at her hands, wrapping them around the heavy mug and hauling it to her lips. She inhaled the scent of coffee and cream before taking a sip.

The lords had agreed to the display—the pretending. Pretending was something Morana was used to, and she did it well. She pretended that her mother's absence didn't sting at all for the sake of her father. She pretended to be fine as her father unleashed his wrath and sorrow upon her. He used to run his hands through her hair when she was young, telling her how much she looked just like her mother. Morana could still smell the stale whiskey on his breath. Her nose wrinkled in disgust as she placed the mug on the table, pushing it further away than necessary.

Some of those memories had left her in the presence of the god of death. She had laid those memories to rest; ghosts of her past, unable to hurt her in this new realm. But with his abduction, the ghosts seemed to return—hellbent on haunting her until there was nothing left beyond bone and sorrow.

She leaned forward, shoulders tight. "We need to get him out," Morana spoke, her voice rasping as she fought to keep her tone steady. "You are ruling in his stead, but we need to get him back."

"I know." Elivira laid a hand over Morana's forearm. She glanced at the woman's deeply tanned skin, flawless in the flickering faefire from the iron chandelier overhead. Morana's eyes rose to the woman. She wondered how Elivira seemed so calm. There had to be something akin to fear beneath those brown curls tied in a bun atop her head. Morana noted the loose strands—wild and untamed as they framed her face. Maybe she wasn't as unfazed as she appeared.

There was a burning intensity in Elivira's eyes when she spoke. "We need to think this through, Morana." Her tone was hushed as she leaned forward. "A mortal man was able to kidnap a *god*." Elivira's lip pulled back. "What else did the Basar show you?"

Morana sank into her chair, a huff escaping her lips as she stared at the mug on the table, anxious to cease the feeling of idleness. Morana dragged the cup closer, toying with the elegant metal handle. "It's hard to remember," she admitted. "I was fighting to get out."

The sarcasm leaked out before she could think better of it. She didn't take it back but wore it like an armor.

Elivira's jaw clenched, and her shoulders stiffened at the remark. As if deciding on a course of action, the lord looked off into the distance, observing the crackling hearth at one end of the tavern. "Then I may need to go fishing."

Morana's attention snapped back to the woman's face; her full lips pressed together. "What do you mean?"

"We need more than details of his kidnapping," she informed, eyes burning like hot earth. "Morana, we need to find out exactly where he *is*." Elivira swallowed. "Something feels off about this situation. Matthias might already be gone. He might—"

"Don't," Morana growled. Her gray eyes went smokey as dark shadows caressed her arms, swirling in a violent mist. "He's alive." The mist crept up her trembling body until her blond hair blew wildly around her face. "That motherfucker, Axton, was a *mortal,*" she spat. Morana leaned in—her brows drawn together. "Axton wielded no power. He didn't *kill* Matthias." Her throat burned on the last statement, clogging with tears at the mention of his name. Morana held onto the anger and hoped it was enough to keep the vulnerability at bay.

Elivira didn't say anything. She didn't move. Those burning eyes had dulled in intensity and now widened in shock. She tapped a finger on the table, and her tongue ran along her teeth. The lord assessed Morana as if she could see through the anger.

Beneath her gaze, Morana felt the sting of sadness pierce through her mask as tears threatened to work their way out. She inhaled deeply, the tears now gathering at the corners of her eyes. Her exhale stilled her tremors and sent the shadows back beneath her skin. She brought the still steaming mug to her lips and gripped it as if it were her only tether to this life—this realm.

"You need to rest." Elivira's face softened, and the harsh angles of her brows relaxed. "You'll think better once you've rested. I have things to take care of in Matthias's absence." She cleared her throat and looked away briefly. "Questions to dodge, but I think Ronan should have things cleaned up. You should come back to the castle."

"Of course." Morana looked down at her cup, running a finger over the rim. Her body was slowly giving in to the idea of rest. Elivira was right. "I'll rest," she began, "but you don't go to the Basar until I can come with you."

Elivira smiled, unleashing a wicked expression. "You were merely playing queen. What makes you think you can give me orders?"

Something about the remark pierced her heart, a dull pain forming at the barb. Morana didn't let it show, guarding herself against the fae in the room. She wouldn't leave space to be judged here. While she trusted Elivira, for whatever reason, Morana didn't want to *feel* anything else. Brooding over her situation wouldn't get Matthias out of The Wastelands. "I will go with you when you jump into the fountain." Morana leaned forward, punctuating her next statement with the same fiery determination Elivira had shown upon entering the tavern. "And I will go with you to retrieve him."

Elivira smirked, but didn't make another comment. There was a knowing look in her eyes as she got up and glanced at the red skirt with black overlay draped over Morana's tired legs.

"The black suits you, too." Elivira turned to exit the tavern.

Morana looked down at the dress, fingering the layered fabric. She could see Axton's blood coating every inch of the throne room, feel the shadows as they engulfed her the moment she pulled the trigger.

"Is meeting with the lord of Namid a regular occurrence for you?"

Morana's head snapped up, greeted with the image of a lean man, long auburn hair loosely tied back. His features were sharp, almost foxlike as he leaned with his hands on Elivira's chair.

Her throat tightened as she fought to formulate a response. Had he been listening?

"Elivira's an old friend." She forced a smile to her lips, eyes holding steady to uncover how much this man had heard or knew.

He sat down at the table, uninvited. The three golden rings lining his pointed ear glistened as they caught the light of faefire when he leaned forward.

Morana flinched, uncomfortable in the man's presence. Something about him unsettled her, but she longed to piece together why he was here. Morana's eyes widened when light gathered at his fingertips, twisting in the way the shadows usually did around her. She cursed the paralyzing feeling as her jaw locked. It reminded her of her time in the dungeons with Inara.

She swallowed, fear taking over and draining her face of color. This man had to be of the Court of Light.

There was a roaring in her ears and the memory of a slashing pain across her unmarred back. She could hear light crackling and whipping out from the hands of the rose-eyed monster who forced her into submission.

The man chuckled. "I'm not here to hurt you."

Even if she believed him, she couldn't fight through her panic. She became hyper-aware of the damp floors and her hollowed stomach. Every memory from her time in the

Court of Light came back, swirling faster around her mind than she could handle. The room was suffocating her, pulling her under the surface of churning waves that wanted to drown her. All she wanted was to leave.

She stood up abruptly. Morana was ready to walk out when a warm hand gripped her wrist. Shadows swirled around her legs, helping ease the fear. The comfort of her power dampened the sound of roaring in her ears and halted the swaying of the room until the patrons came into focus. The fae scattered across the room were looking in their direction as she tugged against the steel grip wrapped around her wrist.

Shadows slipped from her skin and circled his hand.

"I said I'm not here to hurt you." The fae man looked up at her, his voice low. "Sit down before you cause a scene. I just want to talk."

"I don't want to hear it." Morana lifted her chin, still pulling against his grip, begging the shadows to make him release her. She didn't know how to do such a thing, and she prayed to all the gods that the whispering darkness would show her how.

"Inara sent assassins after you. Did she not?" He was almost whispering. "She hunted you down. Tortured you." The lines on his forehead tightened much like her stomach as memories of Inara's cruelty surfaced. "She defied the rules of Mabon, and now the King of Shadows is missing." Morana's eyes widened. She commanded the shadows, refusing to allow her powers to be useless. Who was this man, and why was her panic so difficult to shove down?

"I don't know what you're talking about." She gritted her teeth. He was knowledgeable—painfully so. Morana was tired of being the last to know something in this realm. Her incompetence left her powerless, and she would fight to get that power back. Fire burned in her chest, and she pushed it through her magic, making her blood sing.

The man let out a sharp breath, letting go of her as if burned. When he looked up again, he was pleading. "Please." Somehow, his sharp features softened, begging her to listen. "I swear it. I'm not trying to hurt you."

She didn't trust anyone involved with Inara's court, but she couldn't afford to remain naive about the fae realm—not with Matthias's disappearance still heavy on her mind. She sat down with her back rigid in the wooden chair. Looking around, people were still staring, curiosity shining in their eyes. If this man knew that Matthias was missing, she couldn't risk having his court find out. Elivira was working hard to toss that piece of information into the sea with heavy weights attached. The shadows dissipated, but she still let them linger around her ankles, out of sight from others.

The patrons eventually returned to their conversations and coffee. Morana glanced at the wooden walls, void of anything but sconces filled with faefire. She glanced at the man's fingers again and thought about the power he wielded. It sent a shiver down her spine.

"You're from her court." Morana winced and silently cursed herself for allowing her mask to slip.

"I'm more than that, dear." His honey-colored eyes lighted, a smile crossing his angular face. "I'm a lord in Inara's court."

Two

Fear bloomed like ivy in her chest, winding painfully around her heart to still its beating. Those vines tore through flesh gradually, just like the realization tore through Morana's mind. She didn't know how she was breathing or even alive.

As he sat waiting across the table, Morana noticed the satisfaction on his face. He thought he'd won. This *lord* in Inara's court had secured an audience, and something about that had the vines of fear gripping her tighter, their thorns slicing something deep within. He had trapped her— a true predator.

Attacking the lord among the tavern patrons was out of the question. So was responding to the increasing panic she felt. Morana had to focus her efforts on playing along with whatever sick game he roped her into.

His honey-colored eyes reminded her of that fox he resembled. The only question was, which court was he attempting to trick?

"Strange things are happening in the Court of Light." He ran a tongue along his teeth, picking up an almond from a small dish at the center of the table and rolling it around between his finger and thumb. As she watched his fingers move, all she could think about were the tendrils of light that had circled his fingers and made her shiver.

"Why are you telling me this?" Her gray eyes hardened like ice as she tried to find his lie.

"There are whispers about you." He tilted his head, one eyebrow raised in challenge. "But you know that." The almond dropped into the dish on the table, and Morana barely hid her flinch at the deafening sound. All of her focus was on schooling her expression—revealing nothing. She was playing a game—trying to outsmart the fox. "Don't you?" he finished.

"Queen of Shadows," she scoffed, folding her arms across her chest and closing herself off to his suggestion. She longed to appear unbothered by his presence. "I'm aware." Her tongue rolled along her cheek. Morana dug the hole—the same one where she would bury her emotions to get through this interaction.

"Are you aware of what they mean?"

Rolling her eyes, Morana leaned toward him, trailing her icy gaze down his athletic frame. Slimmer than Matthias, but still large enough to be a threat. She assessed him in a way that would make him feel small—she hoped. "No." Her tone hardened.

His head tilted to the side, unfazed by her assessment. "Inara is secretive," he informed. "Even before the lords that rule over her cities. I am lord over Ohriid—

the city to the north. It's a day's journey from the Wasteland border."

Morana fought to hide her reaction and clenched her teeth. Matthias was in The Wastelands. The Basar had shown her as much while they tried to consume her, but they still weren't sure of where.

The man cleared his throat before continuing. He leaned forward and spoke low enough that the other patrons wouldn't hear. They had all but forgotten the little scene earlier. "Creatures from The Wastelands have been crossing over into my city." Dim faefire flickered across his features, accentuating the sharpness of his cheekbones. "It is something unheard of in our realm. The major gods, the ones said to be sleeping, created the creatures."

He waited then, begging her to take meaning from nothing. But for her, there was no meaning to be had. There was nothing she could do about strange creatures crossing borders. Elivira had said it herself. Morana was merely playing queen. One phrase stuck out to her, though. *Inara is secretive.*

"You don't trust Inara," she deduced, brows lowered and serious.

He didn't answer, though it wasn't really a question. He merely allowed one corner of his slim mouth to turn up while he leaned back in his chair, tapping a finger on the wooden surface of the table.

"How can you not?" she asked, no accusation in her tone. "You rule over a city in her court. You—"

"Does that mean I have to trust her?" He spoke slowly, an eyebrow cocked in challenge.

Fair.

"I don't want anything you have to offer me." Morana lifted her chin, looking down her nose at the lord. She fought the oncoming memories of glass and light and faerie wine that made her laugh like a child. Just the memory of the sickly-sweet taste made her stomach sour. She could feel the blood drain from her face as she remembered Axton leading her to the portal just to shove her into a cell. Clothes ripping. Painful slashing. Damp dripping.

Morana jerked her head slightly to dislodge the sensations that arose before they took her under. She needed to keep her composure—see this game through until the end.

"I am looking for an alliance," the fox admitted. And if he were being truthful, she would then know who he was betraying. Nothing was ever so simple. Morana ran a hand down her black and red dress. She wasn't the one he should make deals with. Who did this man think she was to ask her for an alliance? She had played queen earlier this morning, but she was nothing—a charity case, maybe. That thought made her wince, and she tried to hide her reaction.

"I'm not one to give it—the alliance." Her voice was softer now, laced with the stinging of her insignificance. Morana was fighting with her old habits, desperately trying to maintain control. Matthias was gone. She had nothing left in the human realm, and she murdered a man—one she had thought was a friend. When the shadows twisted and turned along her flesh, she felt significant. When Matthias worshipped her and Death surrounded her, she felt powerful.

But now?

She sat in a chair across from the enemy court, forcing herself to play along despite the blood of her ex-lover and friend splattered on her dress. Worn from the events of the morning, Morana failed to shield herself against a predator. Elivira was certainly right. *Playing queen.* What a pitiful reality.

"Who do you think I am?" she asked.

His eyes flicked over her dress while his slender finger stirred the small bowl of almonds on the table. There was nothing heated in his gaze—only careful observation. "The Queen of Shadows," he finally supplied. He met her eyes once more, and a shiver ran down her spine. A small smile tugged on his lips as he caught her reaction. "Something like that," he added.

She really scoffed then, hoping to regain her mask of indifference as she fell back into her chair, her eyes rolling dramatically. "Nothing like that."

"You wield the shadows." He glanced as if he could see through the table, see the comforting presence of darkness that still twisted around her black heels.

"And you wield the light." She leaned forward then, the very beginnings of anger bubbling just beneath the surface. It was something to latch onto and keep her mask from slipping.

"Your ears aren't pointed," he countered.

"I'm not fae, and I despise the light. I've never once *wielded* it." She spat the words like a curse. *Wielding* the light? Hardly. For the first time in this conversation, she saw a game she could win. It gave her a sense of confidence.

"What are you then?" A flicker of amusement danced in his eyes, as if the fox knew exactly what she would say, as if her budding anger amused him. There was nothing he could offer her—no hidden truth or empty promise that could convince her to take his side.

"Mortal." Her statement was absolute. "Now, I'm not interested in a deal with—" She fought for a name, realizing he had never given it. If names were power, she knew it was the one thing she needed from him. To take power from the fae fed her soul—it cast out her fears.

Would he give it to her?

He smiled then. The light of the faefire glinting off perfect teeth. The teeth of a predator. She still didn't know who he was hunting.

"Conan," he offered.

"Right." She stood up then, the chair scratching across the wooden floors. She was done playing this game with him. After all, the one who cared less held the most power, and she would claim that power by not caring at all. Ronan would be done soon, and she wanted to make sure Elivira didn't dive into that pond without her. She needed to be there. "As I said before, I am not interested in whatever it is you came here for. Besides, I can offer you absolutely nothing in return." Morana braced her hands on the oak surface of the table. "You talk of politics between two fae courts. Again, I am *mortal.*" Pushing off the table, she made to turn around, shadows growing and twisting around her legs, swirling higher in the dusty tavern. The shadows eased the tension in her shoulders and wrapped around her like a comforting blanket.

"Come to Ohriid." His voice sounded behind her.

Morana didn't look at him as she halted. She simply turned slightly so he could hear her response. Knowing her complete uselessness, confused at his accusations, she already started picturing her room at the palace in her mind, the one gilded and containing the crackling fire. The one in the tower where she had shared a bed with the King of Shadow, the god of death. What would Matthias say if he knew lords were seeking her out to make deals in his absence?

"I have better things to do."

Her words hung in the air, charging the space and reinforcing her drive to find Matthias to bring him home.

As inky mist coated her body, the world parted and swallowed her whole. Pleasure coated her veins before releasing her and spitting her out in the small hallway in front of her room. The familiarity finally eroded her mask, and she choked out a sob at the sentiment.

Home.

She was home, and she wouldn't stop until Matthias was, too.

Three

Willow stood in Morana's room, wiping down the nightstand with a cloth. The woman jolted as Morana appeared, spinning around with one hand on her chest; the other gripping the stand she had been dusting. Her long black hair hung wildly around her shoulders; smooth pale skin set with subtle frown lines. Willow was always so put together—beautifully warm, but Morana guessed Matthias's absence had unnerved more than just herself.

In the tavern, it was easy to focus inward—to bathe in her own sorrow. The sheer thought of that made her cringe. In the palace, however, memories seemed to creep into her mind.

"It's you," Willow spoke, breaking Morana's spiraling thoughts. Willow's blue eyes closed as she breathed in a sigh of relief. Her tight grip slowly loosened on the wood, and her shoulders sunk into a more relaxed stance.

"Where is Elivira?" Morana stared at the woman, wondering if her flustered state resulted from Matthias's absence. Morana looked flustered herself, especially as those memories fought to break through. Matthias walking through a dimly lit park played on a loop in her mind. She could recall every detail he spoke of his parents—his life. She longed for more of him—who he was.

She knew Willow could see the tear stains on her cheeks, but the woman didn't say anything about it, and for that, Morana was thankful. She wouldn't say anything about Willow's sunken features, either.

Willow shook her head, turning to continue her dusting. "In the throne room, sitting on the steps of the dais." She turned enough for Morana to catch the fae woman's raised brows. "Making excuses about where he is and saying he will be here in a few days."

It was a lie—one marinated in the uncertainty of their situation and spewed from the mouth of a lord despite the extinguished hope of Matthias's quick return. Morana could see Matthias's breathy chuckle, the way he fought his smug smile when she pounded into his chest—calling him names. She pictured him standing in Sarnai's cottage, felt the way he had looked at her in that moment. The longing was fierce—tearing through her like wind ripping across a meadow.

No. No breaking down. He needs us.

Gathering herself, she cleared her throat and steeled her spine. They would find him. "Well," she began. "She's not giving us much time if she is promising a few days until his return."

Morana felt tears stinging at the corners of her eyes. It was becoming more and more difficult to hide in the presence of this woman. The woman whose stare could penetrate Morana's cool demeanor. Willow's eyes softened as if she could see straight through her. Upon entering the room, Morana had pulled the mask back on, but she couldn't bear wearing it anymore—not now.

"Would you like to change?" Willow asked gently.

Morana looked down at the elaborate gown covered in splatters of Axton's blood. All at once, she became aware of how disgusting she felt.

A murderous mortal in a realm of gods and monsters. The odds had never been in her favor. Something was bound to break her. She just didn't realize it would be her own softened heart to do it—the one that had fallen for Death.

She clawed at her dress, peeling it from her body and leaving the fabric pooled on the floor while Willow ran a bath in the other room. Morana's mind was spiraling, sending her tumbling down into her own thoughts. With her dress gone, the cool air bit at her skin. Was this how her father felt when her mother left? Was this the price he had paid?

Morana was now acutely aware of her own weakness.

What are you then?
Mortal.

It had all been an act. Whatever happened in the throne room didn't matter. She was mortal, and for the first time since arriving in Ascella, she hated it.

For Matthias, she wanted to be *something*. She wanted to be someone who could retrieve him from the jaws of the Court of Light, but what use was she?

She dragged herself into the bathroom, the scent of jasmine and coconut invading her senses. The steam quieted something in her, but the tears still fought to escape. Willow made to leave and give her privacy.

"Willow," Morana's voice was soft, causing the fae woman to pause at the door. "Would you stay with me?" Despite her undress, she couldn't handle being alone with the memories.

"Matthias," she said. Her voice was soft as she looked at him, standing with his hands in his pockets, his dark hair falling gently across his forehead. "Would you stay with me?" she asked—unashamed.

"Just until you fall asleep?" he questioned. There was a gentleness to his voice now, something that rounded the rough edges, the deep gravel usually in his tone.

"However long."

Willow came over with a soft smile, grabbing a comb from the counter. When Morana had dampened her hair beneath the water's surface, Willow began brushing the strands gently over the lip of the tub. The motherly affection, the gentle way Willow was comforting her, had the tears finally falling.

She hardly remembered her mother—the one who had left her family in shambles. There was no anger toward the woman—not anymore. There was just a vast nothingness there.

But something about the gentle sensation of Willow's fingers running through her tangled hair made her question what she had missed. Was her mother deserving of hatred? If she hated her, then she had to hate herself. Morana's father compared her to her mother frequently.

Could you hate someone who no longer existed? Her mother was as good as the major gods—sleeping peacefully in the north. Maybe Morana was more like her than she thought. Her three years in the city held no significance. Maybe she had been sleeping too.

Insecurity and fear of oneself were brutal. For as strong and cold as Morana appeared on the outside, she was afraid and loathed herself more for it. She would never let them know, though. Not the lords from Inara's court, not anyone who appeared to be a threat. Willow wasn't a threat, though. Maybe she could allow herself to break—if only for a moment.

"Did you care for Matthias like this? After his parents died?"

Willow laughed, the sound like music filtered through the air. "Are you asking me if I *bathed* Matthias?"

A small smile split across Morana's face. "I suppose not."

Silence stretched between them as Morana closed her eyes, leaning into Willow's tender care.

"I suppose," Willow began, pausing as if she were gathering her thoughts. "Their death lingered long after it was finished." The smile fell from Morana's lips. "His parents, I mean. Matthias is strong. He is a god, after all. He helped me heal from my past, and though I could say I owed it to him to listen—when grief welcomed him—that wouldn't be the truth. The old fae couldn't lie, but we can. You deserve more than my lies, though."

"A true comfort," Morana joked.

"Matthias is like a son to me," Willow admitted. "Not even the gods are immune to grief, Morana. No matter what they would have you believe."

A god. What am I compared to a god? If I cannot find him—help him, am I truly deserving of him—of the kindness he's extended to me? Am I truly deserving of a home?

"I'm nothing but a mortal," she whispered, closing her eyes and leaning her neck to rest on the tub.

Willow let out a breathy chuckle while running her fingers through Morana's blonde hair. It had lengthened slightly since her arrival, now hitting just past her shoulders. "We don't know what you are exactly." Willow shifted in the chair she was sitting on. "That's why you are here, but I suppose you're right. As far as we know, you're mortal."

Morana kept her eyes closed, fighting the tears that threatened to escape. Her eyes were heavy with the weight of emotion. She was used to being so hard. She was so used to blocking people out that she had been cruel to Willow—guided by her frustration and circumstance.

Maybe she was selfish.

"I am nothing," she admitted. A tear fell down her cheek as she kept her eyes closed. "I'm afraid. I have no real skill, and I—" She didn't know what she was going to say to finish that sentence. Matthias had told her that selfishness was hardly a crime, but this? Elivira had told her to rest, but she was afraid of the stillness; caught between her emotions and her duty to act. Whispers of her father's words pierced her ears, reminding her of the one voice Matthias was trying to combat.

"You're selfish to think you could live here without pulling your weight." Her father's slurred words stung as her chest tightened. He was sitting by the table in their old apartment, a beer in his hand.

"And you're selfish to think you can go on like this." Morana was done. She hadn't made enough for rent this time, and his displeasure was as strong as the alcohol on his breath.

"Don't speak to me like that!" Her father slammed a fist on the small wooden surface. "I've been through enough." He got up, wobbling toward her as anger radiated off him in waves. Morana couldn't help the way she flinched.

He slapped her with enough force that her head turned to the side. She clenched her jaw and begged the pain to disappear.

Her father was close now, spit raining down on her as he spoke. "You will watch your mouth, lest you become like her."

The memory was bitter. When she was younger, Morana wanted to hate her mother in the way her father did, but that would mean she would have to hate herself. According to her father, they were one and the same. Maybe that's why she settled on indifference. It was easier to stomach.

Willow stopped brushing her hair, and Morana sat up, water cascading from her shoulders as she turned around to face the fae.

"You've been broken before," Willow reached out with cool fingers, sweeping away a tear that had migrated down Morana's cheek. The woman's gentle touch trailed over the scars of death Morana wore. "You've built a wall of steel to protect yourself, and I'm hardly offended by the way you acted when you arrived."

Willow looked pensive. She wiped her hand on her dress before her wide blue eyes met Morana's once more. "Just be careful of the cracks that are forming. They are good, but when you open up, two things can invade your soul." Willow brushed a stray strand of black hair away from her face. "Healing or a vicious evil that will consume you whole." Willow patted her cheek and stood up. "You decide."

Moving the chair away from the tub, Willow dragged it across the dark-colored floors to return it to its rightful place. Before she left the room, she turned back to Morana.

"Elivira wants you to take her to the land of the gods by nightfall. Without the Beatrix ring, the one that Hames uses and used to get Ax—" she paused, thinking better of speaking his name. "The ring to get the boy. Elivira will need you to shift realms." A soft smile spread across her face. "See," she said. "You're already useful."

Willow exited the bathing chamber as Morana used a towel to wipe the last tears from her face.

A chill ran down Morana's spine at the translucent fish darting beneath the water's surface in the fountain. She fought the bile that crawled up her throat. The last time she was here, the fish tried to consume her.

Elivira was standing with her in the hall of relics with her arms folded across her chest. Her pine-colored dress draped gracefully over her toned figure. She raised a light brown hand and flicked a strand of hair away from her face.

Morana had gotten out of the tub as soon as Willow walked out, putting on a large black t-shirt and the jeans that she found in the wardrobe. It was a reminder of what Matthias had gathered for her before disappearing. The tears were gone, and she didn't want to wallow. The idea of wallowing brought about a new fear, the fear that she would become what her father was. Instead, Morana longed to be useful—to do something in the way Willow had suggested.

"I should go in." Morana glanced down at the fish; eyes fixed on the small glow coming from the water. She turned to Elivira and tried to keep her nerves at bay. She had gotten out of the Basar fountain before. The only problem was she couldn't remember how.

Elivira's face was tight, her dark brown curls pulled into a delicate bun at the top of her head. She looked ethereal, with black kohl lining her eyes, and her face made up for a day at court.

"You got lucky the first time," Elivira scoffed, and Morana winced. There was no denying the truth, and Elivira's appearance didn't do anything to melt the ice of her tone. Morana remembered the image of Matthias being taken. It was the one the Basar had shown her before, the only thing she could remember clearly.

Elivira reached up, untying the hair atop her head and freeing it to hang just below her shoulders. Her black heels came off next, and she squared her stance, pursing her lips. "We're in a time crunch."

It was the last thing the lord said before diving into the fountain. Startled by the quick movement, Morana fought to catch her breath and the urge to jump in after her.

Shadows twisted over Morana's arms as she fought for comfort in the wake of the Basar. She could remember the sting of her lungs and the pain as she fought for the images that held the answers she sought. Yet, the fountain only showed her who had taken him and the barest hint of where that was. The Wastelands were practically another country. Matthias could be anywhere.

The fish darted to the bottom of the fountain, and Morana leaned over, placing her hands on the stone ledge, desperately trying to see through to Elivira. The water was no longer glowing, dimmed in the absence of the Basar at the surface.

Fear fought its way through as time passed. Elivira should have come out of the fountain by now. Every second that passed without the lord surfacing increased Morana's panic. She thought about the way the fish had dragged her under, coaxing her to lose consciousness. *Did they have Elivira?* It was a desperate anxiousness, one that pulled on her recent experiences.

She pulled off her sneakers and climbed onto the lip of the fountain, looking down as her heart pounded in her chest. She was used to fighting off her emotions, burying them in a grave, and moving forward with little thought about how she was feeling. Willow was right. She could be useful. Morana closed her eyes, breathing deeply before she dived in.

The water bit at her skin with a fierce chill that made her chest tighten. She swam deeper, opening her eyes to see the mass of fish at the bottom. Elivira wasn't visible through the bodies of the Basar and Morana's mind went to the worst possible reasoning. Elivira was being consumed. One translucent fish darted in front of her, and Morana fought back the fear as adrenaline took over. When she swatted at it, the fish barred pointed teeth before swimming away quickly. It wasn't as vicious as she had expected, almost as if it remembered her—feared her.

Her brows furrowed as she got closer to the mass of fish at the bottom. They parted, hissing and flashing needle-like teeth, the same small teeth that had dug into Morana's flesh and dotted her skin in pale circles. The marks were long gone, but some scars ran deeper than the flesh.

A flash of brown skin appeared through the mass, and Morana reached forward, the fish moving away from her as she grabbed Elivira. When her vision focused, she noticed the teeth marks dotting Elivira's flesh. Pink swirled from the puncture wounds as it mixed with the fountain's water. The marks brought horror to Morana's throat, but she couldn't scream—not while she was still holding her breath.

Something latched onto her foot, and Morana kicked the creature off, growling as she hefted the lord higher. Elivira's eyes were closed, lush lips parted as small bubbles escaped her mouth. The bite marks on her body seemed more severe than the ones Morana wore during her last encounter with the Basar.

Kicking, Morana swam to the surface. Her lungs were burning and begging her to take a breath as more fish started latching onto her legs, her arms. The Basar were brave now, hardly the timid creatures fleeing from her presence before. Maybe it was the darkness that forced them away. She called the shadows, attempting to coat herself in inky darkness, but there was nothing there. The shadows sat dormant in the presence of the fish—utterly useless. Panic had a firm grip on Morana as the fish kept coming, latching on to any piece of exposed flesh they could find.

They were still attacking Elivira, too. Morana kept swimming as she fought to hold her breath. Her lips parted and a huff of air escaped her. They were dragging her down again, pulling her into the abyss and begging her to let go. She could see the palace in the land of the gods destroyed. She relived Matthias being taken and the sting of betrayal as she watched Axton lure him away.

Something flickered in her chest. The pulsing grew until Morana looked down to see glittering gold light covering her skin. She held on to that feeling, allowing it to slither down her arms and wrap her body in something other than shadows.

The fish reeled back, burned by the searing power. They hissed before darting away. Morana allowed the power to grow, kicking her way to the surface of the fountain with Elivira in tow.

Hope bloomed in her chest. But before they broke the surface, Morana turned to see Elivira's wide, brown eyes frantically taking in the new power that illuminated the dark water. More bubbles exited her mouth, and Morana knew she had taken in water. There was a coppery tang to the liquid as if the blood that fed the fish also fed the magic of the fountain. The Basar were gone, no longer fighting to consume them and utterly afraid of whatever was causing Morana to glow, but she needed to get Elivira out of the fountain.

She shoved Elivira to the surface and struggled to push the bleeding and unconscious woman over the edge into the Hall of Relics. Elivira's eyes were closed again, flesh covered in pale marks. Now that they were out of the water, Morana could see where the fish had completely ripped off a chunk of flesh on part of the lord's arm.

Panic was spinning a constricting web in her chest. She was fighting for clarity. Elivira wasn't breathing, lying on the ground and bleeding onto the stone floors.

"No," she whispered, kneeling over the still form.

She placed two fingers over her neck to feel for a pulse. Morana looked around the room, desperately trying to think—to make a decision. She positioned a hand on Elivira's chest, lacing the fingers of her second hand through the first, and pushed. Tears stung her eyes, and that glowing power still illuminated her skin.

"No, no, no," she repeated. "Come on. This can't be happening." All of Morana's feelings of worthlessness surfaced as she started chest compressions. She didn't know if she was doing the right thing, couldn't think beyond the overwhelming dread.

If Elivira was dead—if she didn't start breathing soon—Morana couldn't handle the sight. She remembered Morton lying in a pool of blood. Elivira wasn't Axton— wasn't deserving of this kind of death.

Elivira heaved, breathing in and then coughing up the water. She sat up, leaning over as she continued spewing water on the floor.

Morana sat back on her heels and quickly wiped the tears from her face. Glancing at the wound on the woman's arm, Morana reached down to tear at her shirt. She wrapped the torn fabric around Elivira's arm. The lord didn't stop her, just stared at her with her full lips parted, her light brown skin paling in the light of the Hall of Relics.

With the fabric bound around Elivira's arm, Morana looked down to see her skin was still glowing. Memories of light slashing into her back haunted her. She was shaking, trembling with the fear of the power she held as it slowly faded into nothing. She called the shadows, willing them to take away the panic in her chest, begging the darkness to comfort her in the wake of her memories. The power was addictive—feeding her in a way that satisfied. When her fears became too much, she needed that power like the air she breathed.

Elivira was still staring; her dress drenched and hair hanging heavy around her shoulders. The white patches from the fish were slowly fading; only the one injury now tied in the scraps of Morana's t-shirt remained.

"I know where Matthias is," she rasped before coughing again. Elivira leaned over, vomiting all over the floor before wiping her arm across her lips.

Morana fought the urge to retch, too. She hadn't almost drowned, not this time. In fact, she had been the reason they had gotten out.

"And I know how I got out of the fountain the first time," she whispered.

Four

Morning light filtered through the autumn trees as Morana stood dressed in leathers, with her weapons strapped to her side. She stared at the three horses, prepared and ready, as she gripped the heavy cloak hanging over her shoulders tightly.

Elivira had called the lords to a meeting the previous evening. She hadn't been able to explain much of what she saw. Matthias was in The Wastelands, kept in the long-forgotten temple of a sleeping god. It was a palace of bone and clay. When Morana had asked how he was, Elivira paled, swallowing hard before refusing to answer.

Something about the situation didn't sit right. Inara had been to The Wastelands. They had learned as much from the blood book, but there was still the issue of the missing pages. Pieces of information that they couldn't glean from whatever had been written. Cain emphasized the significance of the missing pages, but Morana still couldn't fully grasp the things that were happening around her.

Willow knew exactly how she was feeling, and she was thankful for lowering the mask enough to let the fae woman in. There was so much about the realm she didn't understand, and here she was, trying to find Matthias and be a part of his retrieval.

Elivira called her a *liability* the first time they met, and that word dug into old wounds she had covered the day she walked out of her father's apartment. Every time she thought of it, the scabs that formed over her heart, those thoughts tearing at the raw flesh until the wounds were brand new.

Even more prominent than the memories of her childhood were the memories of Matthias. She couldn't stop thinking about him. He was invading her mind—even now.

Still, the scars from her father ran deep. Deep enough that she didn't know how to care for another--how to love them. The thought that she might want to—want that scared her even more.

I'm capable of selfishness. Nothing more.

That thought felt like truth, but as she pictured Matthias atop the restaurant in Ascella, glamoured and hidden from the rest of the world, those words seemed to lose power.

They were losing power.

*"A god," she mused. "A god trying to enlighten me."
She huffed a laugh.*

"I don't think my name has ever been associated with enlightenment." His jaw ticked as if he were about to

smile. "At least not in the way you're saying. I'm always the thing people are avoiding."

Morana knew her powers couldn't stretch across the distance between them now, but she still hoped he could hear her thoughts. *Nobody is avoiding Death. In fact, we are coming to get you. Please stay alive.*

She was staring now, lost in thought. Closing her eyes and breathing deeply, she refocused her mind. If she wanted him back, she'd have to fight for it.

"Déjà vu, don't you say?" Ronan smiled when he appeared beside her. That familiar cocky grin helped keep her mind out of the abyss.

They were standing outside of the palace stables. Horses paced the white fence in the distance, their breath visible as it blew from their nostrils. Sweat dripped off the chest of a black mare as she pawed the dirt—tossing her head.

The entire palace was in distress—even if most of them didn't know it yet.

Morana's eyes flicked to Ronan. "Shut up," she answered, fighting back the tears that were still threatening to escape. She cried enough yesterday and didn't want to deal with the emotions anymore.

"Wow." Ronan's brows shot up; blue eyes still amused despite the harsh remark. He ran a hand through his blonde hair before pulling the sandy strands into a bun. "Someone's in a mood."

Morana huffed a laugh, a small smile breaking through as she folded her arms across her chest. There was something about Ronan's presence—something light. He wasn't all that bad. "Why are there only three horses again?"

Ronan's grin widened. He winked, elbowing her in the ribs. "You're riding with me."

Nope. He is not all that bad at all—he's worse. Insufferable, even.

Morana wrinkled her nose as she watched the stone archway at the center of the stables. She had yet to explore this part of the palace, but she knew the exterior wall. Two narrow structures stretched back from the center of the building like a horseshoe. The stables were a mix of stone and wood with a gabled roof and one large belfry.

Garian approached with the reins of a large, bay mare in his hand. The sunlight streaming through the trees lining the path from the palace illuminated the lord's chiseled features and dark brown skin.

"I'd rather ride with Garian," Morana confessed.

"Suit yourself." Ronan walked away, mounted the dappled gray gelding, and trotted away to where Elivira was now sitting astride the horse that had taken her to Zora.

Wind whipped through the trees, rustling leaves that were slowly turning more colorful by the day. Morana wondered what winter would be like in Ascella—hoped that Matthias could show her.

She hadn't had time to explore the city or even much of the palace. Morana longed to know what

Matthias's court had to offer. She just didn't want to explore the city without him.

Morana turned to Garian, who now wore an unfamiliar expression. It was something she hadn't seen yet from the lord. "And to think," he began, "I was starting to warm up to you."

Tilting her head, Morana squinted as she looked up at him, daring him to speak truth. Her gray eyes examined his features. "And how do you feel now?" she asked.

Garian grunted, those dark eyes looking down at her. They were warmer somehow. "Just don't expect the same treatment from me atop our horse." He cleared his throat. "I'm not Matthias."

He moved around to the other side of the horse and pulled the reins over the mare's head.

Morana's cheeks heated with embarrassment. She pursed her lips, moving around to where Garian was standing with a small smile on his face.

Her lips parted, hanging open in shock. "It was a joke."

He gestured to the stirrup. "Go on," Garian's full lips hadn't stopped smiling. "Get up."

"You actually made a joke." Morana placed her foot in the stirrup, heaving herself onto the horse they would ride to The Wastelands.

Garian mounted and sat behind her, keeping a respectful distance, and adjusted his cloak. Elivira had handed the cloaks out without a word. She had been oddly quiet since the fountain, not speaking of what she saw beyond the basics. Morana supposed she was thankful for the silence. It meant the lord hadn't said anything about the power she held.

"Why the heavy cloaks?" Morana broke the silence as the horses walked beyond the fence surrounding the stable.

"We are going to the North. We don't know if anyone can track our magic in The Wastelands, but the bigger concern is that we have never been there." Garian shifted uncomfortably behind her. "You can't use the shadows to go where you've never been."

Morana's brows pinched together. She had done that very thing in the beginning, when Matthias had been watching her—hunting her. She had shifted realms with ease, while the lords could only stay within the fae realm without the strange ring Willow described.

"Right," she finally spoke, swallowing hard. "No shadows then."

Garian's grip tightened on the reins, and Morana could have sworn she felt his body tense behind her.

"Exactly. Once we get to the border, no shadows."

When Morana glanced back, the lord was no longer smiling.

The Vulcan mountains were rugged and snow-capped, glistening at their backs as they stood before the border to The Wastelands. It was as if they were standing at the edge of the world, a completely unfamiliar landscape laid out before them. Dry, cracked earth went on for miles as a brisk wind twisted over the dust. It was as if any color or life had been leached from all surfaces. There would be nothing of the beauty found in the Vulcan mountains left once they crossed the border.

Morana sat atop the horse with Garian. They had shadowed just outside of Vulcan, traveling through the mountains for a few hours before arriving here. Despite the casual way Elivira led her mount across the border, a tendril of fear still crawled its way up Morana's spine. She could hardly believe Matthias was out here in the vast nothingness.

Her horse stepped over the line, and Morana held the shadows within her. Across the border, there were no protections against being tracked. She would have to survive without the comfort of her power. It made her feel utterly helpless—worthless. Those familiar feelings swam in her gut, fighting to consume any ounce of confidence that she held. It reminded her of the Basar fighting to consume flesh and feeding on anything they could sink their sharp teeth into. Morana shuddered.

"You're sure you know where you're going?" Ronan was smiling at Elivira as the two moved across the cracked earth. "We will have to stop soon." He ran a hand through his blonde hair. "Maybe keep each other company."

"Would you stop talking?" Elivira gritted out. Her tone was harsh as her gaze snapped to the handsome blue-eyed lord. "You haven't stopped moving your mouth since we left."

Morana could see the tension Elivira was carrying, the way her shoulders tightened, and she worried her bottom lip in anticipation of what was to come. They knew little about what she had seen, but it clearly bothered her. It didn't matter. No matter the mission, even if suicidal, they all would have gone to get Matthias.

"I'm quite good at moving my mouth." Ronan turned, blue eyes glistening with wild delight. "What about you, darling?" He was looking at Morana now. "Interested in verifying that little fact? I'm sure your bed is cold."

It was Morana's turn to tense, her eyes narrowing. "I liked you at first, Ronan, but you're slowly becoming an insufferable bastard."

Garian's deep chuckle rumbled behind her, alleviating some of the tension and causing her to let out a small laugh as well. Ronan was a harmless flirt, no matter what he had claimed at Mabon.

"She's got a bite to her." Ronan licked his lips, winking in her direction. In a rare moment of sincerity, Ronan dropped his charming façade. "Nah, you definitely belong to someone else."

Pain shot through her chest at the statement, fierce and unwelcome. It reminded her of the gaping hole that had formed in Matthias's absence. She was desperate to get him back.

"We will have to camp out in the open," Elivira remarked. Morana's eyes flicked over the cracked and flat earth. She didn't believe anything existed out here. "There's nothing else until we get to the temple."

"What kind of temple is it?" Morana asked. Their horse halted as Elivira dismounted. Concern laced her brown eyes when she looked up from the ground.

"The temple of a major god thought to be sleeping." Elivira brushed a hair back from her face. The wind was still skating over the dusty earth and bringing a crisp chill. Morana tightened her cloak before Elivira released the name of the god. "Raidan," she almost whispered.

Morana's brows furrowed, but she could feel the way Garian inhaled sharply behind her. She had heard the name before, and it must have meant something if the name cracked Garian's usual stoic expression. A sharp inhale was all she needed to hear.

Sarnai had mentioned Raidan in her cabin, and Morana had heard it somewhere else too. She just couldn't place where she had heard the name or what had been said. The goddess had been too busy in the past few days for her to bring it up again.

Morana hadn't seen her since the day Matthias had gone missing. Remembering the panic in the goddess's voice, Morana's heart clenched.

Garian dismounted, and Morana followed behind him, adjusting her cloak at her back. Ronan was already unloading bedrolls and preparing a place for them to sit.

Elivira pulled out a large container holding water and poured some out for the horses.

Morana looked up at the painted sky, orange and purple streaked across the vast expanse. Color could exist here as long as it didn't touch the earth, earth she now had to rest upon. She took it as a sign that things would go in their favor. It would be dark soon, and soon, they would be one step closer to finding Death.

White mist was wrapping around the cracked earth, rising and engulfing their camp in an eerie magic. A song started, soft, and lulling—and familiar.

Morana sat up, her hand searching for the dagger she had carried with her at her side. She couldn't see through the thick mist rising around them, and the song was dragging her under, begging her mind to relinquish control.

Her hand relaxed, never finding the weapon as she looked away from the camp. A beautiful woman with skin like the surface of The Wastelands prowled forward. She was naked, save for the long, dark hair that covered her chest.

Morana let out a harsh breath, standing while the Veeden continued its song. The melody promised to take away her worries, and Morana was falling victim to its desires as she stepped forward, drawn to the creature. Her boot parted the mist at her feet, sending the fog dancing around the motion.

"Queen of Darkness," the Veeden called. The entire scene was familiar. Something in the back of Morana's mind begged her to listen, screaming to tell her that this wasn't right, but her heart was quiet and her body relaxed.

She couldn't fight it.

With sleep clouding her mind, creating a thin veil between what she knew to be the wise decision and what the siren's song made her long for, Morana stepped closer. Part of her believed she would find the very thing she had been looking for so long as she got close. She wanted to feel the creature's skin and touch her soft hair.

A cracked smile appeared on the Veeden's dry lips. The siren combed long fingers through its hair, bare feet stepping in time with the song.

Morana swayed where she stood. There was no fight left in her to resist the call—whatever it may be. As the world spun around her, the swirling mist dancing with the melody, something rose in her chest.

"Raidan's calling," the siren spoke through the song. It was a whisper mixed with the sweetest melody that continued to invade Morana's senses. "Do you hear him, child?"

Morana stared with hooded eyes fixated on the long fingers running through dark hair. Her mouth parted as she fought for breath. The Veeden separated the mist. Beyond the mysterious magic, Morana could see nothing of the vast wastelands beyond. There were no lords and no courts in this secluded place the siren had created. There was only peace.

A long nail trailed down her cheek as the Veeden came to stand directly in front of her. It traced over the scars decorating her face, but Morana couldn't fathom why she had fought off the other siren before. There was nothing wrong with giving in to whatever this was. She was sure of it.

The woman—creature—leaned forward. "Raidan's calling," she whispered before pressing her lips over Morana's.

The kiss wasn't soft like the song that hung in the air. It was bruising and harsh—a punishing noise like the call of a war drum. Morana sucked in a breath, and a long tongue shoved into her mouth, skating down her throat. She felt as if she were suffocating. She reached up to grip the creature's hand that was now wrapped around her neck. What once seemed like a peaceful offer, drawing her in while the Veeden's song pulled her in, was now a bruising force only willing to take. The song was a lie—this creature would steal the life from her.

Morana's throat was dry; coated in sand and sadness. She could taste copper as the Veeden shoved its body closer, digging claws into her flesh and taking whatever it desired.

Morana thrashed, but the creature's grip tightened, the strange magic halting her movements. She was losing her hold on her own mind. It was slowly slipping away on a dry desert wind. Morana's eyes closed, losing whatever tether had kept her to reality. It was all fear and harsh sadness mixed with bitter rage.

The feelings shifted as something like pleasure replaced whatever was there before. It was heady as Morana's blood hummed in her veins. Everything felt good. She could feel the Veeden's power invading her, forcing its way into the core of her being. The mist pulsed with a forbidden power that brought something more than the shadows. This power was strong and beckoning. Morana didn't want it to end. She craved it and all that it offered. She leaned in, deepening the kiss and moaning as the Veeden tightened fingers around her neck.

The creature was taking, and Morana wanted nothing more than to let the thing have it all. Hatred and bitterness stirred beneath the pleasure. Morana could see Axton kneeling on the floor of the throne room. She wanted to rip him apart with her bare hands, to feel his flesh tearing, to smell the bones and blood. She moaned again, gripping the Veeden's hip and pulling it closer.

The misty power mixed with the shadows and light in Morana's veins. It intertwined and danced in a way that had her head spinning. A voice called in the darkness, dark and gravely, as it begged for power—her power.

"Answer the call," it spoke. A chill ran down her spine as Morana held the Veeden to her chest, desperately trying to get closer. She wouldn't be satisfied until the creature consumed her—until they became one.

The Veeden jerked forward before separating from her, its tongue scratching as it exited Morana's throat. She coughed, a white mist pouring from her parted lips.

Morana fell to the ground with her hands gripping her chest. She was gasping for air, desperately trying to register where the siren had gone. It felt empty, and she growled, looking up to search for the one thing she wanted most.

When she saw Garian standing and panting with his sword in his hand, sweat was dripping from his temples, and his eyes were wild, flicking around the fading mist of The Wastelands. It was like water crashing over her—icy and cool—replacing the pleasure with the shock of yet another dead body on the ground. Garian had driven his sword through the siren that was now convulsing in the dirt.

Garian lifted his sword once more, bringing it down and severing the head of the monster. The head rolled across the cracked earth, blood dripping from its neck.

Morana was fighting off the urge to vomit when she registered that Elivira and Ronan were standing with swords drawn as well. They looked as shocked as she felt.

Elivira's face hardened, and Morana remembered the truth. She was a liability, saved by sheer luck. Yet, this wasn't luck. Garian's skill with a sword was the only thing that saved her from whatever the Veeden would have done. She didn't dare ask what end those attacked by the Veeden met. Morana coughed again, something like white dust leaving her lungs.

"No luck this time," she rasped. Morana was looking at Elivira. Shame stirred in her gut.

"No luck," the lord responded. Her tone was icy, her lush facial features unreadable. It didn't take long before she disappeared, leaving Morana sitting in the dry dirt and wondering what would have happened if Garian hadn't saved her.

She coughed again, the same white mist leaving her lungs. Ronan helped her to her feet, his warm hand hauling her up as the ground cleared.

Despite the quietness of their surroundings, the air felt different. Maybe she was more tuned into the risk of being here. She certainly didn't want to be reminded of her vulnerability.

If Death could be captured, who are you to save him?

Morana's limbs shook—anger rising in her chest.

"Does it matter?" she whispered, knowing that the nerves coursing through her veins wouldn't settle—not yet.

Sleep would not come again.

Five

Morana could feel the dark circles carved beneath her gray eyes. Dust coated her skin, and the taste of the Veeden's tongue down her throat lingered—a bitter pleasure that had invaded her bones. She hardly spoke as they walked, consumed by hours of silence and hours of dry, cracked nothingness.

Garian walked behind them after claiming he needed to stretch his legs. Morana got the sense that he was just uncomfortable. Sitting atop a horse with a strange mortal woman had most likely gotten the better of him. She didn't mind the solitude.

That was, until the bones started appearing. Resting on the cracked earth was a skull, picked clean and rocking in the wind that rushed over the ground. Morana looked from one bone to find another, and yet another. Farther out, she could see that the ground was covered with them. A faraway building stretched in the distance. It was too far to make out the details, so Morana glanced back at the bones.

"Did you see this?" she asked Elivira. "When you were in the Basar fountain. Did you see all of this?"

Elivira's shoulders went rigid. She nodded but said nothing. The continued silence carved worry in Morana's chest. She didn't want to think about what the lord had seen—what had happened to Matthias in the time since he was taken.

"The bones here are hardly as bad as where he's keeping Matthias." Elivira's voice was almost a whisper. Morana didn't know if she wanted to hear the rest, but a part of her couldn't resist.

"I haven't asked. I didn't want to bother you." She didn't want to admit that she was fearful—afraid of what the answer would be. "How is he?"

"Don't ask." Elivira's tone was a harsh warning. There was an icy bitterness leaving her lips that said enough about the horrors she saw. Her features softened as she looked over at Morana from atop her horse. There was an understanding there as if she saw something on Morana's face—something not so easily hidden. "You'll only cause yourself grief."

"Grief has already been had." It was the truth. A truth she had fought to run from. Sorrow somehow kept finding her. In her exhaustion, Morana looked over at the woman who had tattooed the snake behind her ear. The same woman who had called her a liability. The truth was a bitter pill to swallow, but she had accepted it. Between being shot at, hunted, beaten, starved, and attacked, Morana had learned very little in the way of protecting herself. She hardly understood her power and didn't have the time to process the events of the past months. "I'm barely trained and carrying power I don't understand. I may have played queen back in that throne room, but you have to know better." The admittance poured out of her, eating away at some of the tension in her shoulders. She was finding it hard to admit the inner turmoil—to let people in.

Elivira didn't offer a comforting response. She merely cleared her throat before her brown eyes flicked around the area to make sure the boys were out of earshot. "Speaking of power that you don't understand," she began. "The light—"

"I don't want to talk about it," Morana snapped. Something about the light still caused fear to swarm in her gut, and that fear wasn't something she wanted to touch. The power brought her back to Inara's cell and Axton's betrayal. It reminded her of the fox waiting in his den—ready to strike his prey. Her stomach clenched at the thought of that light winding its way between Conan's fingers in the tavern. She fought the sinking feeling.

Elivira didn't balk. "You'll have to eventually," she stated. "Will you tell Matthias?"

Morana's forehead wrinkled. "Of course." She thought back to the moment atop the restaurant in the Court of Shadows. It was the moment she had opened herself up to the god and given him more than she thought herself capable of. She let him work his way into her mind, watch her past unfold like a movie on a screen. He had seen Inara whip her, too. There wasn't anything to hide from him—not anymore. How could someone hide the darkness from the very being that lurked in the shadows? There was no reason to hide from Death—he had seen her soul and embraced it. That thought would have scared her a month ago. Now? Well, Death had claimed her, and there was nothing she longed to keep hidden from his darkness.

Elivira lifted her nose, eyes glancing at Morana. "Good," she responded.

There was another long stretch of silence, one more unsettling than before. The conversation had gotten Morana's thoughts working, and they simply would not cease.

Elivira's voice broke the silence once more. "And Morana?" There was no hardness left in her features, but Morana still struggled to place the emotion there. "You're not useless, or worthless, or whatever pitiful lie you told yourself."

Morana's lips parted in shock. She stared at the lord, her body moving as her horse strode forward. There was nothing to be said about it. The only thing she could do was fight back the tears.

Elivira's face twisted in confusion. Had she known the way her coldness had come off?

"You're worth something," Elivira began. Indecision played across her features. The fae wasn't used to expressing such things. "Why do you think our damn courts are about to go to war? You getting kidnapped is why we retrieved Inara's blood book from Lux's tomb." Morana swallowed. It was her turn to be unsure of how to respond.

"Assassins are being sent from the Court of Light. Inara broke the rules of Mabon." Her brown eyes flicked to Morana once more. "Someone of little worth could hardly cause so much strife."

Morana fought the tears, placing the mask back over her emotions. There was nothing else she could do in the wake of the turmoil within, so she allowed a small smirk to form on her lips. "That makes me a liability, doesn't it?"

Elivira looked uncomfortable with her casual avoidance. "I don't know what it makes you, but you're currently riding through a field of bones to rescue a god." Respect shone in those intense eyes, and she lowered her voice before continuing. "You hold power from both courts, and that," Elivira's lips peeled back in disgust, "vile Veeden—" It was as if she remembered the creature's head rolling across the cracked earth. "That Veeden should have *killed* you. They—" Elivira pinched the bridge of her nose, the other hand still on the reins. She exhaled. "The Veeden kill people when they get that close."

Morana's luck hadn't run out, then. She kept her emotions controlled, keeping the grin on her face. It was in stark contrast to the dark circles that still decorated her flesh beneath her gray eyes. "Maybe Garian needs a new tattoo." Morana ran a finger over the snake behind her ear. "For killing the Veeden, I mean."

Elivira scoffed, but there was something lighter in her expression as she fought back a smile. "Maybe he does."

Morana had hardly noticed the temple slowly coming into view before them. The stone building was massive. A mist settled over the ground in front of the ivy-covered doors. Ancient magic peered out from the stained-glass windows.

The mist had Morana's stomach churning. Whatever power the Veeden held, she suspected it was similar to whatever coated the cracked earth.

Nonetheless, it drew her in, calling to her. Matthias was in there, and she wanted him out.

Morana dismounted, pulling the reins over her horse's neck. Her hands were trembling, and determination rose in her chest. The horse was pawing at the ground, hesitant to move any closer.

She was walking closer, refusing to tear her gaze from the structure. Upon further inspection, the building wasn't made of stone at all, but pale clay and bone. Morana reached a hand outward, longing to trace the intricate design the bones created.

Garian gripped her wrist, drawing Morana from the spell she was under. "You can't just go in," he scolded.

"I'm not an idiot,"

Garian chuckled. "Right, then the warning must have been for Ronan."

Morna glanced to Ronan, who was now walking up to join them. His features were relaxed, closed off from whatever strange magic Morana had been experiencing before. Elivira was patting both her own horse and Ronan's on the neck. Her shoulders were tense, eyes focused on the temple.

"I'm hardly an idiot," Ronan stated. "I'm the one with the most knowledge about runes." He cocked an eyebrow and held out his hand. "Now. Knife."

Garian handed the lord a blade. Runes decorated the steel, etched carefully into the metal. The hilt was simple enough, smooth, and free of any symbols.

"What will that do?" Morana asked.

Ronan merely flashed a smile, gripping the hilt of the dagger in one hand and holding out his palm. "Protect us." It was the only answer he provided before slicing his palm open. Morana watched as blood welled, and he dipped a finger in the crimson liquid. Ronan knelt, drawing a symbol on the cracked earth before turning to Morana and asking for her hand.

"A marriage proposal?" she joked. It was an effort to ease the nerves settling low in her belly. "So soon?"

"Hilarious." Ronan gripped her hand, his usually light expression shifting into something more serious as he placed the tip of the dagger on her skin. He looked up once, requesting permission. Morana nodded before the sting of the dagger punctured her flesh. The blood welled instantly, and Ronan repeated the process on the ground.

He did the same for each of the lords.

"He's in the basement," Elivira offered. Her expression was tight, fists clenched at her sides. "That's all I know."

"You think the wards will be enough?" Garian asked.

Ronan ran a hand down his face, a nervous gesture, something Morana hadn't seen in the confident lord. "It's worth something. It will conceal our arrival, but Elivira—" He looked in her direction. "Raidan is a major god. This magic is far beyond our—"

"I know," Elivira snapped, raising a light brown hand as if it would protect her from whatever he wanted to say next. "I know," she repeated—softer this time.

Walking into the temple had Morana's heart racing in her chest. She had tied her hair away from her face, but her temples and palms were slick with sweat. She was out of her element, lost in the discussions of runes and wards. There was no comfort here. No matter what they encountered, she couldn't touch the shadows—couldn't risk being tracked by something even worse.

The air was thick—heavy with the weight of something ancient and very much alive. Morana swallowed thickly, forcing the oxygen down despite its heaviness. She may not know about runes and protections, but she remembered the way Matthias's power called to her own— the way the shadows could whisper and guide. They didn't have to be rippling across her skin to be useful. They were a part of her—designed to bend to her will.

The front doors opened into a large foyer with massive staircases of stone ascending on either side. Moss and ivy grew on every roughened surface, and the entire temple looked abandoned and dark, save for the misty light drifting through the stained-glass windows.

Garian stepped in first with his sword drawn. Between the ascending staircases on either side, tucked under a balcony, was where the staircases descended.

"Down, I'm assuming?" Morana looked to Elivira. The lord's lips were pressed together tightly. She had a hand gripping her sword, her knuckles almost white. Sweat slid down her back. It coated her arms and beaded at her temples, running a trail down her neck. She should have felt doubt—should have doubted the fae guiding her through an unfamiliar palace. Garian had admitted they'd never been to The Wastelands before. Despite her better judgment, she trusted them. It was clear in their devotion to their king—their god. She felt the same. Morana wasn't sure she was ready for the horrors that awaited them, but she would crawl through hell to get Matthias back.

The first step down had Morana panting. The spiraling stairs were dark and slick. Morana couldn't help but slide her foot across one of the steps. Her brows furrowed in confusion. The air didn't feel damp, but the floor clearly wasn't dry.

"Something is here." Ronan's hushed voice sounded behind her. "These stairs are slick with some substance."

"Do you know what it is?" Garian asked. Morana could barely make out the tick of his jaw in the dim light. Bile rose in her throat at the thought of what they would find here.

"I have an idea." Ronan's eyes were ice. He drew his blade, the sound of steel echoing off the walls.

Morana pushed forward again but stopped at the sound of something hissing further down the steps.

"Close your eyes," Garian snarled.

"What?" Morana spun, desperately trying to understand if she heard him correctly. The stairs were slick, and she could barely see. Not to mention there was something in here—something making Ronan draw his blade. Eyes seemed pretty important at the moment.

Garian stepped in front of her. "I said close your fucking eyes."

A crash sounded down the steps, followed by something skidding on the stone. Whatever it was, it was massive.

Morana's breath quickened. A white fog escaped her lips at the chill of the temple. She snapped her eyes shut, sensing the urgency in the air.

"A Basilisk?" Elivira hissed. "A fucking Basilisk."

"Morana, don't open your eyes. Not for anything, just keep walking. I got you." Garian grabbed her wrist, the callouses scraping her sensitive skin. Everything was alive. She could hear movement and rustling, taste the stale stench of urgency.

Garian was dragging her down the steps. She moved slowly, desperately trying to keep her footing.

"As soon as you look at it, the Basilisk will know you're here. It will try to kill you. Do you hear me?" Garian's voice was low and harsh, authority echoing in the large stairwell.

"I hear you!" Morana's eyes were still closed, her hair standing on end. The sounds shifted closer. Too many questions clogged her throat, but she couldn't force herself to ask them. How would they fight a monster if they couldn't see? How did a Basilisk kill its prey? What did it even look like?

Fucking massive. Probably ugly.

She kept her mouth shut, matching the pace of the lord in front of her.

A slick sound rang in her ears.

Closer.

She heard a grunt from Ronan, who was now ahead of her. Then she heard the slick slide of metal slicing flesh, felt Garian's grip disappear on her wrist, and felt Elivira's scream vibrate in her bones.

Without her sight, the sounds were deafening. Morana stepped forward quickly, losing her footing. She held her eyes closed despite the chaos around her. More metal and a loud screeching noise. When she stood up, something moved past her, air blowing stray strands of hair around her face. Whatever it was kept moving, and by the way debris fell around her from the ceiling, she could tell the creature was exactly as she imagined. *Fucking massive.* Could it see her?

She pinned herself to the wall, breath coming out in harsh pants. The creature disappeared, and all went silent.

Something was wrong. Something was—

Morana opened her eyes. "No!" Garian screamed from higher up the steps. His shirt was sliced where a cut leaked blood at his arm. Dirt streaked his face, and panic shone in his eyes as he ran toward her. A monstrous snake with spikes jutting from the top of its head reared up behind him. Elivira's blade stuck out of its body. Morana's mouth opened to release a silent scream.

"Close your eyes!" Garian shouted.

Morana stepped back; eyes caught on the glowing red gaze of the foreign snake. Slick slime dripped from razor-sharp teeth. The Basilisk hissed, and Morana stumbled, losing her footing and screaming as she tumbled down the steps.

Her limbs were on fire, bruises forming upon impact. When she caught herself on the landing, she looked up to see Garian shoving his sword through the belly of the beast. Morana screamed again, and this time, it nearly made the walls tremble. Clamping her hand over her mouth, Morana pushed backward, crushing herself against the wooden wall. The wall opened. *A door, then.*

Her chest heaved with every labored breath. Satisfied that she was hidden away from the beast, Garian shoved his sword through scaly flesh, searing the image in her mind.

She slid back on the floor, still sitting as her legs trembled. Morana couldn't stand or move. She couldn't think beyond the sounds of the battle raging just outside the door.

She needed to get up, needed to do something.

"Queen of Darkness." A gravelly voice sounded behind her as the door slammed shut. Faefires flicked on in the sconces lining the hallway she was now sitting in.

Her head whipped around, a puff of cold white air exiting her lips.

Morana's eyes landed on the broad man wearing a navy suit, his black shoes polished and firmly planted on the stone floor. His gray hair was past his shoulders, and he stood with his hands clasped behind his back.

Morana bit back the scream building in her throat.

"Excuse my pet," he spoke. Chills ran down Morana's spine. Something like immense power pulsed in the hallway. She needed to get out and help the others. She needed—

"Come," he commanded.

White mist gathered at her hands and wrists. It was foreign, yet familiar. Morana couldn't fight what happened next. Her body obeyed, summoned like a dog by the man taking up so much of the limited space.

Black shoes clicked on the stone floors, and Morana was powerless to do anything but follow. Her stomach roiled as she stared at the monster's broad back.

At the end of the hall was another door of solid wood. It opened with a creak before the man stepped inside the small but neat office. Tall bookshelves sat behind the cherry desk, polished to perfection.

"Sit," the man barked. He sauntered around the desk, standing, and observing her with careful concentration. His amber eyes held menacing promises of what was to come.

The pale fog still wrapped around her—shadows different from her own. She staggered on the way to the chair while trying to fight whatever compelled her to obey. Morana suddenly sat opposite the hulking creature, unable to control her own heavy limbs.

Morana thrashed internally like a beast trying to free itself from a cage. Her arms jerked, but the motion was hardly comparable to the effort. To be bound was worse than death, and Death was exactly what she was here to look for. Her neck was straining as she fought her near-invisible restraints, to no avail.

The more she fought, the tighter his power held. She was trapped and suffocating—just like many of her past experiences. Inara's dungeon, her father's apartment, all of it sent her into a frenzy as she grunted furiously.

Her limbs were burning, and she ceased fighting—at least physically. If this was another game, she would play. Though this time, the predator was nothing like a fox. He was a demon.

The monster chuckled darkly. "You're a murderous thing, aren't you?"

She wouldn't dignify that with a proper response and snarled. Her hands clasped the arms of the wooden chair in front of his desk.

"I am, of course, referring to the boy you killed."

Morana gritted her teeth. Anger was still moving through her like a vicious thing, wild and threatening to burst from her chest. "How do you know about Axton?" she asked. If he had something to say, she might as well hear it—use it to her advantage. It could give her the upper hand.

The demon across from her gave her a pointed look, picking up an intricate silver goblet from the shelf behind him. He turned his back to reach for a bottle of wine from the same shelf. Pouring himself a glass, he turned around, his amber eyes vibrant in the dim lights of the study.

"You really believe I'm not aware of what happens in this realm?" he asked. "I am a god, Morana. More powerful than your little pet. The one you call Death."

Dirt and grime were coating her hands and face, adding to the chaos of the storm building in her gut. Morana's lip peeled back as her fury consumed her like a beast starved. "Where is he?" she ground out.

The monster took a sip of red wine slowly—it was as if he were savoring it—as if Morana's presence was merely an unpleasant surprise. When his amber eyes met hers once more, he wagged a finger and made a clicking noise before continuing. "Patience," he scolded. "I thought you wanted to know how I knew about Axton."

Morana jerked against the power holding her once more. Every ounce of rage built up from the past few months poured into her attempts at releasing herself. It was no use.

"Very well." He set the wine down. "If you must know, the man you killed is the one who woke me up."

Raidan. One of the sleeping gods.

"You're lying." Her face paled. After what had happened at Mabon, Morana couldn't trust Axton. Raidan could very well be telling the truth. If he was the sleeping god, Morana would have been better off with the Basilisk.

He chuckled, and something about the noise made her skin crawl. "I assure you; I am not." Raidan lowered himself into the black wooden chair, amber eyes glittering with amusement. "It doesn't surprise me that the goddess of life sent a mere mortal to do her dirty work almost a year ago." He ran a finger along his thin lips. "Much too concerned with herself, if you ask me. Whatever will she do now, though?" He was smiling.

"Axton made a bargain involving me after I was taken by Death." Morana threw out the only truth she knew. "That wasn't a year ago."

"I suppose you believe it all started out with good intentions, don't you?" He was enjoying this conversation too much. Raidan picked up the goblet, taking another drink of wine. "That bargain had been in place long before Death collected you from the mortal realm. That boy had been trying to get close to you since the moment you set foot in that city."

Morana tensed. She didn't believe what he was saying—couldn't. Three years. She had been in the city for three years working at Ashford. Her mind traced over every detail. When she had run through a dark alley in the mortal realm, hunted by one of Inara's assassins, Axton had shot him. He watched the fae walk off—hardly dead from the wound that should have killed him. Axton hadn't even flinched. He didn't respond, and he didn't seem surprised to see something so strange. Alarm bells should have gone off in her head, but she was too busy moving from one task to the next—too busy surviving to notice.

The white mist wrapping around her flesh grew. A heady pleasure took over her, much like her passion with the Veeden. It was the kind of pleasure that danced with bitterness and rage—the kind that demanded vengeance. She could see Axton's realization as he knelt on the floor of Matthias's throne room—taste his panic all over again. Her mouth watered as she longed to relive the moment when she murdered the man who betrayed her.

Morana shook her head, snapping out of whatever bloodthirsty haze had settled over her emotions to scowl at the god across from her.

"You can believe me to be a liar, but that boy is already dead." He gestured to her ear. "Nice tattoo, by the way. Remind me again why you're here in my temple?"

Morana nearly growled. If he knew all of this, he damn well knew why she had come. Why they all had come.

"Oh, yes." He laughed then as he sat back in his chair with his hands folded across his body. "Your pretty little god." His eyes darkened and skimmed over her figure, stripping her of the dirt and clothing she wore. Morana wanted to vomit. "A nice plaything for a woman like you." Raidan scratched at his gray beard, licking his lips. The demon allowed silence to stretch, his raking over her. "Your god is downstairs."

One more attempt and the restraints snapped. Morana shot to her feet. As she stood, her eyes narrowed suspiciously. He was letting her go. But why?

No god could forfeit a game so easily. The only answer was that he was still playing. He *wanted* her to retrieve Matthias. The hungry look in his amber eyes let her know she was right. If she walked away, if she found Death, she'd be doing exactly what this monster wanted.

She stared at him; lips pressed together. Morana knew she was going to play into his hand. She'd get Matthias, regardless. Strategy would be far easier if she could ensure her freedom. A chance to walk away was something she'd never deny herself. It got easier every time.

"Go on," Raidan waved a hand. "Now that you're here, I care very little for Death." A thick fog coated the floor, ghosting over her feet and legs. It must have been whatever power he possessed—whatever had held her to the chair.

Morana turned to leave slowly. She didn't trust the god but couldn't see how he had the upper hand. Maybe she needed to find her way to the court's libraries—learn strategy. Dumb luck would only get her so far.

"Oh, and Morana."

She snapped her head around, meeting his eyes with her own iron gaze. He was still sitting in his office chair, unbothered, and running his finger casually along the rim of his goblet.

"I *will* see you again." He shifted forward in his seat, placing his elbows on the table. "And the next time we meet, I will have a proposition for you."

Anger birthed a new beast in her chest, fiercer and more powerful than before. It thrashed at the cage she built for her emotions and begged to be released like a fire set to a forest. Raidan was letting her walk away, and it felt like another trap. The emotions roaring through her body made it difficult to concentrate on anything aside from leaving. If she lost control now, there was a chance he wouldn't let her go again.

Raidan dragged his gaze down her frame, and something heated in his amber eyes.

"Fuck you," she spat.

"I suppose consummation would be a perk of my proposition." A feral smile cut his features, and Morana fought the urge to vomit. "You can play around with Death, but don't forget where the real power lies." He tilted his head back slightly, eyes hooded as they lingered on her body. "When you're done with your pet, I'll show you what it really means to scream the name of a god." Raidan ran a finger over the surface of the desk. "Don't worry. I like it when they fight me, and I promise I won't be gentle."

Morana swallowed hard, trying to force herself to calm and keep from expelling the contents of her stomach. She didn't look back and didn't think beyond the opened door to the study or the empty stairs she now descended at a full sprint. There were no signs of the Basilisk—or the lords.

Even if there were, there was nothing and no one who could stop her from where she was headed.

Six

Morana was frantic as she bounded down the staircase. The quiet chamber held no sign of the Basilisk or the lords. Her racing heart guided her as she ran, her skin crawling from the god she had escaped moments ago.

No. Not an escape. Morana didn't think it counted as an escape. He let her go willingly. He called Matthias her *pet.* Her stomach churned at the vile way he spoke to her and the promises he made over her body. Raidan was a powerful god—one she didn't want to meet again for fear he might collect.

At the bottom of the dimly lit steps, faefire flickered in sconces along a narrow hallway made of hardened clay and protruding bones. There was no telling who the bones belonged to, but it said enough about Raidan and what he was truly like.

Morana whipped her head around, looking for any sign of the others or a sign she was heading in the right direction towards Death.

A low voice skittered along the stone floor. Morana stopped. *Ronan.* He sounded serious—frantic.

Without thinking, Morana sprinted down the dimly lit hall lined with barred cells. She could feel the magic in this place. It made her skin crawl and her limbs weak. The sound of dripping water echoed in her ears as her boots hit the floor. The sound rattled around her head, calling forth the memories of Inara's dungeons.

Something about it took her back to that place as her heart pounded like a war drum—a call to battle. After waking in Sarnai's cottage, Morana had realized what was happening in her mind—her heart.

Matthias wasn't Axton. He wasn't an escape, though she could have made him out to be one—considering that he provided a realm to flee to. When she was with Axton, she had been concerned about her freedom—desiring an *out*.

There was no *out* with Death. He had consumed every part of her being—seen her for what she could be and not merely what she was. While she may be a weak mortal, desperate to find some kind of usefulness in this unfamiliar place laced with magic and gods, Matthias had never made her feel weak. The memories were swirling faster now.

After all she had endured, after all she had doubted and believed, Matthias was here; looking like he had ripped apart the world to find her.

Without thinking, she moved forward, wrapping her arms around his waist and burying her face in his chest. Matthias tensed but welcomed her just the same by crushing her against him. His hand was gentle as it brushed a strand of hair back. He inhaled, taking in the scent of whatever soap Sarnai had used. He needed this, too. She felt like a ridiculous child—vulnerable and needy, but she had so very little left.

Morana remembered the way he stood in Sarnai's cottage, disheveled but hopeful. He was willing to tear the kingdom apart to get her back, and she would do the same for him—regardless of the strength she possessed—or didn't. None of that mattered.

Only him.

Her heart pounded like a drum, slowly increasing in tempo. Her breath was coming out in harsh pants as Ronan's voice grew louder. Whatever state he was in, he could not be dead.

Death cannot be killed.

Morana looked right, following the sound of voices. An unconscious Matthias sat on the floor of the cell. The stabbing pain that ripped through her caused her to gasp, forgetting all control.

Ronan was crouched over him, drawing images on the iron cuffs cutting into the god's wrists. Death's eyes were closed, hollowed circles etched in the skin beneath them. Dirt and grim smeared his face—his once vibrant tattoos dull in the dungeon light.

You have to move. You have to do something.

Morana blinked to dispel the tears running freely down her face. He was here. Death was alive, and her mind screamed to get him out. To get them both far away from here.

Morana scrambled toward Matthias, grasping one of the cuffs around his wrists to seek a pulse. She needed to feel it—to know. It was irrational. She knew she was being irrational but no longer cared for control. Spending so much time masked and focused while sorrow and fear brewed in her chest had left her emotions bubbling over. Though she didn't want to understand the depth of her relief when she felt his beating heart, she could still no longer keep herself in check.

Ronan reeled back, giving her room, but he continued tracing blood over the other piece of iron.

"Where were you?" Elivira's tone was sharp behind her, sending barbs into her back. When Morana turned, she saw the disheveled lord covered in splatters of black blood. Her sword was dripping the inky substance onto the dusty floor by her feet. Morana winced before looking away, not wanting to touch on what had happened with Raidan.

They had propped Matthias up against the wall, sweat dripping from his hair, sliding down his temples. She noted how pale his skin looked. Morana ran her hands over the exposed flesh of his arms. There were no visible marks, nothing aside from minor scratches and a few bruises. His chest was rising and falling slowly.

Morana ran the pad of her thumb over his cheek, feeling the clammy skin. Her desperation slowly shifted, changing to anger as she thought about the monster sitting floors above them, waiting to continue their game. If Raidan could transform a powerful god into this—someone who looked almost mortal, it made Morana question what exactly he had done.

When Matthias shifted slightly, it drew her out of the storm of rage that threatened to consume her—bringing her back to the present.

"Matthias?" Her voice rasped. The god of death didn't respond. He lay still on the ground—a shell of the powerful entity he had been.

That anger bubbled over again, reminding her of the way Raidan's amber eyes lighted at her struggling form. She recalled the way he made promises of collecting his prize. Cold and callous and utterly unstoppable. That's how the god saw himself. He saw himself as untouchable—unshakable. No wrath or vow could cause him to crumble. Arrogant men believe they are something to be feared, but beneath whatever power they possess is something far weaker. They thrive off of the way those around them tiptoe—fearful of consequence and death.

Morana was no longer afraid of Death, and she had spent her entire life overcoming her own fears. She knew how to ignore them—how to act unfazed.

That fucker is going to die at the hands of a mortal.

"He's going to be okay." Ronan placed a comforting hand on her shoulder, reminding her she wasn't alone. When his ocean blue eyes met hers, the dam burst. Hot tears were tumbling over her cheeks in a mix of rage and sadness. Ronan paled before running a finger along one of the iron cuffs. While internally she warred with her disgusting emotions, it wasn't like her to cry openly. Not like this. The iron opened and clanked on the ground. "These cuffs just drained his power," the lord offered. "There are some in the Hall of Relics, too."

"We have a long journey ahead." Elivira shifted on her feet behind them. Her arms folded across her chest—expression hard and unreadable. Where Ronan spoke to comfort, Elivira spoke to remind her she couldn't break down. Even so, she didn't know if she could help it any longer. "I'm not convinced he can make the journey out." She gestured to Matthias. "I mean, look at him."

"We can shadow out." Morana turned away from Elivira. She ran a sleeve across her face in a useless attempt to soak up the salty sorrow running out of her like a river. "He already knows we're here." Morana sat back on her heels, unable to take her eyes off of the image of Death. "The major god, I mean."

"You saw him?" Elivira stepped forward with her hand gripping the hilt of her sword. The lord was all steel and unforgiving ice. Morana couldn't bear it—couldn't bear the discussions. She just wanted Matthias out of this hellhole without explaining what happened in the study. The lords would have questions, and rightfully so, but there wasn't time. He could stop them at any moment, and the reality of that sentiment crashed into her, stirring urgency and bitterness in her chest. Whatever strategy Raidan was using to play this game, he could change it at any moment, and while Morana promised herself that the god would die a humiliating death, she hadn't the first idea on how to make that a reality.

"He's letting us go!" she snapped, turning to the lord, who was standing in shock. "I care about very little else." Morana could feel the shadows building along her skin, rippling and preparing to move them through space with a mere thought. The power brought that addictive and heady pleasure, numbing her ridiculous display of emotion. Something within her fed on the anger, and though that rage wasn't justified, it was already unleashing itself unbidden. Beneath it all, beneath the draining adrenaline, she was exhausted.

"Morana," Garian finally spoke. He cleared his throat, approaching her as if she were a wild animal that had escaped its cage. "You really should—"

"I'll deal with it later!" she shouted. The words becoming her default for every problem in her life. White clouded her vision, and her lip peeled back.

The second chain hit the floor, and Morana could have sworn she saw a familiar pale mist rising on the stone ground. Her eyes widened. The shadows sent pleasure along her flesh as she willed them to take her to the horses. She grabbed Matthias, not thinking of the others before the world parted, and she could see the three horses still standing on the cracked earth and dried bones of The Wastelands just outside Raidan's temple.

Ronan and Garian were there in an instant. Grabbing the reins of their horses. Elivira followed. Her stance hardened in the wake of Morana's outburst.

Guilt and shame climbed up her throat, constricting her breathing and replacing the anger. Morana still had a hand on Matthias's unconscious body. She stared at Elivira's brown eyes, the way her lush lips somehow formed a thin line. It was then that Morana did the only thing she knew how to do. She ran.

The reality of the darkness was that it consumed. It provided the perfect armor and the best kind of hiding spot to get away. Morana couldn't confront the lords who had helped her. In the turmoil after Raidan had spoken to her, she couldn't bear the weight of how she fucked it all up.

When the dark mist faded and her room at the palace in Ascella appeared, the striking figure of the flora goddess, dressed in shimmering gold with the silver webbing glowing across her forehead, greeted Morana.

Sarnai's jaw hung open, and Willow stood behind her, wringing her hands with a similar shocked expression. Willow rushed forward, registering who it was Morana had brought to her room.

Coated in sweat and smelling of decaying bodies, Morana blinked once—twice. Her breath was coming out in harsh pants. She was sure she looked like a madwoman to the fae in front of her.

"Where are others?" Sarnai's honeyed voice had crystalized into something sharper—something that demanded attention.

Morana stared at the goddess. The previous guilt tightened around her throat to suffocate her in the wake of what she had done. Matthias was on the ground, his tattoos illuminated by the fire in the hearth at the center of her room. Shadows twisted over his skin; his lips parted.

Morana remembered how those lips felt, the way felt pressed against her throat, her chest. His appearance tainted the memories. Raidan had sucked the life out of Death.

Her eyes snapped back to Sarnai as she fought for words. "I left them." She was speaking slowly at first, hardly able to get a breath down as the tears made another appearance. "Tell them I'm sorry. They have every right to be here. I don't know what I'm doing." Morana was wiping her tears and shaking her head. She was speaking faster now, desperate to get it out and fighting with the urge to melt into the earth. The heavy weight settled over her. "They have more of a right to be here. More than me. I—I don't know what I'm doing." She was gasping for air, trembling, when Sarnai walked up to her, placing a cool palm on her cheek.

"Morana," Sarnai spoke. "You've been expecting perfection from yourself. You forget how much you've been through." Sarnai's hand disappeared, replaced by the warm air of the bedchamber. Morana looked up through tears at the goddess adjusting the gold dress that draped over her toned figure. The color made her brown skin stand out. She looked radiant—beautiful. "We can take him to his rooms, but you need to rest."

There was no room for debate. Morana could feel her legs giving in. Exhaustion slammed into her and threatened to pull her under all at once. She nodded. A small sob burst from her lips. Elivira had told her the same thing in the tavern. It had only been a few days ago—only a few days since Morana had taken a gun and killed the only friend she had made in years. Maybe they were all right. She could only bear so much.

Willow was on the ground, running a hand across Matthias's forehead. Strands of her black hair broke free from their binding, framing her concerned face as her brows stitched together. She assessed the King of Shadows as a mother would upon the return of her child. It eased some of Morana's fears. The woman looked up, wide, blue eyes softening at the sight of the broken mortal in the room.

Her steps were graceful as Willow ambled across the room. A pale hand rested on Morana's shoulder to steady her.

"You've been useful," she whispered softly. Her thumb stroked Morana's arm. It was such a motherly act that another sob escaped Morana's lips. "It's time to take a break, dear."

Flames danced in her vision as Morana held a cup of steaming tea in her hand. Willow brought it in and claimed that it would calm her nerves—some concoction Sarnai whipped up. The flora goddess had an herbal remedy for everything. Apparently, this was her remedy for losing your damn mind.

Morana could feel the deep purple marks etched under her eyes. The velvet armchair cradled her, and she pulled her knees up, feet resting on the gray fabric. She spent so much time running from her emotions and moving to the next task that she barely took time to slow down and think of all she endured over the past months.

Death and Life had both hunted her, sending assassins and murderous men to wherever she was. Inara had kidnapped her, whipped her, and starved her. Axton had betrayed her, and now she sat with the knowledge that the man she thought she knew was the one responsible for waking Raidan—the god that now had his sights on her as well. Morana closed her eyes, inhaling deeply. The scent of lavender invaded her senses, easing her worries and organizing her thoughts.

She had killed one Veeden, almost taken by another, and then accosted by a lord of the Court of Light. She fought an overgrown dog in the ancient tomb where she stole a blood book. Morana chuckled at the memory. Hardly trained, and she still managed to drive that sword through the animal.

There hadn't been a moment's pause. Maybe Sarnai was right. Morana just kept running, and her body was crying out for rest—a break. Her mind was haunting her—taunting her with all the ways she was a pitiful mortal. The worst part was the power she had felt in the throne room was the fleeting ghost she could no longer see.

In the mess she had left back at the temple, she had reminded herself that acting despite her emotion was far more than what her father had done, but maybe suppressing it at every turn was making it bubble over until she was more a mess of a human than she wanted to admit. She was more like her father than she realized—and that reality made her loathe herself all the more.

A soft creaking of the door interrupted her thoughts, keeping her from spiraling down into the abyss of self-hatred. It was far deeper than the grave she shoved her emotions into, begging them to die. They never did, but if she fell down into the abyss, it might take her captive and make good on the desire to rid herself of this constant torment.

Morana glanced to Elivira, who was now wearing leggings and a white t-shirt, hair tied back in her usual messy bun. Morana couldn't keep her eyes on the fae woman. She couldn't deal with the guilt.

"I'm sorry," she rasped, her gaze fixed on the swirling herbs in the cup before her.

Elivira gave a curt nod in response. The lord wasn't as graceful as the flora goddess, but she was just as captivating. No wonder Ronan had made advances toward her on their way to The Wastelands.

Shifting in her seat, Morana forced herself to look at Elivira—to confront the truth. "You once said you didn't *dislike* me. I'm sure that sentiment no longer holds true."

Lavender and chamomile tea coated her tongue, the warmth running down the back of her throat and comforting her in the face of all she had done wrong. How pitiful did she sound? It was as if she was fishing for some denial from the lord. Morana narrowed her eyes at the scalding liquid, scolding herself for the ridiculous attempt at an apology.

"Morana," there was something softer in Elivira's voice as she lowered herself into the adjacent armchair. Elivira ran a finger over the soft gray fabric of the furniture. "I'm no fool. We can all only take so much." A crease had formed on her brow when she spoke.

Morana's eyes left the cup in her hand. Orange light illuminated Elivira's high cheekbones and lush features. She was equal parts sharp edges and soft curves. "Because I'm mortal," Morana offered, a half-smile pulling at her lips. "Right?"

There was a time she had felt sorry for her father, the man that had lost control of himself after her mother abandoned them. Morana stayed and nursed him, feeding herself the lies that it was her responsibility to give all of herself to him. He had raised her, clothed her—given her life. He had also convinced her she owed him for existing.

Watching her father refuse to act and completely bury himself in sorrow and liquor etched scars into her heart. It was the same heart that saw even an ounce of feeling—an ounce of sadness and descended into the darkness of shame. That was what she felt now as Elivira looked at her with compassion. Shame.

"It has very little to do with what you are." Warm brown eyes bore holes into Morana's soul, forcing her to stay present—to stop hiding. There was a long pause before Elivira cleared her throat, fidgeting on the chair. "I never thanked you for saving me from the Basar." She tucked a wild curl behind her pointed ear. "I had a uh—" Elivira cleared her throat again. "A hard time with what they showed me. It seems we both need the rest."

Morana saw it then, the puffiness to her eyes that she was trying to conceal. She remembered the hollow way Elivira had existed on their journey to The Wastelands. "What exactly did they show you?" Morana asked, her voice low in the whispering night.

Elivira closed her eyes and breathed deeply, leaning back in her chair. "The torture he withstood."

Morana knew better than to ask about what Matthias had suffered. She could ask Matthias himself—as long as he was alive. "Any word on when I can see him?" It was a ridiculous question, considering what her emotions had been earlier. She was in no state to watch the unconscious god sleep off whatever cruel treatment he had received in Raidan's temple.

"You can see him whenever you choose." Elivira ran a finger across her full lip. "Sarnai is convinced that he will be awake by morning." Elivira waved a hand. "Something about the power of herbs and all that shit. I see she has you drinking her tea." Elivira sat up and leaned forward, sniffing the air. "Be careful with that stuff. It knocked me out the last time I drank it."

Morana nodded, glancing at the cup before putting it on the golden end table sitting between the two armchairs.

"I'll wait until morning." She looked down to where she was playing with the fabric of her leggings, pulling the black material away from her knee nervously. "You're right." She smiled. "Not about the tea, well, maybe about the tea. I'm talking about needing rest."

"I know this is not the time." Elivira leaned forward again, resting her elbows on her knees. She kept her brown eyes on the fire as she spoke. "We need to talk about Raidan and what happened while we were fighting the Basilisk."

Somehow, she knew this was coming. Morana sighed. "He made me a," she paused, trying to find a word to describe the encounter—a word that didn't make her skin crawl. "Proposition." Her brows lowered, and a chill ran down her spine. "Inara used Axton to wake him up. I found that much out." She looked to the fae lord to gauge her reaction, but all she saw was a hardened expression. It seemed to be the way the woman took any kind of news. It was something Morana knew well. Where her responses were fire, Elivira's were stone—cool and solid.

Morana continued, "Everyone keeps calling me the Queen of Darkness." She ran a finger along the outside of her teacup, leaning over the arm of the chair. "Raidan even mentioned it, as well as Inara. What does that mean?"

Elivira looked up through the strands of brown curly hair falling in her face. The hardness softened as she admitted, "I honestly don't know."

"I wasn't thinking in the temple," Morana began, changing the subject slightly. "I just wanted to get out—I wanted to get *him* out, and I panicked. It felt like it was my fault to begin with. Raidan said he would come back and the next time, he would have that full proposition." Morana remembered the way he had leered at her. "It was—" She winced. "Disgusting. I think he wants *me*. I just can't seem to figure out why."

"You *do* seem pretty desirable to everyone around you."

When Morana looked up, a small smile appeared on Elivira's full lips. They both broke into a quiet laugh.

"I wish I weren't," Morana admitted. She realized she knew very little about the lord. "What is Namid like?" she asked, referring to the city Elivira ruled over.

Elivira slouched down in the chair, resting her head on the back of it before sighing wistfully. "Beautiful." Her eyes were closed, thick lashes kissing her cheeks. "Winter is my favorite time in Namid."

Morana knew Garian was married with a young toddler. His family lived in his city, but she didn't know if Elivira was married as well. It didn't seem like it from Ronan's comments, but with Ronan, one could never tell.

"Do you—" Morana tried to formulate the question. "Do you have someone there?"

Elivira chuckled. There was a richness to her voice. It reminded her of the soil of the earth. "No."

"Someone here, then?" Morana's pulse quickened at the thought. Maybe Matthias had been with her at a time.

"Also, no." Elivira grinned and cracked one eye open. "I'm too wild and opinionated to have anyone, really." She closed her eyes once more. "I would never change that for a man."

"Ronan insinuated some things when we were traveling." Morana didn't know if it was a step too far, but she asked it anyway.

"Now *that* man knows what he's doing." Elivira licked her lips. "He certainly wasn't lying about that."

Morana's mouth hung open. The silence stretched on until Elivira opened her eyes and laughed again. Ronan had slept with Elivira. She had seemed so against it.

"He's not for me, though." She tapped a finger on the arm of the chair. "I'm sure, however, if you wanted a ride, he'd—"

"No," Morana shot back. Her eyes were wide. Ronan was certainly attractive and charming, but she had no desire to be with him.

"Ah, right." There was wicked delight woven into her expression. "I haven't slept with Matthias, but I'm certain Ronan, even with how spectacular he is, could never compare."

Morana flushed. "He is your king." She cleared her throat. "Should we be discussing this?"

"Matthias is one hot fucking king," the lord admitted. "I've been nothing but respectful of his power and position." She winked. "It doesn't hurt to look, though."

Morana laughed, some of the tension easing in her shoulders. She hadn't realized all that was missing from her life before. She had never talked to a girl like this. It felt foreign. This was how friends talked about boys—or was it? She didn't really know. It felt—normal.

"He definitely knows what he's doing." Heat rushed to Morana's cheeks, and she picked up her tea, desperately trying to find something to do with her hands.

Elivira laughed loudly then, a sound that was so joyful in the wake of all they had endured. "I'm not surprised." The fae woman gave Morana a knowing look. "I'm sure he'll be back to himself in no time." She stood up, wiping her hands on her leggings. Elivira started walking away but paused before exiting through the door. "Morana?"

"Hmm?"

"You pretend to be hardened to the world, but your emotions can only stay hidden for so long. I've seen plenty behind that mask you choose to wear, and I know one thing." Morana shifted uncomfortably. "You need to stop being so hard on yourself."

Elivira didn't wait for a response before she walked out of the room.

Seven

Anxious energy pulsed through Morana's veins as she paced outside of Matthias's bedroom in the palace of Ascella. She was an emotional mess in Raidan's temple. Thank every god Matthias was unconscious when that happened.

Morana continued pacing, building up the courage to enter. If she didn't soon, she would wear a hole in Death's floors. The crying victim wasn't who she wanted to be. It was pitiful. Morana steeled her spine and turned to the double doors, inhaling deeply before turning the knob.

When the doors opened, Morana thought of the palace in the land of the gods. The interior didn't match the dark walls and floors of the rest of Ascella's castle. Instead, lush red carpet and dark wooden walls surrounded her. A balcony window was open at the back of the room, letting in light that highlighted the carvings on the four-poster bed at the center.

Morana blinked. The bed was empty.

Running water sounded to her left, and she saw faefire drifting in from a bathroom. Taking a tentative step,

Morana inhaled again to get her bearings. The scent of mint and deep shadows engulfed her senses, calling to the power pulsing through her veins.

A large, rounded tub sat empty in the center of the bathroom. The gray stone flooring met the steps of the monstrous bath seamlessly. Morana's gaze left the intricate mural painted on the wall behind the tub to see Matthias standing before the sink.

His back shifted beneath a white button-up when he placed his hands on the edge of the counter. Matthias's obsidian eyes met Morana's through the vanity mirror as the water poured from the faucet, causing her heart to tumble and fall. The top button on his shirt was undone, hair damp and falling across his forehead.

Elivira wasn't kidding. He was already up and looked like he was getting ready for something.

"Shouldn't you be resting?" she asked.

"Kings don't rest." Matthias reached over the sink to the black-colored tie hanging on the towel rack. He wrapped the fabric around his neck, letting the ends hang loose while he buttoned the rest of his shirt. His jaw was tight. "You shouldn't have come."

Morana stiffened, her stomach dipping. She expected anything but that. "What do you mean?"

He turned around, leaning against the sink. His hands gripped the granite counter tightly. "You shouldn't have come to get me." He was facing the mirror and looking down. While the position should have softened his features, they looked almost hardened. Was he angry? "You shouldn't have been in Raidan's temple, Morana."

The faefire highlighted the dark circles etched beneath his dull eyes. Shadows were skating over his arms like the tendrils of night itself. Morana noted he had lost weight in the few days since his capture. She didn't even believe that was possible, but Raidan was a major god. There could be no limit to his power.

Folding her arms across her chest, Morana lifted her chin. His words stung, but she had lived in her emotions long enough. "Well, that's a ridiculous sentiment." Holding his gaze when he looked up, she kept her tone firm, keeping the truth of how much the next words burned her throat carefully hidden. It was one thing to think of herself as a weak mortal. It was another for Matthias to insinuate it—especially after how much she had shown him—mind-to-mind. "I understand I may not be the most useful. I am still untrained, but I—"

"It's not about that," Matthias interrupted. His hardened expression softened, pain entering his gaze. Maybe they were more alike than she realized. She longed to know what he was thinking—feeling. The muscles in his forearms flexed when he pushed off the counter. His black shoes tapped the stone floors until he was standing just in front of her. The moth tattoo on his hand shifted as he pushed a strand of hair behind her ear.

Shadows pulsed in the room, his power reaching out to her mind. She could hear his voice there.

I was afraid. I've failed to protect you enough as it is. You put yourself at risk.

One corner of his mouth turned up. "It seems everyone wants you."

Heat washed over her at his nearness and the words he spoke. She remembered Raidan's gray hair and amber eyes. Morana wanted to scream at the image of the monster—so clear and menacing in her mind. Matthias didn't want her in the temple because he was *afraid.*

What did he do to you?

"Including Raidan," she whispered.

The shadows around Matthias swelled as his shoulders went rigid. "Especially him." He clenched his jaw. "He could have found you, Morana." Matthias's voice darkened—a vicious threat woven into his tone. "I intend to keep that from happening."

Morana cocked an eyebrow, fighting the small smirk forming on her lips. Despite her fear of the major god, there was still the fact that he had let her go. She had stood in his presence and walked out—walked out with his prisoner, no less. "Too late."

Matthias merely stared at her with his brows lowered in response.

"He already pulled me into his study." She fought the way her skin crawled at the memories. "I already confronted him."

Matthias's chest was rising and falling.

She smiled. "What?" she asked. "You didn't think I would leave you there to rot, did you, Matthias?"

"I hoped you would."

Morana leaned towards him, her voice a whisper. "I *couldn't* leave you there to rot." She licked her lips. "Not very agreeable, that god. I wonder if he'll let me kill him."

Matthias's brow rose. Darkness coated her flesh in inky black mist, and deep pleasure rolled through her at the touch of his magic. Morana closed her eyes and breathed deeply before taking a step forward. His tie was still hanging around his neck, and she moved her fingers over the fabric to pick up the tie.

Her body became aware of his nearness and the darkness in the room. She wanted to touch him—if only to confirm he wasn't dead. Something about him made her want to bare her soul—consequences be damned. He hadn't judged her yet—and something about that was healing—safe.

Swallowing, Morana avoided Matthias's eyes when she made her next confession. It had nothing to do with him and everything to do with her own shame. "I don't want to feel so worthless," she whispered, knowing exactly how it would come across if she let him into her mind. The hatred she felt for herself never ceased, and despite her best efforts, her emotions were still lurking beneath the surface. As much as she wanted to appear strong in the eyes of a god, he could see everything anyway. She might as well tell him. Death's shadows knew no secrets, and there was no way to hide the truth. "I've felt like that a lot recently—since Raidan. Being here has—" Her voice trailed off when she met his gaze.

"Don't," he whispered. "Whatever hatred you want to speak of yourself, just don't."

"There are things we need to discuss." Morana continued. She could feel the small flicker of light in her chest as she spoke. She shoved it down, afraid of what the power might do—what it could do. "When Elivira was in the Basar fountain, we learned something about my power." She cocked an eyebrow. "Something that you'd be interested to discover. You were trying to train me and figure out what I could do after all."

"What did you learn?" Curiosity shone in his dark eyes. Matthias had the shadows, but there wasn't a flicker of light there. Her training would become more complex—more intriguing. Morana finished tightening his tie and folded the collar of his shirt down.

"Matthias." The light stirred, flickering over her skin briefly, and she quickly called the shadows. "The shadows aren't the only powers coursing through my veins." She smoothed the fabric over his chest. "I have the power from Inara's court, too."

When she looked up, he was staring at her. If he was shocked, she didn't see it. Matthias gave no reaction, save for the straightening of his spine and a subtle tick in his jaw. "I want you to keep training with Garian," he finally responded.

"What?" A crease formed between her brows. "He's from your court. That has nothing to do with the light."

"It doesn't, but you said you've already seen Raidan. I want you to continue learning to fight with Garian. We will figure something out for the rest. I, of course, can still help you with the shadows." Matthias ran a hand down his face. His tan skin was now pale, the purple marks beneath his eyes still visible. He gave a half-smile as if he knew what she was seeing. "It seems being a god doesn't make a damn difference when it comes to my ability to protect you."

Morana looked at him, her heart picking up in pace at the thought of what she wanted to do. He had wanted her before and shown her exactly how much he wanted her in the river. But something felt different about this. It had been different then, too. He was home, and she was afraid of how much relief that gave her. She didn't know how to love someone—didn't know if something like that could be returned. She hesitated a moment before standing on her toes to press a gentle kiss to his lips.

Matthias gripped her face, fingers of his tattooed hand twinning in her hair. He stepped forward, pressing their bodies together to deepen the kiss. It felt as if Death were claiming her, so long as she would have him, but it wasn't until his fingers tightened in her hair and his tongue trailed along her bottom lip that she realized she may be deeper into whatever this was—lost in him.

Matthias pulled back and whispered, "I have something I need to deal with first." He pressed another gentle kiss to her mouth. "Court politics and stuff."

Despite his words, Matthias didn't stop, and heat wrapped around her as he pulled her closer, pressing his body to hers. His lips crushed against hers again, lighting her body on fire. What started tender was now something else—something laced with desire. Morana gasped when his tongue trailed along her lower lip again, asking her to open. She ran her hands through his dark hair, swallowing his low growl.

He pulled back again—just slightly. "Garian will be in the training room in an hour." His breath was coming out in harsh pants, and she could feel the evidence of his desire against her stomach.

She nodded, drawing him in again. "Mhm."

He kissed her softly. "I'm expected in the throne room in five minutes."

Morana ran her hands up his chest and over his shoulders, allowing the heat to rush to her cheeks. He bit her lip gently, and a moan escaped her throat. The dark rumble in Matthias's chest made her toes curl.

Morana pulled back, stepping away before it could escalate. "Okay then." She smiled, folding her hands behind her back and taking one more step away.

"Okay, then what?" he growled. His lips were swollen and pink, his cheeks flushed. It fed a primal part of her knowing that she could get him going like that.

"You need to go," she answered, her voice holding a taunting musical quality as her eyes burned with amusement.

Matthias grabbed her wrist, hauling her forward until their bodies were flush against each other. "I may have been tortured and starved." His voice was low and menacing. A shiver ran down her spine at the spark of adrenaline that coasted through her veins in response. "But I *am* a god, Morana." His lips broke into a wicked smile. "I'm fully capable of—things."

She sucked in a breath—her body aware of the tight grip around her wrist. "What sort of things?" she asked.

Matthias nipped at her bottom lip with his teeth, his dark hair falling across his brow. "Wicked things," he answered.

The shadows along his arms swelled until a cold, empty room replaced the heat of Death.

Matthias had gone, and Morana swore she heard him chuckle somewhere hidden.

"Unfair!" she yelled. "I was supposed to be the one driving you wild and then vanishing."

Hot breath ghosted over her neck as Matthias reappeared behind her, his lips dangerously close to her ear.

"Oh, trust me," he trailed his hands over her shoulders and down her arms. She tilted her head to give him more access as she smiled. He placed a gentle kiss on her neck. "You're driving me wild, and now I have to go play king while thinking about those soft lips of yours."

Her breath halted when he licked up the column of her neck. The wet heat had her mind spiraling into a lustful haze. She couldn't speak—could hardly breathe when he finally spoke again.

"And now you'll be left thinking about what else my tongue can do."

Then he was gone again. Despite his time being tortured, he still played the same games they had played upon Morana's arrival in the fae realms. She enjoyed it. The taunting and teasing left her feeling lighter, and the way Matthias had trailed his lips over her skin had her feeling—

"Fuck," she whispered as she walked out of Death's bedroom.

Eight

Sweat covered every inch of Morana's frame. They had been at this for hours, and she felt the burn in her muscles as she lunged toward Garian for what felt like the hundredth time. Moisture ran down her back, between her breasts, staining the fitted black t-shirt now sticking to her skin. Her army green pants were just as disgusting, but despite the grime and her aching body, Morana threw all of her weight against the lord, and Garian met every stroke of the wooden sword with ease.

Garian was taller than Matthias, and she didn't mind his calming presence. He was encouraging, if not a bit irritable. Every movement of her sword, every hit of her training sword against his sent her into a frenzy of reliving her behavior in the temple. She hated herself, hated her feelings, and while having Matthias filled the crater that appeared in her chest when he disappeared, she couldn't stop reminding herself how utterly loathsome she was.

Too emotional. Too weak. Too much and somehow not enough.

Each invasive thought was punctuated by her sword blocking Garian's attacks. There was no way to beat this mountain of a man—and there was no way to beat herself.

Raidan had broken something in her—rattling her beyond measure. His words leeched her very essence from her soul. She failed the game, and as soon as she left that ghastly study, her weakness leaked from her like poison.

And what *was* that with Matthias? As soon as he told her she shouldn't have gone, her first thought had been that he thought her fragile and incompetent.

"I've felt like that a lot recently—since Raidan. Being here has—" Her voice trailed off when she met his gaze.

"Don't," he whispered. "Whatever hatred you want to speak of yourself, just don't."

Garian's movements quickened, but her rage pushed her to move faster. When the blows reverberated through her aching forearms, she couldn't help but think she deserved it—every ounce of pain.

Where was the girl who was so good at burying her emotions? Where the fuck was her head? And what was she *thinking,* shadowing herself and Matthias out of the temple without taking anyone else's advice? It's not like she defeated the Basilisk. She didn't *do* anything.

She certainly didn't deserve their kindness.

It all reminded her of her father. The way he let his mess invade every relationship, the way he only ever thought of himself—a vicious hurricane desperate to destroy everything in his path. That's what Morana was becoming, but she would try to stop. She would prove herself to be more than what her father was.

She gripped the wooden hilt with both hands, wishing she could graduate from the ridiculous training blade. A frustrated scream tore from her lips when she brought the sword down again. It made contact with Garian's, and he grunted as the wood splintered. White mist clouded her vision, suffocating her own shadows as she slammed the sword down again—again.

"Stop." Garian ducked sideways, throwing the wooden sword away from them. Morana finally halted, her breath coming out in shallow pants. There was a commanding presence to the lord, something that cleared her vision. "You're being too reckless." His brows pinched together. "You need to stop using brunt force and start using your mind before you hurt someone who doesn't deserve it."

Morana dropped her sword and scoffed. "I'm trying to get away from my mind," she muttered, looking at the black mat beneath her feet. When her gaze met Garian's, his expression was still unreadable. "Isn't this supposed to be a healthy way to deal with my problems?" The corner of her mouth pulled up, and her eyes lighted.

Garian grimaced. "Technically speaking?" He wiped his forehead with the bottom of his burnt orange shirt, and Morana got a flash of the abs beneath. He was built, probably as a result of all the training, or maybe all the fae had cut abdominal muscles. It came with the pointed ears.

Morana felt the heat of embarrassment creep up her neck as she caught herself staring for too long and looked away.

"Technically speaking, yes," he finished. Her eyes met his again as she tucked a strand of hair behind her rounded ear, a sign of what she was—and wasn't.

"Then I'm dealing with my problems." She tilted her head to the side, allowing the smile to fall in place. Garian never responded to her barbs; the same way he didn't respond to whatever attack she had dealt him this morning. He was unmovable.

Morana picked up the wooden sword again, twirling it in her hand. "If you can't keep up, Garian, just say that. However, we may need to talk about your incompetence as my trainer, if that's the case."

Garian chuckled, and it lit something inside of her. She liked the lord, and she had to admit he was helping her. The fae realm made her feel worthless, and he was helping her learn something to change that.

Morana walked to the rack to put the training sword away. She ran her hand over the real sword there; the one Reese had made for her. Even now, it responded to her touch. Shadows crept from her fingers to kiss the blade. She still didn't understand how it worked with her shadows. It was something to ask Matthias about.

She spun to face Garian. "You've been in Ascella for a while. Do you plan on returning home?" Morana thought about the carving Garian had made when they went to retrieve the blood book. He had a wife—a child. He had to miss them. She was just starting to understand what that felt like—home, that is.

"This evening, actually." Garian picked up his sword. There was something there, something breaking through on his face—sadness?

"You miss them?" she asked.

He grunted. "Of course." Garian placed his wooden sword on the rack next to Morana's. He was standing in front of her now. The tone shift made her uncomfortable, but she wanted to press. She had been using training to run from her problems and wondered if he was doing the same. Deciding against it, she searched for something lighter to talk about.

A devious smirk appeared on her lips as she looked up at the lord. "Miss your wife?" She waggled her eyebrows, hoping to get at least some reaction.

Garian offered her a flat look. Not biting then.

"Fine." She rolled her eyes, walking over to the water station set up on the side of the weapons rack. She filled a cup, keeping her eyes on the cool water pouring from the large metal jug. "I didn't realize you were such a prude, Garian."

There was a pause. Morana took a long drink of water and set the cup back down on the table.

"My wife would highly disagree." Garian's low voice rumbled.

Morana spun—her eyes wide. He was holding two actual swords now. One of them was her own.

"About me being a prude, I mean." Smugness took over his features, and Morana burst out laughing.

He handed her the sword as his expression became serious. "We're going to use the real one now. It's useless to only work with the training swords. You need to get used to the weight of your own, especially with how often you've been forced to use a blade lately."

Morana winced. She could picture the Veeden's head rolling. The one she had killed the first time. She traced a finger over the small scar on her cheek, the one below the larger scar from the assassin she killed.

Garian explained what they were about to do. She would practice different moves, bringing her sword down and focusing on her form. He would block her, and she would keep going over and over—until it felt natural.

When they began, Morana could feel the same furious energy take over. Something about swinging a sword, wooden or steel, made her weakness fade into the background. It quieted her mind. The harder she swung, the farther her feelings retreated. Her thoughts were finally receding.

Metal clanked, and Garian actually grunted against the force.

"What has you so worked up?" he asked, though she was certain he already knew. Faefire glinted off of his blade.

She slammed the sword down again, growling with the force of metal meeting metal. "I hate myself," she admitted. Morana could feel the tears working, and so she kept moving, hoping the exercise would outrun the river suddenly chasing her.

Garian grimaced, but it didn't look like it was from the effort of blocking her blows.

The dam broke, words barreling out of her. "I'm becoming so—" her brows furrowed as she brought the sword down again. "I'm wallowing. Sad all the time, and I completely snapped in Raidan's temple." She could feel the burning in her arms and stepped back to lower the sword. Garian's gaze pinned hers. "What was I even thinking? Just leaving you all there like that and yelling at Elivira." She used the collar of her damp, black shirt to wipe the sweat gathering on her lip. "I practically stole Matthias away, and everyone is being so unnecessarily nice to me. You're all excusing my behavior, as if you *know*." He didn't know what she was referring to. His brow creasing as he stood straight across from her, sword lowered. "You're excusing me like you know I'm weak." The next sentence came out as a whisper. "I'm becoming my father."

Garian looked thoughtful. "Did you ever think that we all just like you? Maybe we have all lived long enough to learn something about the trials of life." Her gaze flicked to one of his pointed ears, unable to meet his face for fear of truly breaking in front of him.

"I can't find one good reason why you would like me. And Matthias?" Her voice nearly cracked. "How could he ever love someone like that?"

Garian's brows shot up.

Her cheeks flushed. "Like, I mean." It was a useless correction. The damage was already done.

"Have you talked to him about—"

"No." She cleared her throat—uncomfortable. "Let's just ignore that."

"Morana." Garian stepped closer, his swords still gripped tightly in his hand. "If you just let yourself *feel* without overthinking it for a second, maybe you wouldn't find your emotions so consuming. Hiding them only makes them stronger."

"Right." Was he referring to her emotions in general, or her previous slip? If it was the latter—

"We *do* like you." Garian cleared his throat uncomfortably. He was used to parenting a toddler—not an adult woman. "You should know that." His tone was gentle.

"You're babying me," her tone was flat.

Whatever softness he had expressed slowly dissipated. "Then pick up your sword."

"What?" Morana gripped the hilt tightly.

"If you don't want to be babied, pick up your damn sword, Morana."

She lifted the sword, completely unprepared for what came next. Garian lunged forward, bringing his sword down with brunt force. Adrenaline pulsed through her veins as she blocked him, using the moves he taught her this morning.

She could barely keep up with each swing of his sword, and her muscles burned.

Garian spun, moving behind her and kicking her legs out from beneath her. She fell on her ass, and Garian's booted foot kicked at her chest, pinning her to the mat as he put the tip of his sword right at her collarbone. A small cut formed, her flesh stinging as blood trickled slowly.

"You don't want to be babied, then so be it." Garian snarled, and for the first time, she realized exactly whose presence she was in. Matthias was a god, but the fae were powerful, too. Maybe Garian had a point about them liking her.

"We were giving you time," he spat, "but if you're done wallowing and tearing down everyone you encounter, then get your ass up and stop acting like a helpless mortal."

He took his boot off her chest, stepping back and pulling his sword away.

Morana propped herself up on her elbows. "What am I supposed to act like if a helpless mortal is what I am?"

Garian wrinkled his nose, and she saw a glimpse of his power coating his dark skin. The shadows twisted over his arms. "*Raidan* captured and tortured Matthias. Now Matthias is up one day later, taking care of his responsibilities at court." His jaw ticked. "So that's an idea." He wiped the sweat from his brow with the collar of his shirt. His eyes darkened when he looked at her again, menacing and vicious. She felt fear in his presence now. "Act like a fucking god."

Shadows swelled, and Garian was gone, leaving Morana panting on the mat alone.

A fucking god?

Morana got up and put her sword on the rack. She grabbed another drink of water and strapped her dagger to her leg. Her mind was reeling, but in her spiraling thoughts, she found a kernel of something she had lost after leaving the throne room. Mortal or not, she was powerful, and she intended to prove it.

Nine

The halls were blessedly empty. Morana could feel the weight of her dagger against the burning muscles in her leg. The exercise had cleared her mind, and the conversation, well—

She took a deep breath, thankful for time to think—to be alone. Morana had never seen the lord angry. In fact, she had seen very little from Garian apart from his usual stoic demeanor and an occasional quip. He was never hot-tempered. Though for a moment there, Morana believed that he really intended to harm her. It served as a reminder that Matthias wasn't the only one in the fae realm with immense power. There was a reason the fae considered Garian a warrior—a reason Matthias wanted him to train her.

Low voices jarred her from her thoughts as she passed the doors to the throne room. A guard stood outside the closed entryway. He nodded; his expression unwavering as he regarded Morana. He didn't balk at her presence, didn't question why she was here, or where she should be.

Morana made note of his gray uniform with the embroidered crow placed over his chest. He didn't say anything when she placed her hand on the double doors to the throne room—didn't react—as if she had permission to go where she pleased in the palace. Morana wondered what the guards knew about her—what Matthias had told them.

She snuck in, recognizing Matthias's voice immediately. Her heart skipped a beat at the authority in his tone. It was louder now that the barrier of the walls and doors had disappeared. The room was full of fae spectators lining the walls and fixing their eyes on the front of the room.

Matthias was sitting on the throne and taking a long drag from the cigarette balanced between his lips. Her blood heated at the image of shadows swirling and twisting over his flesh—the menacing god and authoritative king he was playing. A black crown sat atop his head, coated in the shadows that lurked in his presence.

Morana fought for oxygen as she took in his menacing presence. The room was entirely too hot.

Wicked things.

When the door finally clicked shut behind her, she peered through the silent crowd. Nobody dared to move. Nobody dared to speak. At the base of the dais stood a fae man, chains hanging from his wrists. Morana struggled to assess who the man was, but by his clothes, he appeared to work in the palace.

"A Beatrix ring went missing from the Hall of Relics," Matthias spoke, his voice sending power rumbling across the dark floors and through her body. The caress of it made her shiver.

Wicked indeed.

The servant didn't say anything, and Morana could see the sweat rolling down the back of his neck. The bead of moisture shone in the flickering faefire, burning from the sconces on the walls.

"Why did you steal it?" There was no room for debate. Matthias was confident in the way he spoke the question. His voice was commanding the room to take heed of what he said—to obey. Morana's toes curled at the sight of him leaning back on the throne. It was the same place he had kissed her.

"I didn't—"

"Don't lie to me." Matthias's booming voice cut the man off while he leaned forward, his elbows on his knees. His dark eyes promised vengeance. Morana could feel her power stirring in his presence, the deep pleasure running down the length of her arms. "The shadows know no secrets."

It was a truth she now knew well.

"Inara made some promises." The servant's voice was barely audible, but the spectators gasp at the admittance. Inara, the queen of light and goddess of life, must have made this man a deal. But what deal would be worth Death's anger? Morana's brows furrowed, her heart pounding in her chest. Death was more than angry. He was hungry for retribution, and the shadows felt called for the same.

What was happening?

"Speak up," Death demanded.

"Inara, sir," the servant's voice was shaking now.

Morana pushed through the crowd to get closer, finally able to see his profile through the masses. His features were vaguely familiar with the small scar that ran across his left brow. "She promised a haven for my family." His voice lowered again, still shaking in the presence of the god of death and king of shadows. "There were whispers of war." He swallowed. "My mother is sick."

Matthias leaned back, his expression unreadable, resting one arm on the gilded throne. The tattooed crows on his skin shifted with the motion. "So," he began, "Inara told you how to get the ring and had you deliver it to her?" His eyes darkened; a warning woven in his gaze. "Giving her the ability to allow anyone from her court to shift realms." He licked his lips and shadows swelled at his feet. "Giving anyone access to the palace where you worked. Access to the land of the gods?"

Morana was piecing together what Matthias was saying. She looked around the room at the fae gathered to watch. This man had stolen the Beatrix ring—the ring used by the fae to shift realms. She knew that much from Willow's mention of the relic regarding Hames. It was the very reason Morana had to take Elivira to the Basar fish. The ring must have given Axton access to the palace and access to Matthias. Anger burned in her chest, rising like a forest fire desperate to destroy.

She looked again at the fae man, his chains moving slightly as he shifted on his feet. The memory of Matthias chained and unconscious flashed in her mind, pulling that blinding anger further to the surface. Morana could feel the dark shadows, the pleasure of their presence, pulsing at her fingertips. She could feel the gentle tug of something unfamiliar, something hungry for vengeance. If this was a trial, she hoped his punishment was harsh.

The fae man nodded.

Matthias stood up, striding down the steps of the dais slowly. "Your mother," he began, "will be spared." Something in the room shifted, a darkness settled over the castle walls, encasing them in the power of their king. Morana thought she saw the prisoner trembling. "You, however, have committed treason." His eyes locked on the servant as shadows spread out around him. "It will be swift."

Tears were streaming down the man's cheeks as he accepted Death. All movement ceased aside from Matthias's power—the power reaching out to caress the man awaiting his end.

"I can't promise it won't be painful," Matthias added. A dark smile appeared on his lips right before the man started screaming.

She didn't know how long it lasted. Time slowed as she watched Death consume and conquer. Her eyes strained to see within the darkness, but as her power wound over her flesh, the image cleared, and Morana watched as Matthias drove a dagger through the fae man's heart.

There were no sounds, not in the abyss she had fallen into. Her rage swirled in her chest—a storm ready to break. As the shadows shrank, revealing a very different image of the king she had come to know, Morana could feel that unfamiliar something rising—the thing that demanded blood—the thing that longed for the man's screams. She blinked, her hands trembling at her sides. Guilt wound around her heart, squeezing her chest until the air had been sucked from the room.

Fear took root, and she raised a hand to run over the scar on her cheek.

"Tell me this, Morana," he began. "Why do you want to keep these scars? Aren't the ones on your soul enough?"

Her mind flashed to the park where Matthias had asked the question—her response.

"I was just thinking if my soul becomes so scarred that I can no longer feel the sting of death, if I have my skin marked too, it will be a reminder that I can choose to never be too far gone."

When the darkness cleared, Matthias looked up, onyx eyes locking onto hers through the crowd. There was no kindness or softness there, only the power of a menacing god.

The adrenaline of watching him—knowing what he could do and seeing it for herself had heat washing over her. Good thing Death wasn't one to judge, and neither was she. Morana had felt the same overwhelming desire to see the man suffer for what he had done.

"You're dismissed," he spoke, and spectators filed out of the room immediately. She held his gaze momentarily, her finger still gently running over the marks that marred her face. Morana dropped her hand before turning to exit with the crowd.

She could feel him then. In her mind.

Stay.

She turned back, stepping aside so the rest of the fae could move past her. Guards came in, taking care of the body crumpled up on the palace floor. The only thing she could hear echoing in her mind was that one word. *Stay.*

Their gazes remained locked, time still creeping along unbearably slow, fae moving around them until the room was empty save for Death and the mortal that had just witnessed his darkness.

Morana traced back over that conversation, the way she had witnessed a man die in the mortal realm. Matthias had eased the pain of loss there—revealed his compassion. This execution was different. Matthias was living up to his title.

He stood across the room at the base of the dais. His demeanor shifted to something she couldn't quite decipher. "You're not going to say anything?" he asked. She could be wrong, but she thought she heard vulnerability in the question.

"What is there to say?" She was still staring at him as he turned and walked up to sit atop his throne. There was nothing she could say. What would he say if he knew what she had felt—if he saw how she had gotten rid of Axton?

He threw himself in the seat, running a hand down his face. "Plenty." His finger traced his bottom lip, brow furrowed. "There are certain things required of a king." He cleared his throat. It was a crack in whatever mask he wore to perform. She could see that now.

He looked uncomfortable—as if he hadn't intended for her to watch him kill a fae man in his own throne room. Morana had done the same thing to another man just days ago. In fact, old blood was probably still smeared on the floor.

The insecurity in his eyes weighed heavily on her. They were one and the same. Memories of Axton being pulled across this very floor invaded her mind. She could smell the sweet tobacco and relished the lingering feeling of a trigger being pulled.

"I want to show you something." Morana walked forward, avoiding the blood of the servant on the ground.

"The words every man wants to hear spoken from those lips." He smiled, but it didn't reach his eyes.

Morana let him in then and played out the events that took place while he was gone. She had sat on his throne, pretended to be queen, and shot the man that had betrayed her.

Matthias didn't react. When it was finished, she was standing at the bottom of the dais, staring up at the image of the King of Shadows.

"Again," she breathed. "What is there to say?"

The silence was deafening, coating the walls in uncertainty. She didn't know what to say or do, just waited for him to react. Her eyes flicked to his lips, heat suddenly washing over her at the memory of his promises this morning. The memory of the Matthias that bit her lip and made her want to beg for more. Tension crackled with the force of alighting in a storm.

Matthias broke the silence. "There is one thing to say."

She jolted, tilting her head and fighting off the heat pooling at her core.

"The sight of you on this throne is still enough to bring me to my knees."

Her breath caught in her throat as his gaze turned heated. Desire wound her stomach into a knot that begged for release, but she stood perfectly still, caught in the gaze of a hunter and unable to break away. A smug smile pulled at his lips.

"How was training?" he asked.

She could barely speak. Her voice came out as a whisper. "It was good." He knew he was affecting her and was dragging it out.

Bastard.

Morana thought she was affecting him too, but then Matthias shifted on the throne, leaning forward. He ran a hand down his face and pain flashed in his eyes, replacing the heat of his stare. "We are going to war."

"I know," she said, taking a step forward.

In the faefire, she could see the care and concern he had for his court, the way he didn't shy away from his own darkness. The mask he had worn broke, falling to the obsidian floors below. She could *see* him, and it awakened something within her.

Morana walked up the steps slowly, until she was standing between his knees, Matthias looking up at her.

"You look like a god." The heat in his gaze returned, his eyes trailing over her neck, down her chest, and to the dagger strapped to her thigh. Her breath caught as her body cried out to his, begging to touch him.

He chuckled then, sitting back on the throne. "I am a god." The rumble of his low voice stirred desire in her.

Morana couldn't wait as she placed one knee on the chair, climbing up until she was straddling the god of death. She fought the moan that wanted to escape at the way his eyes turned to fire—burning as if they would engulf the entire room in flames.

Matthias licked his lips, resting a tattooed hand on her thigh just above the knife.

She observed his features, suddenly realizing how tired he truly looked. It cooled the fire in her. Matthias had hardly rested, and God or not, exhaustion was taking over. She didn't know what had happened in that temple, but it was enough to make him look like this, no matter how hard he tried to hide it.

Her features softened at whatever she saw there, and concern replaced her emotions. "What scars did you earn, Matthias?" She ran a finger over the long scar on her cheek.

She could see it all—the truth laid bare—the pain of circumstance. Morana wanted nothing more than to give him someone to lean into. Even if she believed her own troubles to be too heavy to carry—she would forever make space to carry his as well.

"What?" he asked.

"Whatever Raidan did to you." She swallowed, biting her lip. "What scars did you earn?" Morana placed her hand over the left side of his chest. "Here?" she whispered.

Shadows deepened and twisted over their skin, joining them together in a cocoon of darkness. Matthias looked away, running a ring-covered finger along his lips.

"He tried to break me," he whispered.

Morana could feel his pain. Inara had tried to break her, too. Here she was—a mess—but she was here. And Matthias was a god.

She leaned forward, running her thumb along his jaw. "Impossible," she breathed.

"I can't find one good reason why you would like me. And Matthias?" Her voice nearly cracked. "How could he ever love someone like that?"

"Have you talked to him about—"

"No."

"Garian and I were talking about you." Morana's heart was picking up in pace. She hated how nervous this conversation made her—but she wanted to tell him, regardless.

His lip pulled up at the corner. "I can't imagine a circumstance in which this would be good."

"It was." He finally looked at her, dark eyes swimming with something other than pain. *Finally.*

"Well," he said, impatient. "Tell me."

"I was going on and on about how I couldn't think of one good reason as to why you would like me."

"That's ridiculous."

Morana held up a hand to silence him. His mouth snapped shut, and something about it satisfied her. "But now, I'm starting to see why you might—like me, that is."

Matthias cocked one eyebrow, begging her to continue.

"Because," she began, "you understand what it is to mask your pain. Though I must admit, you're doing a much better job of it than I am. I've been insufferable."

"I hardly believe that."

"I'm not done." She allowed a small smile to break across her face. "You were the first person to really *see* me. You took on my memories as if they were your own. I don't think you understand what sharing that burden did for me."

She couldn't read his expression but barreled on anyway. "If you'll let me, I'd like to help you carry some of the weight of what happened. However, you need me to do that.”

“Don’t you think you’ve carried enough on your own?” His face was soft—a stark contrast to the menacing god sitting on the throne when she had walked in.

Morana rested her forehead against his. “Not if I can’t carry something for you.”

A comforting silence stretched between them.

“I’d like to take you somewhere,” he finally said.

She smiled then—leaning back and attempting to lighten the mood. “You’re not going to kill me, are you? Word is everyone wants me. I’m certain most of them want me dead.”

Matthias chuckled. “I may be the god of death, but no. I’m not going to kill you.” His eyes met hers and in them, she saw the truth of his words.

“What is this, then?” She cocked an eyebrow. “A date?”

He smirked and covered the expression with a finger over his mouth. “Possibly.”

“Will you still be wearing this tie?” Morana traced over the knot she had fashioned this morning. “I think I’d prefer it off.”

Matthias’s hand on her thigh rose, gripping her tightly. “I live to please,” he almost growled.

She climbed off him, stepping back. “You’re tired, though.” The humor left her tone. Despite her casual banter, she could still see the exhaustion in the hollowness of his features and the way his shoulders sagged when he sat down after the execution. "You should rest."

"Later," he sighed. Matthias glanced to a sconce on the wall and lowered his brows in thought. "I have a few more things to work through. We're sending troops to Zora."

The admittance surprised her. Morana knew nothing of war. She fought the familiar feeling of helplessness, reminded of Garian's suggestion that she act like a god. She didn't want to seem weak and unknowledgeable about this realm anymore. "So soon?" she asked. Maybe there was information in the library to help her.

"Death doesn't wait for things like this." Matthias stood up, running a hand through his dark hair. "Dress for the human realm tonight. Something casual." His brows rose. "I was serious about that date. I need a break from all this nonsense."

Morana huffed a laugh, tucking a stray strand of hair behind her ear. "They told me I needed the same thing."

Matthias looked at her, shadows pulsing in the way they did before he disappeared. She knew what he was about to do. A small smile pulled at her lips. Disappearing seemed to be his favorite trick.

"They're probably right." The last thing she saw was his own half-smile before the god of death vanished.

She chuckled at his show of power before turning to walk out of the room.

Ten

She didn't bother using the inky darkness between destinations to move about the castle. In training, Garian had told her not to. She needed to learn how to wield a blade without the power coursing through her veins. When it came to exploring the palace, Morana simply had time to waste and desperately needed to know how to navigate the elaborately decorated halls in Ascella.

She stopped briefly, glancing at a large painting hanging from the wall. She had admired the artwork on her walk, but this piece caught her eye. The image showed a woman, cloaked in the night sky, kneeling by a river. Her face was soft, and her expression pensive as she trailed a finger over the water's surface. A blanket of pure stars was gripped tightly around her bare body.

Morana tilted her head as she analyzed each brushstroke, the blonde hair cascading down the woman's back in delicate waves. The way the sky above was black—as if every good thing in the night sky wrapped around the woman instead.

Queen of Darkness, she thought. If she had painted it. That was the name she would have given the woman. Maybe this was who everyone was referring to. A woman on canvas—a myth. It would have eased Morana's worries if that were the case.

The low rumble of her hollow stomach interrupted her thoughts.

After working so hard in the training room, she was desperate to find food.

Turning away from the artwork, Morana wandered down the hall, her boots tapping the darkened floors of the palace. A guard dressed similarly to the one that had stood outside of the throne room approached, meaning to walk past her. The emptiness in her stomach made her wince. Her stomach was practically eating itself.

"Excuse me?" Morana stopped, turning to the unfamiliar fae guard. The man halted, nodding once. "Uh, the kitchen," she stammered. "Which way should I go?"

The man laughed, a gentle sound. It was soft, like the low murmur of a gentle summer wind. He raised a pale hand to point down the hall and briefly explained what turns to take.

Morana fought to remember exactly what he had said as the guard walked off. She supposed if she got lost, she could let the shadows take her there. It would certainly be quicker than navigating the castle, but again, Morana had nothing but time to kill while she waited for Matthias.

She could feel the shadows call as her thoughts wandered to the god. The darkness twisted over her skin, pleasure lining her flesh at their captivating presence. She reveled in it, taking comfort from the addictive power. Morana inhaled deeply as she drifted through the castle. Her mind flashed with images of the Veeden and Raidan and her brow furrowed, anger suddenly swirling in her gut. She wanted—

She didn't know what she wanted, but the fury rising had her nearly moaning in pleasure. Something about the bloodlust satisfied her, pulling her under like the current in a raging sea. It was the same way in the throne room. Watching the man scream had brought a certain pleasure. She *wanted* him to die.

When Morana looked down, she thought white mist danced with the dark shadows running along her arms, but as she lifted her hand, observing their movement, only the inky spill of shadows remained.

She blinked, shaking off whatever sudden haze had pulled her under. That white mist kept returning. At first, Morana thought it to be left over from the Veeden, but the longer it lingered, the more she wondered. At least the shadows were familiar.

"Morana."

She turned abruptly; the power dissolving into her skin. Ronan ambled down the hall, his dusty blue button-up undone at the top. He ran a hand through his blonde hair, smiling as he approached her.

"How are you?" he asked. He didn't look put together, and something about it made him more handsome. No wonder Elivira had given him a try. Ronan had a reputation, and one look at the crystal blue eyes, the straight white teeth, and the stubble lining his square jaw spoke of exactly why he was so successful in upholding that reputation.

Morana blinked. "Fine." The pleasure she had felt slowly faded, and her mind cleared.

Ronan propped an arm against the wall, leaning toward her with a smile on his face. He was close now—too close. She could smell salt and amber. His blue eyes were glittering in the faefire. "Care to join me for a drink?" He was shorter than Matthias, but Morana still looked up at him, her nose wrinkling in distaste. He was a hopeless flirt.

"Don't you have a job to do?"

He frowned. "I do." Something shifted in his expression, and he sighed, taking his arm off the wall and straightening away from her. Annoyance broke his casual flirtation as he shifted where he stood. "Something about seeing a blacksmith about weapons for our troops."

Right. Matthias was going to attack Zora.

"Ah," Morana smiled. "You're going to see Reese."

"Is he a hard ass?" Ronan asked.

Morana chuckled at the worried expression decorating the lord's face. Reese was hardly worth worrying about. "*She* might take you up on the drink offer." Morana's smile widened, though she wasn't sure if it was the truth. Reese didn't seem like the type to give in to someone like Ronan. She was too timid. "If you don't scare her off with your advances first."

Ronan gasped as if offended, but could not mask the smirk breaking across his features. "Not you taking me for a common whore." Morana rolled her eyes. He knew what he was. "I don't offer drinks to just anyone." He winked.

"A harlot, Ronan. You are, in fact, a harlot."

Ronan brought a fist to his chest. "You wound me so."

"It's charming." Morana patted his cheek and turned to walk away. She still needed to find her way to the kitchens to eat something. Her stomach gurgled again, just low enough that Ronan couldn't hear.

"Morana." There was a stiffness to the tone of his voice, all lightness disappearing and replaced with a worried quiver. It was a side she hadn't seen from the lord before; didn't think he was capable of anything but his signature charm and bravado. Morana's chest tightened, a knot forming in her throat when she turned around and saw the concern creasing Ronan's brow. "When I asked how you were," he continued, shifting on his feet. "I mean, are you all right? Back in the temple—"

Her throat worked. They *were* being overly nice to her, and this conversation had her feeling weak—mortal.

Act like a fucking god.

There was no reason for him to treat her so kindly, nothing beyond the reasoning Garian gave to their kindness. His concern made her believe he truly liked her.

"I don't want to talk about it." It would only lead to more wallowing—something she had no desire to do anymore.

"I'm here," he offered. He rubbed the back of his neck in a nervous gesture. "You know, as a friend."

"I know, Ronan." Morana offered him a small smile. "You don't need to look after me, though. I can handle myself."

"Ah," the wicked grin returned to his lips. "Right. I had almost forgotten about the way you tore a hole in the training room mats." He chuckled. "Garian actually cracked a smile when he told us that story."

"Well." Morana lifted her chin. "I also handed Matthias his ass."

Ronan leaned in. "Yes, darling." He raised a brow. "You did so by cheating."

"Is it cheating if you're simply using the power afforded to you?"

"Now, now. You don't see me using my power to get every little thing I want."

Morana laughed then. "You seem to use your title to get every woman in the Court of Shadows."

"Absolutely not." His grin was wicked. "For that, I use my charm, my wit, and my good looks."

Morana rolled her eyes. "Yes, while you go off and find a mirror to admire yourself in, I just need to get food."

"I wouldn't dream of keeping you from a quest like that." Ronan stepped away, bowing at the waist before walking off.

Morana shook her head as she navigated her way to the kitchens. The smell of rosemary and garlic wafted up the steps as she descended to the smaller of the kitchens in the palace.

Willow stood at the counter, chopping onions with a shorter redheaded girl standing next to her and kneading bread. The scent of baked chicken and spices rose from the oven behind them. The lights flickered across the brick walls, lighting their faces as the women laughed.

"Tea's on the counter."

Morana whipped her head around to see Sarnai draped over a wooden chair in the corner next to a lit fireplace. Her crimson-colored dress hung off her shoulders gracefully as she drank steaming liquid from a blue cup. Her fingers trailed over the delicate flowers embroidered on her bodice.

"Sarnai." Morana turned to see an identical steaming cup on the butcher-block counters in front of Willow and the other girl on staff. "What is it exactly?"

Sarnai didn't look up but grinned behind her cup. She looked at the green thread that outlined a tiny leaf on her skirt thoughtfully. "Past due herbal tea." One brow quirked up. "You know. Since your god has returned."

Morana flushed, her nails digging into her palms at her sides. "We haven't," she answered, glancing sideways at the two women cooking in the room. They didn't bother to look up, and Morana was thankful for that.

"You will." Sarnai's umber eyes held Morana's.

"Please," Morana huffed, rolling her eyes and grabbing the cup on the counter. She took a sip of the familiar tea, not arguing with the goddess in the room.

"See," Sarnai stood up, her long legs flashing through the slit in her elaborate gown. She leaned on the counter, the silver webbing on her forehead glowing in the light of the flames in the hearth. "You're drinking it. Is he still living up to everything you've ever hoped?"

"I told you we haven't." The cup warmed her hands as the crimson staining her cheeks became more vibrant.

"Pity." Sarnai straightened. "War is terribly dreadful. Sometimes it's nice to find a good way to relax. I should find Ronan. He understands what I'm saying. And I know for a fact the man can perform."

Morana gaped at the goddess. "Has Ronan honestly slept with everyone in this court?" Morana asked.

"I've never met lord Ronan," the red-headed girl chimed in. She didn't look any older than seventeen. The smattering of freckles across her face crinkled as she wrinkled her nose. "He sounds like one giant red flag."

"He may grow out of it," Willow's smooth voice settled over the room. She had a calming presence about her. Willow turned to open the oven, using a mitt to pull out the baked chicken and potatoes. "I have also never been with Ronan." She tucked a strand of black hair behind her pointed ear. "Can't say I haven't thought about it, though."

Morana laughed then, joined by Sarnai and the young girl's snickering.

"What's your name?" Morana asked as she glanced hungrily at the food Willow was preparing.

"Kit," she answered with a wide smile on her face. "I'm Cain's sister."

Morana's brows flicked up in surprise. "Does his whole family work here?"

The brightness from the girl's face faded, and a shadow seemed to cross her features. "Cain is my twin." She swallowed, looking back at the dough she was assaulting. "We only have each other."

"Kit, could you grab a plate for Miss Morana? She's practically drooling all over the kitchen." Willow cut into the chicken with a knife and fork, checking to make sure it was done. Morana noticed the way her eyes slid to Kit's, checking on her discomfort, and Morana was thankful for Willow's attempt at changing the subject.

The somber girl nodded, grabbing a plate from the cabinet and handing it to Willow to dish up.

"I didn't mean to upset you," Morana finally spoke.

"You didn't." There was a hardness to the girl's face now. Her features were soft, but something in her expression spoke of the strength that resided deep in her soul.

"Right." Morana cleared her throat. "Thank you for the food." She grabbed the plate in both hands. "I may take this back to my room, and I should be in the library this afternoon. I still have a lot to learn, and time to waste." Morana also wanted to ask Cain about his sister—his background. He never mentioned a twin. Then again, Morana had never asked.

"Of course," Willow answered.

"I'd love to join you." Sarnai was shoving a small pastry in her mouth. "However, I'd like to go home for a while."

Morana could almost smell the cardamom and see the plant life crawling up the walls of Sarnai's cottage in the Flora realm.

Shadows danced in Morana's vision as she pictured the cushioned chair in her room by the fire. Within moments, the world parted, and Morana was thrown through space and seated on the couch, devouring the lunch Willow had generously prepared.

Eleven

Sitting at the table in the lower levels of the library, Morana scanned the books littering the wooden surface. She had collected enough reading material to last her centuries. She sighed, tucking a damp strand of hair behind her ear. Her muscles ached from training, but her body was clean, and so were the band t-shirt she had found in her wardrobe and the cut-off shorts the garment was now tucked into.

"If you're going to huff, then I will gladly take my work elsewhere." Cain didn't look up as he scribbled on the parchment, copying something down from the tome in his lap.

"I didn't ask for your opinion," Morana snapped.

"No." He raised his brows, still focused on the work before him. "But *you* asked *me* to sit with you."

Morana could see the thin smile cutting across his face. She leaned back, folding her arms over her chest as the wooden chair creaked beneath her. She let out another dramatic sigh.

Cain's eyes snapped up, but Morana found only humor in his gaze. "That was rude," he commented, his nose wrinkling as his smile widened.

"Isn't there some fountain of fish that can just give me all of this information on gods and war?" Morana looked up at the ceiling, the dim faefire flickering in the sconces and casting dancing shadows on the walls. She smiled.

"Some things take actual work." Cain almost chuckled as he went back to his copying with predatory focus.

Pompous asshat.

"How old are you, anyway?" Morana asked, leveling her gaze at the fae before her. "You have to be young. Fae or not."

"I'm not the one sitting across the table huffing like a child because of a little reading assignment."

Morana leaned forward, her elbows on the books strewn across the wooden surface. The sound of rustling paper and distant footsteps echoed off the charcoal walls of the library. She narrowed her eyes. "There are a lot of books here. This will take hours."

"And you keep saying you have nothing but time."

"You can be kind of an asshole. You know that, Cain?" Morana crossed her legs beneath the table.

Cain looked up again, his expression flat. "You just called a fae child an asshole."

Morana watched as his jaw flinched. He was fighting to hold back a grin. Morana smiled at that. "Thanks for keeping me company."

"I can't very well not." He ran a hand over the red curls atop his head. "Matthias would have my head. We had specific instructions. Something about an esteemed guest."

Morana flushed. It explained the guards allowing her to roam the castle, Willow's assignment to her, and the way her wardrobe kept growing the longer she stayed in the Court of Shadows. "Oh." She slid a book across the table's surface and cracked it open, searching the table of contents for anything about the major gods—or anything about Lux and Inara.

Her thoughts strayed back to Cain's sister and the dark past they carried. She hadn't asked Cain about himself when they first met. It was difficult to be concerned about others when your entire world felt as if it was imploding. Guilt stirred in her gut at the selfishness. It resurfaced feelings she didn't want around. Morana looked up again. "Tell me about your sister, Kit."

Cain threw his pen down. "Good god woman, is it just that you *can't* read?"

Morana snatched the parchment in front of Cain and snapped it in front of her face as she read. "Blood books detail the histories of gods. Deep magic instilled in the book by the Oracle allows for memories to be recorded as they happen." She glanced around the paper, still holding it aloft. "This is about blood books?"

"It's just an entry for an encyclopedia of sorts," Cain grunted.

"So, are you recording the location of Matthias's blood book?" She cocked an eyebrow. It's not that she wanted the book for malicious purposes but saying she had it or even knew where it was. It would be a perfect opportunity to goad the god of death. Morana remembered the way it had felt to get under his skin as she sat in the dining room in the land of the gods—discussing Axton and the dream she had crafted entirely from a bitter lie.

Fear crawled up her spine at the idea. The thrill of watching the god of death so unhinged made her stomach flutter.

Cain snatched the paper. "No. That isn't to be recorded. I'm just updating information."

Morana narrowed her eyes suspiciously. Cain seemed to know more than he let on. She didn't believe this was an exception. "You know where his book is."

"No."

The boy wouldn't look at her. His pen was already in his hand again, scratching carefully along the page, slim letters delicately traced onto the parchment. Morana didn't tear her eyes away from him. He didn't acknowledge her, merely put a hand on a book in the sizeable pile toward her side of the table and slid it in her direction.

"If you want to know about war, this is the book to learn from. It discusses the goddess of life." He winced as he said the last word. "It'll explain the conflict between the courts." Cain cleared his throat, a red strand of hair falling across his forehead. "As for Kit and me, we came here not long ago. Inara had—" He swallowed. "She had executed our parents and sent me away to live with a powerful woman in the mortal realm. Kit didn't go with me. She didn't display the same—gifts."

"Who was the woman?" Morana thumbed the delicate binding of the book he had slid toward her, trailing her fingers over the gold embossed on the spine. She shoved the other books out of the way and placed the new one—the helpful one flat on the table.

A dark expression came over Cain's face. "She's the goddess of divination. A major god left in the mortal realm. She lives in some cabin in Appalachia." He still refused to look at her. "She's an oracle."

"So, she tells the future?" Morana asked.

Cain finally looked up, his mouth a thin line. "She sees it. She also seems to just *know*. Inara thought I had that same gift. She wanted me to train and wanted to use me for her own personal exploits. Matthias was there on business and got me out. He found my sister when I was fifteen. That was a year ago."

Morana felt some satisfaction at her accurate guess of Cain's age. He had a good read on her, even. She observed him carefully—thoughts swirling around in her head and dragging her to her next question.

"And do you?" she asked. Her voice was low, concealed between the shelves of books on either side of their worktable. "Do you have that ability?"

Cain dipped his pen in ink, looking up as a sinister smile pulled at the corners of his mouth. "No," he answered.

Morana didn't believe him, but she figured that was as much as she would get out of the scribe for now. She opened the book he had handed her and started thumbing through the pages, frantically reading any information she could find about the conflict between the courts.

One page stuck out to her, detailing Inara's rise to power. According to the book, Inara had lived in a small village north of Ohriid in the Court of Light while it was still called the Seelie court. There had been an incident. Malicious creatures from The Wastelands—creatures unseen for thousands of years—had somehow descended on her village, and this small fae woman defeated them all with power more immense than was normal for the fae.

Lux, the god of Life at the time, invited the woman to the Palace of Glass as an esteemed guest, where, over the course of a year, the two fell in love.

Whispers surrounding Inara's inexplicable powers led the Unseelie Court to attack following her coronation. In that battle, Inara killed her lover, Lux, and struck down the king and queen of the Unseelie, leaving their twenty-year-old son to take up the throne and the place as the god of death.

Matthias.

Morana read his name four times before she registered what happened. Inara was the reason for his parents' deaths. Her heart was pounding in her chest, fists clenched on the table.

"I take it you learned something you didn't like?" Cain asked. There was no sarcasm in his tone—only a serious question.

"Inara killed Matthias's parents after becoming queen."

"Ahh," Cain leaned back in his chair. "So, you're realizing that for a goddess of life, she's really quite fond of murder?"

The rage was consuming, laced with a separate emotion, one that crept in through the shadows of her heart. "Why didn't he tell me?" Her voice almost cracked as she spoke. She instantly regretted it, cursing herself for laying it all bare before a sixteen-year-old fae scribe. More and more, her control seemed to slip. Since coming to this realm, holding her composure proved nearly impossible. It was ridiculous, but the pain still sliced deep. Matthias had walked with her—told her about his parents but had omitted this piece of information.

"Don't take it to heart," Cain spoke gently, his eyes knowing. "Some memories are too painful to rehash over and over." He sniffed. "No matter how long you live."

He was right. It was selfish to expect Matthias to lay out his entire life before her. It would have been irresponsible on his part, anyway. They hadn't known each other long, and he was still trying to figure her out. He was still trying to piece her powers together.

"Right," she whispered, the pain dulling to a small ache.

"Cain?" a male voice echoed from behind the stacks where a slim boy in the same robes as the scribe peered out. The faefire illuminated his ebony skin, the light flickering over his broad features.

The boy looked up, noting Morana's presence.

"Oh." His cheeks flushed. "I didn't mean to interrupt."

"Amit, this is Morana." Cain placed his pen on the wooden table as he shifted uncomfortably. "She's Matthias's guest."

Amit grinned, his white teeth flashing. "The girl who was kidnapped."

She kept her expression blank and her tone flat. "That's a touchy subject."

Amit stepped back, clearing his throat. "My apologies." He rubbed the back of his neck, his voice sounding a bit flustered. "Um, Cain. I just came to ask about dinner."

"I'll be there," Cain responded. They stared at each other in the long silence that stretched between them.

"Right." Amit turned, quickly stalking off into the bowels of the library.

Cain didn't respond, but Morana smiled as she began organizing the books in front of her. "Dinner?" she inquired.

Cain deadpanned. His gaze shot shards of ice in her direction. The silence stretched taut. Morana swore she could hear herself blinking. She glanced away, making to stand up and gather the reading material.

Cain placed a hand over hers before she could finish stacking the books.

"I'll take care of those," he started. "I did find something in Inara's blood book I wanted to share with you, Morana."

Morana's stomach twisted. The last time she had opened that god's awful journal, she had stumbled across a page detailing Inara's sexual exploits. The memories of her time with Axton.

"It's about Axton," he added.

Rage simmered in her chest, bubbling slowly as her wrath heated from the inside. Her tongue tasted bitter in her mouth. Hearing his name was enough to set her off. "I'm not interested in reading about their sexual encounters," she snapped.

Cain winced. "It's not that." There was a pause before the pained look crossed his face. "It—" he swallowed hard, gathering his words. "It predates what you believed Axton's involvement to be."

"What are you saying?" Morana closed her eyes, inhaling deeply to calm the mixed emotions swirling in her gut. There was pain, anger, sadness, and fear—all swirling to make a torturous cocktail.

"Axton was involved with Inara soon after you arrived at the gun club. That's when he made his bargain." Cain's hand was still resting atop hers, warm and reassuring.

She tried to pull strength from it, but her knees felt weak. "His bargain was to watch you—get close to you."

The sinking feeling threatened to drag her under, to bury her beneath the earth in the same grave she housed her deepest feelings. She fought desperately to hide them. Cain knew that this would sting. She could tell by the way his thumb stroked gently over the back of her hand once—twice. Morana couldn't bear for him to know the full scope of her feelings. For as open as she was becoming with Willow, there was still a part of her that felt the need to protect herself—encase her heart in a steel chamber. Axton's betrayal being the reason why. She thought of him as a friend, and he lied to her face with such skill for so long. Her steel heart would be a fortress to keep people out of the very feelings that made her feel chaotic and worthless—the feelings that whispered in her ears at night telling her it was all too much—that she was too much.

I'm not here to take your freedom, Ana.

Memories flashed briefly in her mind. Painful and harsh.

"At some point, I'm going to need a straight answer." He was so close that her back arched over the countertop. "I can see right through it all, Ana."

Her eyes widened in surprise, the smell of sweet tobacco invading her senses.

Morana closed her eyes to fight against what she knew was coming and the feelings that would burn her at what he said next. The memory continued on—unbidden and unwelcome.

"A straight answer to what, Axton?"

He had been using her—watching her. The one soul she had trusted in her time after leaving her father had betrayed her long before the whip of magic lashed across her back.

"A straight answer to how you feel about me."

Bile rose in her throat, threatening to expel the contents of her stomach on the books littered in front of her. She snatched her hand away from Cain's, steeling her spine and schooling her expression. She looked him in the eyes, summoning as much strength as she could muster.

"Thank you for telling me." Her gray eyes hardened, entrapped in the same metal casing that she was building around her heart.

"I know this isn't the right time to ask." Cain shifted in his seat once more, tapping his pen once on the table before setting it back down. "Why did you go with him? At Mabon, I mean."

It was a valid question, but somewhere in the storm of her emotions, Morana could only see white mist and twisting shadows. She pulled her power back to herself.

"We cling to what's familiar." She lifted her chin. "Sometimes we cling to it until it becomes the very thing that binds us."

Cain chuckled, desperately trying to lighten the mood. "You sound like an oracle."

Morana smiled, the expression feeling foreign. "I don't see the future," she began. "My ears are rounded. I'm just a sad mortal with strange powers from a broken home." Something bloodthirsty stirred in her chest. She remembered the way Axton had looked the moment before he died—utterly afraid. "Just a mortal playing at being a god."

There was a flicker of something in Cain's gaze—something she couldn't decipher. "Just pretending?" he asked. There was a moment of silence. "Right?"

Morana pushed her chair in, and the screeching of wood sliding across the stone floor echoed through the library. She licked her lips. "Right."

Morana turned to leave, allowing the shadows to twist down her arms as she climbed the stairs to the main floor of the library. To the exit.

Twelve

The tea was bitter and cold. Morana stared at the liquid in her cup, desperately missing coffee and thinking about all she learned in the libraries.

Inara had been the reason Matthias's parents had died. She had killed them, along with Lux. She had killed Cain's parents—kidnapped Morana and Matthias. There was nothing the goddess of life wouldn't do to leave a trail of ash and smoke in her wake. She had even been willing to send an assassin to Axton's apartment.

Something about that thought made fear churn in Morana's gut. Matthias wanted to take her to the human realm, and Morana wondered if Inara could find her there, too.

There were things she needed to wrap up, though. This could be an opportunity for that. She didn't plan on returning to her human life.

Morana took another sip of tea, her mind continuing to wander. If she took this as an opportunity to pack up her old life—her mortal life, she would need to figure out how. Her phone had been lost in the car accident, but her laptop was probably still sitting on her bed.

Shadows twisted along her flesh, reminding her of the reasons she couldn't go back. The inky darkness trailed along her skin, sending pleasure shooting through her veins. She watched their comforting presence—the way the shadows consumed and caressed every broken part of her. Maybe returning to her old apartment unsettled her more than she cared to admit.

A glimmer of white mist joined her dark power, dancing with the shadows in a way that caused Morana to stiffen. She willed it away, but her power swelled instead. It sent something stirring deep in her gut. A small moment where she felt out of control—addicted and consumed.

When the shadows and mist finally dissipated, she looked up at the crackling hearth, breathing deeply. She took another sip of tea. Sarnai had provided it, convinced that it would be exactly what she needed before her date with Matthias. She peered into the cup, contemplating what blend made you prepared for a date. Sarnai had already provided contraceptive tea, but this tasted different. She didn't know what the goddess made—what the tea was preparing her for. She wasn't certain she *wanted* to know.

Shadows eclipsed the flickering firelight. Morana jolted in the armchair, turning her head to see Matthias dressed in a white sweatshirt and jeans. He ran a tattooed hand through his black hair as the rings on his fingers reflected the light from the flame. The dull exhaustion had left his gaze as he stared at her—replaced with something like excitement.

"Ready?" he asked, pulling his hood over his head.

Morana set her cup down on the end table, unfolding her legs from on the chair and toying with the rip in her jeans. She had found a black ribbed corset in the wardrobe. She was certain it was part of some elaborate fae court dress, but she threw a large flannel on and the jeans instead. She supposed it was casual enough.

"Where are we going?"

"To get away." Matthias sidestepped around the chair, placing both hands on the arms and caging her in. His dark scent invaded her senses, and she swallowed while looking into his onyx eyes. "This is familiar." His jaw ticked as if he were holding back a smile. "You, sitting on a chair beneath me while I can picture nothing but your lips on mine." Her breath stuttered before the darkness grew, coating her flesh and whispering promises in her ear.

This magic was black—dark and brooding—and utterly void of the white mist. Part of her missed the way the shadows danced with whatever was haunting her. She didn't want to think on that too deeply.

Morana's lips parted as she held Death's attention. His eyes flicked down, noting her attire, and taking in the way her corset lifted her full breasts.

"You said the human realm." Morana raised a brow and ignored the lust swirling in his eyes.

"I did." Matthias chuckled. "I also said casual."

"I took that to mean casually enticing."

"And how do you suppose this date will end, Morana?"

A smirk pulled at her lips. "I envisioned at least one of us on our knees."

Matthias groaned, looking away and gripping her wrist as he pulled her to stand. The world parted, throwing them into a dark parking lot.

Shades of purple and blue flickered from the glowing neon sign on the building in front of them. It looked like a warehouse, busy and littered with people exiting their cars to walk toward the pounding music. Morana could see games glowing under the black lights of the interior, and she watched as a young teenager stood focused on one of the pinball machines toward the front.

"An arcade?" Morana smiled.

Matthias grabbed her hand, pulling her along toward the doors. "They have go-karts and laser tag too. I thought it made a nice escape. Something different."

Morana's grin widened, excitement building in her chest. "It was a good idea." She cleared her throat as a knot formed in the pit of her stomach. She hadn't had to worry about things at the palace. Willow made her food. Her room was stocked, and she had access to the entire castle. The human realm was different. "How much does this cost?" she asked.

Matthias glanced at her, a soft chuckle escaping his full lips. "I'm a king, Morana. It will cost *you* nothing." His eyes narrowed. "This is also a date. I hope to never meet the man who made that kind of question even cross your mind."

"Point taken." She leaned into him, seeking his warmth as a brisk night breeze flitted through her hair. She held her flannel tighter around her body, hoping to keep out the cold.

When they got to the glass door, Matthias stepped around her and opened it, gesturing for her to enter. Sounds and sights assaulted her senses as she made her way into the arcade.

The black, tiled floors shone under the blue and purple neon lights suspended above them. The black at the entrance made everything seem more vibrant, and Matthias's sweatshirt was almost glowing.

When they stepped forward into more normal light, Morana noticed just how massive the warehouse was. It held every game imaginable, including the large sign suspended from the ceiling at the back indicating go-karts. The engines revved, and Morana watched as a group of teenagers started racing around the indoor track, laughing and tossing inappropriate insults toward one another.

"Is that what you want to do first?" Matthias was watching her, his fingers weaving between her own. He was cleanly shaven, his hood now lowered since they were inside the building. Something sparked in his dark gaze. He didn't look nearly as tired or worn as earlier.

Morana gazed up at him, fighting the anticipation building in her stomach. She didn't want to seem too excited, but the thought of escaping—the thought of being here away from the madness and the constant threats from Inara and Raidan gave her a sense of security. The real danger was a world away. "I mean, they usually put a limit on how fast they go, but it's still fun. Would *you* want to race?"

"I have a better idea."

Morana smiled as he licked his lips, dragging her toward the desk at the entrance of the arcade. Music blared through speakers overhead and the scent of burned popcorn and cotton candy filled the air.

"How much?" The brunette at the counter popped her gum, her manicured hand hovering over the keyboard. She looked unamused as she stared at the screen. When she finally looked up, her eyes widened. She stood up straighter, her lips parting while her chestnut-colored eyes roved over the god in the room.

Morana tapped a finger on the hard surface of the counter impatiently. Jealousy was sharp and piercing. Her heart ached from its unexpected barb. She could hardly hear the transaction beyond the roaring in her ears. Malice dripped from her tongue as she looked back at the arcade employee and let her words run free, spurred on by the rage building in her chest. "Do you always throw yourself at your customers, or was this just a one-time act of desperation?"

Shadows spilled around her ankles, slowly creeping their way up her legs as they twisted with the white fog. Morana scowled at the woman, wondering what it would be like to feel a blade run across her—

Matthias laughed quietly, sliding the loaded card across the counter. "Thanks for your time."

The woman's mouth was practically on the floor as Matthias dragged Morana toward the go-karts. She couldn't stop looking—couldn't stop envisioning a painful and gruesome punishment.

"Get control of your power," Matthias whispered, his breath ghosting over the shell of her ear.

Morana looked away from the desk and at the magic receding from around her legs. She noticed that familiar tangle of white mist—that new coloring that kept appearing. She wondered if it had to do with the light pulsing through her veins—mixing with the shadows.

"Sorry," she mumbled. "I don't know why I acted like that."

Matthias wrapped an arm around her shoulders as he turned his head so that his lips brushed her temple, his face soon buried in her hair. His closeness sent sparks across her skin. "It was bloodthirsty. I thought you were going to murder that woman." He nipped at her ear. "I'd love for you to feel what that did to me," he whispered.

Morana bit her lower lip, her stomach twisting with desire. Her blood now heated for less murderous reasons. She could feel every place where Matthias touched her—desperately wanting more. Her mind wandered to the broad planes of his chest—the ink painted on his skin. She thought of the way his body had pounded into her beneath the surface of the stream while they were traveling to Lux's temple.

"Calm down, we just got here." His voice rumbled, making it harder to control her lust-filled thoughts.

"Maybe I don't want to calm down."

"Then the adrenaline rush of these fucking go-karts will help you release some pent-up energy." Matthias unwound his arm from her shoulders and walked up to the counter where a young teenager was running the desk, hunched over, and scrolling through videos on his phone.

"How fast do these things go?" Matthias's deep voice startled him. And he frantically put away his device.

The kid cleared his throat. "Sixty, but we don't let them get up to that speed." He gestured to the controls. "How many did you say?"

"I didn't," Matthias grinned, and the boy became more flustered at his presence. "Just two, though."

"Will you be racing or sitting together?"

Morana watched as shadows skittered down Matthias's arms, pushing across the desk and dancing over the boy's skin. The darkness danced in the neon lights of the arcade—consuming and powerful. Her brows creased as she watched them, letting her own shadows pool around her hands—reaching out to decipher what Matthias was doing. "One car, and forget about the controls."

The kid nodded and didn't acknowledge the strange power circling him. He simply agreed with the request to forget about the controls. "All right, just your card, the waivers, and you're all set."

While signing the waivers, Morana couldn't stop the way she kept glancing at Matthias and the smug look plastered to his face.

They walked away from the desk, and Morana pushed open a glass door that led out to the track outside. Streetlights flickered overhead, illuminating the tire-lined path painted with red and yellow markings.

"Did you really just manipulate him?" she asked as the cool night air bit at her cheeks.

The smug smile hadn't disappeared from Matthias's features as he guided her to the cart where they would ride. He trailed his tongue along his teeth and looked down—trying not to laugh. A strand of black hair fell across his brow, and he quickly brushed it back with a tattooed hand.

"Merciless," Morana whispered.

He leaned in, speaking low. "You sounded disappointed when you mentioned how slow these went." His fingertips trailed along her jaw before he lifted her chin. "We couldn't have that now. Could we?"

Her stomach twisted with desire at his words, her breathing shallow. Maybe this *would* be a good way to release some pent-up energy. He had her wound so tightly she couldn't think straight.

"I suppose not," she nearly whispered.

Matthias's hand dropped, his smoldering gaze finally leaving hers, but the satisfied smile held firm. He knew exactly what he was doing.

A blonde with a ponytail gestured to the cart as she began spouting the rules of racing. It didn't matter, though.

Death didn't follow rules—clearly. Her gum popped when she glanced at her painted nails, completely unamused by her job.

When they climbed into the car, shadows crept toward the girl, wrapping her in the same familiar inky spill of darkness. Matthias buckled the harness around himself. "I hope you still plan to go fast." He glanced sideways at her. "Because I live to please."

"By bending the rules for me?" she asked.

"By whatever means necessary." His hand reached for her harness, skimming between the strap and the skin above her corset. He slowly worked his way down, his warm hand keeping contact with her skin until he was brushing over the swell of her breast. The blonde didn't pay attention to them, held captive by whatever Matthias's shadows were doing.

Morana's heart pounded—her breath shallow and rapid. Her stomach twisted as heat washed over her. His closeness was driving her out of her mind. When he leaned over to grab the second strap, she smelled the mint on his breath—the bergamot and shadows scent that was just *him*. She could feel the slickness between her thighs as he moved to clasp the buckles and tighten everything in place. Every touch—every whisper of flesh across her body—was slow and calculated.

He held her gaze a moment before placing his hands on the wheel. His tendons flexed beneath the moth tattoo, and Morana swallowed—hard.

"Ready?" he asked, a knowing look in his eyes.

"For what exactly?" she asked.

She could hear the low rumble of his chest—the noise he made betraying him. He was just as wound up as her. "Right now? A race."

"And later?" She cocked an eyebrow.

"Later, we try to find some closet or dark corner. Literally anything." A smile still sat on his face, holding a wicked edge that had her envisioning every last detail of *later.* She fought to compose herself as she smiled, looking out to the track beyond.

"Seems like you're the one that needs to burn off some energy now." She squeezed her thighs together in a useless attempt to relieve some of the pressure.

His shadows brushed her skin, trailing down her neck then her arms. As he caressed her with his power, the pleasure rippled along her flesh, forcing a small whimper to escape her lips.

Matthias shifted gears. "I have an idea far better than racing." He cleared his throat, a knowing glint in his eyes that were still pinned to the track. "Don't get the seat wet, love."

When they took off, Morana fought to catch her breath. The wind whipped at her face as they accelerated. Matthias sat casually in his seat with one hand, directing the car seamlessly through the track. Her blood was pumping, adrenaline moving through her veins and pushing the thoughts out of her head. With her mind deliciously empty, she forgot about her worries for the first time in months.

You look happy. Matthias's words echoed in her mind as they took a sharp turn to the left.

She let the shadows reach for him, finding the depths of his mind completely open to her. *I am.*

Morana looked over through wild strands of hair, her eyes lighted as they took another turn. She could see him glance back at her—watched the tick of his jaw beneath the streetlights.

The shadows ran over his arms. *There is one sight I enjoy more than the image of you seated on my throne, then.*

With her mind blessedly empty, they rounded another turn, adrenaline feeding her soul. There was no fear here—with him. Only the thrill and rush of unbreakable bliss.

When the cart came to a stop, she was breathing heavily, smiling at Death. "That was so fun." She rested her head on the back of the seat, closing her eyes and sucking in a deep breath. Matthias shifted, unbuckling his harness and offering his hand when she had undone hers.

Stepping up onto the track, Matthias pulled her closer, trailing his thumb across her bottom lip. The air crackled between them—her eyes pinned to his dark gaze.

Later.

"Let's go," Matthias wound a hand around her wrist, nodding once at the employee on the track before pulling Morana back into the arcade.

Her steps were quick as she fought to keep up with him. She huffed a laugh. "Where are we going?"

Matthias didn't respond. He weaved through the different games and bodies littering the floor space. His eyes were searching, whipping around the room until he locked on the small 4-D theater. An *out-of-order* sign hung on the front of the entrance. Shadows flickered, and darkness encased them, ducking under the sign and entering the dark, shut-down theater.

Morana glanced to the exit. "This thing isn't even working. Nobody is working the—"

A bruising kiss swallowed her words. Matthias's hand cupped the side of her face, fingers twisting in her hair as he pressed his mouth to hers and let out a hungry groan.

She fisted his sweatshirt and dragged him closer until their bodies met. The warmth of his body ignited fire in her veins as his scent invaded her senses—making her mind dizzy. When his tongue traced her bottom lip, she opened for him, moaning at the contact.

"Fuck," he whispered against her mouth.

Matthias guided her back until her legs hit one of the chairs in the theater. His mouth chased hers, following as she lowered herself into the seat with her hands frantically running over his arms—his chest.

His fingers trailed over the button of her jeans, toying with the metal as he nipped her lower lip. Before he pulled back, he lowered his mouth, trailing kisses along her neck. As he retreated, his dark eyes swam with desire. "I need your yes." His body was nearly vibrating with tension. "I'm dying here."

Panting, Morana tried to ignore the need crackling through her body as best she could. Her lips pulled back at the corners. She couldn't help but torture him a little. "You're *dying.*" Her eyes blazed with mischief—ready to repay him for the stunt he pulled in the go-kart. "I didn't think that was possible. You are the god of death, after all."

He groaned, leaning closer. "You once asked me how to go about killing a god." He nipped at her lip again—his teeth pulling, and she welcomed the subtle sting. "This," he said. "I'm not entirely sure you weren't crafted from darkness—a goddess created from the shadows with the sole purpose of ending death itself."

Her breath caught, her fingertips now tucked into the waistband of his jeans, pulling him closer. Another dark sound exited his lips. She let her nails gently graze the skin just below his waistband. "Are you saying I could kill you with one word?" Morana cocked a brow, sliding her fingers lower still. "We wouldn't want that."

Matthias sucked in a breath when her fingertips grazed the head of his length. "I think you're already trying to kill me." He pushed forward, begging for more contact, but Morana pulled away.

She reached up and ran her hands through his dark hair, savoring the softness of the strands. Her lips met his again, urgent and seeking before breaking apart. "It's a yes," she breathed. "In fact, I'm starting to get pissed you're taking so long."

Shadows twisted in the already dark room as he growled—deepening the depths of blackness until there was nothing but their harsh breaths and Matthias's fingers pulling her jeans off her hips.

His mouth was on her neck—tongue swirling as he trailed kisses down lower. He kissed her collarbone, then the swell of her breast. He licked—sucked—and she was certain she was going to break apart. When his thumb moved down to find exactly where she needed him, he circled gently. She gasped for breath, her mind zeroed in on that one wicked finger.

"Where would you have me kiss you tonight, Morana?" He circled again—again.

A moan dragged from her lips, and her back arched as she gripped the arm of the seat. "Everywhere," she whispered, circling her hips and barely able to function. She felt hot and out of control.

Matthias licked the column of her throat before whispering a soft promise. "Anything you want. You can have it all."

She whimpered when he broke contact, his hands moving to her waist. He knelt, his fingers digging into her hips as he dragged her further down the seat. The first brush of his tongue set her world alight. She fought the noises dragging from her lips as he worked her, one finger dipping into her core and curling as he pulled it out.

He huffed a laugh, his breath ghosting over her sensitive flesh before his tongue assaulted her once more—moving and coaxing pleasure from her until she was climbing—her release just within reach.

"Don't stop," she begged. "Please don't stop" She was moving now, her body chasing every promise his movement was making. Her mind repeated the request like a song. *Don't stop. Don't stop.* As shadows worked toward her mind, she was certain he heard that request again—again.

Matthias moved his mouth over her until her world exploded, and she was gasping as he wrung out every ounce of pleasure that had coursed through her blood, his grip tightening painfully on her thigh—holding her open.

When she settled, Matthias pushed the button that moved the chair to a reclining position, startling her before his mouth was on her neck again. Morana writhed beneath him, coaxing him closer to the need building all over again. "I need you inside me," she gasped.

"Eager to fuck a god again?" he chided. "You're vicious."

"Says the man who just licked me within an inch of my life." Morana looked at him then, noticing the absence of pain. Whatever was haunting him in the throne room had disappeared. "You should know, though," she began. "I'd still want you, even if you were powerless."

Emotion flashed in his eyes as Matthias pulled his sweatshirt over his head, dragging his shirt along with it and exposing his bare chest. The crows inked on his arms twisted like the shadows that now surrounded them. Morana didn't know when their power started mixing, but it sparked something in her chest. She reached out, letting the shadows take her as she unbuttoned his pants. Glancing up at the god before her, Morana shoved his waistband down, freeing him and pulling him down until he was over her, his thick length brushing against her soaked entrance.

He kissed her once—twice—something she couldn't name dancing in his gaze. "You know, you're the first person to truly ask about my family the way you did."

She laughed low and gently. "That can't be true." Matthias teased her entrance, the seriousness never leaving his face, and she hissed through her teeth.

"People are concerned with me being king. Garian—the other lords. They already know my history. So, yes. It's true."

They stared at one another—the silence stretching taut between them. Morana tried to read his expression, to understand why this was so important to bring up now. She accepted every part of him—his past—his present. Didn't he know that? The shadows pulsed around them, her power working on its own.

He kissed her again, his lips gently brushing over hers. "Thank you," he whispered. The gentleness—the intimacy—if there were any pieces of the wall around her heart left, he had shattered it completely.

He moved slowly, entering her inch-by-inch as she stared into his eyes. Their breath twisted together like their powers, shadows cutting them off from all else. When he was fully seated, he began pulling out slowly.

When it was just his tip teasing her entrance, he nipped at her lip, chuckling briefly before he slammed back into her.

She gasped, nails digging into his spine as he started moving. She was already climbing again, the pleasure building in her body faster than before. He kissed her harder, and she gripped the dark strands of his hair, if only to hold him there.

Morana could feel the shadows swirling around them as they called her, twisting with something relatively new. Matthias was moving, his harsh breaths feeding her desire. She kissed him back, feeling the heady power that was taking over her senses. Biting his lip, the coppery taste of his blood coated her tongue. It fueled something in her, a dark desire to taste more—consume more. She longed to drink of Death.

Her release crashed through her, and Matthias picked up his pace as she licked the remaining blood from his lips. He groaned, slamming into her with one final thrust.

The blood coated her tongue and awoke the beast in her chest. All she could see was death. Morana could feel the blade slicing through the Veeden's neck—the way its head rolled across the forest floor. She could feel the power swirling around her as she pulled the trigger of the gun pointed at Axton's head. The images fueled a deep desire to kill and destroy.

When she opened her eyes, the inky blackness had faded, white mist twisting in the air and encasing them instead of the shadows. Matthias stared at her, his expression hard.

She reeled back as he pulled out. Matthias was now standing and looking down with a curious expression. His gaze cold and haunted.

"What is that?" she whispered.

The mist swelled, growing and filling the small theater like a thick fog. Matthias didn't move. His chest heaved, and she saw fear in his expression. She desperately tried to drag the power back to herself, remove it until it was, at the very least, a mere whisper across her skin.

When it disappeared, heeding her command, they simply stared at each other. Matthias looked as if he were consumed by memories, and Morana was reminded of Raidan's power holding her in his temple.

"I'm sorry," he apologized, shaking off whatever trance he was in. "That's—"

Morana stood up, pulling her jeans back over her hips and turning away while Matthias dressed, too. A heavy weight settled in her gut. She couldn't get the taste of his blood out of her mouth.

"Raidan," she finally mumbled, her voice barely audible. The strange power—so similar to the gods—had kept her company since The Wastelands. This, however, was the first time it had been difficult to draw it back.

Matthias grabbed her arm, twisting her to face him. His eyes were void of judgment as they flicked over her face. "It's all right." Her chest squeezed at the sincerity in his voice.

The white mist had faded, disappearing until there was nothing left. "It's been happening since we went to the temple to get you. I have no control over it. I don't know what he did."

"Probably nothing." It was an assuring statement, one that she could tell he didn't believe. Ghosts entered the room with the look he was giving. They were the ghosts that spoke of the torture he'd experienced. They haunted and lurked, joining with the concern in his eyes—concern for her. Despite everything he had been through, and the torture Raidan had put him through, Matthias was still here, concerned about *her.*

"We came to escape all of this," she said, worry stirring in her gut. She shoved it down. "Why don't we forget about it, and I can kick your ass in some arcade games?"

A small smirk pulled at his mouth before he kissed her softly. "I'd like to see you defeat Death."

Morana brushed a hand over his jeans, feeling the length of him beneath the fabric. "I'd like to think I already did."

With a wicked smile filled with promises of the many ways she would wipe the floor with him, she turned to duck out of the closed theater.

Thirteen

Matthias had beaten her at every game except one. They had spent nearly an hour standing in front of the large screen swiping and cutting fruit because it was the only game he had actually struggled with. She'd lost everything else. It was infuriating. Mostly fun, but still infuriating.

The streetlights flickered over the sidewalk as Morana's sneakers tapped the damp concrete. The night air smelled of weed and stale beer. It was the familiar scent of her crappy apartment complex in the city—the one she was about to leave for good. There was nothing left for her here, and she couldn't put it behind her fast enough.

Matthias's fingers wove through hers, the hood of his white sweatshirt pulled over his head. "You really kicked my ass at all of those games, huh?" There was sarcasm there.

She bumped him with her hip. "I will not admit defeat. I will go on pretending I won until you believe it to be true."

He sucked on his teeth. "Sounds a little like gaslighting to me. I believe mortals call that a red flag. I'm not sure if I'll ask you out again."

She cleared her throat. A part of her knew he was joking, but something still had her halting at the statement. Morana glanced away, trying to hide her own insecurity by looking at the run-down brick building to their right. The light by one of the doors flickered ominously. The next building was hers.

Matthias leaned over, pulling her closer before he whispered in her hair, "I was kidding." *Of course.* The shadows knew no secrets. "One, I enjoyed winning too much, and two, I think we should find another theater very," he nipped at her ear, "*very* soon."

A flush colored her cheeks, and she squeezed his fingers, feeling the metal of his rings.

He halted and turned to face her, pulling her close as his hand traced her jaw. His gaze snapped to her lips before he drew her in for a kiss. This one was slow and coaxing, tasting of summer rains and smoke.

When they broke apart, she looked up at him, refusing to hide herself. In a way, it was comforting. "I'm sorry," she said. "What you said—I don't know." She looked away, hardly able to find words to express it.

Morana knew she was a mess—knew her weaknesses more intimately than anyone. His words triggered that awareness, making her want to cave in on herself—to disappear.

Matthias waited, trailing the pad of his thumb along her jaw.

"I guess I don't understand how I deserve this—any of this. The date, the kindness of your court, *you*." The truth burned like acid on her tongue, but the only way to ease the pain was to get it all out. "I want all of those things. There's nothing I want more than to be a part of your world, but my mind keeps reminding me of how weak I am—how much I don't know."

Matthias's brows drew together. "You think I believe you to be weak?"

"A burden," she whispered, the truth of her biggest insecurity hanging in the air.

"How can you see yourself that way?" he asked, but he didn't allow her to answer. "You gave up so much of yourself to care for your useless father. Look at all you've accomplished in a realm so ready to devour you whole. Morana, you've defeated assassins, the Veeden—you've even endured torture."

She shook her head. "That was all dumb luck."

"No." He held her face in his hands, his touch gentle and warm. "Garian has told me how hard you've worked in training, and don't think for a minute I haven't noticed you frequenting the libraries in the palace." He placed an encouraging kiss on her forehead before looking into her eyes again—truth swirling in his gaze. "You are motivated and intelligent. No matter what life has thrown at you, you've continued to fight. How could you ever refer to yourself as a *burden?*"

Morana stared at him with a burning desire to see herself the way he saw her.

"My mother would have loved you." She could feel the sorrow in his words, allowing it to seep into her bones. The declaration warmed her chest, and she leaned forward to kiss him.

When his lips met hers this time, there was none of the urgency of the theater, only the slow slide of their unhurried movements. He kissed her like he longed to leech the insecurities from her heart—to patch it up and help it heal. And in that moment—she believed he could.

Shouting caused them to break apart. Two men ran down the steps leading down from the apartment flats just ahead.

Time slowed as the man screamed and pulled a gun from his waistband, raising it to the man in front of him and pulling the trigger. Morana jolted, some memory swirling around her mind and freezing her in place.

"Morana." Matthias was shaking her shoulders. The roaring in her ears subsided and his features came into focus in front of her. "Shadow into your apartment."

"What about you?" Her heart was racing, sweat beading on her brow while fear stirred in her stomach.

"That gun can't hurt me, and I'm—" he glanced back at the body that was lying in a pool of blood. The other man had disappeared. "I'm needed. So, go."

Morana nodded, hardly able to speak as she let the darkness take her, parting the world and throwing her into the entryway of her apartment.

Landing on all fours, she shifted to sit with her back against her front door. The apartment smelled like paint and new carpeting. It always did. It was as if she had never actually taken the time to *live* in this space—only using it as a place to stay.

Morana inhaled deeply and fought to steady her shaking hands. She drew her knees to her chest and felt the sting of tears forming in her eyes. As one ran down her cheek, she wiped it away with the back of her hand, smearing her makeup and leaving her empty.

She steeled her spine, unwilling to let the last shooting she had been in consume her like this. She would overcome these feelings and move forward—act like a fucking god and not a pitiful mortal cowering in her apartment while Matthias was out easing the sting of death.

Morana braced her hand on the floor, pushing herself up to stand. Her hair was a tangled mess after their racing and the brisk wind that twisted the strands during their night stroll.

At least she could escape to court. There was no one hunting her here, nobody to bother or find her. Death would come for her soon. The thought settled the anxiety twisting in her chest, cutting off the roots and preventing the fear from blooming in her chest.

The apartment was bare. No decorations hung on the walls. No personal photos, only thick layers of beige paint coating the walls to hide the scratches and stench of weed from the tenants before her. Despite maintenance's valiant and poorly executed efforts, the smell was still there, resting beneath the fresh scent of clean brown carpets. Even the perfume she had spilled in the bathroom months ago clung to the surfaces of her apartment like they were a sponge.

Morana glanced to the galley kitchen to the right, her living room with the old futon she had found in the dumpster on the left. She walked down the hall to where her bedroom and bathroom were. Nothing had changed. She didn't bother flicking on the lights, just walked into her old bedroom, utterly detached and void of any emotion.

Her laptop was still on her bed, plugged in and waiting. She opened it quickly, finding the contact information for the apartment complex to draft an email explaining that she was moving—figuring a different realm would be far enough to not worry about her leftover things.

"Here to wrap up your human life?"

Morana's gaze snapped behind her to the doorway. Fear crawled up her spine until it lodged itself in her throat. There was no way she could forget that voice, but there was also no way he would be here. The white mist drifting across the floor confirmed her fears and guided her to the image of Raidan standing in the darkness of her apartment— menacing and utterly wretched.

Fear felt like a consuming abyss, one that she was now free-falling into—the descent ripping the breath from her lungs, and all hope shattered. Even here, she could be hunted. Morana didn't let her emotions show. Raidan didn't deserve the satisfaction they would bring him. She buried them deep, hardening her gaze.

"Why the fuck are you here?" she asked.

"Overwhelming hospitality, really." He sauntered to her dresser, fingering the wilted flowers in front of the vanity. Raidan's amber eyes met hers in the mirror. "I told you we would meet again." He licked his lips. "My proposition."

"I'm not interested in any proposition from you." Shadows spilled down her arms, eating the white mist of Raidan's power, awakening with the anger now bubbling in her chest.

He crushed one of the dried petals and turned, leaning against the wooden surface and staring at her with such intensity that she fought the bile rising in her throat.

She needed to get out. Morana drew on her powers, willing the shadows to encase her and readying herself to escape. Something latched onto her magic, dragging it under until it was lost to her entirely. She felt nothing—no comforting shadows, no light flickering in her chest.

Her fear took root, sending panic through her veins.

"Pity," Raidan tsked. "The shadows don't serve you when bound by my power. You've insulted me, and I haven't even gotten to my offer yet." His lips peeled back in a feral smile.

Morana didn't respond. She could feel his magic wrap around her ankles and hold her to the floor. The mist caressed her, rising higher until it was gently brushing against her throat and coating her entire body.

"There's nothing you could fucking offer me—"

Her breath left her lungs as his magic tightened, choking her until she was clawing at her neck, eyes wild.

Raidan's own eyes narrowed. "You have quite a mouth on you. I'm not sure I like it." He stepped closer and trailed a finger over her shoulder before the pad of his thumb rose to drag over her lip. She was still fighting to breathe, her hands now pinned and grasping her neck. He was keeping her from moving. "I still present you with my offer. You'll need to be of sound mind to accept."

Air flooded her lungs, and she coughed and hunched over. Raidan had stepped back, giving her space but keeping her feet firmly planted. He clasped his hands behind his back, his dark suit stretching across his broad chest.

"As I was saying." His tongue clicked impatiently. "I want to take you as my queen."

Morana looked up through a damp strand of hair. She was sweating now, panting, with her hands still gripping her knees. "Your what?" she rasped.

"Queen of The Wastelands." Raidan circled her, sizing her up with his hungry gaze. "You're powerful. I want you to rule with me in The Wastelands."

"I thought Inara was your pawn in this game. She's the one that woke you." Morana stood up, rubbing her neck. "Isn't she?"

"Useful as it was, I've already returned the favor. I owe her nothing." Raidan stopped in front of her again. "You, now. You would be quite the prize. And after I let

you retreat with your pet in tow, you just happen to owe
me."

And there was the reveal—the game he had been playing in the temple. "I am no prize," she snarled. Her anger was a sentient being, wrapping around her and begging for blood. It whispered dark promises in her ear and encouraged her to fight the demon.

"Debatable." He stepped forward and returned his thumb and finger to her jaw, stroking gently as his power held her in place. Her stomach roiled. "I believe you would be a valuable prize." His gaze burned with intensity as it trailed over her features. "I am certainly eager to rule with you. You could be queen, you know. Death isn't the only god to lurk in the darkness, and I know you have a taste for it." The mist rose around the room—a deep and impenetrable fog.

"I have not agreed to anything."

"Maybe not, but as I mentioned before, you owe me a favor. Fae work in bargains, but so do the gods." He leaned in slightly. "Can't you feel my power inside you?" He licked his lips as his eyes traveled to the swell of her breasts. She wanted to crawl into the earth—bury herself beneath the soil to escape the menacing monster in her room. "I *am* inside you, Morana."

A loud pounding on the door drew her eyes away from Raidan. Matthias's voice followed. He sounded frantic. "Morana!" His fists hit the wood, and his presence settled something inside her.

"Death can't get in," Raidan whispered. He leaned forward, his tongue trailing along the flesh of her cheek. He smelled like lilacs and storms—so contradictory to the vile scent of rot and pain that followed wherever he went.

Morana closed her eyes to keep the tears from escaping. It was useless. When she opened her lids, a tear trailed down her cheek, mixing with his saliva. She was shaking now—still bound by magic and helpless.

Matthias's shouting grew louder, assaulting her senses. She was begging him to break through whatever Raidan had done to keep him out—begging him to save her.

Raidan leaned forward again, pressing a kiss to her lips. Something broke at that touch. She could feel the same magic, the one that called for destruction, swell within her. The fog became dense, twisting in her bedroom with an unquenchable thirst. She could see blood and death—ravens flying overhead and promising destruction.

The fog responded, and she pulled on that power, shoving it into the god's chest until he was staggering back. He smiled then, placing a hand over where she had hit him. "There it is," he began—voice smooth. "You're already coming into my power, I see. Ready to become the queen of The Wastelands."

Morana saw the exit and sprinted, running through her apartment. The door was rattling so hard she thought it would splinter. All she could hear was Matthias's shouts and the fear in his voice. "Morana, what the fuck is happening?" His voice nearly cracked with emotion.

At the sound of boots on the floors, Morana ducked into the kitchen, sliding with her back against the cabinet after grabbing a knife. It wouldn't save her, and she wasn't even sure it would help her, but she couldn't sit and do nothing. No more being a useless, helpless mortal.

She called on the power and found the shadows responding again. She let them spill over her as tears streaked down her cheeks. Raidan's footsteps moved closer, and she was trembling, sweat dripping down her back.

"You can't hide, Morana."

She called on more of the shadows, willing Matthias's voice to give her strength. As a black boot stepped in front of her, the door behind Raidan's towering figure burst open, and darkness engulfed the apartment.

Raidan turned and took a step toward her entryway, just out of the galley kitchen. Morana stood up, her hands pushing against the tile floor. When her eyes locked with Death's, she was met with an overwhelming image of power.

The darkness spilled over Matthias, consuming the room as he plowed toward Raidan, gripping the major god's throat with a bruising force. Morana could see his fingers dig into flesh and hear the wheezing sound exit Raidan's lips.

"We have unfinished business," Matthias snarled, his face inches from Raidan's.

Morana stepped forward, watching Matthias slam Raidan's back against the wall. The shadows pulsing in his wake. He was power and darkness—a death god craving blood.

Raidan smiled manically. "Good to see you. I was just coming to retrieve my queen."

"Fuck you," Matthias snarled, pulling back and slamming him against the wall once more. The force of it rattled the walls of the apartment.

Morana's grip tightened on the knife. She knew it was useless, but she still held it as she got closer. The darkness begging her to kill and destroy—calling her like a vicious lover.

"Yes," Raidan spoke. "That's exactly what I was hoping your woman would do."

Matthias growled, practically lifting the god off his feet before he threw him across the room. Raidan was on the ground, blood trickling down his temple, when Matthias charged him, grabbing his throat again and baring his teeth. His shadows twisted, sucking their way into Raidan's skull.

"I will rip whatever image of her you have in that useless brain."

For the briefest moment, Raidan looked afraid.

"Get out of here," Matthias growled before slamming Raidan's head to the ground once more and walking away.

He was standing in front of her now, power radiating off him in waves while Raidan still lay on the ground behind him.

Raidan's amber eyes burned as they locked onto Morana. "I'll be back to retrieve what's mine."

He smiled and disappeared.

Matthias grabbed her wrist quickly, dragging Morana's body against his and causing her to drop the knife. Her body shook as she let out gasping sobs, soaking his chest with pent-up tears.

"I'm not leaving you again," he whispered. His voice was so strained that she thought it might break.

"Let's go home." Her words were barely audible. Matthias pulled her closer as the shadows twisted around them, pulling them through the darkness until they were in the gardens of the palace in Ascella.

Fourteen

Delicate white flowers wrapped their sleepy limbs around the wrought-iron fence in the palace gardens. Their vines climbed the metal, shielding the bench from the rest of the elaborate landscaping.

Morana rested her head on the brick wall behind her, sighing and fighting off the demons circling and whispering—eager to coat her veins in fear.

Morana closed her eyes and willed the tears to dry. "He's not going to go away."

Another billow of smoke. Matthias was staring at the statue in front of them. They had found this small alcove to hide from the world and the responsibilities that await them. The implications of the night were huge. Morana wasn't ready to face that reality just yet.

"Then I'll wage war on The Wastelands." Matthias looked up at her with his jaw tightened. "War was inevitable with the Court of Light. I don't think including The Wastelands would make much of a difference."

Morana nodded as the silence stretched between them briefly. The wooden bench creaked when Matthias shifted, leaning back to blow more smoke into the night air. The scent of tobacco invaded her senses. It wasn't sweet in the way it was with Axton. There was something else mixed into the scent, something with more substance than empty promises wrapped in pretty words.

"Why didn't you tell me Inara was the one to kill your parents?"

Matthias chuckled, but there was no mirth to the sound. "You've been reading, I take it?"

She didn't answer, hoping that the quiet would spur him toward a further explanation.

"Old stories," he spoke. Matthias cleared his throat. "Painful stories." He turned to her, offering her the cigarette. Morana glanced at it briefly before looking back into his eyes. She took it from him with her hand, brushing against the warmth of his fingers.

Morana brought the cigarette to her lips and inhaled deeply. Smoke invaded her lungs as the tip burned bright in the darkness. She halted, coughing and waving at the smoke in her face before handing it back to Matthias. There was some reprieve there—something to relax her, though she never smoked before. The corner of Matthias's mouth quirked up as if he had known.

"I've never done that before," she admitted."

His smile stretched wider. "You don't say?"

"Shut up."

Quietness filled the space once more, leading her to ask the questions swirling in her mind. "Were you there when it happened?" she nearly whispered. "When they died, I mean."

A dark strand of hair had fallen across his creased brow when Matthias turned to look at her. There was pain in his expression. The chiseled planes of his face covered with the hardness of someone desperately fighting off haunting memories.

"They were the first of those I've given peace to in death." He was staring at her now as his face twisted. There wasn't anything she could say to wipe the pain off his face, but she wanted to be there—carry his memories as he had carried hers.

The shadows twisted down her arms, and she found herself with access to his mind. *I'm sorry.* Saying it aloud didn't feel as intimate. Here, in his mind, it was just them. She could almost feel her words echo in her own head too—as if, in this moment, they were one. *I'm sorry you had to endure that kind of pain.*

Morana reached up, brushing the strand away from his eyes. He caught her wrist, holding her there and gripping as if he could siphon strength from her very presence. Matthias didn't speak as he leaned forward to brush his lips over hers.

There was a difference in this kiss, something gentle and coaxing. It was as if he wanted to learn the very depths of her soul, and in return, have her learn the depths of his. When his mouth opened, she tasted mint and smoke. Their pain was wrapped in a space that didn't need words—one where she could feel all of his thoughts as if they were her own. She sensed the thanks he longed to give her for listening—for being there to carry the burden. It was the least she could do, after all.

Matthias brought a thumb up to brush her cheek, and Morana stiffened. She could feel Raidan's tongue licking up the side of her face. Her brows pulled together, and she reeled back with tears now stinging at the corners of her eyes.

Matthias looked at her, shadows dancing around them. She could feel him in her mind again, speaking. *What did he do to you?*

She let him in.

His face hardened, and wrath rippled over the tension in his shoulders. Inky darkness pulsed around him, and she got a glimpse of the god she had seen bursting through her apartment door.

"He touched you." Morana couldn't look away from his intensity.

"It's fine," she whispered. *It isn't.* She knew the thought to be true, but somehow, she couldn't bring herself to feel it just yet.

Matthias ran a ringed finger over her cheek—over the exact spot Raidan had licked her. His touch was gentle, eyes seeking as if he could erase whatever lingered on her skin.

This was one scar she didn't want to wear.

Tell me how to fix it, he spoke into her mind. *I will do anything. Do you want me to kill him?*

No. She closed her eyes, leaning into his touch.

Do you *want to kill him?*

She smiled. *I may have promised him a gruesome death already.*

Then it is death we will deal.

When she opened her eyes, he was still looking at her, his magic still sending words into the space designed just for them.

Please, he spoke. *Tell me what I can do for you. How do you want me to take the pain away?*

Morana turned, leaning her head against his broad shoulder and gently taking his hand in hers. She placed his palm on her chest, over her heart. Closing her eyes, she inhaled deeply.

"Stay," she spoke aloud. "Stay with me."

He turned to place a kiss atop her head.

Always.

The gate opened, and they broke apart, gazing at the flora goddess's ethereal presence. There was an urgency to her steps. As her crimson dress wound around her legs, the flowers in the garden seemed to open up in her presence, as if she was the sunlight to sustain them. They only needed the glowing woman bathed in moonlight and finery.

"Cain found something in the blood book," Sarnai began. The silver webbing on her forehead glimmered in the darkness.

"If you've come to explain the full extent of Axton's betrayal, then save it." Morana folded her arms over her chest.

Matthias cast her a confused glance before they both returned to the panicked creature before them.

"Listen," she hissed. "Inara is on her way to the palace."

"Here?" Matthias was standing in an instant.

"Why?" Morana asked.

"We haven't the slightest idea. Cain is still looking for that information in recent entries. She should be here for dinner. She will expect to be hosted." Sarnai pulled the dark strands of her thick hair over one shoulder. Her umber eyes were burning with fierce intensity.

"What do we do?" Morana asked, leaning forward on the wooden bench.

Matthias schooled his expression—the bitter cold of his voice biting in the night air. "We go to bed." Command laced his voice as he spoke to Sarnai. "Morana is not to be alone," he added. "Then tomorrow, we will host a monster for dinner."

Morana huffed a laugh and licked her lips. "So much for a fucking break," she added.

The earth was dry and cracked beneath the rising smoke of the fires in the distance. Thick fog coated the ground in ancient magic.

Morana stood in the field with bones crunching beneath her boots. In her hand was a sword. The weight felt different from the one Reese had made for her. This one was heavier—reminding her of a time she had pierced the skin of a wolf-like creature in the tomb of a god.

Closing her eyes and inhaling, Morana breathed deeply, letting the white mist invade her body—her mind. She could see blood and bone and chaos. It fed some beast deep in her soul—the one thrashing and begging to escape. It had escaped before and fed the monster within.

As she opened her eyes, the fog lifted and revealed the bodies of each lord from The Court of Shadows.

Garian's eyes were open—shock still written on his cold face. She hungered for the fear that he had shown when she drove the sword through his gut. Morana stepped forward and crouched next to Garian's body, dipping a finger in his blood, spinning the crimson liquid and mesmerized by the sight. Memories filled her mind of the way she had cut the lords down, leaving them in this wasteland of bone and ash.

"Do you like the taste of blood?"

That voice echoed behind her and brought a sense of comfort and solace—belonging. When she turned, Raidan's amber eyes locked with hers. Armor-clad with his gray hair braided down his broad back, but she wasn't afraid.

Morana stepped forward; her eyes dead as she approached the god. "I do," she admitted. It was the truth. The scent of copper filled her nostrils, and she relished in the bloodlust that filled her chest—her mind—consuming her entirely.

Elivira, Ronan—all of them slain by the sword still clutched in her hand. She had caused this destruction, and she longed for the power that swelled with each slash of metal against bone.

"Wouldn't you like to drink of Death, Morana?" Raidan brushed a finger along her jaw. "Aren't you curious about how Death's blood would taste on your lips?"

For a moment, Morana wanted nothing else.

Morana jolted upright as sweat trailed over her skin, staining her cheeks with salt and sorrow. She was panting—surrounded by the black walls and gilded accents of her room in the palace of Ascella.

Only then did she register the presence of Death in the room. He had refused to leave her alone after what had happened in the human realm. He promised to stay.

Matthias was sitting shirtless in the velvet chair by the fire and staring at the flames. He quickly stood up when she shifted and caused the bed to creak. A pained expression creased his features when he faced her.

"I tried to wake you." His low voice was raspy in the late hours of the night. Moonlight filtered in from the window, illuminating her room in a silvery glow. "Your mind was closed off to me. I couldn't reach you. I was worried—" He ran a hand through his hair. "I was worried that Inara was in your mind again."

Fear tightened her chest at the memory of the dream. Inara hadn't been there, but someone else had. Morana slaughtered everyone in that dream—standing on a battlefield surrounded by Raidan's power. She had run her finger through Garian's pool of blood and relished in the coppery tang that coated her tongue when Raidan asked her if she wanted to drink of Death.

Morana swallowed. "I don't think he was actually there with me."

Matthias's expression darkened, and he moved to sit on the bed next to her. Anger surrounded him—pulsing and begging for vengeance. "What do you mean by he?" he asked. There was no doubting Matthias already knew by the timbre of his voice.

"Raidan," she whispered.

"You dreamed of Raidan?" Matthias's voice held no softness or comfort.

"I dreamt of slaughter."

Matthias reached up, running a thumb along her jaw. She flinched. The memory of Raidan's tongue still burned into her mind. Breathing deeply, she leaned into the touch. This was *Matthias.* Matthias was safe. Shadows rippled over her skin, and with them, she felt the comfort of power.

He observed her carefully, tilting her head to one side. His gaze scalded her and burned the same as a wrathful fire. She wasn't afraid of what she saw there—the desire to kill the god that had tortured him. His dark thoughts were hers and he knew that.

Matthias leaned forward and gently lifted her chin, swiping at a tear on her flushed cheek. "Will you let me see?" he asked. Closing her eyes, she nodded. "Morana." A softness entered his voice at the sound of her name on his lips. "Let me see the dream that's haunting you. Let me carry the burden."

Matthias allowed his power to ripple and reach out to her. She let him in. Despite her fear of what he would think, the bloodlust he would feel, she laid it all bare.

When the dream ended, Matthias brushed a gentle kiss on her lips, then her forehead, and finally her nose. He did not balk at the villain standing in his presence. That's what she had felt like—a villain.

His eyes met hers in the dim light of the crackling fire. The darkness of night and shadows surrounded them. It was in that darkness that Morana found strength.

"It's nothing," he breathed. "We will figure this out."

Morana wanted to believe him. She wanted to believe that the strange power and dreams meant nothing, but there was a part of her soul that knew it wasn't true. Raidan was inside of her. The scariest part was that for the briefest moment, as she beheld the bodies of those she had learned to care for, Morana had relished in the power of destruction.

She reached up to touch the scars on her cheeks and then her tattoo. They were reminders of the cost of death and the reality of who she wanted to be. Death had to mean something at her hand. If she stopped caring, there was no telling what lay beyond that kind of callous evil.

"I'm scared," she whispered into the night.

Matthias laid down, and she cradled next to him, resting her head on his bare chest. Tears flowed freely in his presence as he stroked her hair, his steady breathing slowly bringing her back to the present. There was still fear there. Inara was to be in the palace at dinner. They would have to host her as if Death wasn't waging war on their court, and Morana would have to pretend she didn't feel the phantom sting of slashes of power across her back in the goddess's presence.

Matthias never responded—he simply allowed his presence to bring peace until the shadows settled. He had kept his promise to stay—to be here. She should have been afraid of how much she trusted him. It was the last thought she had before sleep took her under.

Fifteen

Morana stared at herself in one of the mirrors in her room at the palace. Shimmering black vines climbed up her dress, barely covering her breasts and stomach—leaving very little to be imagined.

It was beautiful, though. A dress she could never afford during her previous life. The one filled with caring for her drunk father and working multiple low-paying jobs.

Her hair was pinned up, loose strands framing her made-up face. Willow had outdone herself in preparation for this dinner. Morana's stomach roiled—anticipating who she would have to face.

"Matthias wanted you to wear this." Willow appeared behind her with the crown of rubies and obsidian stone that Morana had worn before retrieving Matthias from The Wastelands. The crown had belonged to Matthias's mother. Morana's heart fluttered in her chest at the implications of wearing the crown to a dinner hosting the Court of Light.

Her voice dropped to a whisper. "Why would he want me to wear that?"

Sarnai laughed from where she was perched in a chair by the fire. Her long legs draped over the arm, and she smiled over a cup of steaming tea.

Sarnai and Willow exchanged smiles. "I believe that's something you should ask him for yourself." Willow stepped forward as Morana's eyes returned to the mirror. She placed the crown on her head, carefully pinning it to keep it from shifting or moving.

"How is this dinner going to work?" Morana asked. "None of the lords are here. We have no idea what she wants. Matthias is about to send troops to Zora. He is about to start a *war*." Her thoughts were racing as she tried to piece together what her role was in this entire thing. Of course, she wanted to be involved. She wanted to prove herself useful—to find some semblance of control after what Inara had done to her during Mabon. Yet, some part of her continued to believe she contributed nothing. After last night with Raidan, that control was even more important. Morana allowed the shadows to pulse around her—snuffing out the light that lay dormant within. She hadn't touched that power since discovering she had it—couldn't bear it.

"Personally," Sarnai began from the other side of the room. "I think that's exactly why she is here." Sarnai trailed a black and red painted finger over the rim of her cup. The firelight danced over her brown skin and illuminated the silver webbing etched into the goddess's forehead. "What better way to stir the pot than to show up where you aren't welcome?" The disdain dripped from her lips like thick honey—honey with a bite to it.

"I agree." Willow was adjusting a stray strand of Morana's hair. "Inara knows she violated sacred laws during Mabon by taking you and imprisoning you." The fae woman's blue eyes burned with fire. "She likely knows something is coming and is looking to show up to figure out exactly what that *something* is."

A wicked smirk split Sarnai's face. "She doesn't have Matthias's blood book." Sarnai cocked a brow. "She can't see our moves the way we see hers."

The nerves were still crawling up Morana's spine and filling her with anxious energy. "So, she's coming for information about where we stand in relation to Mabon." Willow had stopped fiddling with her hair, and Morana reached up to trail a finger over the crown atop her head. She looked like a queen—seated and awaiting an opportunity to give orders. "Doesn't the crown make some sort of statement? If Inara kidnapped me, and now I'm here in the Court of Shadows dressed in black and wearing Matthias's *mother's* crown—" She didn't finish explaining what that implied.

"I'll admit," Willow began while taking a seat on the corner of Morana's bed. "It is a statement." Her brows rose as Morana met her eyes in the mirror. "Again, you will need to ask Matthias about that."

As if summoned, shadows swirled by the doorway, parting to reveal Death dressed in a suit, the moth inked on his hand shifting as he ran his fingers through dark strands of hair. He looked every bit a king and a god—his clothes fully changed from what he wore in the human realm.

Matthias's obsidian gaze didn't break from hers. He placed his hands in his pockets, leaning casually against the door frame.

Willow bowed as she made to exit the room—taking the hint that she was no longer needed. Morana hoped the woman found time to rest. Willow had been with her nearly the entire day. Matthias had been serious about Morana not being alone, and while he had kept his promise to stay with her whenever he could, the constant presence of others was becoming suffocating.

"Sarnai." Matthias didn't bother looking at the goddess as he spoke. "A moment."

Sarnai made no move to leave. "I'd rather not." She leaned back, trailing a finger over the edge of a vase on the side table. Flowers bloomed, and the vase instantly filled with life at her touch. Vines spread from the floor, wrapping up the legs of the table and sprouting deep green leaves.

Matthias looked at her with a dark expression. Sarnai simply rolled her eyes and stood up.

"Fine," she huffed. "I *suppose* I have places to be." She scowled at Matthias before disappearing out the door. Morana swore she saw his jaw tick as if he were holding back a smirk.

"The crown?" Morana asked.

"Looks beautiful on you." Matthias pushed off the door frame and took a step forward.

A flush crept up her cheeks as Morana's gaze flicked around the room. "Why am I supposed to wear this?" she asked.

Matthias moved forward again, stopping just inches from her when her eyes found his. He reached up, running a finger along the top of the crown and then gently fingering a strand of her hair. "I'm asking you to eat dinner with the monster that tortured you," he began. "The least I can do is gift you some authority."

"I don't need a crown to have authority to speak in her presence." Morana's eyes narrowed.

"No." Matthias smiled. "But I still like the look of it, regardless." He slowly leaned forward, the scent of mint and bergamot invading her senses. Her lips parted—a shuddering breath escaping them at his closeness. Matthias whispered, "That crown makes me want to place you on my throne and show you what it truly means to worship."

Her breath left her. Morana swallowed as images of Matthias kneeling before her in the theater flashed through her mind. She could feel his hands trailing over her thighs, her waist, her breasts.

Matthias chuckled—a dark sound. "We have a guest," he spoke. "It would be rude to keep her waiting."

Morana felt his fingers thread through hers as if he were trying to give her strength. It was strength she would need as she faced yet another monster in less than twenty-four hours.

The tall doors opened with a groan to reveal a long dining table stretched across a room fit for receiving guests and hosting monsters.

Matthias gestured for Morana to walk in first. Her black heels clicked on the dark floors of the palace as she crossed the threshold. Four guests stood upon her entrance into the dining room—one of those guests being a honey-eyed fox with narrow features and his mouth pressed into a thin line. Morana tried to keep from reacting at Conan's presence, but when she noticed the fifth guest still seated and running a finger over a silver chalice, her white hair draped over one pale shoulder, anger thrashed against her ribs—begging to be released from the cage like a wild animal.

Inara's brow cocked. Her bored gaze flicked to the crown atop Morana's head and trailed down the sweeping gown glittering in the faefire that streamed from a crystal chandelier overhead.

Morana broke her gaze, fists clenched at her sides as she walked down the long end of the table. She halted midway, positioned behind two unfamiliar guests. Inara was across the table and still seated just beyond the crimson rose centerpiece that Sarnai must have fashioned. The heavy doors clicked, and Morana knew without looking that Death had entered the room. Shadows spilled down her arms, kissing the floor and swirling like a thick and consuming fog.

Morana turned to look at the monster, and rose-colored eyes narrowed in challenge. Refusing to balk, Morana lifted her chin.

Matthias's voice sounded behind her. "Shall I force you to stand and show my future bride an ounce of respect, Inara?"

Her stomach bottomed out, and Morana halted, keeping her expression neutral and reaching for the shadows once more.

Future bride?

She nearly choked on the word, even speaking mind to mind with Matthias.

Play the game.

His blank expression and short response told her he wouldn't give her anything else.

With her stomach twisting painfully and her eyes hardened toward the goddess in the room, Morana questioned whether she was more offended that Matthias hadn't informed her of his plan to announce her as his bride, or if the offense was coming from the fact that he had called it a *game.*

This entire fae realm is just one fucking game after another.

Inara stood begrudgingly. "I did not realize things had progressed to such a level. My sincerest apologies." The lies dripped from her pink mouth like sweet poison.

Morana continued her trek forward as Matthias trailed her. He pulled out the chair at the head of the table and gestured for Morana to take her seat. When she did, Death slid the chair into place before leaning down to kiss her temple. While he was there, his hot breath tickled the shell of her ear when he spoke. "I'm sorry." His voice was low and pleading. "I'll be on the other end. Just keep your mind open to me."

Morana nodded. Matthias walked to the other end of the table, and she watched his movements. Her chest was tight, and the crown on her head felt unbearably heavy after his surprise declaration.

"It's good to see you, Inara," Morana spoke after everyone was seated. She picked up the silver goblet filled with sweet red wine in front of her, twirling the liquid casually.

"Likewise," Inara spoke gently. There was a melodic quality to her voice. "You look well."

Morana nodded. The sticky, sweet lies spilling from their mouths covered the walls, blocking out the air and making the atmosphere suffocating.

Leaning back in his chair, Matthias took a sip of his own wine, the rings on his fingers catching the light reflecting through the crystals on the chandelier.

You're doing great. His voice entered her mind seamlessly. *You look like a queen.*

Morana fought the urge to flinch, keeping her reactions contained. *I wish you would have told me your plan. I suppose it is my fault for not realizing why you brought the crown. Were you simply trying to throw me off?*

She swore she caught the corner of Matthias's mouth turned up behind his goblet. *Of course not. Though I must admit, I like how flustered your mind feels. I'd never know just by looking at you.* His eyes met hers. *There are no secrets when I can be inside your mind.*

Is that a threat? She cocked an eyebrow in his direction. The servants were buzzing about and placing roasted lamb, mint jelly, and rosemary potatoes on the long table, distracting Inara and most of her guests. The only guest whose eyes flicked between Death and his bride was the fox's.

Hardly a threat when I've given you the same access to my own thoughts. Shall I show you what they are? The echo of Matthias's voice in her skull dropped lower, as if he were whispering in her ear. She felt the shadows ghost down her neck, giving her the sensation of his lips there. *I must admit, they're quite scandalous for an official dinner. I would love to see how your mind reacts to the image of my head between your thighs.*

"I've actually come to apologize," Inara interrupted. "I wanted to apologize for my behavior during Mabon. I made a bargain with that boy, and he defied me when he brought—" Inara glared at Morana. She almost spat the next words. "Your *bride* through the portal. He accused her of all sorts of treachery against our court." Inara picked up her fork and began prodding the potatoes. "He mentioned something about the girl's intentions to start a war between our courts." Inara's gaze slid across the table to Matthias. Her eyes were so sharp they could have cut through glass. "During a peaceful time like Mabon, I simply couldn't allow it."

Anger was a vicious animal. "Interesting sentiment," Morana began. "Do you always whip and starve those you capture based on false accusations from human boys bound to you by a bargain?" Death set the tone of the evening with his games, and two could certainly play this one. Morana's gaze rivaled the sharp blade of the goddess's own eyes. If she wanted to sell her sweet lies as honey, Morana would expose them for what they were—black tar—thick and ugly. "That doesn't seem like a sound way of leading." Morana licked her lips and looked down at her plate, stabbing into a piece of lamb with the force of the angry beast thrashing in her chest.

She swore she saw Matthias's jaw tick at her comment. If he was fighting back a grin, nobody would know it. Nobody aside from the mortal occupying the depths of his mind.

You're awful quiet, she said.

Matthias did smile then, licking his spoon clean. The seductive slide of his tongue against metal made Morana's stomach twist with desire. *You seem to handle her quite well. Why would I steal the show from you?*

"Forgive me." Inara's lips peeled back into a delicate smile. Her white teeth flashed. "You aren't acquainted with the pressure of protecting a court yet, but that will not be for very long, no?" Her voice climbed at the end, entering that melodic higher register, the one that sounded almost mocking.

Morana's fist clenched around her fork.

"My future wife fully understands the demands of protecting a court. That is why she is questioning your decisions so thoroughly." Matthias licked his lips, his dark eyes swirling with the power lying dormant within him. "I believe her questioning proves that she's well suited to lead."

Inara grunted at that.

The fox finally spoke, filling the silence that had descended on the room. "When did the proposal occur?" he asked. The faelight overhead flickered, casting shadows over Conan's sharp features. "I'm sure Death was quite romantic."

Panic swept through her chest like the wind that billowed between trees before a violent storm. Morana didn't know how to respond.

Relax. Matthias's voice in her head soothed her. *Spin a pretty lie. Just tell them it was private and just before Mabon.*

Morana cleared her throat, flicking the food around her plate. She forced a delicate smile to her lips. "It was a private proposal," she answered. "Just before Mabon." Her eyes trailed over Matthias's form as she allowed lust to show through the mask on her emotions. The attraction wasn't a lie. "He even gifted me the dress."

"Interesting." The word sounded like a question on Inara's tongue. "I didn't realize you had known each other that long." The goddess allowed light to twist over her arms, sending Morana's stomach roiling.

"I didn't realize how long you had known Axton," Matthias interjected. "Three years, was it?" His mouth closed around a piece of lamb, and he chewed before continuing. "That information just came to light. I'm so sorry for your loss."

Inara's mouth was a thin line stretched taut across her face. "Yes, well, sometimes vengeance can be overpowering."

Morana didn't have to guess her meaning. The only question was how Inara knew who had killed him. Morana was grinding her teeth, fighting the swelling of shadows in her chest. They whipped out, sending air blowing over the room. The two guests who had been eating silently, guardsmen, Morana guessed by their attire, sat stock still.

"Not so overpowering." Morana's voice was low and menacing. "Considering you are still sitting before us unharmed."

The goddess didn't balk at her flagrant display of power. Her melodic voice simply rang in the dining hall, bouncing off the chandelier but sticking to the lies dripping from the walls. "Don't be fooled." Her voice was too sweet for a warning, but the warning still shone through. "Evil lurks within us all, Morana. I think you've yet to discover what truly lies in the realm of the fae."

There was silence, and then there was the crawling sensation of white mist swirling around Morana's ankles. Blinding anger followed.

"What is that supposed to mean?" Morana practically growled.

"Enough." Matthias's booming voice snapped the tension and dragged Morana from the fiery pits of rage. "We should enjoy our dinner, shall we not?" he asked. There was power mixed in his words, something authoritative that commanded Inara to bow down and submit.

The doors clicked open, and Sarnai sauntered in wearing an elaborate forest green gown decorated with delicately embroidered flowers and parting along the vast slit that ran to her mid-thigh. Her smile was wide as she entered the dining hall and threw herself in the chair on the side of the table near Morana.

"Apologies for the delay," Sarnai said. "I was busy tending to the gardens." Sarnai's umber eyes flicked to the goddess of life. They were bright in the faelight. "Inara, my love." She nodded in acknowledgment. "It's so good to see you."

"Goddess," Inara gritted out, and Morana raised a brow at the queen's reaction. She knew Sarnai preferred to stay away from the Court of Light, but she didn't realize how deeply the hatred ran.

"Did I miss anything good?" Sarnai asked. Her tone was bright.

"Nothing worth mentioning." Morana's tone was tight and unamused—the direct rival of Sarnai's. "I actually may need to step out to use the restroom."

"By all means." Matthias gestured for her to rise. "You're to be my wife soon—I cannot tell you no." He was smiling up at her—something predatory and hungry in his gaze. Morana's breath nearly halted before she rose from her chair.

The room was shrinking—she was certain of it. There was no room for her to think clearly when she had to be so guarded. She had hardly had time to breathe after Raidan's attack. Maybe she had gotten used to taking the mask off in front of those in Matthias's court. It didn't suit her the way it used to. She needed to get out.

Sarnai's shocked expression showed she was clearly uninformed about Matthias's plan to announce his soon-to-be bride. Morana still wasn't sure whether she understood the purpose behind his strategy, but she assumed it had something to do with the authority Matthias longed to give her in the presence of her tormenter. She couldn't be sure, though.

"You did not know?" Inara caught on quickly. Conan was nursing his wine, amusement shining in those golden eyes as the two guards in attendance dared not speak.

Sarnai cleared her throat, gathering herself. "I did not know it was public knowledge yet." She smiled gracefully and collected herself. "The lamb looks delicious." She scooted her chair back with an abrupt skidding noise. Sarnai promptly placed her feet on the table with her goblet in hand, throwing all etiquette out the window. "You brought out the good wine, Matthias. I'm glad I could take part."

She guzzled the crimson liquid as if she were trying to chase her own shock away. On the outside, the goddess appeared unfazed, but based on her alcoholic consumption, Morana knew it had rattled her. She didn't dare consider what Sarnai was thinking, allowing a demure smile to stretch across her face before exiting to the hall.

Sixteen

The lights were dim and Morana was finding it difficult to catch her breath. As she hunched over, gasping for air, she gripped the railing of the narrow staircase for support. Her nerves were seeping through the cracks of hardened cement she had used to maintain her composure in the dining room.

For one, the very presence of Inara was pulling at deep-rooted memories of torture and imprisonment that she longed to wrestle away. Second, Matthias's strategy had left her confused. There was no real purpose to the announcement. If he wanted Morana to have authority in that room, he should have allowed her to demand it herself. She was fully capable of putting Inara in her place.

Morana was so engrossed in her own thoughts and the subtle shaking of her hands that she didn't hear footsteps approach. It was Conan's voice that startled her out of her shock and forced her to lock her feelings away again. She grabbed for anger—the emotion that would allow her to cover her fear.

"Queen of Darkness," Conan said by way of greeting.

The words made the anger easier to grip, and Morana allowed ice to enter her tone. "Don't," she snapped. "Don't call me that."

Conan's foxlike eyes narrowed. "It is what you are."

"You don't know what you're talking about." Morana was standing straighter now, lifting her chin to challenge the lord. She allowed the shadows to fill the room, but she didn't dare let them touch him. Not with the queen of the Court of Light in the other room. "Why are you here, Conan? Is it to torment me?" she said through gritted teeth. "You seemed fairly useless in the dining room. Entertained—but useless."

She expected a reaction, but he didn't give her one. Conan merely raised a brow in her direction. "Have you thought about my proposition?"

Morana released a hollow laugh. "To go to your city?" she asked. "Yes, in fact. The answer is no."

Conan's expression changed as something pleading entered his eyes. Morana nearly reeled back at the sight of it. "Morana, please reconsider." He stepped forward. "There are things you need to see—things you could *help* with."

She was having none of it.

"Inara isn't actually here to make peace," he warned.

"Oh, really?" The sarcasm spilled from her lips. "You're just now figuring that out?"

"Listen to me!" The urgency in his tone startled her. He was talking in harsh whispers and desperate to get her to understand. Morana couldn't help the way her stomach dropped at the seriousness in his voice. She couldn't help the way she believed him. "Inara is here to check on *you*. Your powers, that is. There have been whispers you hold more than merely light and shadow. I could *feel* it, and I'm certain she could too."

He stepped closer, gripping her shoulders. Morana couldn't fight the shocked look that overcame her face at his words.

"How did you know that?" Morana's voice shook as she spoke, and she internally cursed herself for being so obvious. The first time she had encountered the fox, Morana could maintain her façade despite the swirling emotions inside her. Now? Something had changed, and she didn't know if it was good or not. He could lie and take advantage of her with this kind of obvious vulnerability without her realizing it.

It opened her up to be used as a pawn, and something about the way Conan had insisted that she was this *Queen of Darkness* made her chest tight. If he believed her to be whatever that was, then there was motive.

"Does it matter?" His eyes were piercing. "There's something else stirring in you, isn't there?" Conan shook her gently as he asked the question.

Morana didn't respond. Her eyes flicked wildly around the room. She could feel that white mist rising within her. Morana remembered the way it had appeared in her dream—muddying her mind and forcing her to depths of anger and rage she had never touched before. She should have been afraid of that power, but she longed for it.

"You cannot let her see it," Conan warned.

His grip loosened and eventually fell away. Without another word, the fox turned, leaving her to listen to the tap of his black shoes across the polished obsidian floors of the palace.

With her heart racing and panic stirring in her veins, Morana walked back to the dining room.

Seventeen

Inara's departure to her room was swift following dinner. The knowledge that she was in the castle, and the warning Conan had issued in the hallway, sent Morana's mind spinning with a thousand questions.

She didn't have time to ponder it all on her own, though. Ever since Raidan, Matthias had someone in her room—*always*. She was certain that there was a guard stationed outside as well.

After one full day of it, she was desperate for some alone time, but Morana planned to address it later.

For now, she was thankful for Willows's calming presence and the delicate scent of jasmine permeating the room from the steaming bath.

Morana crawled into the tub. She didn't mind Willow in the room. In fact, her company kept many of the swirling thoughts at bay. It gave her a wonderful distraction—someone to talk to.

"Engaged!" Sarnai shrieked as she entered the bathing chamber with the door slamming behind her. Even

Willow started at the sound of her storming into the bathroom. "You're engaged?" she asked.

Sarnai hadn't changed out of her dress from dinner. Her eyes were bright—face frantic—as she placed her hands on the edge of the tub and demanded answers.

"No." Morana deadpanned—her tone firm.

"I can't believe that motherfu—" she halted mid-sentence. "What?"

"We aren't engaged," Morana answered while sliding deeper into the tub. Willow took up combing her hair gently and chuckling at Sarnai's reaction. "I'm not exactly sure why Matthias told her that."

"Oh," Sarnai began, "I know *exactly* why he may have said something like that." She threw her hands in the air, causing vines to form on the ceiling and grow until they hung loose and decorated the bathroom. Morana reached out to touch the one now in front of her face and winced when a sharp thorn poked her finger. She sucked the blood from her flesh as the vine retracted back up to the ceiling. "Maybe he was feeling you out. You know, testing the waters and trying to see how you'd react to a proposition like that."

Morana released a harsh laugh at that. She hadn't known Matthias long enough for that to make sense in the slightest. "Inara is still here," she warned. "Be careful what you say."

"Oh, please." Sarnai was behaving as if Morana was exasperating. A small smirk pulled at the corner of Morana's mouth. It was, perhaps, comical. Willow was still chuckling behind her. "She's heavily guarded."

"By whom?" Morana sat up abruptly, water sloshing over the lip of the tub as the strands of her hair pulled from Willow's gentle grip. "The woman is more powerful than your average fae. Who would guard her?"

Sarnai's lip peeled back in disgust. "Matthias had a god that owed him a favor."

Curious.

Morana cocked a brow. "I take it you don't like this god?"

Sarnai's face twisted. "He's an absolute *animal.*"

"I don't know what that means," Morana admitted.

Willow was now laughing openly, clearly amused at the interaction. "He's not an animal," the fae woman added.

"Well." Morana looked between the two. "Who is he?"

Sarnai shuddered as she nearly growled the word. "Fauna."

"I take it you don't frequent *his* realm," Morana taunted, feeding into Sarnai's obvious distaste.

"Gods no." The stump of a tree slowly began rising from the floor, with roots stretching out over the tile. Sarnai twisted her hand in the air and threw herself onto her new seat.

"You're making my bathroom a jungle," Morana protested, but Sarnai didn't acknowledge her.

"His realm is a mountain retreat filled with wild beasts from every realm imaginable. It's horrid."

"So," Morana questioned. "*He's* guarding Inara?"

"No," Sarnai responded. "He sent some kind of powerful guard dog." She licked her lips. "*Literally.*"

"Will I see them?"

Willow was now setting out a pair of night clothes on the sink. Morana saw the flash of black silk and lace. Her brows creased.

Willow was the one who chimed in with an answer. "You should hope not," she said, her hands gently smoothing down the fabric. "I hardly believe Inara feels welcomed here now. I overheard those two useless guards she brought with her discussing a swift departure by morning."

"Good." Morana nodded as relief washed over her. She didn't want to spend another moment in the goddess's presence.

A vine stretched out into the bedroom, gliding back into the bathroom and setting a steaming cup on the small table next to the tub.

"I brought you some tea," Sarnai was smiling. "It was meant to be an engagement gift, but on account of you being a fraud." There was humor in her tone. "I maybe wouldn't drink it."

"What does it do?" Morana asked, staring at the cup. Sarnai was constantly forcing various teas on her. If she weren't a flora goddess, Morana wouldn't have minded. The only issue was, Sarnai knew what she was doing when it came to herbs. Whatever her intention—it was bound to work.

"Nothing you wouldn't want." Sarnai had a wicked glint in her eye. "I wouldn't drug you or make you do anything you didn't want. It just—" she paused, trying to find the words. "It makes things more enjoyable, is all."

"Okay," Willow interrupted, a towel in her hand. "Up you go."

Morana stood and wrapped herself in the plush towel, stepping carefully onto the cool tile. "What is that supposed to mean?" she asked.

Sarnai waved a hand. "Doesn't matter."

"I think it does."

The eyeroll Sarnai presented was almost impressive. "Fine," she huffed. "The tea will intensify any feelings you may be having."

Morana's brow furrowed. "Like my emotions?" Her nose wrinkled in disgust. "That's the last thing I would want."

"Physical feelings," Sarnai added as she fought off the smile threatening to break through. "You can thank me later."

Physical feelings. Morana's cheeks flushed, the pink tint deepening as she heard Willow's chuckle. The fae woman was enjoying herself far too much.

Walking over to the sink, Morana caught a glimpse of the nightgown waiting for her. It was short, low cut, and absolutely *not* her usual leggings and t-shirt.

"Where did my other night clothes go?" she asked, spinning to see Willow and Sarnai standing with innocent expressions. Morana hardly believed them.

They had conspired against her for a *false* engagement. It was ridiculous.

Willow coughed, but Morana swore she heard a laugh hidden in the sound. "They're in the wash," she supplied.

Morana's gray eyes narrowed. "Liar."

"Well," Sarnai started. Her voice was bright again. "We must be off. Death knocks at the door!"

Just then, Morana heard a knock sound in the other room as Sarnai and Willow hustled to exit the bathroom. Morana swore she heard giggling as she ran the towel over her legs to dry them and begrudgingly pulled the nightgown over her head. It came to mid-thigh, and the thin fabric pulled at her chest—barely containing her breasts.

"Great," she muttered, glancing back at the tea. It was tempting. She carried it with her to the nightstand before setting it down.

"Can I come in?" Matthias's deep voice sounded from the doorway of her room.

Morana's heart quickened at the sound as she thought back to dinner and Matthias's announcement. She hadn't pondered the event since returning to her rooms, preoccupied with Willow's company, but now that he was standing at the door, frustration bubbled in her chest.

He could have *told* her what he planned to do. After everything, he knew better.

"Not sure why you'd ask. I *am* your future bride." She couldn't keep the bitterness from her tone and instantly regretted it. Morana winced, squeezing her eyes together before turning to face the god now entering through the door.

Matthias was frowning. "I—" He ran a tattooed hand through his hair. "I should have told you."

Morana's eyes widened. She didn't know what she expected him to say—but not that. She also didn't expect to see him appear so nervous—as if he were afraid of her fury. Or maybe it was something else. Her rejection?

"You're right," she whispered.

Matthias stepped forward, shadows twisting in his wake. "I wanted to give you power over her here," he cringed as if he knew how ridiculous the sentiment was. "I can see now; it wasn't the best way." He reached his hand out and tucked a strand of damp hair behind her ear. "You demanded authority without title or rank." His jaw ticked. "You didn't need me at all."

Morana's breath caught. His fingertips were warm as they continued their journey lower—slowly trailing over her neck. The contact sent goosebumps rising from her skin, and Matthias swept his dark gaze over her nightclothes.

"Well," she swallowed. "Apology accepted."

Matthias's gaze flicked to the small, wooden nightstand where she had left Sarnai's cup of tea. His brows furrowed and his hand fell away from Morana's collarbone.

He strode across the room and placed one finger in the liquid before bringing it to his mouth and licking it away. Morana tried not to stare, but the way his finger moved between his full lips had her stomach curling and heat rising to her cheeks.

"Did you make this?" Matthias asked.

"No," she admitted. "Sarnai brought it. I haven't tried it yet." Morana cleared her throat. "And Willow picked the nightgown."

Matthias turned to face her, and his dark shoes clicked on the floor. "Trying to seduce me?" he asked, voice low.

Morana smiled when she noticed the way his eyes were glittering in the light. "I would never," she whispered.

Matthias shrugged, dragging the cup upward and drinking. She watched his throat work as he consumed whatever Sarnai had concocted. His eyes never broke from hers, and she couldn't help but think of what the goddess said.

"Fine," she huffed. "The tea will intensify any feelings you may be having."

Morana's brow furrowed. "Like my emotions?" Her nose wrinkled in disgust. "That's the last thing I would want."

"Physical feelings."

Morana watched him drain the cup before setting it back down. *He has to know.*

He cleared his throat. "I talked with Garian," Matthias said, changing the direction of the conversation. "The lords are to return tomorrow." A pained look crossed his face as his gaze flicked everywhere but her eyes. "I wish I could have given them more time. Especially Garian, since he's been away from his son for so long."

Morana nodded, not knowing how to respond. Her mind still catching up to what he was saying after watching him drain whatever pleasure tea Sarnai had left them.

Dark eyes laced with humor returned to her own. "Garian said he lashed out at you during training. He apologized."

Morana huffed, but there was no genuine frustration in the sound. "He should be apologizing to me." She trailed her tongue along her teeth before continuing. "That's a lie. I encouraged his reaction."

Matthias touched her chin gently and lifted her head. "Are you telling me you were goading him?" he asked in a sarcastic tone. "I am surprised, Morana."

"Oh, shut up," she quipped, pulling her face free from his grip. She turned back to him, allowing her eyes to trail over his full lips and down to the top button of his shirt. Heat pooled at her core. "If you're jealous, I could give you a turn," she taunted. Morana trailed a finger over Matthias's chest—down his abs and halted at the waistband of his pants. "You did drink that tea, Matthias. I wonder, what is it you're feeling exactly?"

He shuddered as she let her finger pull him closer. He smiled—masking the way she knew she made him weak. "Wouldn't you like to know exactly what I'm feeling?"

"No, no. I'm content to goad *you* a little. Get you all worked up."

"Is that what you were doing during training?" Matthias tilted his head. "I mean, Garian's abs are irresistible."

Shadows twisted in her vision, and Morana was swept away. She felt strong arms wrap around her in the darkness, and before she knew it, she was being pinned to the bed of her room. Matthias's hands gripped her wrists above her head as his body held her down.

She was breathless. "You can't do that," she contested.

Matthias leaned down, skimming his lips over the swell of her breast. His hot tongue swirled on her skin before he pulled away and looked at her. "I don't think you can control me like that. Tea or no tea." His smile widened. "You can certainly try, though."

Morana laughed, a low sound. "I'm still the one that held a fire iron to the throat of Death himself."

Matthias's eyes darkened, and he nipped at her lower lip. Her breath caught and her back arched, pressing her body closer to his. She could feel the solid length of him beneath his pants. It sent her mind spiraling with lust.

"I can control you, however," he taunted. His lips brushed against the shell of her ear, and his voice dropped to a low whisper. "When I play your body like an instrument, and these lips part to release such beautiful sounds." He ran a finger over her mouth and then kissed her gently. "Then you'll willingly give control over to that same god you threatened."

Morana arched even more; her wrists still pinned above her head. A small noise escaped her.

"Exactly," he chuckled. "Good girl."

He was driving her wild, but she still gathered fire for her rebuttal. "I won't be giving you control."

Inky darkness swelled, and suddenly Morana was moved to the chair by the hearth. Matthias was kneeling between her legs and running his hands over her thighs. She whimpered. "So," he began, "on my knees, it is, then? Maybe that will encourage you to give in."

Morana stared at him; lips parted as he kissed her thigh. She could feel the power pulsing in her chest—feel the way the shadows rippled along her skin. She took hold of them and willed them to bend at her command. The world folded, and suddenly, Matthias was thrown into the chair. Morana kneeled before the god of death.

She smirked up at him and licked her lips. "No," she said. "On my knees." He sucked in a sharp breath. Morana allowed the shadows to float over his skin, no doubt sending pleasure shooting through him. Matthias groaned at the contact of magic, and Morana was drunk on the powerful feeling that invaded her.

Reaching for his belt, she carefully unclasped it. Matthias's head lolled back against the couch while she dragged the zipper down. Shadows danced over his neck and trailed down over his rapidly moving chest.

When she freed him, Matthias's hooded eyes peered down at her, fully aware of where this was going. She licked her lips again and held firm to his thick length. As her mouth parted around him, Matthias reached a hand into her hair, guiding her while she licked up his shaft. He practically growled when she swirled her tongue.

Morana pulled away abruptly. "I have one request before I continue."

Matthias's thumb trailed over her bottom lip and pulled at the flesh there. "Anything."

"If you truly believe I can handle myself, then you don't need to constantly send people to watch me in my room." His lips parted to protest, but she dragged her thumb over the tip of him and gently swirled the moisture that beaded there. He hissed.

"After Raidan—"

"No." Morana's thumb stilled. It was a command thrown at the god of death. There would be no argument as Death, himself, would bend to her request.

Matthias grunted, his other fist clenching at his side. "If you wish to be alone, I can grant you that."

"Good," she whispered. "Though I don't wish to be alone now."

Lowering her head, Morana parted around him again and began sucking, dragging her tongue along Matthias until he was muttering curses—or praises. She didn't know. His hand fisted in her hair gently as he lifted his hips, losing control of himself and sending dark rumbling noises through the room. He bucked into her mouth, and she deliberately pulled back on his length without releasing him. His thrusts turned frantic, and when

Morana moaned her approval, Matthias let himself break apart.

Morana licked her lips, standing and staring down at the god of death.

"Next time, you're drinking the tea."

She chuckled. "Do you feel powerful, Matthias?"

He smiled, hair mussed, and eyes glazed over with satisfaction. The expression sent chills down her spine. "All the power is yours, my queen."

Eighteen

Light streamed in from the window, casting the room in a gentle glow. Morana opened her eyes to watch dust swirling through the air. It took her a moment to realize she was alone. At first, she sat up abruptly, scanning the room for whomever Matthias had commanded to keep watch of her.

When she realized no one was there, Morana slouched on the mattress, breathing a sigh of relief. Matthias had listened to her request—though it wasn't fair how she had gone about ensuring his cooperation. Morana ran a finger over her lips as heat crawled up her neck to her cheeks. She could remember the noises that tumbled from Death's lips and the way his hand clung to her hair.

Before she got carried away, Morana threw off the comforter and made her way to the bathroom where a silk robe was draped over the sink. Wrapping it around her shoulders and sliding on the slippers by her wardrobe, Morana stepped delicately on the cold floors and made her way to the door.

Peaking her head out of her bedroom, she wasn't startled when she saw Elivira sitting in a chair just outside the door. She was armed with a sword, two daggers, and the book that lie open in her lap.

"Matthias said I shouldn't disrupt you." Elivira hadn't looked up from her reading.

Frustration burned like fire in Morana's chest, growing faster than her attempts to snuff out the flames. "Matthias is an asshole," she responded coldly.

Elivira looked up then, eyes wide. She cleared her throat as her brows lowered in confusion.

Morana sighed. "I told him to stop sending people to watch over with me." She tucked a strand of hair behind her ear. "I'm allowed to be alone." Looking away briefly, Morana muttered, "I'm not a caged animal."

Elivira chuckled, closing her book and slipping it beneath her chair. She stood up with her arms folded across her chest. "And he still sent me, regardless."

"At least you're *outside* of the room."

Elivira lifted a brow. She was wearing fighting leathers, her hair piled atop her head in her typical bun. "They set the war camps up at the border near my city since Namid is closer to Zora." She scowled, looking at nothing before continuing. "My trip home wasn't much of a break. I'm expected there today."

Morana nodded. "Who is replacing you as my babysitter?"

Mirth returned to her expression, and Elivira let out a low laugh. "No clue. Inara's gone though, as well as her guard dog." Morana swore she saw Elivira shudder at the mention of the creature. "You could—" she spoke with caution, allowing the words to roll out slowly. "You could come with me."

Morana's gaze shot to hers, and her heart leaped at the thought of escape. Matthias meant well, but she couldn't help but feel trapped. "You're serious?"

"I don't see why not."

Morana took a step back and slammed the door in the lord's face while anticipation and excitement shot through her. It was an opportunity to flee the useless feelings she had avoided when she had realized Matthias was coddling her after Raidan's surprise visit to her apartment. Not that she didn't appreciate the concern, but he had promised. When she had asked him to stay, she didn't mean *this.*

Scrambling to the wardrobe, Morana got out her training clothes. She assumed they wouldn't expect her in the training rooms this morning if the lords had just returned, but she would need to retrieve her sword and dagger.

Throwing half of her hair up into a bun to get it out of her face, Morana opened the door to the hallway. Elivira was still standing there with a shocked expression as Morana turned to close the door behind her.

"I'll need to stop in the training rooms for my weapons." She smiled brightly. "We *don't* tell Matthias."

As Morana started walking down the spiral staircase leading into the bowels of the palace, Elivira trailed behind her and muttered under her breath, "I wouldn't dream of it."

Namid was filled with tall trees stretching sleepy limbs upward to the sky and babbling brooks running through the mossy undergrowth of the forest. The war camps, however, were not set up in the city of Namid. They were further north along the border of the Court of Shadows, just where the deciduous trees transformed into pines and began crawling up the low mountains of the mountain range that divided the courts.

Morana's boots struck cool earth when they emerged from the shadows after leaving Ascella. Elivira's commanding presence shone as they weaved through the endless supply of tents and smoke floating up from the fires of the camp.

As they prowled through the masses, fae men and women bowed toward Elivira, muttering words of her return and the preparations for war between the courts.

"If the fae hold powers," Morana began as she trailed the lord and dodged a fae woman with harsh features. "What does war look like?"

She didn't care to admit that she hadn't thought about the damage of a war between beings as powerful as the fae. Throwing the gods into the mix—throwing Raidan into the mix—and Morana could see the coming bloodbath. Her stomach twisted in knots. Families lived here, and her mind ruthlessly whispered insults about her part in bringing the war to the court.

Something like this would destroy her *home*. Even though Matthias was a god, knowing the kind of danger it would throw him into had her gut twisting. Gods could be murdered. Maybe the whispers were right. The war would be her fault.

No. It wasn't the truth. Inara had *killed* Matthias's parents. To believe that her presence was the only reason for the war would be selfish and irresponsible, but to deny her role as a catalyst would be naïve. Elivira had called her a liability, and as she watched the hardened gazes of people who may die in the coming battle, Morana couldn't help but feel the weight of that statement fully.

Elivira winced, parting the fabric of a large tent ahead of them and gesturing for Morana to enter. Maps littered the dirt floors and spilled over the large table set up at the tent's center.

"It's war," Elivira supplied. "There will be blood." She rested her elbows on the table, her brown skin illuminated by the faefire glowing in a nearby lamp. "It's certainly no place for a mortal." Elivira lifted a brow, and Morana deduced her meaning.

"You mean to say that war is no place for me?" Morana stared at the lord—unrelenting and challenging.

"I'm saying it's no place for a mortal without power pulsing through their veins." Elivira trailed a finger over the table's surface. "You, on the other hand, could be quite powerful if Matthias would return to training you properly. You could be an asset."

"And here I was thinking you believed me to be a liability." Morana smiled. "So much so that I nearly believed it myself."

"It's not my fault that you're stupid enough to believe that after everything."

There was a pause, and Morana could hear the stomping of boots beyond the canvas tent. The air was cold, warmed very little by the fires erected around the site.

"What are you meant to do here, anyway?" Morana broke the silence.

Elivira pushed off the table and grabbed a map from its surface. She moved around the table until she was standing directly next to Morana before unfurling the map in front of them.

The word *Zora* stretched across the bottom of the parchment in bold letters, and streets littered the entire map with their names and various buildings.

Elivira cleared her throat. "I'm meeting with the general to discuss our options for invading the city." She clenched her jaw before continuing. "We want to take the city because it's close to the border, and Lux's tomb is close. If Inara was keeping her blood book there, Matthias believes there must be something of interest in this location. It wouldn't make sense for her to store the book in his tomb merely out of spite."

"Forgive me if I'm wrong." Morana's mouth lifted into an insulting smirk. "I've met the woman. She definitely seems like one to do things out of spite."

Elivira chuckled at that. "Maybe so, but if there's something here that could help us with our goal—"

"And what is your goal?"

Elivira turned to Morana, her warm eyes shining with an intensity that suddenly shifted to something more painful. "Do you know about Matthias's parents?" she asked.

"Inara killed them."

Morana remembered the details well enough—remembered the reasons he had to hate the woman.

Elivira nodded once. "She was a random fae girl that suddenly began showing immense power; power only achieved by the gods. You've noticed her ears are pointed, and Matthias's are not?" Elivira wiped the wild strands of hair from around her face, sweeping them back toward her messy bun. "We would be fools to think there was nothing in her rise to power. She not only killed Matthias's parents, but she has pages of her blood book missing, something that reeks of deception, and there are stories from her court detailing the atrocities of the way she treats her people."

"Cain?" Morana questioned.

"Willow too." Elivira sighed and looked back at the map. "I was harsh with you. But breaking the rules of Mabon was exactly the excuse we needed to begin this war. It's a war of both justice and vengeance. So yes, there will be bloodshed, but that is the cost."

Morana's chest tightened. There were so many things about the court that she didn't understand—a history that was unfolding before her and revealing how small of a part she truly played in the things happening around her. There was something like sorrow, too—a deep well of sadness with no identifiable source.

"Why did Matthias bring me here?" The last part was a mere whisper. "Truly?" Morana fought the doubt creeping into her mind about Matthias's intentions.

Elivira was looking at her now, but Morana couldn't bring herself to meet her eyes. The pain was too deep, the well overflowing with all the things she didn't want to touch. "There's something inside you that feels important, Morana. You hold more power than you know how to handle. If you could just look around and see the bigger picture—see how your powers could be used for good—" Elivira paused abruptly. "I'm not saying that was his reasoning," she continued. "You hold immense power. Matthias isn't one to use you for that." A softness overtook her features—one that Morana hadn't seen in the lord before. "He cares for you. Now, whether he admits that, that is up for debate. I don't claim to know the mind of a god, but I can say that what began as a curiosity and a deep desire to protect his court quickly became admiration for your strength and character."

Morana winced at the words as if they had struck her. Despite Matthias's encouragement, she still couldn't see herself as someone with good *character.* Hearing Elivira mention it made her uncomfortable.

Even so, there was *some* truth there. Matthias did seem to care for her—for people. He showed it in the human realm back when the older gentleman passed. Morana also recalled her conversation with Willow during what felt like a lifetime ago.

"Has Death been kind to you?" Morana finally looked up into the woman's pale face. There was a wisdom there in her eyes, the look of someone older than she first appeared.

"Death has not been kind to me." She sat down in the chair to Morana's left, leaning forward. Her mouth was a firm line. "Matthias has." She paused for a moment; sincerity trapped within her gaze. "He's been kind."

Blinking away the memory and the tears that worked behind her eyes, Morana realized the truth that Garian had spoken. These people *liked* her, even when she didn't like herself. Her throat tightened with the weight of her emotions. "He brought me here for my power."

"Initially, yes," Elivira confirmed. "But he keeps you for who he's found you to be."

Morana let out a bitter and breathy laugh. "Selfish."

When she looked up, Elivira's gaze was hardened. She gripped Morana's chin and forced her eyes to hold there. "You don't get to decide if you are selfish when all your decisions are based on trying to *survive*. People do stupid things when they are lost, Morana." Elivira's tone became commanding, and Morana caught a glimpse of the lord that she truly was—the way she ruled her city. "You are here now. You are allowed to *feel,* to start moving forward."

Morana fought the tears as Elivira released her chin. She became aware of the medley of power that resided in her—the powers that had served her as she transitioned into the world of fae, gods, and magic. Matthias had promised to continue training her, but time hadn't allowed it yet. If she could practice on her own, learn more about her abilities, then she could participate in dealing death to the woman who had hurt all of those she had grown to care about.

White fog gathered at her feet, and for a moment, Morana could feel Raidan's power awaken within her. She tried to pull it back, as it was fierce and angry, meddling with her emotions and causing a sea of rage to stir in her chest. She clenched her teeth and looked up at Elivira's shocked expression.

That was when a scream rang out from beyond the tent.

Nineteen

Morana was out of the tent in an instant but halted when she saw a creature descend from the sky. Large, feathered wings stretched out and eclipsed the light as the large bird swooped low. When Morana glimpsed of the gnarled face of a woman, and sharp fangs attached to a humanoid body covered in feathers, adrenaline skated through her veins.

The strange creature gnashed pointed teeth at the fae woman Morana had stepped around upon arrival. White fog floated in the air, and the fae woman lashed out with shadows, hurling her hands in the bird's direction.

"What the fuck?" Elivira was standing at Morana's side, her sword firmly grasped in her hand.

"What are they?" Morana asked.

Elivira shook her head. "Some kind of harpy. I've never seen these before."

The monster flew back as the shadows pushed into its chest. The fae woman was panting as troops started gathering around them. When the bird swooped again, teeth pierced the flesh on the fae woman's shoulder, and she cried out.

Morana grabbed her sword, desperately trying to remember all Garian had taught her. Fear was real and deep—an ocean churning and ready to consume. She wouldn't let it stop her.

A stray arrow flew through the air, blazing with fire and parting the thick mist that had descended on the war camp. The bird—woman—whatever it was, shrieked as it fell to the ground and made the earth tremble.

All was silent.

There were fae men and women dressed for battle, standing around the tents, looking up into the sky at the swirling fog. Morana could feel the tug of power within her. She could feel the bitter rage as she watched the fae woman on the ground, holding her shoulder as a man stood next to her.

"Can he heal her?" Morana asked.

"Not like Matthias." Elivira's expression was grim. "The fae heal fast, and we can do some, but Matthias is much more capable. She will bleed for a while with a gash like that."

Morana's stomach twisted and churned with bile.

A loud screeching sound rang out over the mountains. Before they had caught their breath, thousands of shadows hovered over their heads, moving rapidly and approaching the war camp.

Elivira was staring up into the sky with widened eyes. "Matthias is going to kill me," she whispered just as another scream broke the mist.

Morana was running—chasing anything and everything that faintly resembled feathers. Sweat beaded on her brow as she sprinted forward on legs that burned from the exertion.

The fog had thickened, and it became difficult to see anything beyond the sweeping dark figures dragging fae into the sky. Morana heard wings rustle behind her and twisted, calling on the shadows and begging them to guide her as she threw them out toward the harpy.

The darkness spilled over feathers, and Morana found she could access the mind of the creature, finding nothing but burning rage and a desire to destroy. She pulled more power from within, trying to mold the mind of the harpy until it truly believed it could not move. Matthias had explained that the shadows affected the mind. She hadn't tried something like this, but she had to *try.*

There was no stopping the monster as it descended again with sharp teeth that cut through the murky air. Morana lifted her sword, striking upward with a move Garian had taught her. The creature screeched, spreading its wings and gliding out of the path of the blade.

Morana's heart was hammering in her chest, nerves zapping through her body like lightning. Those nerves didn't cease as her mind wandered to all the ways she had *gotten lucky* before. This time, she would need to fight her way out.

As the bird tried to strike again, Morana gripped her sword tightly, forcing the shadows to engulf her. If she couldn't manipulate the mind of the bird, she could certainly use her magic to *move.*

Morana appeared at the back of the harpy moments later. She was in the air, descending toward the ground faster than she could make sense of. The bird had moved again, and Morana quickly grabbed at the darkness and readied her sword.

She fell again, shoving the weapon down until she felt flesh stretch apart around the blade, black blood dripping from the bird's wound as they were both falling to the ground with sounds of battle echoing through the clearing.

Morana tried to pull up on her sword as they continued their descent, but the weapon was lodged so firmly in the bird's back that she couldn't grip it. She parted the world, landing on the ground just feet away from the bird.

When the ground ceased its shaking, Morana scrambled for her sword, placing her boot firmly on the monster lying sideways on the ground. She grunted, using all of her weight to haul the metal out of flesh and feathers. The stench nearly sent her vomiting, and when the sword finally broke free, Morana stumbled back and landed on the ground.

A dreamy feeling overtook her, and she could hear a familiar soft song carrying through the trees. The lilting voice grew closer, and mist swirled in front of her when Morana looked over her shoulder.

A Veeden approached her, song rising and begging Morana to give in to whatever the creature wanted. She wouldn't, though. Rising to her feet and wiping the black blood from her face, Morana faced down the Veeden that had come for her.

Mossy skin and eyes like silver moonlight glided over the moist earth. The creature's long, black tongue snaked from between sharp teeth before it spoke. "Raidan's done waiting, Queen of Darkness."

"Go to hell."

Morana lunged forward, pushing her sword toward the heart of the monster only to slash at white mist. The Veeden had disappeared into the clouds.

Spinning around, Morana noticed the screams had grown more distant—the sounds of battle fading into the background. There were no more demons lurking between the trees, and Morana couldn't see enough to remember how to get back. She begged the shadows to guide her.

"You naïve girl." Inara's voice parted the clouds, carrying that taunting melodic note.

"Inara," Morana snarled.

As the fog faded, clearing Morana's vision, she saw the goddess approaching. Her soft pink gown matched her rose-colored eyes and billowed in the wind swirling through the forest.

"An interesting development for Matthias to announce you as queen," she said. Morana could hear the mocking undertones of the statement. "You really are being used by Death."

Light crackled in her chest as Morana beheld the monster far worse than any creature she could have faced. Her power pulsed through her veins—begging to be released. Morana only wished she had a better grasp of her magic.

"I am not following, Inara."

"Pity," the goddess leaned against a tree, bringing her hand in front of her face to inspect her long nails. "I would think after everything, you'd realize when you were being used to start a war. I'm not a fool." Inara looked up at Morana, her eyes sharp like blades. "I knew war was coming. It was only a matter of time. I've lost count of all the reasons Matthias hates me."

"I think I can help you remember those reasons if you've forgotten," Morana seethed. Anger was thrashing behind her ribs—wild and untamed.

"No need." Inara waved a hand. "But if you are aware of all those reasons, it's a wonder you haven't realized that your kidnapping was simply an excuse to attack my court." Inara's tone soured—all sweetness dissolving behind those lips. "You're an insignificant pawn in a game you don't even understand."

Morana lunged. Fury was a sentient being begging for blood. She could feel the fog thickening as she dropped her sword and grabbed Inara's throat. Her skin was cold, and Morana squeezed as the goddess fell to the ground.

Morana was instantly on top of her, hoping her grip left bruises and blood trailing down the queen's flesh.

"A sore subject," she wheezed, but Inara was making no attempts to fight Morana off. The goddess laughed manically, and Morana tightened her grip. "You won't win this war. You're up against far more than you realize."

"Did you hear all the details regarding Axton's death?" Morana asked. "Did you hear how I killed him?"

"Axton wasn't a god."

Yellow light shone beneath Morana's fingers, burning the flesh there. She pulled her hands away as more light emanated from the goddess—scorching.

Morana called the light within herself—unafraid. She allowed the power to crackle along her arms and dance with the shadows. The white fog rose at her feet.

"You must think you're powerful," Inara laughed once she was standing on her feet again. "All the more reason to be used by Death."

In an instant, Inara was gone, replaced by the descending form of another harpy. Morana didn't have time to think. She grabbed her sword and turned to run, but the bird latched onto her calf, sending blinding pain blasting through her limb.

Morana screamed as the bird rose into the sky, those sharp fangs digging further into Morana's leg. She tried to use the shadows to fold into the darkness, but something stopped the power. Tears and dirt were streaking her face, and she twisted, fighting against the searing pain to fight. Morana allowed the light to burst from her palm, lashing toward the bird and sending them careening toward the ground.

When they landed, Morana lost her breath before regaining her wits. Her face twisted with pain when she tried to stand. The bird was already getting up, stretching its vast wings to shoot back into the sky.

Morana spotted her sword through the mist and quickly grabbed the hilt. She stood on her good leg, grunting against the pain that shot through her. With the teeth now out of her leg, Morana could feel the shadows return, and she grabbed onto them. With the last of her strength, she willed herself just in front of the bird and stared at the gnarled face of a gigantic woman-turned-bird as she plunged her blade deep into its chest.

As Elivira's fast footsteps sounded behind her, Morana pulled her weapon out of the bloodied body and turned around just before collapsing in the mud.

Twenty

"That's where you took her!" Matthias's voice boomed through wherever Morana was. She could hardly open her eyes. Her limbs felt weak, her breath difficult to catch hold of—as if she was chasing the wind itself.

"It's not her fault," her voice cracked like the dry earth of The Wastelands. Morana's eyes blinked open into slits, and she saw the blurry figure of Matthias standing over her. Across from him and on the other side of the bed was Elivira, still covered in dirt and blood.

"She wanted to go," Elivira defended.

Morana's heart sank as she realized they hadn't heard her. Everything hurt. The walls were dark and gilded, letting her know she was in Ascella's palace. She just didn't know the exact location.

"I don't fucking care what she wanted to do, Elivira. You *knew*. It doesn't matter how much power she has, she's not fully trained, and she hardly knows anything about this realm!"

"Then let her learn!" Elivira shouted.

"By getting her killed?" Shadows swirled around Matthias, speaking of the powerful god held within. Morana had seen the way he had thrown Raidan against the wall of her apartment.

"It wasn't her fault," Morana tried again, her voice barely audible.

Matthias looked down abruptly, his hands clutching the sides of her face. She couldn't see past the pained expression he wore, or the panic in his eyes. Matthias quickly let go when she winced at the contact of his hands on her face.

"You'll be fine," he assured her. There was a hardness to his voice—as if he was trying to command it to be true.

"How do you know?" Morana allowed a wane smile to her cracked lips. "Are you the god of death or something?"

Matthias let out a strained laugh. "Something like that."

"Leave Elivira alone," Morana said. "I wanted to go."

She didn't catch his response. Her eyes closed, and the pain eased as the darkness finally pulled her back under.

A gentle humming sound woke Morana from her deep slumber. When she opened her eyes, delicate morning light filtered through the window of her room to greet her, and Willow's slim figure perched on a chair next to the bed.

The fae woman was embroidering, her gentle voice floating like a morning breeze, calling the world to life.

Morana sighed, and Willow chuckled softly, her eyes still fixed on her work.

"Good. You're awake."

"Where's Matthias," Morana rasped. Her throat was so dry, reminding her of the cracked earth of The Wastelands. "He hasn't killed Elivira yet, has he?"

"Hm," Willow pondered. "I was hoping you'd be happy to see me."

Morana winced when she tried to sit up in bed. Her leg stung. Willow threw her embroidery on the side table and stood up so quickly, Morana barely registered that the woman had moved.

"You give yourself away," Morana smiled as Willow helped prop her up on pillows. Her head was pounding. "I am happy to see you, and you're not as indifferent about me as you were pretending to be."

Willow chuckled softly, the sound like music. "You got me," she confessed. "Matthias is talking with Hames somewhere in the palace. The troops have already taken Zora, so don't worry about your failure at the war camps."

"Brutal," Morana scoffed, but there was a lightness to her tone. Her eyes caught the steaming cup on the nightstand. "Wait." She looked back at Willow; her brows pinched. "The troops took Zora. How long have I been out?"

"It's been a week." Willow smiled then as she sat back down. "Sarnai brewed some strong herbs for you. Kept you knocked out while Matthias worked on healing you."

Morana threw the comforter off herself, her muscles stiff. Her legs were bare, and she saw a half-moon scar decorating her calf.

"He said you'd want to keep the scar. The healers thought he'd lost his mind."

"He didn't." Morana allowed a soft smile to appear on her face as Willow stood up again from the chair.

"I suppose I should find you some food. I should probably get Matthias as well."

"No," Morana snapped. Her heart picked up in pace. "I—" she didn't know how to explain her reaction. All she knew was that she appeared weak. Again. She swallowed—shoving down the awareness that this was the second time she had been left in bed after something had gone wrong. When Matthias had returned from Raidan's temple, he hadn't been this ridiculous, and she didn't plan to be this ridiculous either.

Act like a god, Garian had said.

Morana fought the pain as she moved to stand. The pain dulled to an ache, and her muscles were stiff as she got up.

"I don't want him to come in here while I still look so—"

"Mortal?" Willow supplied.

"Yeah."

"Suit yourself. I should still get you food." Willow walked to the door and smiled once at Morana before exiting into the hall.

In the bathroom, Morana noticed that vines still decorated the ceiling. A vase of flowers sat on the stump Sarnai had fashioned next to the tub. She smiled at the delicate blooms before placing her hand on the metal handle and turning it to send steaming water into the tub.

When she crawled into the bath, the scent of jasmine permeated the room. Morana allowed herself to scrub away whatever dirt and blood remained and washed all weakness away with it.

Twenty-One

Breakfast was bland since Willow was convinced her stomach wouldn't tolerate anything heavy, but Morana had to admit that plain toast was the last thing she wanted. In fact, she could hear her stomach growling for something sweet and fattening as her boots shuffled through the palace to the training rooms.

Morana rolled her shoulders, impressed at Matthias's healing work. She needed to learn how to do more than heal minor scratches and bumps, especially if this was to be her life.

A very shirtless Ronan sparring with an equally shirtless Garian greeted Morana when the doors opened. Sweat was dripping from both as Ronan threw out a precise punch that Garian dodged at the last second. It wasn't until she glanced over at the weapons that Morana noticed Reese staring.

The Blacksmith wore fitted black pants, brown boots, and a gray t-shirt. No flowing dresses covered her thin form, just a simple outfit, and soot decorating her temple along with the freckles across her nose and cheeks. Her long brown hair was loose, flowing in waves as she leaned over to pick up a small dagger from the floor. Those green eyes never left the men sparring, specifically Ronan.

Morana walked toward her, startling her with the sound of her footsteps.

"Morana, I didn't see you come in." Reese stood up straight and looked away from the lords. "I—" her brows furrowed. "Ronan said you were injured in battle. Did you have the weapons I crafted you?"

"Ronan, huh?" Morana smiled and tilted her chin toward the mats. "I heard he was supposed to talk to you about weapons."

Reese wrung her hands, her gaze flicking wildly around the space. "Right, yes." She cleared her throat. "He did. He's very thorough."

Morana raised a brow, meeting Reese's eyes. That was a word many women here associated him with. The girl flushed.

Reese's eyes widened. "Oh gods, not like that." She chuckled, but the sound was tight. "I mean to say he's checked on the progress of the weapons frequently. Full of questions, that one. I showed him how to make a sword."

Morana was smiling now, her arms folded across her chest. "Of course," she said.

"The weapons." Reese was talking quickly now, trying to dig her way out of the hole her words dug her into. "The ones I crafted. Did you use them?"

"Yes." Morana sighed and looked just as Garian landed a blow to Ronan's abs. He grunted and spat to the side before squaring up once more. "Garian's been teaching me the basics of swinging them around. Thank you again, Reese."

Her brows furrowed as if Reese were pondering something. "You know," she began, "those weapons were designed for more than swinging around. You should be able to filter the shadows into them. There's a reason Matthias came to me."

Morana's eyes widened. "I—" She tucked a strand of hair behind her ear. "I didn't know that. Well, I vaguely remember that being mentioned, but I'm not good with any of these things." She waved a hand around to gesture to—she didn't know what. "With any of this, really."

"Well, if you need help, I can always work with you on using the weapons. I made them, after all."

"That would be nice." Morana offered an appreciative smile.

"Hate to break it to you." Ronan was walking toward them, holding his shirt and using it to wipe the sweat from his forehead. Beads of moisture drifted down his abdominal muscles—the same muscles Reese was now staring at. "I think Matthias planned to train her with the weapons you made, Reese."

Ronan smiled at the blacksmith, licking his lips as her gaze snapped from his abs to his face. Her tan skin was flushed, and Morana could see the glimmer in Ronan's blue eyes.

"Oh, of course." Reese ran her hands through the brown hair hanging at her waist, combing through it before looking toward Garian on the mats. "I should help him put those things away."

The blacksmith scuttled off, leaving Morana with Ronan.

"Really, Ronan?" she scolded. "That poor sweet girl. You've already sunk your claws into her."

"I'm glad to see you're feeling better, darling." Ronan leaned in, the smile splitting his face. "Unfortunately, nothing has *sunk into* that poor girl." He leaned back and put his arms through his shirt, pulling it over his head in one swift motion. "It isn't for lack of trying."

"With the way she was staring at you, I don't see how you had to try. The girl must be made of steel or something. She had me fooled." Morana was watching her lift the mats on the ground and move them to the corner with Garian.

"I—uh," Ronan suddenly sounded bashful. Morana's gaze flicked to him as he rubbed the back of his neck. "I don't really want to—" He was stuttering. "I—"

"Out with it."

"I don't want to go about this one the wrong way."

"My goodness." Morana tapped her chin, her eyes lighted with amusement. "Have you finally found the woman your mother has longed for you to find?"

"Shut up." He shouldered her gently, momentarily tipping her off-balance as Morana laughed.

Ronan was still smiling when he moved to take Garian's place, finishing cleaning up the room with Reese. She seemed pleased to have him close.

Garian approached with a sword in his hand. "You're here," he said. His expression was solid, but she could see the flicker of relief in his eyes. Garian reached up to place the sword on the rack next to her.

"I was going to practice, but you're already packing everything up." Morana looked down and gestured to her training clothes, very similar to what Reese was wearing. "I even dressed for it."

"I think Matthias was waiting for you to feel up to things, and then he was going to take over. He wants you to learn to better use the shadows. Said something about it giving you a better chance than your abilities with a sword."

Garian looked behind her, and Morana scoffed. "What an asshole. That is such an insult. I do just fine with a sword."

"Depends on what kind of sword we are talking about."

Morana's head whipped around to see Matthias standing a few feet behind her. His black button-up was rolled at the sleeves, dark hair neatly in place, and silver rings decorated the fingers of his tattooed hand.

"Gross," Garian muttered before walking away.

"Where were you?" Morana asked. "I mean, I know you were with Hames. Willow told me that much, but what were you doing?"

Matthias sighed. "Hames has connections to another god because of the creatures that roam the Vulcan. That god helped me out when Inara was here, and if Raidan and Inara are sending creatures with their troops, we need to meet that kind of force with something greater." Matthias glanced at her, as if he were fighting the urge to check her for more scars. There were none he didn't know about. "Anyway, we are thinking of going to this god to ask for aid. He still owes me—but he owes Hames more."

"Fauna?" The corner of Morana's mouth turned up. "Sarnai didn't seem to like him much."

Matthias chuckled, and the sound washed over her like a warm night breeze. "Yeah, she hates him. We don't have a choice, though."

"So, we are going to visit the god of fauna, retrieve some creatures that can fight for us, and continue the war?" Morana knew that Matthias had become protective, especially as he yelled at Elivira when she had been injured. Deep down, she knew he would never keep her caged, and she refused to sit on the sidelines wallowing while the courts were at war. That kind of behavior only left him to carry his burdens alone. And after talking with Elivira near Namid, she realized just how much was at stake. She couldn't sit back and let it all happen. She was done allowing things to simply *happen* before dealing with them. "When do we leave?"

Matthias's scowl could have melted the metal Reese worked with. She could have saved money by selling her tools and using Matthias's death glare instead. "You don't have enough training."

Morana stepped forward, crowding his space to run a hand over his chest, slowly feeling the muscle beneath his shirt. His eyes didn't leave her as she traced his solid form.

She cocked an eyebrow. "So," her voice was low. "Train me, Matthias."

Despite taunting him, she held firm, raising her chin and daring him to tell her no. Her shadows stretched toward him. *I told you I would carry some of the burden. Let me. So far, this is the only way I know how.*

"You already saw what happens when I get stir crazy." Morana lifted a brow. "You might as well train me and then let me do whatever the fuck I want."

"So bossy," he said, licking his lips. She could feel him there, in her mind as well—the shadows trailing over their skin. *I'm afraid,* he admitted. *I can't lose you—not now.*

"You did happen to promote me to future queen. Queens aren't meant to be locked in palaces and protected as if they were made of glass. You would think a *god* would know that."

Matthias moved his hand to her cheek, running his thumb over her jaw and leaning in. She could feel his hot breath against her face, and it had heat pooling at her core.

"How could I ever tell my queen no?" Matthias pressed a soft kiss to her lips.

When he pulled away, Morana was lightheaded. She didn't know if it was the ease at which he allowed her to make her demands, the injuries she suffered while in Namid, or that they were talking of her becoming queen like it wasn't a power play in the war, but as if it were real?

She didn't want to think too hard on that last one.

As far as she knew, their engagement was still fake. Though she wasn't sure she wanted it to be. That probably scared her the most.

Twenty-Two

"I won't lie to you." Morana was smiling while striding through the castle behind Matthias's massive form towards the training rooms. After the attack on Namid, he insisted on a lesson on healing. "The tiramisu the kitchen staff made was absolutely foul tonight."

Matthias glanced back briefly; his brows pulled together. "I will fire the staff immediately." There was a hint of humor in his voice that clued her into any sarcasm.

"Or you could simply have them practice every night until it's perfect. I would be happy to taste test all the tiramisu they can bring me."

Matthias spun around to stand over her. He was so tall, Morana had to look up at him. "I am finding it hard to believe you were telling the truth."

"I said I wouldn't lie, didn't I?"

"If the tiramisu was so awful, then why are you suggesting you continue to eat copious amounts of it?"

A grin split Morana's face. "Out of the kindness of my heart. As future queen, my only desire is to help the kitchen staff perform their best." Morana's smile widened. "And, of course, eat cake."

Matthias scoffed, mirth dancing over his features. "You're ridiculous."

"More like hungry. This training has me eating more than Garian."

"I highly doubt that."

The lights were dim in the training room, mats still leaning against the far wall where Ronan and Reese left them. Two chairs sat in the center of the room, facing each other. On one of them was Morana's dagger.

Matthias gestured for her to sit down as he picked up the weapon and leaned back in the metal seat.

"Unfortunately," he began, "you have to be injured to learn how to heal yourself."

Morana's eyes widened as she looked from the dagger to Matthias's onyx eyes. "You—" She swallowed the knot forming in her throat. "You want me to cut myself?"

Leaning forward with his knees brushing against hers, Matthias placed a hand on her thigh. The touch was warm and comforting. "I'd rather you get a minor injury in a controlled environment than be forced to heal yourself during another impromptu battle."

Morana's heart was quickening in her chest, her palms sweating. "I—"

Act like a god.

"Okay," she whispered, gripping the cool metal hilt. The weapon had grown familiar to her, the weight in her hand bringing comfort.

"Do you—" Matthias's brows pulled together. "Would you like me to do it?"

She licked her lips, pretending that his offer wasn't a relief. "That's sadistic."

The corner of his mouth quirked up. "Maybe a little."

Turning the dagger over in her hand, Morana thought about having to drag it across her flesh. It's not that she couldn't do it, but while the image of her blood dripping onto the floor entered her mind, she could feel an unsettling white mist pool around her ankles—the same fog that begged for blood. She feared losing control.

"Here." Morana held the dagger out to Matthias, and he took it. "Make sure you don't mar me too much. I don't want to be ugly."

"No, no." His eyes were smoldering. "We wouldn't want that for my queen."

There was a pause—brought on by the lack of oxygen now in the room at his words. While she was certain her joking remark was exactly that—a joking remark about a fake engagement, something in the way he said it made her stomach twist in knots. When he called her his queen, the words felt loaded. They hadn't discussed it, and she had no clue if it would amount to anything. She wasn't sure she wanted to discuss it just yet—not when she wasn't sure about his feelings. Hers were becoming more obvious, and she was fearful they wouldn't be returned.

Morana didn't break eye contact as she tried to piece his words together. Maybe she wanted to talk about it—if only to confirm what she suspected—the very thing that would sting. If he was about to slice a hole into her palm, she might as well allow him to slice one into her heart, too. At least if she found out now, it wouldn't hurt as bad as finding out later. Dating and sex were one thing. *Marriage* was another. She didn't deserve that.

"The engagement is fake," she stated. "Right?"

Matthias looked down at the dagger, his elbows resting on his knees. He twisted it in his tattooed hand to observe the carvings on the hilt. "Do you want it to be?" he asked, voice unsure.

Morana swallowed. "I hardly know you." It was a pitiful last-ditch effort to give him an out. She didn't deserve him, and she knew it. No sense in getting her hopes up.

Matthias chuckled and gently took one of her hands, turning it so her palm was up. The tip of the dagger was cool against her flesh, and Morana wanted to close her eyes. The white mist was begging her to close them, but, if she couldn't conquer the pieces of Raidan's power within her, what did that make her?

Weak. Undeserving.

She could prove her fears to be wrong.

Morana stared as Matthias drew a deep cut across her palm. Blood welled and slid over her skin, warm and thick as it dropped to the floor. She clenched her teeth at the biting pain of the blade and the stinging that refused to go away long after it was done.

Earn him, she thought.

"Okay." Matthias shifted uncomfortably. The gentle run of his thumb along her wrist soothed her. "You'll need to call the shadows over the skin. This isn't a small cut. You need to use the shadows to feel this area of your body, much like when you enter my mind and feel around for all the dirty thoughts I have about you." One corner of his mouth turned up. "Picture what you want—how you want your palm to look when it's unmarred. Do this in the same way you picture where you want to go when you shift realms."

Morana closed her eyes, drawing the shadows over her flesh. The tingling sensation washed over her hand, coating her skin with dark magic. The stinging had persisted, though. And something in her stirred, pacing and prowling and waiting for release. That *thing*, the white fog, broke free, mixing with the shadows and causing anger to build in her chest. Morana tried to push past it, to picture her palm completely healed, but all she could think about was blood. She could feel the way Garian's blood had coated her finger in her dream.

A sharp pain had her eyes snapping open and looking at her hand. The gash was longer now, stretching across her entire palm.

Matthias was looking at it with his eyes wide. There was no hint of suspicion there, and she didn't see the white mist in the room as she had before. It was as if he hadn't seen it either. He merely thought she had messed up.

Figure it out and fucking earn him.

"You'll stay injured until you can learn this." Matthias leaned back in the chair, crossing an ankle over his knee. "We leave for the fauna realm in a few days, and you'll need that hand for a sword." His jaw ticked.

Morana ground her teeth together. "You can't heal me?" She didn't really want him to heal her, but as she asked the question, she could see the temptation in his eyes.

"I can."

"You won't."

Matthias leaned forward and placed a gentle kiss on her forehead. "I once told you I wasn't here to coddle you. What use is it if I heal you now?" His shadows stretched into her mind. *It is tempting though.*

Morana deadpanned, calling the shadows once more. "And to think, I was beginning to believe you cared for me."

Matthias licked his lips, his eyes hooded as his gaze raked over her. "I do."

"But you won't heal me?" She leaned forward. "You were awfully heated while you were yelling at Elivira. I was injured then. I don't really believe that you *won't* heal me if I can't do it myself."

They were both leaning forward, sharing breath as Morana clenched her hand between them, fighting the persistent stinging and still calling the shadows to the injury.

She heard his voice again in the quiet place belonging to them, and only them. *You're not wrong.*

The corner of her mouth lifted. *I don't want you to heal me. I can do this.*

So persistent. Why is that? His eyes were locked with hers, begging her to answer the question.

I want to deserve someone like you. I want to be worthy of a god.

His eyes widened; mouth parted in surprise.

"When you were yelling at her, you seemed pretty disheveled for a god," she whispered.

"And you seem pretty divine for a mortal." He leaned forward. *You've already proven yourself worthy of far more than a god of death.*

I haven't.

His voice was a gentle caress to her thoughts. *I'm the one fighting to deserve* you, *Morana.*

Her stomach dipped, heat washing over her at his words. She leaned back—more determined now as she closed her eyes.

Matthias's voice rumbled across from her. "Heal yourself, Morana."

She could feel the tingling sensation in her hand, and for a moment, an intense itching. Picturing her palm unmarred, she opened her eyes to see her skin healed.

Morana flexed her hand, testing it out. All the stinging had subsided.

"This means I can go to the fauna realm, correct?"

Matthias had one arm resting on the back of the chair, his knees wide. "I don't think I could stop you."

"You're right about that. So, when do we leave exactly?"

"A few days." Matthias moved to stand, pushing the chair back behind him. "I want you to get better at healing, and then I want to learn about your weapons. Ronan said

Reese offered to show you how to use them. I think it might be good to have her show you. Since she made them, of course."

Morana bit the inside of her cheek. "You're too busy for me?"

Matthias leaned down, kissing her lips. The contact was warm—slowly building until she was melting into him. He pulled back before she could get lost. "Never." Matthias winked before he turned to leave the room. "I'll see you tonight."

His shadows reached out one final time. *You don't need to prove yourself worthy. I already want you.*

Her breath hitched, and Morana nodded, her grip tightening on the dagger. This time, she dragged it across her forearm, grunting at the pain before sending shadows to repair the wound.

If she was going to act like a god—like she belonged in this realm, she'd have to start here.

Twenty-Three

"Seems kind of morbid, if you ask me." Cain was scribbling something down on the parchment, copying words from the book on the wooden table.

Morana had stayed in the training room late into the evening. She could heal gashes deeper than what Matthias had put on her hand but couldn't bring herself to do anything worse. Cain was right. It *was* morbid.

Worse than that, after a while, that white mist pooled at her feet, and alone in the darkness, she thought of Raidan. The worst part was how much she longed for that power—longed for it to consume even her shadows. It was fear that led her to stop as the dream she had about Matthias's court flashed in her mind. Morana didn't want the bloodlust she had experienced in that dream space to become real.

She furrowed her brows, her hands folded atop the table while she stared at the freckles across the scribe's face. "It is."

Morana leaned back in the chair, tapping her fingers on the wooden surface and glancing at her hand. She flipped it over, observing her palm. The callouses that had been there from training with Garian had disappeared, too.

"Still thinking about how morbid it is?" Cain asked.

Morana laid her hand flat and leaned forward again. "So, we are going to the fauna realm. What should I know about it?" She smiled, hoping it would earn a simple answer. "What should I know about the fauna god?"

Cain looked up through the red curls hanging in his face. His pen halted. "Again." He pursed his lips before continuing. "Can't you read?"

Sighing and rolling her eyes, Morana leaned back in the chair again. "I can read just fine," she defended. "When it's informational, it's easier to have someone just tell you. Someone you trust."

It was true. She had grown to trust Cain. The boy was kind, and she enjoyed their time in the library. There wasn't much else for her to do aside from going to war camps and almost getting killed.

Cain rolled his eyes, returning to his scribe work.

"She has a point." Sarnai's smooth voice floated into the room as she appeared between the stacks. Her gown was yellow today. "When it's romance though," she continued, "That's when we all become avid readers."

"I almost forgot you read sweet romance books in your free time," Morana remarked.

Sarnai threw herself into an empty seat, stretching her long legs out and placing her feet on the table as she leaned her chair back. "*Sweet* isn't what I would call them."

"Gross," Cain muttered.

Sarnai's smile was wicked. "As for your questions about the fauna realm and its god, he's a collector. He dabbles in many realms to acquire various beasts. It's disgusting."

Morana scoffed. "Your house is covered in plants, Sarnai. Isn't that the same thing? To collect plants the way he collects creatures? You even made my bathroom into a forest."

Sarnai deadpanned. "That's different."

"Okay."

"His realm is full of dangerous animals, and—" Sarnai's nose scrunched up. "He smells." She pretended to gag, Morana and Cain both chuckling at the dramatics. "Like an animal." She threw her legs off the table and leaned forward, pointing a finger covered in red-tinted soil at Morana. A vine wrapped around it like an intricate ring. "And don't you *actually* gag at the stench, or he *will* be insulted." She waved a hand. "He loves Hames though, so I'm sure he won't pay much mind to you with that lord in the room."

"Fantastic." Morana's lips pressed together.

The scratching of pen on paper filled the silence, and when Morana glanced at Cain, the scribe was smiling and shaking his head.

Sarnai's gaze whipped to him. "What?" she asked— her tone sharp.

"For someone who reads so much romance, you'd think you would see the enemies-to-lovers arc before I would." Cain wasn't looking at her.

"What arc?" Sarnai almost growled the words, her eyes fixed on the fae boy.

"The enemies-to-lovers one," he supplied. "Between you and the fauna god."

Sarnai slammed a hand on the table, and a thorny plant sprouted abruptly beneath the paper Cain was writing on. It stabbed through the thin parchment, sending Cain reeling back, his eyes wild, before turning toward the goddess.

"You're delusional," Sarnai spat before standing up to waltz out of the room, her yellow dress billowing behind her.

"Take this death plant back!" Cain shouted. "You ruined my workspace." He pinched the bridge of his nose. "And my paper," he added.

"Absolutely not!" Sarnai threw over her shoulder. "Enjoy rewriting that little story." She smiled brightly before disappearing.

Morana held in a chuckle, looking at the frustrated scribe. "You really pissed her off," she commented.

Cain leaned over the side of his chair behind the table, getting a new piece of paper from the floor. "All you have to do is bring up fauna, and she's done for."

"What's his name?" Morana asked.

"Hm?"

"The fauna god."

Cain looked up with one brow raised. "Callum."

Fire crackled in the hearth while Morana sipped tea and flipped the page of the book Sarnai provided in her hand. The goddess was certainly right about being more motivated to read when the book was like *this.*

Morana's thoughts halted when she heard the door to her room slam shut. Something in his appearance had her shaking off whatever *feelings* her novel inspired. Matthias's white button-down was wrinkled, the sleeves rolled, and the top buttons were undone. He clenched his jaw as he ran a hand through his hair. Before she knew it, the god was pacing between the hearth and the sitting area where Morana sat curled up in her chair.

He halted, turning to her with shadows whispering against his flesh. "We need to talk."

Her stomach dropped. Nothing good ever started with those four words.

I already want you.

Had he changed his mind?

Morana placed her tea carefully on the end table. "I—" She uncurled her legs from the chair and sat up straight. "Okay."

"*Fuck.*" Matthias ran his hand down his face. "The court—" Morana was staring at him, her heart beating a wild rhythm in her chest. "Inara—" He struggled finding the words. "The entire fae realm believes us to be engaged. They know about the engagement." Matthias stopped pacing and his stance and expression hardened.

"The *fake* engagement." Her brows lowered. He never really *did* answer her question before. Being worthy of him didn't necessarily mean she was worthy of being queen.

"Yes. The—" Matthias halted, his shoulders tense. The flames from the fireplace sent light dancing over his features, but the rising darkness surrounding him soon swallowed it—the shadows were growing as he fought to control whatever he was feeling.

"What does that mean, exactly?" Morana's brows lowered. "Matthias?"

He pinched the bridge of his nose. "I would never force something on you." He resumed pacing, wearing a hole in the floor beneath his black shoes. "I told you once you weren't a prisoner, so it doesn't have to mean anything." He halted in front of her. "Inara will know that we lied, but I can figure it out."

Morana swallowed, her mind swirling with the idea of going through with an engagement to Matthias. "And the other option?" she asked.

Would she *want* the engagement to be real? The bigger question being if Matthias would want that too. The answer scared her. She was falling—fighting desperately for an opportunity to prove herself worthy of him—and hoping he would find it to be true. Morana *wanted* him. She wanted this realm. The people and places were slowly becoming a home.

Her nerves were frantic as she longed for an answer, but the doubt in her mind—the nagging voice that reminded her how weak and *mortal* she was, wouldn't let up. For a while, that voice had disappeared. In the face of this question hanging between them, it had grown louder—braver.

"We can go along with the fake engagement." Matthias's voice interrupted her swirling thoughts.

Fake. Of course.

He barreled on. "We'll hold a ball to announce it. You would attend." Something broke over his features—pain, maybe? "I'm sorry, Morana."

She cleared her throat. He hadn't said he wanted it to be real. It was all too easy to put a protective border up around her heart. She kept her expression blank. "For what?" she asked.

"It seemed like the right decision during that dinner. Inara would realize you had both authority and protection and after Raidan, it—" He pinched the bridge of his nose and squeezed his eyes shut. "*Fuck.*"

"It's fine, Matthias." A small, sharp pain pierced her chest, her wall of protection doing nothing now that they had grown this close.

Better now than later.

For a moment, during training, she thought maybe he wouldn't oppose a real engagement. Whatever this engagement was, it had to be fine. It *was* fine. Even as tears worked behind her eyes. She wouldn't let them show.

A softness overtook her features—one that Morana hadn't seen in the lord before. "He cares for you. Now, whether he admits that, that is up for debate. I don't claim to know the mind of a god, but I can say that what began as a curiosity and a deep desire to protect his court, quickly became admiration for your strength and character."

Elivira couldn't know the validity of her words. It didn't matter. The lord explained the reality behind what they were doing—its significance. Morana couldn't get wrapped up in senseless emotions. Not anymore.

They needed this war, after all. Between the missing pages of Inara's blood book, her work with Raidan, and what she had done to Morana, the engagement *was* a good idea. It gave them more reason for the war that was starting.

Maybe she had been selfish, and this was her opportunity to fix it—to act like a god. Something settled within her. Morana could do a fake engagement. She had already played queen once, and she didn't think it would be difficult to continue, but one question still hung in the air—tense and unrelenting.

Nerves coasted down her spine, reminding her that Matthias *had* made those comments about it being real. She wouldn't settle fully without a clear answer.

"It is fake though," she spoke. "Right?" Morana cleared her throat, trying to calm the way her stomach was twisting with anticipation of what his answer would be. She gripped the sides of her chair with an unrelenting force, hoping it would chase the threatening tears away. "The other night, you said—"

"Morana." His voice was soft as he took a step forward. Could he see it then? Could he see how she felt?

Vulnerable and weak, and so completely— undeniably at Death's mercy.

"It doesn't matter," she said, allowing a tight smile to form on her face. The shadows knew no secrets. He had to see it.

He cares for you. Now, whether he admits that, that is up for debate.

"I've been inside your head," Matthias began— stepping even closer. He rested his hands on the arms of the chair where she sat, just next to her own. Her grip was still punishing, and as his breath fanned over her face, as he looked down at her white knuckles, he seemed to realize how tense she was. "I've seen your past, so forgive me if I feel as though I've been acquainted with the deepest parts of you. Forgive me if I believe that watching you these past weeks has given me insight as to who you are." He lifted his hand, gently skimming his knuckles over her heart. "In here."

Morana's lips were parted, her grip loosening as she stared into the eyes of Death. Shadows rose around them, their power mingling.

It wasn't a declaration, but it was something.

"I'll go through with it," she whispered. "The ball, I mean."

Matthias nodded, glancing briefly to her lips before standing up. "I'm going to get some food."

And with that, he disappeared—leaving a thousand questions still hanging from the ceiling like stars in the night.

Twenty-Four

The dining room table stretched out before her, decorated with an assortment of breakfast foods delivered by the kitchen staff. While tiramisu was absent from the table, the scent of eggs and sausage had Morana's mouth watering. Since training, she had been eating more, and while she wasn't *overly* petite, despite her shorter stature, she was noticing more muscle definition on her body.

Morana sat at the head of the table across from Matthias, recalling when she had been in a similar position in the land of the gods. Only this time, Hames's broad form sat at the table with them, his white hair pulled back in a braid, his long beard moving as he ate his food.

"You get along with the fauna god?" Morana attempted to break the silence. "Callum?"

Hames looked up, freezing with his gripped fork hovering over his plate. His blue eyes reminded her of winter frost—cold and indifferent.

"I do." His response was curt—final—as if he were shutting down any further conversation.

Morana walked into the hallway, heading for her rooms after finishing breakfast. She didn't want to forget the dagger Reese had given her. When they got back from the Fauna realm, she would have her first lesson with the blacksmith.

Hames's figure appeared down the hall in front of her, and she quickened her steps to catch up. Morana grabbed his arm, forcing him to halt. When his blue eyes slid to hers, they felt like shards of ice raining from the sky, ready to pierce the nearest piece of flesh.

"I—" She didn't know what to say or how to start the conversation. "I just wanted to say thank you—for being in the throne room when Axton—"

"You're welcome." He had a subtle accent—something different from the other lords in the court—an accent she hadn't noticed before. "However, I didn't do it for you."

Her stomach dropped as his eyes froze her where she stood. She felt off-balance.

"Forgive me," he began, though she didn't think he meant it. "I am loyal to my king, and I trust he is making wise political decisions as it pertains to you."

Morana let the icy presence of this man harden something within her. She lifted her chin, refusing to balk.

Political decisions.

She had to cling to Matthias's words.

I already want you.

The words twisted in her mind. He wanted her, that much he had said.

For political decisions, she told herself.

Morana fought the voices in her head, willing herself to hold his gaze despite her torturous thoughts.

Hames stood like a mountain above her—one that could never and would never crumble. "But I am not as foolish as the other lords. If friendship is what you seek, then go speak with the blonde one. I'm sure Ronan would be happy to warm your bed if you asked him nicely."

The lord ripped his arm from her hand and walked away.

Morana stood in the hall, painful gashes carving themselves into her heart. If she had doubted Matthias's feelings before--

Standing in the throne room as Morana pulled the trigger, Hames hadn't acted like he hated her. But it was clear, now, he had been bound by duty.

It unsettled her. Especially with how much the fauna god was said to admire Hames. Morana pressed her lips together, fury building in her chest. She wouldn't be weak when it came to the lord. Morana would earn his trust.

Even so, the consuming doubts spun a web inside her mind—something that sparked questions—if only a few.

Morana sat next to Matthias as the wooden boat coasted along the misty water of the fauna realm. She could see large, jagged rocks in the distance, slowly appearing through the thick fog.

Everything smelled like fresh water and fish, reminding Morana of Sarnai's distaste for this realm—specifically, this god.

"Wherever this god lives," Morana stated. "It doesn't seem like it's easy to get to."

Staring out at the vast nothingness beyond the choppy waves and mist, Morana strained to see something—anything.

Matthias glanced down at her from where he sat. His arm provided a steady weight over her shoulders, settling her as she looked toward where Hames was seated at the other end of the boat, picking at his fingernails. If he didn't agree with Matthias's casual affection—the lord didn't show it.

The small craft rocked, propelled by the current guiding them to wherever they were headed. They had no paddle—as if the magic of this place was enough to set them on the right course. Morana could almost taste that magic—thick and bitter—like the taste of burnt coffee. The power felt ancient, mixing in the blue-tinted air like the churning waves beneath them.

"It's not as difficult as it looks," Matthias said, a devious smirk splitting his face. "Though Callum tries to scare people off."

"How so?"

Hames grunted before gesturing to the mist-covered rocks appearing through the haze. "Those aren't rocks," he supplied.

Morana looked to Matthias for confirmation.

"Not rocks," he confirmed.

The water sloshed against the side of the creaking vessel, licking the planks and pushing them forward faster. As the fog split in the distance, Morana saw what Hames was referring to. The large, jagged rocks were, in fact, not rocks. They were tall stone structures stretching hundreds of feet into the air on either side of the watery path. Carved like stone dragons. Moss covered the structures until the bellies of the dragons changed from stone to iron bars—cages for whatever the fauna god collected.

Drifting past one of the statues, Morana peered into the dark cage. She was staring into yellow eyes, so menacing they had her hairs standing on end.

The beast inside lunged—a giant, snarling animal that resembled a cat slamming against the metal. Morana flinched and Matthias gripped her tighter, chuckling softly in her ear.

"You're not scared, are you?" he asked.

"No."

His breath was hot against her hair as he placed a gentle kiss on the side of her head. His shadows rippled over her skin, caressing her until she let him in.

Liar.

She could feel him smiling as his lips lowered to her ear. His whisper sent goosebumps rising over her skin—goosebumps that had nothing to do with the eerie and ancient magic.

"I bet you're terrified," he said.

"No," she repeated, her body heating at the distraction. "I'm not."

"Why are you lying to me?" he asked, his voice still deliciously low. Hames was busy with his knife.

"I would never." Her voice was near breathless.

Shadows rippled again, and she was met with something new. Matthias was now standing in her mind, distracting her from the caged beasts lining the sides of the water.

"Just tell me you're afraid, so I can have an excuse to soothe you." Matthias was standing behind her, hands resting on her shoulders.

She squeezed her thighs together—liquid heat swirling in her belly. "I'm not afraid."

"Then pretend," he whispered, his breath hot against her neck.

"Okay." She leaned back against him. "I'm afraid, Matthias."

He placed a kiss on her bare shoulder. She wasn't wearing a tank top, but she supposed in her mind, she could wear anything.

"We can't have that." His lips pressed higher on the side of her neck. "Would you like me to distract you?"

A shuddering breath exited her lips as she ground against him. Matthias groaned, the sound vibrating along her skin.

"Please let me distract you."

She took a steadying breath, preparing herself to taunt the god in her mind. "Are you begging, Matthias?"

Matthias shifted, circling until he stood tall in front of her. Slowly—so slowly—he lowered himself. His fingers trailed down the sides of her waist—her hips—her thighs.

Morana couldn't breathe, not as he knelt at her feet, and not when his dark eyes peered up at her. When he placed a gentle kiss on her hip, she thought her heart stopped completely.

He looked up again, eyes burning with desire. "I would like nothing more than to beg at the feet of my queen."

She was back on the boat, Matthias's shadows retreating back into his skin. The smirk on his face was smug.

Morana looked to Hames, still busy with his knife.

He had called her his queen. Morana took a deep breath, reminding herself of their arrangement. The engagement was real—but not completely. She fought the pain that tightened her chest.

Morana peered into the cage of the final dragon, noticing how close they were to the rocky shore. Inside the belly of the beast sat cold stone and emptiness.

Her mind settled, breath returning to normal after Matthias's blessed distraction. Her brow furrowed as she questioned the empty cage—curiosity dragging her back to the present.

"What belongs in that one?" she asked.

"Better not to think about it," Hames chimed in. His icy eyes were now on her—hardened and unfeeling. "Callum collects all kinds of beasts. I'm sure it's something terrible."

She could have sworn she saw the corner of his mouth lift—just slightly. Morana didn't know what that meant.

When they dragged the boat onto the shore, Matthias gripped her hand, warm fingers intertwining with her own to drag her toward the path in the forest.

It was dark beneath the canopy, a cacophony of sounds surrounding them. The trees stretched their limbs overhead, breaking the mist apart. Leaves and moss-covered logs littered the forest floor.

A skittering sound drew Morana's attention into the forest. Out there, in the darkness, she could have sworn she saw a massive creature with wings. Before she could give it much thought, it was gone. That didn't change the way her limbs weakened beneath her. Her heart thumped loudly in her chest; her eyes wild.

"The forests are filled with creatures, too." Hames was walking ahead of them, moving with long, confident strides over the muddy path. "They shouldn't bother us, though. Some may try to scare you."

By the time they reached the top of the forested hill, Morana had heard screeching and baying. Even more frightening were the sounds of laughter echoing from between the trees. She was jumpy, but Matthias kept his hand in hers, reassuring her every step of the way.

The fauna god's cabin looked exactly as she imagined—eerie and ancient—just like the feeling of the magic in his realm.

Scratches decorated the wooden door along with one large gash cut through the center.

"Clearly an animal," Morana whispered.

Matthias squeezed her hand once in confirmation before Hames opened the creaking door.

Upon entering, a small rodent-like creature with giant eyes scuttled across one of the wooden beams on the ceiling while Morana's eyes adjusted to the light. She jumped back, heart picking up in pace, before the creature disappeared.

Dust settled over the narrow entryway—all wood and musk and creaking floorboards. Morana only imagined that more horrors awaited her as she stood in the god's cabin.

Matthias chuckled again, the dark sound stirring anger deep in her belly. At first, she had been amused, but now? Every turn made her jump. Maybe it was making her appear weak.

"You don't have to be so rude," she hissed.

"It's comical." He shrugged, eyes glittering in the dim lights as Hames walked to the wooden stairwell just beyond the entryway. "The fauna god owed me too much to put you at risk. For all the creatures he collects, he isn't one for violence." Matthias flashed white teeth at her. "He wouldn't test me by allowing harm to come to you."

Tapestries lined the walls of the dark stairwell, stitched with delicate depictions of wolves and dragons—every creature imaginable. Morana paused by one, looking at the roaring mouth of a lion. This lion—however—was massive. When she turned, Matthias and Hames were gone.

Morana watched her steps as she bounded up the stairs but halted abruptly when she reached the top. Fear crawled over her skin, making her limbs shake. At the top of the stairs, a great beast huffed hot breath behind the bars of a cage just beyond the landing. Morana couldn't make out its form, but its presence captivated her.

When a creaking sound drew her attention back to the present, she looked in both directions. The hall stretched equally to the left and right, with several doors on either side. She didn't know what way they had gone.

It reminded her of the fear she felt stranded alone in Sarnai's realm for the first time, though this time, it was even more potent.

"Act like a god," she whispered to herself.

Turning left, Morana moved down the hall, her boots scuffing on the wooden floor. She tucked her hair behind both ears, glancing for an open door—any open door.

There was one, but as she got closer, she could hear a distinct growling sound. Morana squeezed her eyes shut and kept walking past it.

A three-headed dog, larger than her, emerged from the room and crowded the small hallway to prevent her from retreating the way she came. Each head had a set of eyes as bright as the sun, warm and fiery—like madness.

Morana gripped the dagger at her thigh, planning to turn and run. The dog stepped forward, lunging, and she ducked to the side, taking her chance to sprint back down the hall.

She halted.

Just beyond the beast, Hames and Matthias stood next to a tall man with lightly tanned skin and eyes slightly turned up at the corners. "Easy," the man said, causing the dog to sit. It was so large that the motion rattled the floor beneath Morana's feet.

"Did you take a wrong turn?" he asked. The embroidery on the man's elaborate vest depicted animals of all kinds. Similar images wound around one arm in ink, the tattoos detailed and—

Morana squinted as the ink on his arm twisted and moved, alive and speaking the story of the creatures depicted on his skin.

Matthias looked unamused and moved to stand next to her. "Try not to get lost," he whispered.

He didn't seem angry, but he also didn't seem pleased. Morana simply nodded.

Who she assumed to be the fauna god spoke again. "He won't hurt you."

Matthias had a warm hand on her lower back as he ushered her down the hallway to follow an amused Hames. An even more amused Callum walked next to the lord—relaxed as if they were old friends. Morana glanced back at the dog retreating into its room.

Passing the beast at the top of the stairs, they continued on in the other direction, moving until they reached the singular door at the end of the long hallway. For a cabin, the building was immense.

When the door opened, Morana's eyes caught on the large wooden desk at the center and the bookshelves lining what appeared to be a study of some sort. Skulls and skins of different animals sat above the shelves—as if the god wasn't just a collector, but a hunter as well.

Flames shot out, small and ferocious, from a tiny dragon sitting in a golden cage to the side of the desk.

Callum sat in the chair opposite them and tapped on the bars to scold the creature.

Matthias stood at Morana's side as she took her own seat, thankful for his hand resting on the back of her chair. Its presence helped ease some of the tension through her shoulders.

Hames leaned against the opposite wall; his arms folded across his broad chest.

"Excuse the dragon," Callum said, a wide smile breaking across his face. "These creatures belong to another realm and are typically used as—" His tongue rolled along his mouth in search of the correct word. "Familiars," he provided. "That's what they call them there. It's a great realm full of all kinds of beasts. Most of them are half-human though, so not worth my time."

The god tapped a finger on the desk while Hames chuckled behind him, running a hand down his thick, white beard.

"So," Callum began, "you're here for more aid, I presume." A wide smile stretched across his face.

If Matthias was uncomfortable, he didn't show it. "Inara is using creatures in the war."

The god raised a brow. "What creatures?" He was clearly interested. Whether that was in using them as décor for his office or collecting them in cages, Morana didn't know.

"The Veeden," Matthias said. "As well as others."

"Any I would be interested in?"

"They were all created by Raidan."

Callum grimaced, the smile quickly disappearing from his face. His clear disdain for the major god settled something in Morana and made her feel more comfortable.

The longer she sat in his presence, the calmer she became. Maybe it was how he tamed the beasts he collected.

Still, she couldn't fully grasp why Sarnai hated him so much. He seemed—fine.

Callum sucked on his teeth. "A pity," he said.

"You do still owe Hames. He brings the creatures from the Vulcan frequently for your use."

"That he does," Callum said, smiling once more. "What you're asking, though, would be a grand sacrifice. If I'm understanding correctly, you would like animals to be fighters."

Turning in his chair, Callum took a giant tome from the shelf behind him and slammed it on the desk. The small dragon skittered to the corner of its cage, away from the book.

Callum flipped through pages, making a show of reading its contents. "I have some that would work, but again, the cost would be tremendous."

Morana licked her lips, glancing between the two gods in the room. There were no shadows surrounding Matthias—as if he didn't feel threatened by the god before him. She didn't dare call on her own, afraid of making the wrong decision and insulting the god. They were his guests, after all.

"Name your price." Matthias's tone was authoritative, yet calm.

"That desperate?" Callum's brown eyes winked in the dim light.

"Desperate isn't the correct word," Matthias offered. "Maybe motivated."

Callum smiled, and this time, the gesture sent fear pulsing through Morana's veins. Whatever calmness had worked over her before was gone. Here sat the predator that acquired the skins hanging behind him. She could feel Matthias's grip tighten on the chair behind her.

"You could bring me a beast in exchange for a legion."

Matthias schooled his features into a careful mask.

"What beast?" Hames asked.

Callum looked back at the lord still leaning against the wall. "A high-value creature." His teeth flashed white and Morana swore she saw fangs. His gaze flicked briefly to her and back to Matthias. If Sarnai was right about one thing, it was that he had hardly paid attention to her during the conversation. "The dream-eater," he said.

Morana could feel Matthias tense behind her, but Hames laughed. "You're insane," the lord said. Morana didn't know what a dream-eater was, and Hames's reaction told her she didn't want to.

"That's my price. Take it or leave it." There was something in Callum's tone that let her know he wouldn't budge on his demand.

"We will do it." Matthias's voice echoed in the room and all mirth fled Hames's features.

"Matthias," the lord warned.

"We will capture it," Matthias continued. "If you tell us how, provide us with what we need to make it happen, and prepare a legion for our war. We will capture a dream-eater."

Callum tapped a finger on the desk, clearly pleased with the direction of the conversation. "Making bargains like the fae you rule, Matthias? I didn't think a god would stoop so low."

Matthias just stared at him—unmoving.

"Very well." Callum sighed, standing up and turning to the shelf next to Hames along the back wall. He pulled another book from the shelf, and a latch clicked on the floor to the left of the desk. Rising from the open hole was a column, and atop it sat an iron collar with webbing that glowed blue and pulsed with power.

"I've been prepared to ask someone for this creature a while," Callum began, a feral smile splitting his face. He picked up the collar and handed it to Hames. "You'll need to put this around the creature's neck while it is still alive. That will subdue it enough to get it back here. I'll be placing it in my last dragon." He clicked his tongue. "You saw the empty cage on your way in, I suppose."

"And what does this dream-eater do?" Morana asked, finding the courage to speak. Callum glanced down at her, small wrinkles forming at the corners of his eyes.

"It finds the worst of your nightmares and makes them a reality." As he spoke, fear crawled across Morana's skin. "If only to feast on your terror."

Morana recalled dipping her finger into blood— anger—Raidan.

"And where does this creature live?" Her eyes were locked to the fauna god's.

"The Vulcan mountains, of course. I've made it rather simple for you all."

"Simple enough," Hames grunted.

Callum sat back at his desk, glancing at the small dragon with immense admiration.

"Bring me the dream-eater, and you can have your legion. Now—" he waved a hand as if to shoo them away. "Leave me alone. With this many creatures, I have chores to complete. Use your shadows. I've lifted the restrictions regarding travel."

Matthias nodded, and Hames pushed himself off the wall.

Shadows twisted, and Morana was thrown out of one realm and into the next. The comfort of Ascella washed over her—helping her to forget the conversation they just had.

Twenty-Five

"The shadows manipulate the mind, but I'm sure you know that." Reese shook her head, the brown hair braided over her shoulder moving with the motion. She was staring at the dagger in her hand—Morana's dagger. "What I mean is that if you can filter your power into the hilt of the sword, it can do more than maim others." The way she spoke was logical and assured. Something about her work dissolved the timid creature that had once existed upon their first meeting. "If you can do that, your opponent will believe that the injury is worse. When done right, they can experience more pain, or—"

Reese looked up, her eyes finally meeting Morana's. The woman was still wearing an apron covered in soot—most likely from working earlier in the day. Reese's nose scrunched—highlighting the freckles that decorated her flesh. "You won't think poorly of me?" she questioned.

Morana gave her a curious look, tilting her head to the side. "Poorly of you? I'm the one learning to wield a weapon." Morana licked her lips. "Trust me, whatever you're about to say probably won't shock me." Not with all she'd seen and done since coming to this realm. Morana had no room to judge.

"When done correctly, you can convince your opponent to give in to death, even if their injuries don't warrant that kind of fate." There was a slight discomfort on her face, as if she were more impressed with the technology and less impressed with its ability to kill.

"Is this how Matthias became the god of death?" Morana asked, raising a brow. "Just like a *man* to take all the credit."

Reese chuckled, some of the tension easing from her shoulders. "No, no. He does, however, capitalize on the technology. I'm the one who invented it or discovered it or whatever." A blush rose on those freckled cheeks, and Morana saw what Ronan observed in the blacksmith. Reese was brilliant and kind. And still, there was a fire hidden within her slight frame.

Morana sucked on her teeth. "You're certainly intelligent. Too smart for Ronan, I'm afraid."

Reese cleared her throat as a flush on her cheeks deepened. The pink tint broke through a small smudge of black grime coating one side of her face. "Right." She shifted uncomfortably. "So, let's get started."

Morana's brows furrowed. "Um—" Something in her mind flashed to death—not the god she had come to know, but the death she had dealt over the past weeks. "I— I'm not going to injure you. How will I know if it works?"

Reese pointed to an obsidian stone embedded in the hilt of the dagger. "Here," she said, her expression serious. "This will glow with whatever color the dagger believes fits your essence. Kind of a fun mood ring." One corner of her mouth turned up at that.

Morana nodded, closing her eyes and allowing the shadows to coast down her skin and send ripples of pleasure over her flesh.

At first, nothing happened. Darkness only grew in the training room.

"Think of the dagger as fae. Work it as you would work into another's mind."

Morana nodded, keeping her eyes screwed shut. She felt for the dagger in the way she had felt for Matthias's mind—stretching her power out to the metal.

Queen of Darkness.

The metal hissed; Morana's mind filled with the whispering noise as she dropped the weapon. The metal clattered on the floor—the sound echoing across the training room. Somehow, that sound wasn't as loud as the words whispered into her mind moments ago. Morana stiffened.

Reese's lips formed a tight line. "Did something happen?"

"No, I—" Morana's heart was racing and pumping adrenaline through her veins. She bent over to pick up the weapon. The metal was now cold in her hand—lifeless. "I'll try again." She sat up straighter, rolling her shoulders and preparing to master the dagger.

Act like a god, she thought.

Reaching out to the weapon once more, Morana used her power to feel for the consciousness that was there. It wasn't long before she heard the voice again.

Queen of Darkness, it whispered. *You are only half awake.*

Morana winced, attempting to communicate in the same way she did with Matthias. Mind to mind. *What do you mean?*

You've hardly touched your power. I will accept what you offer.

Just like that, Morana felt the shadows pull from her chest and run down her arm to be sucked into the dagger. She gasped, sweat beading on her brow. Losing her power to the weapon caused fear to churn in her stomach. For a moment, she believed the dagger would swallow her whole.

When the sucking sensation eased, the feeling shifted. Shadows were running through her and the dagger, spinning like a closed circuit. Opening her eyes, Morana realized no shadows were coating her flesh.

Reese smiled; a look of genuine satisfaction highlighted in shades of burgundy flickering across her features.

Morana looked to the stone embedded in the dagger, now glowing in a deep shade of red. Her eyes widened.

"Perfect," Reese whispered. "You made my job easy. I think we are done here as long as it feels natural."

Morana's eyes were still wide, glancing from the blacksmith to her weapon. The power ran through her veins like flowing water. "Nothing about this feels natural." She had come a long way from the mortal realm. Morana was now playing with magic. She felt power she never thought existed, and the channel was easy to keep moving, as if the dagger longed to share her abilities. The burgundy gem swelled with light before settling again. "It feels—good," she admitted.

"Good."

Just then, the doors of the training rooms slammed shut, causing both Morana and Reese to jump. The connection to the dagger was severed as the weapon clattered back to the ground.

"Engaged?" Elivira's tone was icy. "You mean to tell me you are engaged to Matthias? You are set to be queen." Her hair was loose, wild strands of brown hitting just below her shoulders. She looked frantic—her charcoal dress hanging from her toned figure.

Morana stiffened in her seat. "What do you mean?" She spoke slowly, unsure of what the lord knew.

Elivira stopped right in front of her, her features confused. "Matthias just announced to the court that there will be a ball in a month's time to celebrate his new *engagement*." She spat the last word like a curse.

Morana couldn't hold eye contact. Guilt seeped from her like an old wound, bringing a painful confusion. Certainly, Matthias would tell the lords the truth. Sarnai knew the truth. The engagement wasn't real, and while Morana knew Matthias cared for her in some sense, he hadn't admitted to actually *wanting* her as his queen.

Hames's words circled her mind, causing the pain to slice sharper across her chest.

She glanced at Reese. "Could you excuse us?"

"Oh—um." The skittish girl returned as Reese quickly stood and bowed as she moved toward the door. "Of course," she mumbled.

When the training room was empty save for Morana and Elivira, Morana whispered, "It isn't real."

"What do you mean, it isn't real?" The lord seemed almost angry now.

Bile rose in Morana's throat. "It—it's a political thing." She winced, afraid that her words didn't do it justice. "Matthias shocked even me when he told Inara over dinner. It is good for my *protection*." Morana cringed. "And more importantly, it provides more fuel for the war. I agreed to go through with it after what you told me in Namid. This entire—" Morana could barely finish the words. "I'm a very insignificant piece of what is happening here."

Her heart twisted painfully in her chest at the admittance. It was true, though. She was far more vulnerable now. Conan sought her out in that tavern. Inara showed up at the palace, and Raidan—

She closed her eyes, unable to look at the lord. For as much as she wanted it to be real, to be wanted despite her mortality and her weakness, she wasn't sure Matthias would ever give her that satisfaction. She convinced herself that it didn't matter, telling herself that the longer she waited to accept the truth, the more the rejection would hurt.

That wasn't entirely true.

It still hurt.

When she opened her eyes, Elivira's face was blank. If she could see the truth of Morana's feelings, she didn't show it.

"Okay," the lord began. "Okay, well—" She didn't seem to know what to say. Her blank expression shifted to something like confusion. Her brows lowered, and her eyes flicked around the room. "I suppose that makes sense." Something in her tone didn't seem convinced.

Morana cleared her throat, wringing her hands together. "He didn't yell at you, did he?"

Elivira paused, warm eyes turning toward Morana. A small smile tugged at her lips, and she huffed a laugh, folding her arms across her chest. "He only threatened to kill me."

"Tell me how to kill a god, and I'd be happy to threaten him back." Morana smiled; one brow raised. It was easier to toss taunting remarks than sit with the weight of her feelings for the god of death.

"Of course." Elivira rolled her tongue along her cheek. "As soon as I discover how to kill Death himself, I'll be happy to let you know."

Morana chuckled, picking up the dagger and sheathing it on her thigh. She tightened the strap there and tucked a strand of hair behind her ear. It had grown longer since coming to the fae realm. "We leave for the Vulcan tomorrow. Hames doesn't seem to like me," she confessed. "So, the trip should be interesting."

Elivira did laugh then. "Hames likes no one other than that fauna god and the strange creatures he captures from the mountains. Don't take it too personally. He's loyal, though, and once he sees the steel in you, that loyalty will extend to you as well. Currently, his only view of you is the strange emotional girl that showed up, got kidnapped, and spurred a fae war."

Morana grimaced. "I can see how that would leave him to think poorly of me." She thought poorly of herself, even.

Elivira patted her arm. "Don't take it to heart."

Morana nodded, making her way to exit the training rooms. The looming journey worried her more than she cared to admit. A creature that would taunt her with her deepest fears wasn't exactly what she needed. The strange white mist was already doing that work.

The solitary image polluted her mind. It was the image of her kneeling beside Garian's corpse and swirling the blood with her finger. If the dream-eater was everything Callum said it would be, she didn't know if she could stomach the reality of her nightmares.

Even more worrisome were the hidden fears within her—the ones she hadn't even recognized herself. There was no telling what the dream-eater could unearth. Morana spent years hiding everything she hated about herself, and while she was working to wade through the mess of her loathsome qualities, she didn't know if she could handle confronting herself head-on.

Elivira thought her made of steel—Morana wasn't sure that was the case.

Twenty-Six

Standing at the base of a snowy mountain, Morana pulled the heavy cloak tighter around her body. Matthias had given her thick layers to wear to prepare for the journey into the Vulcan mountains. The chill still found its way through the layers, leaving her yearning for a cup of Sarnai's tea.

Shadows dissipated slowly, eaten by the frigid breeze whipping through the frost-coated evergreens. Morana felt for the dagger strapped to her thigh and the sword sheathed along her back as she pulled the hood of her cloak up.

Hames grunted before pressing onward. The massive man looked immune to the cold, like he'd acclimated long ago. Or maybe the icy chill had found its way deep into his soul. Maybe it was a part of him. Morana figured that could be true, too.

"Do you know anything about the dream-eater?" She couldn't fight the nerves circulating through her body— not knowing if the shivering was from the cold or the fear.

Matthias's features were stern beneath the hood of his cloak. "It's not all bad," he began, though there was a tightness to his tone. "The dream-eater is less beast and more human in its interactions. It forces you to walk through nightmares and feasts on them." His eyes slid sideways to her. "That being said, once it drinks its fill, your dreams should be peaceful."

Hames's shoulders shook, and he turned back. "Until your mind crafts some other terror to torture you with. The beast will keep coming back."

Allowing her power to stretch toward Matthias's mind, she found it blessedly open to her, as it always was. *Who will try to capture the creature?*

He winced. The movement was subtle, but Morana caught it, nonetheless. *Don't worry about it. It's not going to be you.*

Why not? Matthias had agreed to bring her, and she was thankful for that. It didn't stop the unsettling feeling that led her to sleep in Matthias's room last night. Knowing she wasn't the one facing the dream-eater did nothing to settle her—especially if Matthias was the one willing to take the risk.

Matthias's shadows caressed her inner world. *I could never willingly put my queen in danger. What kind of king would I be then?*

She was certain he could sense her unease. He was in her mind, after all. *It would make you a king willing to do what was best for his kingdom.*

Morana could almost feel the way he paused. Tension was tight, his entire body stiff. *Is that what you think?* His voice was soft, even as it echoed in the quiet place belonging to only them. *You must know—you have to know. I care for you, Morana.*

They continued climbing, those words circling like a vulture in the sky. Morana played them on repeat, and with Matthias's power still lingering in the corners of her mind, she knew he must sense it too.

You didn't know.

Morana looked to him as they walked, the snow crunching beneath her boots.

How could I not?

Even in her mind, she couldn't help the way she longed to ease the pain by blocking off some of her true worries. *I wouldn't be here if you didn't care. That doesn't mean my presence or our fake engagement can't be useful for political reasons.*

Matthias was in front of her now, and she couldn't see his face. The shadows pulled back abruptly, leaving her with cold far deeper than the chill of the wind.

Either she was wrong, and he didn't care about her in merely a political sense, or she was painfully, irrevocably right. While he cared for her, there was an underlying motive—just as Hames had insinuated. One of those options gave her hope—and the other?

Morana grunted as the mountain grew steep, giving way to sharp rocks and more snow descending from the heavens. Morana had to use her hands to climb, her fingers numb within the black gloves she wore.

"Does this thing exist at the top of the mountain?" she asked.

"There's a cave up here." Hames gestured to what Morana could only describe as—up. "We will need to enter the cave and then wing it."

"Wing it?"

Matthias pulled back, slowing until he was beside her. He leaned in, lips brushing against her ear. There was no hint of their previous conversation—as if it had never happened. Heat washed over her regardless, warming her from the inside out. "You are in the presence of a god," he spoke low. "You don't trust me?"

The words felt loaded—two meanings twisting together in her mind. She tried not to think about it.

"Well, I don't have your blood book." Morana raised a brow. "I do, however, have access to your mind."

That you do. Matthias's voice surrounded her again, but there was no sound running through the tall pines. *You have access to all my secrets without a book. You now know that my parents are buried in Nashira where Garian is lord. The city includes the largest library in our court and their tomb beneath it. My mother always loved books and hated winter. It only seemed fitting.*

He leaned in again, placing a kiss on her temple. *You also have the answers to any questions you wish to ask.* His voice was so loud now. *I just don't know if you'll like the truth.*

Morana nearly slipped on a rock, catching herself before glancing at Matthias who was now further away. Something flickered in his gaze. She willed the shadows toward him to speak, ignoring the last statement. She didn't even want to think about how it made her feel. If she wasn't going to like the truth—

A library, she said instead.

A smile split Matthias's face. Morana couldn't look away, helpless to the way her body responded to him. The physical distraction was pleasant, considering all that warred within her.

Morana was panting by the time they came to the cave. All that training with Garian, and a hike up a mountain could still take her out. It was a gaping mouth of black and mystery yawning in the face of the bitter mountains of the Vulcan. Hames lowered his hood, his white beard decorated with flakes of snow and ice.

Fitting.

"Do you have any idea what it looks like?" Morana asked him.

He kept his eyes on the cave, pulling a small lantern from where it was hooked at his side. Hames didn't acknowledge her. He took green leaves from his pocket, chewing on them before placing them in the lantern. The emerald light erupted from the glass, illuminating the entrance to the cave.

Even so, the light only went so far.

Hames turned to her then, holding the lantern in front of his face. "You'll know it when you see it," he said, his accent thicker than before. "Maybe you'll see your worst nightmare first."

A chill worked its way down her spine, sending shivers through her entire body. Matthias grabbed her hand, squeezing once before they all entered the blackness of the cave.

They were wandering—swallowed by the darkness and cold stone. Morana wanted the comfort of her power, but in this place, the shadows struggled. It was as if the darkness of the cave was a void, a place where even the night couldn't exist. For in the night hung the stars.

There was no light here.

"How are we supposed to find this thing?" Morana whispered.

With every passing second, fear rose in her body until she was almost choking on its presence. In the darkness, there was no way to see the creature. No way to know how far or how close it was. Were they prepared for this?

Matthias was certain he would be the one to face the creature, and that unsettled her even more. She wasn't just afraid for herself—but for him. Gods were harder to kill, but they could still die. Matthias's parents proved that to be true.

A tapping sound echoed ahead of them, causing them to halt in their tracks.

Morana's heart was pounding in her chest now, sweat forming on her brow as adrenaline took over. Her shallow breaths were the only sound aside from the growing silence of the cave. In that silence, the echoes of that singular tapping lingered.

Even the dripping of water had stopped.

"You've come for me."

The low groaning voice surrounded them, and Morana swore she heard *something* step forward. Hames's faint light did nothing to illuminate what was speaking.

Matthias stood in front of her. She could feel his power ripple in the air, but the cave was too dark to see it.

"Ah," the creature began. "I will gladly go if it is the girl who agrees to be tested. I can already taste her terror."

Matthias's shoulders stiffened. Green light illuminated his features and mixed with the darkness of the cavern. "She's unavailable," he said through gritted teeth.

Morana thought she heard the creature breathing. It was a sound that had her knees shaking. "I have chosen *her*, god of death." Morana swore the deep voice contained a smile—if this creature could even smile. "You don't have a choice."

Hames's expression was blank, the lantern still held in front of him. "There are no negotiations here, Matthias."

Matthias looked back with something like pain in his eyes.

Act like a god. Morana allowed the words to rattle in her mind, giving her the strength to agree. She nodded. This was what she wanted. She would do this.

"No weapons," the beast hissed.

Morana obeyed, giving her sword and dagger to Matthias. He took them, but she could see the hesitancy in the way he gripped each hilt.

Even a god couldn't command the dream-eater. Morana didn't know what that meant. Every ounce of adrenaline racing through her body fed the shaking of her hands. This was the one true test of hiding her emotions, though all of her darkest worries would be revealed soon. She would hold on to the control while she could.

Hames handed her the metal collar. It was cold against her fingers, larger than she would like for a creature she couldn't see. Tightening her grip, she willed the ice of that metal to make her hands stop shaking, drawing strength from the one thing she could hold on to—the reality that the dream-eater could be captured.

As soon as she turned around, the lantern light disappeared, leaving her alone in the darkness with the nightmares she never wanted to face. Morana started digging a grave—the one she could bury her fear in.

Not that it will help.

"This will be delicious," the beast growled.

Under the weight of magic flowing toward her, Morana could do nothing but fall to the floor and squeeze her eyes shut. When she opened them, she stood in a shitty apartment, and a familiar man slouched in a chair, tapping his finger on the kitchen table.

"Dad?" she whispered, stepping closer.

She was wearing her old pajamas—the plaid ones with the hole in the knee from when she was twelve.

Lifting her hand, Morana realized her hair was longer, hanging around her waist the way it did before she learned how to cut it herself. Her father was too busy wallowing to care, so she would use kitchen shears and do it herself. The first few times left her crying as the kids at school made fun of her, but after a few helpful videos she found using a computer at the library, she managed.

"Dad," she whispered again.

He didn't look up, his eyes swollen and red, unmoving. Even as a beer bottle rolled across the floor, hitting Morana's bare foot. She winced.

These memories—this place—it was all too much. Before her were pieces of her past she hadn't dared touch. The root of her insecurities sat before her, and she was positive those insecurities were about to erupt from their grave—unearthed by the dream-eater calling her emotions to come out and play.

"It's your fault," her father spoke.

"What?"

"It's your fault she left." His eyes finally slid to hers. In them was nothing but wrath and desperation. It had tears welling in her eyes. "If you weren't so troublesome. If you didn't have so many needs. If you would have made her life easier."

Morana flinched when his fist hit the wooden table and caused it to splinter. She closed her eyes briefly as a tear rolled down her cheek. The feelings slashed through her chest, cutting her too deeply. These weren't things she vocalized, and they weren't things that she had thought about in years, but there was truth here. Maybe it was her fault. She didn't want to be a burden.

Too emotional. Too weak. Too much and somehow not enough.

"Why did you have to be so selfish?" He was standing now, prowling toward her like a lion ready to attack.

"Dad, I'm sorry."

The slap rang out in the apartment. The sting of it felt real. It broke something in her.

"You selfish bitch," he spat. "You earn your keep here, because you are owed nothing! How could you take her from me?"

His eyes were wild as he brought his hands up to her throat. Morana was clawing at his hands and pleading. The tears rolled faster down her cheeks as the air left her lungs. She gasped, but nothing helped ease that he was suffocating her.

She deserved this. Morana deserved every ounce of pain and loathing he gave her. In this place, there was no one to turn to. She was the only one who could do anything about her situation, and as her vision spotted beneath his squeezing fist, she wasn't sure she wanted to fix it.

A burden. This is better.

As Morana's hand trailed upward to her face, she gently brushed against a scar—two scars. They were the proof of the realm she was in—who was waiting for her outside of the cave.

"This isn't real," she tried to whisper.

"What did you say?"

"It's not real."

Just like that, her father vanished, leaving Morana to collapse on the floor.

She expected the cold ground of the cave, but instead, all she felt was a soft carpet between her fingers and under her bare knees.

Shaking, Morana stood up, her toes sinking into the soft texture. A light flipped on—illuminating a bedroom she was unfamiliar with. Her brows creased.

"You're supposed to be sleeping, little one."

Morana turned to see a woman, much taller than her, with blonde hair pulled over her shoulder and hanging to her waist. She was beautiful, her gray eyes sparkling in the purple bedroom. Her presence reminded Morana of a blanket of stars, peaceful and present—if only for a moment.

"Morana, you know that once the lights go out, you need to be in bed." The woman smiled, and something clicked. It was her mother—in the flesh.

Morana cried then, the sobs sounding as if they were coming from a small child no older than four. "Mama, stay with me," she howled.

Her mother sighed, moving to sit on the bed and gesturing for her to come forward and sit on her lap. Morana snuggled into her mother; her body dwarfed by the adult woman.

She could smell the scent of wildflowers, feel her mother's arms warm around her shoulders.

When Morana looked into her eyes, dark circles were painted beneath them. She looked thin and hollow—much different from the woman who had just entered her room.

"You can't possibly need me this much." The woman rolled her bloodshot eyes.

"I do," Morana admitted. "I *do* need you."

"No." Her mother's tone was scolding. "You do not. I can't do this anymore. It's too much. *You're* too much."

"Mama, wait."

Morana was thrown from her lap, landing on the floor with the same pain clawing at her chest. Her mother was gone, the door slamming behind her.

Screaming through tears, Morana curled up into a ball. She cried for what felt like hours until her sobbing ceased, and she was left numb on the floor. Darkness greeted her when she closed her eyes, reminding her of a palace—dark and gilded—home.

Morana sat up in a dungeon with the sound of cold dripping hitting the stone. For a brief moment, she expected to see Inara or Axton through the bars of the cell. It was a reminder that she was dreaming—or something. She didn't quite know what anymore.

Boots clicked on the stone, a tall figure coming into view.

Death had a cigarette between his lips and a white button-up rolled at the sleeves. His tattoos shifted when he brought his hand to his mouth to remove the cigarette, throwing it on the floor and stomping out the flames.

"Useful," he mused, tilting his head to the side. "Powerful, and certainly useful."

Morana's heart sunk. She couldn't speak. Power radiated off the god, reminding her exactly where she stood.

He tilted his head to the side. "Isn't that what you wanted?" he asked. "You wanted to be useful—to play the game. Well, here you are—playing." He leaned down, brushing a cold finger over her scarred cheek. "What does it take to kill a god, Morana?"

"What?" She finally forced herself to speak.

"I said, what does it take to kill a god?" The voice was coming from behind her, and now Raidan loomed over her like a demon of the night. He held out a dagger—her dagger.

"Don't you want to drink of Death? Tell me you do."

"I don't." Morana's head whipped back to Matthias, now crouching in front of her as she remained sitting on the ground.

Raidan pressed the dagger firmly in her palm. "You want to," he whispered. "You want to become queen. The only question is—queen of what? Drink of Death, Morana."

White mist danced in her vision, taking her under with rage and chaos. The beast inside of her thrashed and howled—ready to attack the injustice she had suffered.

Morana gripped the dagger tighter, lunging forward with a snarl to drive it straight through Matthias's heart.

The last thing she could remember was how delicious his blood would taste coating her lips.

"Stop."

She was in the cave again and surrounded by darkness. Sweat beaded on her brow and dripped to the floor as she sat up. Morana was panting, her heart pumping so quickly, she wasn't entirely sure it wouldn't burst.

A lion-like creature prowled forward into the light. It had a small trunk for a nose, and large eyes—eyes that she swore could see everything.

"You won't be having any more of those, Queen of Darkness." The creature was speaking again. "Though Raidan's power is strong within you."

Morana couldn't draw her gaze away. She couldn't function after everything she had witnessed.

She had tried to kill Matthias.

Morana leaned over, hurling until the contents of her stomach were coating the cave floor. She wiped her mouth with her sleeve, coughing and looking back at the beast.

"I have to admit," the creature started. "Your nightmares were brutal—delicious. You've earned the right to put the collar around my neck."

Morana blinked. "You long to be captured and put into a cage?"

"I long to be fed." She swore she could hear the dream-eater smile. "The fauna god feeds his collection well. I'm sure I will be fat by the end."

Morana looked around, spotting the metal collar lying open on the floor. She crawled toward it, wrapping her fingers around the cool surface before standing up and walking to the dream-eater.

She could still taste the vomit on her tongue and smell the coppery scent of blood. Gripping the collar for strength, she turned to the creature.

It was larger than she expected, but not so large that she couldn't reach its neck. Hooking the metal around it, she nodded once, and the dream-eater bowed in response, its soft fur rustling in the wind that ghosted through the cave.

They walked out together—woman and beast. And though Morana felt powerful after facing down her fears and the lies she told herself during the darkest of nights, there was nothing left inside of her but an empty shell, only serving to heeding exhaustion.

When the light came from outside the cavern, Matthias rushed to her, cupping her face and scanning her for injuries.

Morana merely nodded, too tired to do anything else. "Let's go home," she breathed.

Twenty-Seven

Matthias's bed was warm, with its lush red comforter, thick blankets, and the scent of bergamot permeating the room. She still couldn't shake the chill that settled deep into her bones after capturing the dream-eater.

Morana had bathed and eaten, crawling into bed as soon as they returned. It had only been two in the afternoon when they arrived back at the palace in Ascella, but exhaustion weighed heavy on her, leading her to fall asleep with damp hair and a loose t-shirt that belonged to Matthias hanging from her shoulders.

Matthias and Hames had gone to the fauna realm to deliver the dream-eater, and though Morana was set on making something of herself and refraining from wallowing, she was grateful Matthias hadn't asked her to go.

Useful, he had called her in the nightmare. It was as if her value was based solely on what she could do for him. The power coursing through her veins, the way she could move through realms and tame the beast in the cave. Their entire situation served his kingdom, and the revelation brought with it a painful, searing thought. Her emotions were a part of the game—a way to secure her compliance.

None of that actually mattered, though. If it did, she knew it would break her, and she wasn't willing to touch that thought—not yet.

It was dark when her eyes opened again, awoken by the sound of the creaking door.

"We are sending the legion to Zora. Callum kept his promise."

Morana was silent as she sat up, staring at Matthias. He looked exhausted too, and she wondered if he ever took time to slow down—if anyone took care of him the way he was taking care of her.

He sat on the bed next to her, lacing his fingers through hers and bringing the top of her hand to his warm lips. "How are you?" he asked when he broke the fleeting contact.

Morana huffed a laugh.

Matthias cleared his throat. There was something heavy hanging in the air—something like vulnerability. "I've ruined your life so fully," he whispered.

Morana tilted her head to the side. "Why do you say that?"

"You've been attacked and beaten—tortured. You were forced to face your worst fears in that cave because I couldn't protect you. And now?" He paused, looking away. "I'm forcing you into an engagement you couldn't possibly want. How could you want that?"

Something in her chest cracked at his words. Her shadows reaching out to trail over his skin.

"I have." She nodded. "Been through those things." There were no lies she could tell. Despite the wrongness of his feelings regarding the situation, the list of what had happened to her was true, but when it came to their engagement, he had it completely wrong.

Matthias's voice was strained when he broke the silence. "Morana."

His mind was open to her, as it usually was. *You're wrong about the engagement.*

She gave him a small smile. "I'm trying to stop wallowing and feeling sorry for myself. You don't need to remind me of what I've been through." Matthias was leaning against the headboard now, and she placed her head on his chest, listening to the steady beating of his heart. "I'm trying to earn you," she whispered.

"Earn me?" he questioned. "I'm the one who put you through most of it." There was pain mixed in his voice, threatening to shatter her completely. His tattooed hand came up to brush her hair.

"Does Death feel guilty now?" humor laced her tone—desperate to find some other expression besides pain and sadness on his face.

"I—" Something heavy cut through her humor like a knife sliding through butter. His hand dropped away from her hair. "I haven't been completely honest."

Her stomach dropped as she sat up. The silence consumed them entirely. There was something in the crease of his brow and stern expression that had nerves coursing through her blood.

"I was watching you because I had—" Matthias grunted, looking away with his brows furrowed. "I had done business with the oracle who is tucked away in the human realm. It's where I found Cain. I was looking for information on Inara, and instead, I was told that I would find my answers—" He looked up at her. "I would find my answers with you."

She could hear her own heartbeat, the only sound in the nearly silent room. When Morana hadn't trusted Matthias, when she had been sitting on his throne, he admitted to sending someone to kill her. He knew she wouldn't die. Now, after everything, finding more to the story, she struggled to wrap her mind around his meaning. Morana spoke slowly. "That makes very little sense."

Useful. Political decisions. Weak.

Whispers about her being the Queen of Darkness were weaving their way through the court. She had heard about them, been confronted with them. Was there something he knew about that?

"Does this have to do with me being the Queen of Darkness—or whatever people are calling me?"

Matthias shook his head. She watched the tightness in his shoulder and feared that he would say more. What could Death hide from the living?

"I'm not . . . whatever they are saying. I'm also not entirely sure how I'm the answer to anything." Morana swallowed the thick lump forming in her throat. Her heart was beating wildly in her chest—her fingers shaking. "Why are you telling me this?" He was going to reject her.

Doubt was creeping in like a swallowed poison. Morana had believed she had access to his mind—to anything. And here there were secrets. Maybe she hadn't been cautious. Maybe she jumped at the one person who had seen her darkness and refused to judge her. In fact, she had seen the same darkness in him.

She shoved the feelings aside. He was telling her things now and confessing that he believed she was significant. It didn't mean he didn't feel for her. He omitted information. He didn't *lie*.

Morana breathed deeply and let him continue.

"When I went to the oracle, there was someone else there—" Matthias stopped abruptly, rerouting and shifting what he said. "I don't know. I'm still trying to figure you out. You're a mortal that can avoid Death himself, shift realms, and you hold the power of both fae courts." He was looking at her now, his gaze so intense it nearly burned through her. "I'm not sure what it means, but the oracle believed you were the answer, and I assume you could be. I'm not sure I understand what is happening."

Was this it? Was he reminding her how fake their engagement was? "You and me both," she spoke. Morana leaned back, releasing a long breath and closing her eyes. She pinched the bridge of her nose, begging her heart to steady and slow to a pace she could keep up with. When she opened her eyes, she asked, "Who was there, Matthias?"

He shifted uncomfortably and ran a hand through his dark hair. "A strange woman." He wasn't looking at her now. "I was convinced she would give me more information about why the oracle was sending me to you, but she was—unhelpful."

Morana nodded. Maybe she was too exhausted to care. There was still one thought echoing in her mind, drawing her to speak.

"Do you actually care for me?" she asked, vulnerability in her tone. "Is this—" She gestured to nothing, that doubt slowly building in her bloodstream like an unwelcomed toxin. "Are your feelings—"

Too emotional. Too weak.

"They're real," he asserted. There was something in the tone of his voice that begged her to believe it.

Her wild heart settled, worries stilling in her mind. Morana stared at him as silence coated the room like thick honey—trailing slowly down the walls.

"What's it like?" she finally asked. "Being a god?"

Matthias closed his eyes, his brows pinching together. "Heavy," he whispered.

Morana leaned forward and fought the ache in her bones. Her body was still crying out after their trip to the Vulcan. She placed a kiss on his cheek, the corner of his mouth, his lips, drawing away after the briefest of touches. "At least you're about to get a good wife." One corner of her mouth turned up.

Matthias smiled, his face still inches from hers. "At least there's that." The comment made her cheeks flush.

"Though the one issue I have is that it was still against your will."

Morana's smile fell. He still didn't believe she wanted this—not fully. "I agreed to it, didn't I?" She sat back, leaning against the headboard. "Though I wish you would have taken me somewhere warm to look at the stars when you asked. Maybe then it wouldn't be so forced. I'm sure I'd fall for you in an instant after a proposal like that."

Darkness covered her. The last thing she remembered seeing was Matthias's smile and the glint in his eye as he drew on his power to move them.

The first thing she heard was water lapping against a wooden dock—the dock she was now sitting on in only a t-shirt.

"I am not dressed for this," she said, frantically pulling at the shirt's hem and trying to will it lower on her thighs.

Matthias laughed, and she relished the sound. Glancing around, Morana noted they were alone and calmed her frantic pulling.

She gave up on her shirt and moved to sit so that her feet were dangling over the dock. Out on the vast sea, glittering water reflected the light of the stars overhead. The calm waves ebbed and flowed as Matthias joined her to stare at the calming sea.

The image was stunning, reminding her of the night sky they painted in the wake of mortal death. The moon shone on the surface of the water, warming her chest with the beauty of it.

"Where are we?" she asked.

"Adhara." Matthias's eyes slid in her direction. "Ronan's city."

"Figures it would be so romantic." Morana chuckled. When the sound disappeared, they sat beneath the night sky, feeling the salt on their skin as Morana took the moment to breathe. Nobody interrupted them, and behind her, she saw city lights in the distance. It almost looked like a coastal town in the human realm. She would have been convinced it was if it weren't for the scent of magic in the air. Morana kicked at the water and closed her eyes.

Matthias's hand slid to hers, gripping her tightly, and for a moment, the questions between them faded, and there was only the settling reality that he could see all of her. He was willing to show her the deepest parts of himself as well. She had to believe that—especially if she was going to marry him.

There was no room for doubts here. That was the truth she believed, despite his admittance of being told she was the answer. Maybe there was a different reason he had followed her. Maybe Death thought she was the key, but it didn't dictate the things that happened after.

Morana thought back to the rooftop restaurant Matthias had taken her to. It was the moment she had seen something different in him. The very beginning of trust. Maybe that was the moment things had changed for him, as well.

Without Matthias or the power that pulsed through her soul, she would still be working at Ashford and living a hollow existence. Axton's involvement would have caught up to her eventually. Who knew what that would have resulted in?

"What would you have liked to happen?" she broke the silence, drawing Matthias's attention away from the sea. "I mean, if your parents hadn't died and if war wasn't—if Lux was still ruling the Court of Light and Raidan was still sleeping?"

There was a long pause. Morana didn't dare look at him as she fixed her gaze on their hands interlocked in her lap. She carefully traced the moth tattoo and the ring that was still on his thumb.

"I don't know that I would change those things." His deep voice finally cut through the quiet.

Morana's brows furrowed. "Why do you say that?"

Matthias sighed. "If everything remained peaceful, I would have become king." He chuckled softly; the sound had her toes curling beneath the water. "A spoiled ass of a king, might I add? I would know nothing but fae and mortal death. One day, I may have stood by your bed helping you pass in your sleep."

"Ah," Morana interrupted, smiling as she looked up to the stars. "But you forget, I can avoid you."

I wish you wouldn't.

She looked at him then, her stomach curling and fluttering at his words. Her breath caught. "You wish me to die?" she asked.

Matthias brought a hand to her cheek, stroking the scar gently. "I would have stood by your death bed. You would have been old and wrinkled, positively ugly." She chuckled. "I would have known nothing of you and your husband. He wouldn't have been a god, and he would have been considerably less handsome than me, of course." His jaw ticked in the starlight. "Your husband would have walked into the room—"

"Hobbled," Morana interrupted. "He would have been old, too. I'm not a predator like you, Matthias."

Matthias rolled his eyes and his hand fell away from her face. "I do not count, in that regard. It's like dog years or whatever you compared it to." He turned to her again. "Your husband would have *hobbled* into the room and cried. He would have shared all the wonderful memories of your life together, and even though it would have been incredibly sweet, I'm certain I would have only felt pain."

"Why is that?" she questioned. "Is a long, happy life so repulsive to the god of death?"

"No." His face was serious. "I would have felt pain because none of that happiness would have been created with me."

Her lips parted—heart fluttering in her chest. It was everything she wanted—everything she couldn't allow herself to have. She had been caught up in trying to earn him, to be good enough for him. It never occurred to her he had meant what he said. She was already worthy.

"I've thought about the engagement," he began. "About if it were real—"

Morana could feel the heat wash over her. "You want me to be your queen?"

"I do."

She didn't know how to respond to that—didn't know what to think beyond the memory of Matthias in Sarnai's cabin after Inara had tortured her. She had called this place home, and she had meant it.

"I hope you have a ring hidden in your damn pocket," she joked, but her voice shook slightly. She *would not* cry. "This was not well thought out. I was the one who suggested this location anyway, so the stars were not even a romantic idea on your part."

Matthias turned away briefly and laughed, hanging his head. The way his smile widened had her heart clenching.

"If I find you a ring," he said, "then what?"

Morana closed her eyes, breathing in the salty air. "I may just let Death take me."

She could feel him shift forward, more hesitant than he had been before.

The kiss he pressed to her lips was sweeter, nothing like the starved and frantic kisses in the theater or the stream during their trip to Zora.

Shadows swelled, pulling them back to his bedroom in Ascella.

It didn't take long before Matthias was over her, peeling her shirt from her body and trailing his lips down her throat—her breasts.

She squeezed her thighs together, feeling the dampness there, and hissed as his tongue flicked over her nipple, sending sparks along her skin.

Morana moaned when Matthias pressed a firm kiss to her lips before he sat back to remove his shirt—his pants.

When he was bare and over her again, his hardened length pressed against her entrance, his dark eyes boring into her own.

"I want to look at you," he whispered.

Morana could only nod as he pressed himself into her—filling her in a way that differed from before—speaking of the confessions he had made on the dock, and promising that she would no longer be alone. Her power was matched in the god of death, and she didn't know what that meant. All she knew was that the doubt from earlier didn't exist here.

In the depths of the night, Matthias moved with her, reminding her that for the first time in her life, she felt as if she were.

Twenty-Eight

Two weeks of training with Garian in the mornings, Matthias in the evenings, and spending most afternoons in the library left Morana exhausted and more muscular than she had been before. But she figured the months leading up to her time training helped with the latter as well. She was just finally seeing the changes.

Morana was sitting at the table in the library, Cain scribbling on parchment across from her. She'd become accustomed to the rhythm they were in. This time, Morana was reading another book recommended by Sarnai—almost forgetting the scribe existed.

"So, you do read." Cain was looking down, but Morana could see the way his lips pressed together to not smile.

"Hilarious." Morana shoved a dried flower into her place in the book. It was one of the flowers Sarnai had placed in the vase when she had healed after Namid. "I can read. I'm just unwilling to do things that bore me."

Cain huffed. "That just tells me you're irresponsible." He looked up then, eyes lighted. "And to think, Matthias is choosing you to be queen. How will you ever function? I hear most royal tasks are painfully boring."

"At least I can tell a man when I'm interested," she mocked. Something in her words felt somewhat like a lie. "When are you going to ask Amit to my engagement ball? I think I will riot if you don't."

His cheeks flushed as his eyes flicked in between the stacks. "Keep your voice down."

Morana smiled. "Of course. It is your choice. I am to be queen, though. I could uninvite you."

"You're a manipulative queen."

Morana sat back in her chair, tapping the romance novel on the wooden table. "Of course, I am. Why would I lie about that?"

Cain let out a low laugh, returning to his work. "I'll think about it."

She could have sworn he was smiling again.

A vine slithered across the wooden surface of the table from somewhere between the shelves of the library and wrapped around Morana's book. She didn't bother to stop the tome when the plant dragged it away until Sarnai was standing near them, the novel in hand.

"A good one," she commented. "I'm glad you're listening to my recommendations."

"Of course." Morana nodded once.

"Here's another recommendation. You need a new dress. Get up. We are leaving."

Morana watched as Sarnai slid the book back over the table, reaching a hand toward her to help her stand.

"Don't dresses magically appear in my room?" Morana stood, rolling her eyes when Sarnai began dragging her away. She waved over her shoulder to Cain's laughing form.

"You're about to be queen," Sarnai scolded. "You should really be more involved in learning about the court. We are going shopping."

"I—" Morana's throat became unbearably tight. "I don't actually have money," she squeaked.

Sarnai glanced back at her with a look that could kill an immortal being. "You're kidding, right?"

Morana bit her lip and shrugged, resulting in a dramatic eye roll from the flora goddess.

"Matthias's pockets are plenty deep, and you're about to be his wife." Sarnai stopped, turning abruptly and staring down at Morana. "I always knew you would marry rich." The intensity in her gaze sent Morana's pulse spiking. "Even if it is *fake*."

Morana hadn't told her of their conversation or the nights she spent in Matthias's room after training, but knowing Sarnai didn't know made her question. Matthias hadn't told anyone either, but maybe he didn't know he needed to. Morana was the one who insisted it was false to begin with. She was in control of the narrative.

Morana cleared her throat. "Right."

Sarnai tilted her head—curious and questioning. "I don't know that I believe you."

A smile pulled at Morana's lips. "That seems like a you problem. Are we to be the only ones going out?"

"Elivira agreed to come."

"Fantastic."

Morana was still wearing her training outfit, which was covered in sweat and grime from the day. She pulled a strand of hair and sniffed, wincing while walking behind the goddess.

"Will I have time to bathe?"

"Just make it quick."

The streets of the Court of Shadows were just as she remembered. Cobbled stones lined with vine-covered houses and smoking chimneys.

Autumn was slowly disappearing as winter began its arrival—sending brisk wind through the buildings where they walked.

Sarnai set a punishing pace; her charcoal cloak covered with silver embroidery that matched the webbing on her forehead flowing behind her.

When the streets became more crowded at the base of the hill, fae turned and noticed the two walking. The way they stared and bowed as Morana moved past them had her stomach churning. She didn't know what they thought of her, but by their reactions, she knew as well as anyone that they recognized who she was—who she would become.

Hustling to stand next to Sarnai, Morana pulled the hood of her own cloak over her head.

"They're staring at us," she whispered. Her tone bit like the wind on her cheeks.

Sarnai rolled her tongue along her cheek. "That's the whole point." Her umber eyes flicked to Morana. "You want to be seen by the court. Right now, you're a mystery queen cloaked in darkness and hidden away in the tower. You're supposed to make them like you."

Morana tensed at that. "Am I supposed to be smiling and waving like some elegant princess?" she ground out.

"No," Sarnai turned to her as they approached a two-story stone building with large windows displaying what looked to be a type of art studio. Sarnai's smile was devious. "That would be false advertising. You can't have them expecting a meek princess when they're getting a bitch queen."

Morana halted, Sarnai standing just inside the studio with the door opened. Metal bells rang on the glass, but Morana couldn't bring herself to focus on the surrounding noises. "Did you call me a bitch?" she asked, though there was no offense loaded into the question.

Sarnai rolled her eyes and gestured for her to get into the building. "Endearingly."

Morana's heels tapped on the hardwood of the studio. She had donned a burgundy dress for their excursion. The color reminded her of the stone of her dagger when she could channel her power through it. Reese had mentioned it matched her *essence*, and as the skirt billowed around her legs, she couldn't help but believe it to be true.

Arriving at Matthias's court, she had initially refused to wear the dresses. Now, though? It reminded her she was home. She *belonged.*

Easels stocked with canvases lined the well-lit room. Carts loaded with paints and brushes lined the studio, ready to be used. Morana grinned as she noted the empty wine glasses by each canvas, understanding what the pre-shopping event was.

"I suppose you're right about the bitch queen thing." She turned to face Sarnai completely. "Are we about to paint while drunk? Please tell me we are about to paint while drunk right now."

Sarnai lowered the hood of her cloak. "Oh, yes," she replied. "Elivira will be here soon."

There were individuals already seated at their stations. A fae male came up to them. He was lean and wearing an apron covered in various colors of paint. His golden eyes shone brightly, pointed ears decorated in golden rings to match. The instructor guided them to their seats, and moments later, the jingling of bells alerted Morana to Elivira's arrival.

Even inside the studio, the fae were staring—whispering and stealing glances every chance they could get. The attention made her uncomfortable, and she supposed she should smile and try to win them over, but Sarnai had made a decent point. They weren't getting that kind of queen, and it was almost cruel to lie to them.

Morana let shadows whisper along her arms and legs, easing some of her worries. As the fae male who had shown them their seats walked to a canvas displayed at the front of the studio, Morana turned to Elivira, who had sat down between them.

Their glasses were full of wine, and the lord immediately reached for the drink, guzzling half the glass in one motion. "I fucking hate war," she muttered. Her hair was wild, pants and shirt covered in dirt and sweat. She must have come directly from Zora. Matthias was having her check on troops often.

"I can tell." Morana lifted her glass, tasting the sweet liquid. "So," she began, "what are we painting?"

"No idea," Elivira said, leaning forward to look at Sarnai on Morana's other side. "What class did you choose?"

The instructor lowered a tarp from a second canvas, revealing the painting beneath.

"Oh gods," Elivira muttered.

Morana couldn't hold in the laugh that burst from her lips, looking toward the front of the room beyond the dozen or so fae taking the class with them. A detailed painting of an incredibly naked man glared back at them.

"We are painting penises?" Morana was laughing now and taking another long sip of wine. "I hope they give free refills."

Sarnai turned to her, a wicked glint in her eye. "They do," she answered.

Elivira finished her glass and picked up a paintbrush, holding it between her teeth as she started squirting paint onto one of the pallets in the cart behind them. The instructor was finally giving directions, explaining that one should be free as they paint. Morana looked at the giant genitalia painted on canvas and realized just how *free* this instructor liked painting.

Elivira pulled the brush from between her teeth, dunking it in the first color. "Good about the refills," she commented as a petite fae woman came around to refill her glass. "I think it is the only way I'll make it through this."

The first brush stroke had been focused and intentional, but after her second glass of wine, Morana was aimlessly swiping the paint across the canvas and trying to follow directions. If the instructor said to be free, the wine was definitely helping.

"We haven't even painted the penis yet, and I'm already sweating," Elivira slurred. She was on her fourth glass of wine and had become more loose-lipped than Morana had ever seen. There was usually a coolness to her. Elivira was more aloof, serious, and hardly one to make jokes, but somewhere in the middle of the third glass, a switch had flipped. Good. The fae lord needed it.

"Oh please," Sarnai chimed in. "It's the hands that had me feeling like a waterfall."

Morana giggled, lifting her glass to her lips and inhaling more of the alcohol. Her body was relaxed, her mind pleasantly empty. The instructor's voice was smooth and rich like soil, but even with his captivating presence, the more wine she drank, the harder it was to focus on her task. She took matters into her own hands, refraining from following the directions he outlined. Morana chose a different hair color for the man she was painting and spent extra time defining his abdominal muscles.

When her art was finally complete, she looked at her work, satisfied with how realistic the man she crafted was.

Sarnai was standing over her shoulder, and Morana flinched when the goddess gasped. Morana could hear the lingering smile in her voice. "Elivira, you're going to die."

"I hope you don't mean literally." The lord was wiping her hand on a towel as she sauntered over to look at Morana's painting. The loudest cackle erupted from her lips, causing the entire class to turn in their direction.

"Shut up," Elivira said. "You painted a naked Ronan." She squinted a bit. "It's really quite good."

Morana looked back and fought the blooming laughter. "I did not."

Turning back to her painting, she took the time to examine her artwork, noting that the facial features were more similar than she had realized. The man she painted was also blonde. He—

"Oh shit," she said, tilting her head back and laughing.

"Look," Sarnai began, pointing at the large member of painted Ronan—apparently. "She even got the size right."

"All I did was make it massive." Morana was crying now, her body shaking with the laughter she couldn't hold back. Tears were streaming down her cheeks, and she wiped them frantically.

"Exactly," Elivira added, a wide smile on her face. There was paint in her hair, on her face, and covering the apron she wore.

"Matthias is going to shit his pants." Sarnai was picking up the canvas, moving it to where the other paintings were drying. "Plus, they're going to send this to the palace. I'm sure everyone will see it before you even get your hands on it."

"Can't we come and pick it up later?" Morana asked, hiccupping.

"Absolutely not." Elivira was standing with her hands resting on the arms of Morana's chair. "You're a fantastic painter. I think everyone should know about your hidden talent."

Morana slouched in her chair, pouting. "You wouldn't treat your queen so poorly, would you?"

"Oh, I absolutely would." Elivira's grin was sharp.

Sarnai clapped her hands together when she got closer before reaching to help Morana stand. Morana was swaying on her feet, desperately trying to keep herself from tipping over as the alcohol had her head spinning.

"Should we be choosing my dress like this?" she asked, steadying herself by gripping Sarnai's shoulders. "I don't think my judgment is going to be very good."

"Don't worry, I'm perfectly sober." Sarnai flashed a winning smile, winking as she turned to exit the studio.

"Don't listen to a word she says," Elivira whispered, falling into line next to Morana. "If the dress ends up looking horrible, you can just show up to the ball naked."

Morana hid her grin behind her hand. "And match Ronan."

"Precisely."

Twenty-Nine

The dress hadn't arrived at the palace yet, nor did Morana's painting. She was thankful, considering that she couldn't remember either very well. The only thing she knew was that the trip to town had been incredibly fun, and Elivira wasn't as harsh as she let on. With enough glasses of wine, she became the life of the party.

As the ball approached, Morana lived in a constant state of nerves, her gut twisting painfully at the thought of being presented to the entire court, even if the ball was necessary. War had begun, and the troops were moving deeper into Inara's court and preparing to expand their territory to the forest in the east. Eventually, the Court of Shadows would surround the capital and take it for themselves.

"What are you thinking about?" Garian scolded, bringing his sword down in an arc to meet hers. The metal clashed together with a loud clank. Morana's limbs were already shaking.

"That I'm already tired of this, and we've been doing the same thing for hours." Morana nearly fell forward, her stomach flipping when Garian stepped away abruptly and left her sword swinging toward nothing. It nearly put her off balance. *Nearly.*

"We need to work on that," he grunted.

"It *was* better," she defended. "I didn't fall that time. Morana allowed a smug smile to pull at her lips.

Sheathing his sword, Garian ignored her comments. "I had an idea for training today."

Morana rolled her eyes. "You say that every morning, and each morning, I hate you more for it." She sat on the mat. When she leaned back to stare up at the ceiling, she let her limbs sink into the floor. Closing her eyes as she focused on her breathing until it steadied. Everything felt limp, and Morana knew that by morning she would be sore.

The soreness fueled her now. It was a reminder of the work she put in. Something about this training room cleared her mind and helped her feel less useless than before—despite Garian's taunts. A smile split her face.

Garian's footsteps disappeared through the double doors, only to return moments later with the sound of wheels rolling across the solid ground.

Morana sat up, gripping her sword, assuming he was about to surprise her—as he had done in previous training sessions.

Instead, she saw Garian pulling what appeared to be a cage beneath a tarp into the center of the room.

Something thrashed behind the metal bars, but Morana could only make out the clawed feet on the floor of the enclosure. It was about as tall as her, a few inches over five feet.

"What is that?" She was propped up on her elbows with one hand on the hilt of her sword. Her heart was thrashing like the creature in the cage. Whatever idea Garian had for training, she was certain she wouldn't like it. If her muscles felt limp now, by the end of this, they would dissolve away completely. Matthias would have nothing to hold when he returned to his room tonight.

A tragedy, she thought. *Garian will surely be on his shit list after this.*

"One of the beasts we have on loan from Callum. You're going to fight it." Garian squared his stance, and she swore he was smiling.

Oh, Matthias is definitely going to kill him.

"Like hell I am!" Morana stood up abruptly, wiping the sweat from her brow with the short sleeve of her black shirt. "I captured a dream-eater, Garian, you really think I need to fight more beasts?"

"This is different."

"I defeated a harpy in Namid, for fuck's sake!" Morana was panting now, anger rising in her chest. The anger mingled with fear—the same fear that lingered after she had found herself inside the cave two and a half weeks ago. There was no way she would fight whatever lurked in the metal cage of hell Garian dragged in.

"That was an accident." Garian was calm and collected, refusing to react to her outburst. "You're going to fight this creature properly with what we've been working on this week. I don't care how tired you already are. As you know, sometimes you have to fight long after the pain of exhaustion has settled into your bones."

Morana straightened her shoulders, pointing the sword in his direction. "Fuck you," she growled. This was low—even for him.

"Act like a god," he spoke.

That statement shook something within her. He had a point, as much as she hated to admit it. Trying to defeat the beast as tired as she was, would prove that she could make it in this realm. She was stronger than when she first came here, rightfully so. Garian knew what he was doing with training—she hoped.

There was so much more at stake now. With war looming and Raidan's presence lingering but hidden, she knew she needed to be ready for whatever the fae courts threw at her. Raidan had made threats nearly a month ago that he would find her and claim her as his own bride. That should have been enough to spur her on. It was enough to spur her on.

What really motivated her was the knowledge that she was to become queen, and it wasn't something she took lightly. Morana had spent the last few weeks considering what the position meant for her. Though she had spent time in the library preparing as best she could, there were still pieces of her insecurities lingering. Deep in her stomach was the churning fear that she would never be fit for the position. She was too naïve—too stupid to hold that kind of power.

When Matthias presented her officially to the court, she would need to be concerned with how they perceived her—the kind of image she wanted to display. It wasn't one of a weak and unknowing mortal, but a fighter—a warrior. She wanted to be someone that made a difference— someone they would accept.

"Fine," she ground out, swinging her sword in her hand, burning muscles be damned.

"I knew you'd agree." Garian gave a smug smile before peeling away the tarp that covered the cage.

The creature was a winged beast with feathers and bird-like features. The pale blue feathers grew darker around the animal's face. Eyes menacing and frightening. To think that Callum kept creatures like this for *fun*?

It lunged forward, biting the metal bars. The vibrant green eyes of the beast swirled with anger—as if it wanted to rip apart the world.

Morana's heart picked up in pace, her palms sweaty as she tightened her grip on the hilt.

"You want me to fight something that can fly?" she asked. "That's a clear disadvantage. I'm not entirely sure you aren't trying to get rid of me, Garian." Morana attempted to smile at her own joke, but there was no humor in her voice—only the slight trembling of fear as she beheld the creature she would now need to fight.

"Well," Garian began, "I suppose it's time for me to sit back and assess you. Consider this a test." He cleared his throat before moving to the lock hanging from the metal door. "Don't worry," he said, his jaw flinching in the faefire of the training area. "I won't let you bleed too much."

With that, a sharp click of metal sounded, and then the creaking of the door that opened, releasing the beast into the room.

The bird rushed out, spreading its wings wide as it ascended to the ceiling, eyes pinned on Morana and looking down. It had found its prey, and it wouldn't relent until she was bleeding and broken on the mat.

She lifted her sword, assuming a defensive stance when the bird swooped down, its sharp beak aiming directly at her.

Morana's limbs were trembling as she tried to stand her ground, but with each passing second, the descent of the bird grew faster, and fear won out.

Morana dodged away, running to the corner of the room before the beast could tear her arm from her body. This wasn't a fair fight. How was she supposed to defeat a creature flying through the air with only a sword?

"Fantastic," Garian shouted, clapping slowly. "You've shown it you're afraid. You're off to a great start."

"I'm going to go ahead and repeat myself and say fuck you, Garian." Sweat was beading on her forehead and running down her temples. Morana squared her stance and called the shadows forward. She fed them into the sword, the gem on the hilt growing a burgundy red.

With power humming through her veins, Morana watched as the bird came for her again, swooping and pointing its sharp beak right at her.

Morana was desperately trying to find a solution when the bird lowered and struck.

Aimlessly swinging her sword, Morana missed, sending the tip of a sharp claw grazing across her shoulder. She grunted against the pain, gripping the wound as blood gushed between her fingers. She bared her teeth against the pain now searing her flesh.

There was no way she could use her knowledge of sword fighting against the animal. She needed something else—something smarter—something powerful.

Morana's eyes flicked around the room, noting that there was nowhere for her to hide from the animal. There would be no surprising the creature in an attack.

Remembering the way she had challenged Matthias in training, the way she used her shadows to move and avoid him. That had surprised him. They were unmatched in that fight, but she had still outsmarted Death. She could outsmart a bird, too.

Hope suddenly swelled in her chest at the opportunity. Morana called on her power, allowing the shadows to dance and swirl around her. The bird was moving to strike again, but this time, the bird wouldn't know what hit it.

Morana allowed the image of where she wanted to go to appear in her mind, but something else muddied the picture. She could see Garian lying in a pool of blood—feel the way her finger swirled in the liquid. Morana breathed deeply, relishing in the copper scent in the air.

Her shadows twisted and turned around her, combined with the mix of a different power—one she hadn't seen in weeks. The anger was an all-consuming wrath that couldn't be quenched.

Morana felt herself falling from the air, descending just above the feathered creature as they plunged to the ground. She screamed, pushing the shadows into her weapon and driving it through the creature's neck.

It screeched as blood spurted from the wound, and they both landed on the hard floor. Morana tumbled off the creature's back. White mist was coating the floor and feeding the bloodlust that still lingered in her stomach.

Garian's eyes were wide when Morana got up, her sword tightly gripped in her palm. Looking at the lord, she wanted nothing more than to see his blood joined with that of the beast. She ran for him, allowing the addictive power to pull her under.

Would you like to drink of death, Morana?

Death would be sweet, and she would plunge the sword through his gut and harvest the blood from inside him.

Morana was all anger and vicious violence as she shoved the sword toward Garian.

He moved quickly, grabbing his own weapon and blocking the attack before kicking his leg out and sending her sprawling onto her stomach on the mats. Morana could feel the blood trickle from her nose as she spat red, turning to launch herself toward the lord once more.

There was no stopping the white mist rising around her, feeding the new beast rising in her chest. She would *kill* him.

He was on her in an instant—kicking her sword out of her hand and pinning her to the floor. Morana had seen some of Garian's power, but nothing like the shadows surrounding him now. He was growling in her face, pinning her chest to the floor with one forearm and holding her wrists above her head.

Morana thrashed beneath his heavy weight, desperate for blood. She caught a glimpse of her sword on the floor and felt a desperate need to retrieve it.

"Morana, stop!" Garian yelled, his voice booming through the training room. "Morana!" He was screaming now, and something about the urgency in his voice jarred her from whatever senseless haze had taken over her mind.

She could see him then, warm dark eyes begging her to return. She was lost, floating on Raidan's power. Morana's movements slowed.

"I—" she stilled beneath him. Tears threatened to break free, and Morana was left panting. Her body felt numb. "I don't know what that was," she whispered.

Garian's brows furrowed. His warm eyes hardened to ice as he assessed whatever state she was in. If she had hurt him—

Somewhere between the sobs that started wracking her body, and the pained look on her face, Garian decided she was no longer a threat and eased off her.

"It's fine," he grunted, "but we need to tell Matthias." He was standing over her now, his own shadows rippling over his skin. Unlike Matthias's, Garian's shadows had a bluish tint.

Morana nodded, wiping her face with her sleeves while Garian extended a hand to help her up.

Garian didn't say anything. His shoulders were tense, jaw ticking. He stood with his hand resting on the hilt of the sword now sheathed to his side—as if he expected her to snap again at any moment.

Just then, Matthias appeared behind them, his steps sure and steady as he approached.

"What's going on?" he asked. Matthias looked at the creature on the floor, bloody and still. He took in Garian's hardened stare, the streaks on Morana's face, and came closer.

She didn't have words to explain it, so she simply reached with her power to draw him into her mind. Matthias accepted, watching the scene play out from her point of view.

He could feel what she felt, she was certain. He would know the consuming wrath that fed her bloodlust. For the first time, she feared his judgment. This wasn't her; it was something else entirely.

When it was over, he nodded once, unfazed by what had just occurred. She should have known no judgment would come. Not from the god of death.

Morana was looking up at him, taking in the way a strand of dark hair fell across his brow—the crows tattooed on his forearm. She knew there were more birds inked on his skin, moving across his chest as one flew in the light of the moon. She'd come to know his body—his soul, and something about having him in her mind when words weren't enough had her feeling that he knew hers as well.

"We will need to see the oracle," he provided. Garian seemed to agree, but he ran a hand down his face as if the idea caused him anxiety. Morana didn't know what that would mean. She knew very little of the woman Cain and Matthias had mentioned in the past. Still, she knew she couldn't go on—especially if the dream she had become a reality.

She was out of control.

"After the ball," Matthias spoke. "She doesn't take to surprise guests well, but I will send in the request."

Morana stepped forward, wrapping her arms around his waist and breathing in the bergamot and shadow scent that reminded her of Death.

Death was a comfort now—more than just darkness and sorrow. Nothing she threw at him would set him off balance, as if he could see the shadows within her and knew that he was capable of the same evil. There wasn't a soul immune from the evils and dark corners within, but it was only those that refused to acknowledge the shadows, that allowed them to grow and to fester that found themselves transformed into something truly sinister.

Even so, Morana now understood that in the darkest night, one could still see the stars.

Thirty

The sheer black corset led to a glittering skirt that flowed from her figure as Morana stood before the mirror of her bedroom in Ascella.

Pins held her hair up away from her face, matching the familiar crown sitting atop her head. She ran her hands over the skirt, gray eyes wide as she took in the image of herself. She didn't feel like a mortal. In fact, she felt more like a queen. The reality of what she was doing crashed into her, nearly knocking her over and sending her heart galloping in her chest.

The door creaked as it opened, and her head whipped to the side to watch Ronan strut into the room. He was carrying something wrapped in a large, plain cloth.

Matthias followed quickly behind him; a scowl etched into his features. He tightened his fists already clenched at his sides.

"Would you like to explain something?" Matthias asked, his tone bitter. Both he and Ronan halted at the entrance, eyes skimming over her.

Morana was wringing her hands and unable to make eye contact with the two men in the room. "Explain what?" she asked. She was a vessel filled with nerves and uncertainty. There was no room for any other emotion, and she struggled to deduce what Matthias was scowling about.

When her eyes met the onyx gaze of Death, he shook off whatever trance briefly held him, and his face returned to that same scowl. "Explain why *this* was delivered to the castle."

Ronan was smiling now, removing the cloth and revealing the canvas painting that looked, oddly enough, like a naked depiction of the lord. There was pride and humor in his face.

The appearance of her painting allowed the nerves to wash away—if only for a moment. Morana fought her smile. "That," she said, "was an accident."

Matthias's scowl deepened; his shoulders stiff in the suit he wore.

Ronan flashed a wicked grin, turning the painting to get a better look at it. "I don't know, Matthias. I think she really captured me well. Especially here." He pointed just below the center of the painting. "This part, where you can see by sheer size alone—"

Matthias held up a hand and walked around Ronan gawking at the artwork. "Stop talking while you're ahead." He stood in front of Morana, grimacing. "You painted Ronan." Matthias winced before adding the last detail—the true problem. "*Naked?*"

His obvious jealousy gave her an immense feeling of satisfaction. Even so, she rolled her eyes despite her inability to mask the embarrassment washing over her, making her entire body feel hot. She didn't know how Ronan got hold of the painting first. It probably had something to do with Sarnai.

The original plan was to intercept the artwork, but that clearly didn't work. She hadn't received any notification that it had arrived. Willow was supposed to watch for it, and knowing the fae woman's friendship with the flora goddess—

Morana's cheeks were warm, and she was certain pink colored her skin. She licked her lips, trying to feign indifference. "It *was* an accident," she supplied. "I was drunk, and the instructor said to be free with our work." She gestured to nothing in particular as she defended herself. "I was making it up as I went. It's not my fault we were positively wasted."

"Instructor?" Ronan asked, his entire demeanor perking up—something she didn't know was even possible. He set the painting down and nearly skipped closer. She was certain his ego grew by the second. Maybe he would hang her work in his home in Adhara. It would look nice— beneath the coastal stars.

Morana smirked.

"You mean to tell me," Ronan began. "There was an entire *class* dedicated to painting naked depictions of me, Morana?" His eyes narrowed without losing the humor sparkling in them. "And I wasn't even invited?" He leaned forward a bit to punctuate the last statement. "I thought we were friends."

Matthias cleared his throat. "You didn't think for a moment that you should have given your—" He gestured to the canvas that was now resting against the wall. "Your subject, *black* hair?"

"Actually." Morana tapped her chin, one corner of her mouth pulling up. "I believe the man the instructor painted had black hair."

Matthias threw his hands up, exasperated. He was pacing, practically creating a ditch in the bedroom floor. Something about his brooding had heat twisting in her belly. Where the embarrassment was subsiding, her satisfaction wasn't. He *was* jealous.

Matthias walked toward her, placing both hands on either side of her face. She was fighting the urge to laugh at his frustration—the dramatics of it.

Placing a bruising kiss on her lips, Matthias startled her, swallowing her gasp. It was fast, lasting only a moment before he pulled back inches from her face. "I didn't realize I would have to work so hard," he spoke low.

Ronan resumed admiring her artwork. Maybe she would give it to him as a gift for the winter solstice. It was an important holiday to the fae, and with the way Ronan couldn't look away from the piece, she figured it would be exactly what he wanted.

Her eyes flicked back to Matthias. One corner of his mouth was turned up, his eyes darkening as he leaned forward. "Tonight is going to be very, *very* long after the ball," he whispered.

Morana's breath caught, her lips parting and heat washing over her. She would be happy to paint all the lords if he continued making threats. Maybe she would even paint him.

Her shadows reached into his mind easily—as if it were natural. *Would you like me to paint you, Matthias?*

His smile told her he was considering it.

She spoke again. *I'd be happy to embellish your size. If that would make you feel more important than Ronan.*

Matthias's smile never wavered. *You wicked, wicked woman.* His words echoed louder than her thoughts. *There would be no need for embellishment. I'm sure you could have guessed that already. If not, I'd be happy to show you again.*

Matthias's eyes were devious as he trailed them over the swell of her breasts. She could almost feel his stare across her skin.

"You know," Ronan cut in from the other end of the room. "If you tire of the brooding death god—"

Matthias practically growled—cutting him off briefly. Ronan didn't react. It was as if he were used to Matthias's outbursts. Maybe he got off on the taunting. It certainly appeared that way as the lord barreled on.

"I was just going to suggest that you gaze longingly at your artwork and simply *imagine* someone else was warming your bed." Ronan was nearly laughing and still smiling as his blue eyes glittered in the light. "I, on the other hand, will be spending the night very much alone because, for the first time in my long life, a woman has decided she *doesn't* want to sleep with me." His humorous expression was gone.

Morana gave Matthias a pointed look. "See—"

"Not you," Ronan corrected, and Morana frowned. "The blacksmith."

"Of course." Matthias didn't even seem surprised by the news when he turned around, pinching the bridge of his nose before gesturing to the lord. "You have been chasing after Reese. I gave you one job, Ronan. Can't you keep your cock in your pants?"

"Well, as you can see from your future wife's depiction, it's very difficult to restrain something so massive."

Morana was really laughing now, trying to fight the tears that threatened to leak out and ruin the kohl lining her eyes. It really was comical. She considered hanging the painting in random places around the palace just to toy with Death.

Matthias leaned in when she settled, kissing her temple before brushing his lips against her ear. "Tonight," he promised, and she was instantly hot—much too hot for the room they were in as she ran her hands down the skirt of her dress.

Death stepped back and by the look on his face, he was still thinking of his wicked promises.

"Is it time yet?" she asked. The nerves returned, but they were no longer consuming.

"Actually," Matthias began, "I was just coming to get you before I ran into Ronan laughing with a few staff members in the palace. We are expected to make our appearance momentarily."

Morana swallowed. Her hands trembled at the idea of being presented to the court as their future queen. Did she know enough about the fae to appear capable? Those nerves coasted through her veins. Nobody had seemed worried that they wouldn't accept her.

Matthias had been preparing her during the past few weeks, letting her know that she shouldn't stress about the ball. He would announce her as his future bride in the beginning. She would be expected to talk to members of the court, but he promised that after the initial introductions, she was welcome to enjoy herself—drinking all the faerie wine she wanted. That eased her worries then, but there was still the nagging truth in the back of her mind. The reminder of where faerie wine led her during Mabon. She wouldn't be so foolish.

The staff had prepared the ballroom, and Morana had hardly set foot in the space. When she had gone in this morning, she saw that the massive room was littered with crystal chandeliers hanging from the ceiling and deep red roses mixed with ferns and other greenery used as floral decorations.

Matthias shadowed her to the doorway, and she worked to take a deep breath, preparing to meet the court she would rule—formally. Would they welcome a bitch queen?

Standing atop the stairs, Matthias gently squeezed her arm as he tucked it gently into his own. The doors opened, and the crown on her head instantly felt heavy. Nothing weighed her down more than the sinking feeling in her stomach when the entire ballroom halted, turning to stare at their arrival.

All was silent as they descended the large golden staircase, guests pausing in their conversation, their drinking, and their dancing to gaze at the face of their soon-to-be queen.

"Maybe I'm not fit to do this," she whispered, so low only Matthias could hear her.

He leaned in, his breath ruffling the strands around her ear. "You're far more capable than you believe, Morana."

Maybe she could believe that. Maybe after everything she had been through—she deserved something good. An entire court was far beyond what she believed she had earned, though. Shadows rippled beneath her skin and steadied her as they stopped on the last step. She felt Matthias's power reach out to her—invading her mind seamlessly. His voice was all around her. *You're the most stunning being in this room. Lady Death, herself.*

Her heart was like a drum, beating loudly in her ears and pounding against her sternum. Morana licked her lips, raising her eyes to look out at the crowd. She spotted Garian in the mix, and something in her shattered at the memory of what happened weeks ago. A woman clung to his arm, her long, white hair braided and descending her back against the deep navy dress she wore. Golden rings adorned her fingers, and her brown skin glowed, the golden highlight on her cheekbones catching the light. It was then that Morana looked to Garian, who was smiling at the woman as if she held his entire world in the palm of her hand.

Is that his wife? Morana asked into Matthias's mind.

The one and only.

Morana kept her eyes on the couple, the easy way they interacted, leaning toward one another as if nobody else existed. It grounded her—showed her possibilities she hadn't dared hope for herself. The comfort they felt with one another was one she had experienced in the past months. This place truly was *home.*

Matthias's voice boomed through the ballroom, announcing her introduction. "May I present my future wife, Miss Morana, future queen of the Court of Shadows?"

Her heart was in her throat while silence hung in the air. The entire room held their breath, but none as much as Morana. She was waiting to see what the unfamiliar faces would do. Her eyes flicked back to Garian and his wife, drawing comfort from the way they were now smiling at her, eyes flicking between her and Death.

Applause erupted in the room, and just like that, it was over. Fae guests returned to drinking their wine, and the stringed instruments started up again from a balcony overhead. There were, however, a few fae making their way through the crowd to introduce themselves.

A man came up to them, bowing before Matthias, and turning to bow before Morana, too. She almost told him it was unnecessary, but Matthias had warned her against such actions. If she was to be queen, she needed to act as queen.

The fae man's pale skin stretched over sharp features, his brown hair hanging to his thin shoulders, and when he spoke, he had a slight stutter. "It's a pleasure to make—to make your acquaintance." He bowed again, and Morana could feel her gut churning with discomfort. Something about his presence unsettled her.

Matthias introduced them. "Morana, this is Jameson. He owns the grand library in Nashira." Matthias raised a brow before turning to look back at Jameson.

"Yes, yes. It's incredibly beautiful. We would be pleased to have you visit." He was nodding profusely, desperate to gain her approval.

Morana contemplated what Sarnai had said. It would be of no use to lie or pretend to be anything other than what she was. In fact, if she were a meek woman, willing to bow to anyone in order to save face, she wasn't sure she would have the crown on her head to begin with.

"I've heard about it," she said, thinking back to what Matthias had told her about his parent's tomb. She didn't know if Jameson knew about that, so she played it safe. "I would be eager to explore what the library has to offer."

Jameson gave Matthias a nervous look, to which Matthias nodded his approval. "Ah, you speak of below the libraries, I take it. I tend to that—" He paused, looking for the right word. "Area as well."

Morana didn't have time to respond before Matthias was mumbling his apologies and dragging her through the crowd. Fae parted for them, leaving a pathway to the dance floor.

A server carrying a gilded tray moved past them, and Matthias picked up a glass of wine. He took a sip before handing it to her to take the rest. His shadows trailed over her as he spoke. *The glass is for you. I only took a sip, so you will think of my lips each time you take a drink.*

"Are you trying to get me drunk, Matthias?" she asked, taking a sip of the delicious liquid. She did, in fact, picture his lips as she did. She imagined them trailing down her neck, along her collarbone—lower. The wine and desire warmed her belly.

Matthias stopped in the center of the dance floor just as the previous song ended. He pulled her close, pressing her body flush against his as she held her wine out to keep it from spilling. Her breath caught in her throat when his face came just inches from her own. His dark eyes were burning with something she couldn't decipher. "No," he finally answered. "I'm trying to get you to dance."

Morana didn't break his gaze. She pulled the glass to her lips, parting them and tilting her head back to drink the entire serving. Matthias watched, his eyes darkening as they lingered on her throat while she swallowed.

When she was done, he took the glass from her hand and placed it on an empty tray passing by them. The music started again, slower this time, and Matthias made a point of holding her to him. She could feel his steady breathing and smell the wine he had drunk, too.

Matthias leaned in, whispering in her ear in a way that sent shivers down her spine. "The last time you attended a fae party, you danced with Ronan."

Morana recalled Mabon and the way Ronan had paraded her around the dance floor in her drunken haze. She remembered giggling and smiling, blissfully unaware of where the night would lead her.

"Is that why the painting made you so jealous?" she taunted.

"No," he chuckled. "This time—" Matthias's voice was dark and laced with promises. "I plan to show you how much better I am at dancing until the memory of him fades so thoroughly, you could never accidentally paint him again." A smile tugged at her lips as he continued. "Then, when we are done, we can see our way out, and I can make you forget about that ridiculous painting, too."

The wine was already working its way through her system, making the world seem inexplicably brighter. Morana felt slickness between her thighs at his words—his closeness—the promise of where they would go following this dance.

One corner of her mouth turned up, and she stretched up to brush her lips right beneath his ear before whispering, "It may be difficult to forget the painting. You're going to have to work a very, *very* long time."

His grip tightened just before he started spinning her around the dance floor. It didn't take long for Morana to lose herself in the crowd.

Thirty-One

Darkness surrounded them as Morana found herself in the crisp night air on the balcony just outside of Matthias's room. After spinning her around the dance floor, Matthias escorted her to a forgotten hallway and promptly used his magic to disappear.

Her back hit the wall—body flushed—as Matthias pressed into her, crushing his lips against hers. He kissed her as if starved, and everything about his urgency had her entire body ignited with awareness.

Matthias lifted her dress, and Morana let out a guttural sound when he pressed his thigh between her legs and tightened his grip on her hips.

"Thinking about that painting?" Matthias asked, dragging her hips forward, so she was grinding against his leg. The motion had pleasure shooting through her.

She tilted her head back and to the side as Matthias's lips trailed down her neck. He bit her flesh, leaving her breathless before his tongue swirled, and he sucked gently at the stinging skin. She couldn't get enough of him—enough of Death.

"If I say yes—" She was panting now. "What would you do then, Matthias?"

He pulled back; the shadows swirling around her as the stars peeked through the wispy clouds above. His smile was as wicked as the dark look in his eyes. Matthias's hair was mussed from all the places she had just dragged her hands through it.

Without warning, his power touched her, sending ripples of pleasure across her skin. Morana threw her head back against the stone wall. He pulled her forward again, providing delicious friction as he dragged her against his leg again—again.

Matthias pulled the cup of her corset down beneath her breast and lowered his head to flick his tongue across her nipple. The shadows were trailing down her torso, lower—lower. She could feel the power as if it were his touch circling just where she needed him. Her head hung forward, resting against his shoulder. "You have to stop. It's too much."

"Really?" he asked. She knew then that he would— if she asked him, but the groan gave her away. She felt hot— out of control.

"No," she said, pleasure building at her core. "No, not really. Keep going"

Matthias's chest rumbled with the sound he released. She felt the vibrations of the noise against her, feeding her desire more. He trailed soft kisses over her collarbone, along her jawline, over her lips. When their tongues met, she could only think of fire—burning hot and consuming.

"The painting," he whispered, his own voice shaking. "Forgotten?"

The honest answer was yes, but Morana knew that the lie would do—how he would respond. "Actually, I am thinking of it more now—"

Matthias pulled his leg from between hers, the sudden movement cutting off her words. She could feel the dampness there. He spun her around, placing her hands on the wall and lifting her skirt. She could hear his harsh breaths in her ear—feel them. The sound of his zipper had her arching and desperate for contact.

Matthias leaned forward, kissing her gently on the shoulder. The motion was in direct contrast with the hungry way he had moved before, and she could feel him at her entrance. She pushed back, chasing the fullness of him, but he moved too quickly.

"Not a chance," he whispered. She could feel his smile, feel his chest pressed against her, as her fingers clawed the smooth stone of the palace wall.

"What the hell, Matthias?" Shadows whispered down her arms, over her neck, sending sparks across her skin.

"I said, not a chance." His hand migrated down, trailing over the swell of her ass. "Beg." His tone was commanding, sending a shiver down her spine.

Her breath was ragged, chest rising rapidly as his magic still twisted over her flesh. She glanced back over her shoulder, smiling. Reaching for her own magic, she sent it trailing over Death, moving downward until her magic was stroking him. His lips parted—face taut as he pressed forward, the tip of him touching her entrance again. "I could never beg a god for anything."

He groaned, hands tightening on her waist as she bent over more, offering herself up to him.

He was just as out of control as she was—slowly losing his mind as he leaned into the touch of her magic. "And why—*fuck*—why is that?"

She stroked him again, relishing in how unhinged he was becoming. She wasn't even touching him—not really. "Because," she whispered, still out of breath. Morana was thinking of how much she had grown over the past months, the things she had endured. Garian had challenged her, scolded her for her weakness—and even as a mortal, it all had to count for something. "I am one."

Matthias grunted when her magic released him, and he slammed into her, stretching and filling her until her mind was dizzy with pleasure. His hand wrapped around beneath her skirts, and he slid his palm against her, setting a punishing pace.

The night air was filled with slick sounds and harsh breaths as Matthias wrung every bit of pleasure from her body. She was climbing, working toward a release she had never experienced before. Matthias used his magic to brush against her nipples, his palm still rubbing, his body still moving relentlessly.

She gasped—breathed his name on a moan before her release crashed over her. Morana was still coming down when his thrusts turned frantic. Sweat was beading on his brow, a dark strand of hair across his forehead as he moved again, groaning and filling her until she couldn't think past what he had done to her—what she had now done to him.

"I suppose we should go back to the ball," she breathed. He was still seated inside her, holding her and kissing her neck. The sensation was enough to have her arching again.

"We should," he said, his voice low. "We've been incredibly rude."

He pulled out, lowering her skirt and straightening it out before fixing his own clothes. Matthias reached a hand up, tucking a loose strand of hair behind her ear.

"I was thinking," she said, her body limp after what they had done. "The ball—Isn't it a bit insensitive with the court at war?"

Matthias tilted his head. His eyes were bright beneath the starlight—pleased and drunk on pleasure. "You would wish for sadness to eclipse everything else?" he asked, trailing a knuckle over the scars on her cheeks. "Can't both sadness and immense joy exist together?"

She was staring at him, searching his eyes for a sliver of doubt at the words he spoke. Morana knew they could. She was experiencing it now. There was sadness twisting in her at the injustice of what Inara had done—the strange way Cain's face became hardened whenever someone mentioned the goddess of life. Then there was this moment—the ball and life with Matthias. A home that filled her with joy and continued to challenge everything she believed about the world prior to being taken to the land of the gods—everything she believed about herself.

"I suppose so," she whispered, offering a wan smile.

Matthias kissed her once, allowing the darkness to swirl around them, returning them to the party to celebrate what was to come.

The new queen of the Court of Shadows.

Thirty-Two

It was as if they had never left. Hundreds of fae gathered in the ballroom, dressed in elaborate clothing, and dancing to the music that continued floating over the dark floors. Faefire flickered in the large crystal chandeliers hanging from the ceiling, casting shadows as the court spun and laughed, drinking until their hearts were content.

Matthias had gone to converse with some court members while Morana desperately tried to hide how flushed her cheeks were. If Sarnai found her, she would never hear the end of it. The goddess would push until Morana gave up the details of what happened.

"I know that look." An unfamiliar voice greeted her, and Morana spun around to find herself face to face with Garian's wife. Garian stood right beside her, smiling in a way Morana hadn't seen before. He was more relaxed—less rigid with his wife around.

"It's so nice to meet you." Morana gripped her wineglass in one hand and reached out to introduce herself to Garian's other half.

Garian intervened. "Zara, this is Matthias's future wife, Morana."

"Please, Garian. I'm not daft." Zara smiled brightly. Her warm hands were gentle, just like the wide grin splitting the fae woman's face. "It's nice to finally meet you."

"Likewise." Morana took a sip of wine, looking between the two fae, unsure of how to continue the conversation.

"I take it you stepped out for a moment?" Zara began. "What a wonderful idea." She raised a brow, causing Morana's cheeks to flame.

The wine burned on its way down her throat. Crystal chandeliers still decorated the room in soft light as sounds of the crowd carried across the floors. The dancefloor was still full, as if the fae were merely getting started. *Creatures of the night.* It only seemed fitting in a Court of Shadows.

"I didn't mean to embarrass you," Zara added, her tone apologetic. "I'm glad Matthias is marrying someone." Her eyes trailed across the room and Morana followed her gaze to where Matthias stood, his suit neatly in place as if they hadn't just spent the last forty minutes clawing at one another and moaning atop the balcony outside of his room on the other end of the castle. She was certain guards heard them, though she hadn't thought about it at the time. His eyes fixed on Morana, still heated despite what they had already done.

"He's clearly in love with you."

Morana's head whipped around, snapping toward Garian's wife. "What did you say?"

Garian chuckled; his lips pressed tightly together. He wasn't denying it—wasn't saying anything. Morana's brow creased.

"The way he looks at you," she began. "It's so very clear how he feels. You must know. You'd have to be blind to miss it." She leaned into Garian, if only for a moment. "In all my years, I've never seen Matthias look at someone the way he looks at you."

Morana cleared her throat, looking down into the red wine in her cup. "Of course," she whispered, though she wasn't sure what to make of the woman's comments. While their engagement was real, while he admitted to caring for her—love was hardly a word spoken between them.

Love. She couldn't get the word out of her head. She experienced very little of it in her lifetime. What was *love?* Looking at Garian and his wife, she thought she had an idea.

"Well," Zara began. "We may go out to the gardens." She had a devious look in her eye—something that told Morana exactly what the woman planned to do with her husband. "Theo is staying with a friend in the court. We don't get out often."

Morana simply nodded, and Garian leaned in as his wife walked away. "What have I said before?" He cocked an eyebrow, daring her to deny it. "My wife would disagree with you. I'm not a prude at all, Morana."

"No," she said. "You're clearly enamored."

His smile was wide, splitting his face and flashing white teeth. "I wouldn't have it any other way."

With that, Garian trailed behind his wife, leaving Morana to her thoughts.

Just beyond where the couple was walking, Reese stood with a strange man next to her. Her brown hair was pulled into a long braid over her shoulder, woven with golden threads and what appeared to be sparkling diamonds sprinkled through the thick plait. Morana had seen her dressed in her work clothes so often that the sight of the woman wearing an elaborate pine-colored dress took her by surprise.

The crowd parted as Morana moved, stopping just before the blacksmith. The man next to her offered Reese a drink. His blonde hair was neatly styled and cut short.

Staring at the man for a moment, Morana turned to Reese. She could feel the wine making her head dizzy, and she suspected that was the reason why the next statement flew out of her mouth unbidden. Very little thought preceded it, and she regretted it as soon as it barreled past her lips.

"Why aren't you here with Ronan?" Morana asked.

The statement jarred the blacksmith, causing her to stumble over words and stutter while trying to explain why she was here with the man at her side. Her eyes whipped back and forth between her date and Morana's confident presence.

Morana took another sip, leaning in to encourage a response. Ronan had been so intensely interested in her, so concerned with doing the right thing and refraining from ruining any chance of a relationship he had. When Morana had emerged during their training session, she had been so sure of Reese's feelings towards the lord. The way she blushed and watched as he sparred against Garian—it all made very little sense.

"I—well—I mean—" Reese looked to the man. "Could you get me a glass of wine?" she asked, smiling as if there was nothing strange about that figure being anyone but the lord of Adhara.

"I just did. Your glass is full." He was clearly confused—and offended. Morana couldn't bring herself to care. The alcohol had her shoulders loosened and her mind was pleasantly empty from all that loomed over the court.

She wasn't thinking of war, Inara, Raidan, or the attack on Namid. She was only thinking of her friend. That's what these once strangers were now—friends.

Reese tilted her head back, guzzling the wine and firmly placing it into the man's hand. "Another." She softened it by looking up at him through her lashes. "Please," she added.

When he walked away, she turned to Morana, face flaming with anger. Her freckles scrunched as her face twisted in wrath. "What do you mean?" she spat. Her tone was nothing like what Morana had heard from the blacksmith before. She was all steel forged by the hottest flame. "You're the one that informed me of his sexual escapades. Of course, I didn't ask him on a date. I haven't thought of him a moment since."

Morana swallowed, realizing what the blacksmith was talking about. "He's slept with a lot of people."

"I know that," Reese ground out.

"I wasn't done," Morana interrupted. "He likes you. This is different."

"And you've known him for how long?" Reese questioned, bitterness seeping into her tone.

"Alcohol makes you mean," Morana commented, taking another sip of her own drink.

"And it also makes you loose-lipped around my date." Her voice rose an octave and nearly cracked on the last word. It was then that Morana noticed the tears gathering at the corners of her eyes.

"I'm sorry, I didn't realize how much you—" Morana fought for words. Guilt poured over her like thick honey, making it difficult to choose a direction. Her mind was still struggling to work properly against the faerie wine. "I didn't realize you cared so much for—"

"I don't." Reese wiped one tear away quickly, gathering herself before more could spill on the ground. "I wanted it to be Ronan." Her voice was nearly a whisper.

Morana's heart cracked in her chest. She had unwittingly done this, and she had every intention of fixing it. Her shadows swirled around her ankles before she reached her power out to Matthias so she could speak with him from across the room. *Send Ronan this way.*

Am I allowed to ask you why? When Morana looked over, Matthias was staring at her, clearly understanding that she was up to something.

You dare question a queen?

Of course not. You're with Reese. He may actually run in your direction.

Just like that, Ronan was parting the crowd and taking hurried steps until he stood next to Morana. His navy suit and white shirt complimented the broad expanse of his chest and shoulders. He had his hair neatly tied back in a bun. When he appeared, his blue eyes were stuck on Reese, as if he was unable to see anyone else in the room.

The date returned with a glass of wine in hand. Morana promptly took it from him, making a show of drinking it. "I am—so drunk," she said. "I can't even move my feet properly." She downed the rest of the glass, and by the time her mind caught up to her, she wasn't sure how much of what she said was a lie. "Will you dance with Ronan for me, Reese? I was so pleased by the sword you crafted, by the way. Anyway, I promised Ronan a dance, but I simply—" She leaned over, pretending to lose her balance and gripping Reese's current date on the arm tightly. He was wearing a scowl, and Morana really didn't care. This was her mistake to fix. This man could go sulk in the courtyard. She had very few fucks to give.

"I—" Reese was looking back and forth between the two men, clearly torn by the decision.

"It would be my honor, darling." Ronan held out a hand, and Reese hesitantly took it.

When they walked off onto the dancefloor, Morana adjusted the crown on her head before turning to the man. She caught Willow standing by a table with intricately displayed pastries, waiting for whatever duty called next. The fae woman certainly deserved to have a good time, too. And unfortunately for this stranger, his date was rather preoccupied.

Pointing at Willow, Morana leaned in to speak, as if she were sharing a deep secret. "That woman over there works for Matthias." She cleared her throat. "Well, more for me if you really get down to it. Anyway, she's talked about you non-stop since your arrival. With your date busy dancing, you should—"

"Ah," he said. "You're playing matchmaker, Queen of Darkness."

Morana looked to him; her eyes wide as his words broke through the alcohol circulating through her blood. "What did you say?" she asked. The room was spinning and barely able to provide enough oxygen for her to breathe.

"That is what you are," he mentioned, nodding once.

Morana watched as light flickered over his shoulders—a preview of the power this man held. She sucked in a breath, fear climbing up her throat and threatening to choke her like a weed consuming a flowerbed.

"I'll ask her," he spoke, keeping his eyes forward and walking away.

Morana couldn't catch her breath. The entire room was closing in, and her ears were ringing. She placed her wineglass on a passing tray and walked through the crowd, holding her skirts in one hand. When she exited out of one of the doors of the ballroom, she found herself in a hallway of the palace. Black floors and the empty space helped her steady herself—though not as much as the decorative table she was now gripping so hard her knuckles turned white.

"Queen of Darkness," a hushed voice danced in the air, and Morana turned to see a fox standing in the room.

She straightened, feeling the dagger strapped to her thigh under her skirt. "What do you want?"

"You need to leave."

"In the middle of my engagement party?" Morana straightened herself, lifting her chin in challenge. "What a ridiculous piece of advice. How many times do I need to tell you, Conan? I have nothing to offer you."

He prowled forward like a beast stalking its prey. His sharp features were highlighted by the dim faefire in the sconces lining the walls. "You once made me believe you were insignificant." He laughed. "Now look at you." He raised a brow. "Becoming queen."

"I am not going to Ohriid." Her tone was firm. "Whatever creatures you spoke of were most likely the same as the ones found in the Vulcan. Go capture a dream-eater and leave me alone."

"A dream-eater?" he questioned. "What have *you* been up to, Queen of Darkness?"

"Stop calling me that." She could taste the bitterness of her tone on her tongue. Her mind was still swimming with wine, making it harder to concentrate. "I'm not *leaving.*"

He took a step forward, causing her to rear back when his hand lifted. He dropped it quickly. "You don't understand." Something in his voice changed. It was pleading now, and Morana questioned the look in his eyes. He was still a fox, but what side was he playing? "You have to leave."

"What do you know?" she asked, her mind sobering slightly as he continued to stare at her. He was warning her of something. Whatever it was, it couldn't be good. Nothing good ever happened at these celebrations.

Silence hung in the air, thick and stagnant. Even the sounds of the ball had faded. His golden eyes were unmoving, lips pressed together in a firm line.

Somewhere amid their staring contest, a sound drew Morana away from the conversation. The scream set off a series of horrid sounds from inside the ballroom.

Maybe he wasn't here to help. He was here to destroy. Anger burned hot as she shoved past the fox.

"You fucking piece of shit," Morana snarled.

Her heart was racing as she lifted her skirt and drew her dagger, running through the doors she had just come from.

Thirty-Three

Chaos.

It assaulted her senses the second Morana moved into the ballroom. Sharp glass littered the floor by the broken windows along the far wall. Harpies flew in from the windows, sending fae scattering across the floor. The creatures moved so quickly that many of the attendees didn't have time to draw on their powers.

White mist coated the floors, followed by Veeden seeping into the room through the broken windows. The Veeden called out, controlling fae that now stood held in a trance—called to their deaths.

Death.

Morana looked for Matthias in the crowd, following the swell of intense dark power as a harpy crashed to the floor. She could feel the vibrations beneath her feet, sweat already beading on her brow as she gripped the dagger tighter. Matthias was snarling, lunging forward to drive his sword through the harpy's neck. The creature thrashed on the ground, sending a table flying across the room before it finally stilled—succumbing to Matthias's blade.

Morana felt a rush of wind at her back and heard the ghostly voice behind her.

Queen of Darkness.

When she turned, she saw the image of a Veeden prowling toward her, its skin like cracked earth. The creature's hair covered its bare breasts as it slowly stalked through the room, throwing its song into the crackling air.

Morana could feel the pull of magic wash over her. Her lips parted, her hand loosening on the dagger. When the Veeden stood mere feet away, she wanted nothing more than to be taken by the beast—consumed entirely.

A flash of metal broke the trance when Ronan slashed his sword across the Veeden's neck, sending its head rolling on the ground. It was then that Morana saw it.

Blood.

So much blood surrounded her. There were pools of it beneath bodies taken by harpies after the Veeden overpowered them. Bile rose in her throat, and Morana fought the urge to vomit while the sounds of metal and the scent of copper drove her to the brink of madness.

With the creatures attacking fae guests, soldiers wearing yellow armor poured in from the windows, followed by even more beasts. Their swords were coated in light and fog as they cut down men and women, dressed for a ball as opposed to battle.

Sickness churned in her stomach, and she called on the training she had completed with Garian. Lunging for the nearest soldier, Morana channeled her wrath and pushed her magic into the blade clutched in her hand. Ronan had disappeared, leaving Morana enraged as she drove the dagger through an unsuspecting soldier's back. She used her magic to intensify the feeling. Her blade had barely pierced the fae man's flesh, but he screamed in agony, falling to his knees and opening an opportunity for Morana to do actual damage.

She screamed, driving the weapon down in a perfect arc and connecting the metal with tissue. She could feel flesh breaking apart as her dagger pushed into the fae soldier's neck. Blood gushed from the wound, and Morana quickly gathered herself before moving deeper into battle.

A harpy came after her so fast she didn't have time to think. Morana moved her way through the dead corpses on the ground and ended up in the hallway before she thought through her plan of attack. The shadows encased her while she pictured the harpies back. She had done something similar in the training room just weeks ago. She could do it again.

In a flash, she was on the creature and driving the dagger through its skull while grunting with the force she used. Morana could feel the shadows dancing over her skin, mixing with the rising white mist that now floated over her as well. The power was addictive—heady. She couldn't get enough. If she needed to cut down every last soldier infiltrating the palace, she would—even if she had to do it alone.

Her heart nearly stopped when black boots clicked on the obsidian floors of the palace. They echoed louder than the sounds of screaming fae and beasts in the other room. Deafening and familiar. Morana turned.

Emerging from the fog was the towering form of the major god who attacked her in her apartment. Raidan's gaze was delighted, and he stopped a few yards in front of her, inhaling as if he enjoyed the stench of battle and blood. His head tilted back, and he moaned, drinking in the death just a wall away.

Morana couldn't keep her heart from thrashing against her ribcage. Her breath was shallow, shoulders painfully tense as she held her weapon and the shadows close. He was here to collect—she knew it.

The god's game was never-ending. He would keep returning until he either had what he came for or lay dead on the ground.

"I've come to claim what is mine," Raidan spoke— his voice making her skin crawl.

"What the fuck is that supposed to mean?" Everything about the god made her stomach churn, but despite those feelings, something like anger rose within her. The anger was different, mimicking the bloodlust she had felt before, and that part scared her the most. The anger had no direction, though she knew through the fog veiling her mind it should have been directed toward him.

"I told you," he chided. "I planned to take you as my bride, and I'm here to collect."

Morana's lip peeled back, sweat rolling down her spine. She allowed the anger to carry her, knowing exactly where it needed to go. Fighting the haze, she screamed. "Go to hell!"

"My pet," Raidan began. He was speaking as if she were a naïve child. "I designed its very depths. You think I haven't been there? You think I don't enjoy it?"

Everything inside her wanted to lash out. She wanted to lunge for him and drive her dagger across his throat, relishing in the way it would tear through his flesh as his blood coated the floor at their feet, dyeing it crimson. She hungered for that kind of release. His power stretched out to her before she could move, holding her to her spot.

"And what makes you think I'll agree to go with you?" she asked, raising her chin. Fear crawled up her spine as his magic wound around her ankles. Her stomach bottomed out, but she refused to let the god know what was going on within her.

"You honestly think I need you to agree?" he scoffed. There was evil in his eyes, something that spoke of a man who was not used to being told no. "I don't. I must ask, though, why are you so hesitant? Can't you feel me inside you, Morana?"

There was no moving beyond his power. Morana's hands trembled at her sides, shaking with the wrath that was building steadily in her chest and begging to be released. That white fog moved upward, and she pressed her mouth firmly together as it tried to snake its way down her throat. She could feel it in her nostrils, feel the anger and senseless desire for complete control invading her body. Raidan was inside her—manipulating her, and as he continued to shove his power into her—around her, she found she was hating him less and less.

"Is it Death?" he asked. "Is he the reason you still refuse?" A pitying look crossed Raidan's face. "He didn't tell you, did he?"

"Tell me what?" she ground out when she was sure magic wouldn't choke her.

"About his visit to the oracle, and who was there working for her?"

"He told me." The words leaked out through clenched teeth. Matthias had told her about the oracle—confessed he hadn't been completely honest with her. In the moment, she saw the conversation as him coming clean, trusting her in a way he hadn't before, but now with Raidan's power pulsing through her veins, something about it clouded her vision. He had withheld information from her. Anger churned like a stormy sea, threatening to pull her like a broken ship, sinking to the blackest depths.

The conversation played in her mind.

I haven't been completely honest.

She could see him with painful clarity, hear Matthias's voice in her head. In his tone was nothing of the comfort she knew. It enraged her, especially as one line began playing on repeat in her head.

Why are you telling me this?
There was someone else there—

Raidan's head tilted to the side—questioning. "So, he told you that your mother was there, yet you still choose him? You're still fighting what I have to offer you?"

Everything stopped.

Morana couldn't register anything in the room, aside from the beating of her own heart. Its slow thumping echoed louder. Her eyes were wide, staring at the demon who had come to take her away. Her body felt bloodless, limp.

"That's not true," she whispered.

There was someone else there—

"Morana." Raidan stepped forward, placing a large hand on her cheek. His white hair hung loose around his shoulders, amber eyes burning with something she couldn't identify. "You are a political pawn to him. A wise decision and reason to start the war he has been wanting since the death of his parents."

Not true, not true, not true.

She didn't know if she was thinking the words or saying them aloud, but Raidan skimmed a thumb over the scars on her face—the reminders of the death she had dealt. Hames's comments, Elivira's explanation of the war while they were near Namid, all of it came crashing into her. Even her own doubts had tried to warn her.

I never claimed to be good.

Matthias himself had warned her.

"You know nothing about me," he chuckled. "I'm the god of death, Morana." His face fell as the mirth disappeared from his features. He narrowed his eyes at her. "There's nothing I wouldn't do."

"Think for a moment, Morana. Inara rose to power—a fae turned god. I can tell you exactly how that happened. She killed Lux and took the throne. She killed Matthias's parents. Matthias has been collecting fae from her court, trying to piece together anything that would warrant a war." Raidan sucked on his teeth, a look of pride etched into his features. She was piecing things together, too, and the god knew it. "Matthias couldn't explain why, or how, but he wanted the key to destroying Inara. He needed an answer."

"I don't know. I'm still trying to figure you out. You're a mortal that can avoid Death himself, shift realms, and you hold the power of both fae courts." He was looking at her now, his gaze so intense it nearly burned through her. "I'm not sure what it means, but the oracle believed you were the answer, and I assume you could be. I'm not sure I understand what is happening."

Matthias had already fucking told her.

He leaned in again, placing a kiss on her temple. You also have the answers to any questions you wish to ask. *His voice was so loud now.* I just don't know if you'll like the truth.

Morana was dizzy. For a moment, she was thankful for the major god's power, the very mist that held her up—the power that twisted in her chest. She could feel the tears trailing down her face, staining her skin with a pain far fiercer than the scars she wore on her flesh.

Raidan continued, his thumb wiping the sorrow leaking from her eyes. "If he convinced you, a mortal with strange gifts, to become his wife, knowing that Inara already had a deal with the boy—" She held onto Raidan's power as if it were the only thing that would keep her breathing. The addictive comfort of anger kept her standing. Raidan barreled on. "The entire thing was orchestrated. Convince you to fall in love knowing you'd be kidnapped. Dangle you in front of Inara during Mabon. Allow Axton a chance to retrieve you. Kidnapping his future wife during a peaceful holiday was the perfect excuse. He could avenge his parent's death."

Anger was its own entity—rising in her like a prince from the very depths of hell Raidan claimed to be from, ready to conquer—to devour.

"Matthias is a *god*. He's smart. He used Inara's senseless need for power against her and used you as a reason for the war he longed for. It was the only way his court would support him." Raidan's amber eyes were shining as if he were pleased with what he found on her face.

The sting of betrayal—she couldn't allow herself to feel it. This betrayal cut too deep. Morana called to the darkness, the strange white fog that existed somewhere in between. Pleasure rippled across her flesh, numbing her pain completely.

Raidan's hand dropped away, and he stepped back, a sinister smile slowly emerging to show his white teeth. "Wouldn't you like to drink of Death, Morana?"

Panting with the force of her wrath, the room crackling with the depths of her power, Morana's lip peeled back into a snarl. She found her dagger and clenched it painfully, shoving every ounce of herself into the blade. The deep burgundy stone turned black, scorched by the force of her sadness—a sadness she could no longer feel.

There was only Raidan—his power seated deep inside her—mixing with the shadows to create a grave far stronger than any she had ever built for her emotions. This wasn't a grave, it was an abyss, and she would gladly cast her feelings for Death into its shadowy depths.

Something like pleasure took over her as if picturing Matthias lying on the ground, bleeding and broken, would bring life to her very being. The image filled her with even more power than what she already had. She moaned at the thought, breathing one word before turning to return to the battle in the other room.

"Yes."

Thirty-Four

Morana's hair had broken free from the pins Willow had used. The crown still sat on her head, her eyes burning like flame and smoke as she entered the ballroom. Shadows and fog filled the air—so thick it was difficult to see.

She willed them to ease until her power was trailing across the floor, light crackling over the blade in her hand. There was nothing but anger and darkness housed in her soul. All that she knew now was the wrath she felt over being used. Her father used her once, and she had vowed to never allow something like that again. It was the entire reason she fled.

Everything halted. Dead creatures and fae alike littered the floor, covered in blood and gore. Raidan's power burrowed deeper into her as it begged to be wielded against those who hurt her. Matthias had used her to start a war. Elivira had told her as much in Namid, and now Raidan confirmed it. She wasn't thinking clearly, not with his power pulsing through her veins.

She didn't want to think clearly, knew, even beneath the deep well of wrath, that if she touched on her emotions, they would break her apart completely. She had *loved* him, and he had used her. The only thing holding her together was the feeling of power—the image of blood.

How she longed to drink of Death.

Matthias stood at the other end of the room, covered in blood, but it wasn't his own. At some point in the battle, he removed his suit jacket. His hair was damp and hanging across his brow. He wiped his mouth and looked up at her—a queen of death—of darkness.

"You're a fucking liar, Matthias!" Her voice was no longer her own. It was loud and sinister sounding, like a blend of many voices together. The distortion in her voice caused him to halt.

Raidan walked in behind her. She didn't need to look to *feel* his presence or *feel* his pleasure. There was nothing but him. Where Matthias had lied and used—Raidan had come to her with the truth. Even if he had awful intentions, at least he wasn't pretending. At least his power mixing with her shadows took away the pain.

Matthias's eyes were wide in shock, but his brows soon furrowed—confused at the raging woman pulsing with magic before him.

She would kill Death. By whatever means necessary.

He walked forward, and as he approached, he gently set his sword down in a sea of blood. The white button-up pulled at his broad chest, dirt-streaked over one shoulder.

"Morana?" he questioned, talking quietly as if one wrong move would send her spiraling. "I refuse to hurt you."

So foolish, she thought. *Easy.*

"Morana," he tried again. "I won't hurt you. Come back to me."

The statement tugged on something deep within her. It pulled at the remnants of who she was beneath her drunken state. The problem was—he had already hurt her. He had started this entire thing by sending a man to kill her at Ashford. Matthias's desire for war and vengeance led him to lie. He lied about her mother—his feelings.

All of it was a lie.

There was no returning from the hell she longed to release.

When he got close enough, Morana lunged, shoving him to the ground with that white magic that pinned him to the floor. He couldn't fight whatever Raidan's magic was. He was powerless to the force she used to bend him to her will.

Morana screamed as she brought the dagger down, aiming for his heart. He shifted at the last moment—the weapon lodging near his shoulder and she spat at him— infuriated that she hadn't stopped his black soul from existing in this realm. His dark eyes were wide and pained as he tried to push her off. "Morana!" He shouted— desperate for her to hear him, but she was too far gone.

She could taste his blood—feel it coating her tongue and feeding the beast inside her. The dream-eater must have felt this kind of intense pleasure as it feasted on her terror. Matthias probably took her there on purpose—longing to break her further so she wouldn't suspect what he was doing or that he was using her.

Too emotional. Too weak. Too much and somehow not enough.

The lords of his court were surrounding him, but Morana unleashed herself to hold them in place. Raidan's hand touched her shoulder, and she yielded to his desires. It calmed the burning in her chest. Standing and pulling the dagger from Death's flesh with a slick sound, Morana leaned into the major god behind her. Matthias gripped his wound, blood leaking through his fingers. It was as if he hadn't expected her to be able to hurt him.

Too emotional. Too weak. Too much and somehow not enough.

There were no secret books or pieces of knowledge that would keep her from killing a god. It wasn't a question she needed to ask anymore. The way his wound wasn't stitching, the way he struggled on his feet. She knew *she* was enough. Enough to kill—enough to destroy—enough to inject fear into the very gaze of Death.

"That's enough," Raidan spoke as a smile cut across his face, making his white beard shift. "All in good time."

Morana yielded.

"Why the fuck are you here?" Matthias was seething, trying to stand but still unsteady. Morana couldn't stop staring at the blood pouring out of him. She smiled.

"I'm here to collect my bride." Raidan's voice was calm. Something about the deep rumble had her shivering in response. "Rude of you to try to claim what's mine for yourself."

"Morana." Matthias was pleading, but there was armor over her now, covering her like the magic she wielded. He had done this. He had tried to kill her—use her.

So, she would play his game, and she would win.

"Don't speak to her." Dark promises laced Raidan's tone. "She knows you met her mother when you went to the oracle. She knows you used her for this war."

He didn't say anything. Matthias was standing now, wincing as he held the wound she had given him. She longed to give him more—to slash her weapon across his body until he was nothing but a rotting corpse.

Morana stepped back, tilting her head and allowing a manic expression to overtake her face. Her voice was calm when she spoke—steady.

"It's true, isn't it?" she asked.

Raidan's grip on her shoulder tightened, and she placed her hand over his. He was claiming her, and she knew it, but something about this headiness—there was no denying what she wanted.

"We should go," Raidan whispered, "but we will be back."

"Of course." Morana smiled then as Raidan's power consumed her entirely.

The last thing she remembered was the salty liquid gathering in Matthias's eyes before Raidan had them moved into a palace made of skull and bone—the one that held nothing but rage and violent mist.

"I have a task for you after you get settled." Morana turned to see Raidan's satisfied face in the dim light of his temple.

"Yes." She hoped he would command her to return to The Court of Shadows—to end Death.

"Matthias's blood book. I want you to find it."

Morana smiled—wicked and vicious. "Not a problem," she said.

I already know where it is.

Raidan nodded and gestured down the long hallway where they were standing. "Your rooms are at the end. Make yourself at home, my queen."

Morana turned, her heels tapping on the cold stone floors, Matthias's crown still on her head.

"And Morana?"

She halted, but she didn't look back at the major god.

"How are you feeling?" he asked.

Morana fought the urge to laugh, the corners of her mouth turning up again. She strode down the hallway of Raidan's palace, already planning on retrieving Matthias's blood book—of using it to halt his ridiculous war. Maybe she would rule his court. Maybe she would rule the realm.

One word circulated in her mind as she turned the metal handle on the wooden door. It creaked when it opened, revealing an elaborate bedroom decorated in red and cream.

That word continued to echo in her mind until she closed the door behind her, staring at her new home as she finally whispered her response.

"Powerful."

ACKNOWLEDGMENTS

This part is always so difficult for me. I have so many people to thank as it pertains to my writing, and I'm always afraid I will miss someone.

I want to start off with my editor, Kenna. I would be lost without you—stranded somewhere between passive voice and comma splices. This particular story was difficult for me. The magic system was far more complicated than anything I have written to date, the fact that this will be a trilogy, all of it. I am eternally grateful for the way you pushed me to dig in and make this book something to be proud of. I will never be able to thank you enough for that.

Then there's the friendship. Thank you for visiting the zoo with us. My son loves you, your mom, and your daughter eternally. It was a grand adventure—even during the crazy rain. You also walked in the rain in search of Dippin' Dots because they are my love language. If that isn't true friendship, I don't know what is.

I have to thank Kate for reading all of my little snippets, and never failing to share in the excitement when it comes to books. I've been terrible at responding because I'm juggling a thousand things, but I am eternally grateful for you and excited about your newest book! You are going to do awesome things, and I love that I get to witness the start of your author career.

To my grandmother, I couldn't be more thankful to have a woman like you in my life. Our phone calls about books and my ideas hold a special place in my heart, and I can't imagine a world where they don't exist. Thank you for supporting me, and for challenging me by never failing to tell me when things are, quite literally, awful. I'm sorry that my books are not *Great Expectations*, but some people don't even like that book, so it isn't really a valid point to begin with.

I want to thank my husband for being the most amazing sugar daddy as I transition from my teaching career to my author career. You are constantly reminding me that this is a career that takes time to build, and I am eternally grateful that you haven't kicked me out of the house yet. I am, however, substitute teaching to fund my bookish habits, so it's not all bad. Thanks for being around for so long. Also, thanks for the ring, I really like it.

I'd like to thank Ronan for being literally the hottest man in this book. It's the confidence for me, my guy.

I am also incredibly thankful to all of my readers and those that have supported me on this writing journey. I would be lost without you. Quite literally. I would have no book sales to speak of, and my sugar daddy husband would think I was the laziest creature on all the earth. Thank you for proving that sentiment wrong.

Thank you to Ali, for being a lovely friend and narrator. You bring all of my stories to life, and you also bring joy wherever you go. I'm so thankful for our phone conversations that end up lasting like five hours because we both have ADHD and really cannot stop talking.

Thank you to Wednesday. You'll probably read this out of obligation, and that's what true friendship is. Also, send me more chapters, bitch.

Thank you, Reanna for proofreading and saving me from embarrassment. I always add typos in the last round of edits because I'm literally so dumb, but it's fine. You went above and beyond combing through the final manuscript, and I literally cannot thank you enough for what you did!

I'd like to thank anyone I have forgotten. This acknowledgments section is so long, but it doesn't matter. I will sit here and thank anyone and everyone because I am deathly afraid of conflict, and I would die if someone felt left out in this little section of the book.

ABOUT THE AUTHOR

Emma Steinbrecher re-writes her about the author section frequently because she has no idea what she's doing. She lives with her husband and son in Ohio, and enjoys hiking, painting, and of course, writing all the stories.

Steinbrecher also writes under the name Emmie J. Holland for her romantic comedy books. It's literally the same person, so see above for hobbies and family information.

A Clan of Wolves Duology
A Clan of Wolves by Emma Steinbrecher (Book 1)
A House of Witches by Emma Steinbrecher (Book 2)

Romantic Comedy Stand-Alone Books
The Unbelievable Misadventures of Olive Finch by Emmie J. Holland
Pride, Pancakes, and Paris by Emmie J Holland (March 6, 2023)

The Death Hunting Trilogy
The Death Hunting by Emma Steinbrecher (Book 1)
The Raidan Awakening by Emma Steinbrecher (Book 2)
The Light Conquering by Emma Steinbrecher (Book 3)
Official release date for *The Light Conquering* TBA

AUTHOR WEBSITE

Don't forget to check out Emma's website for signed books, exclusive content, and a newsletter that is literally so inconsistent, it won't bother you at all. You can, however, get first dibs on ARC sign-ups and other announcements through the newsletter, so it *is* worth something.